John Ashton

Social Life in the Reign of Queen Anne

Taken from original sources. With 84 illustrations by the author from contemporary

prints. Vol. 2

John Ashton

Social Life in the Reign of Queen Anne
Taken from original sources. With 84 illustrations by the author from contemporary prints.
Vol. 2

ISBN/EAN: 9783337094867

Printed in Europe, USA, Canada, Australia, Japan

Cover: Foto ©Raphael Reischuk / pixelio.de

More available books at **www.hansebooks.com**

Social Life in Queen Anne's Reign

VOL. II.

LONDON : PRINTED BY
SPOTTISWOODE AND CO., NEW-STREET SQUARE
AND PARLIAMENT STREET

SOCIAL LIFE

IN THE

REIGN OF QUEEN ANNE

𝕿𝖆𝖐𝖊𝖓 𝖋𝖗𝖔𝖒 𝕺𝖗𝖎𝖌𝖎𝖓𝖆𝖑 𝕾𝖔𝖚𝖗𝖈𝖊𝖘

BY

JOHN ASHTON

AUTHOR OF 'CHAP BOOKS OF THE EIGHTEENTH CENTURY' ETC.

IN TWO VOLUMES – VOL. II.

*WITH EIGHTY-FOUR ILLUSTRATIONS BY THE AUTHOR
FROM CONTEMPORARY PRINTS*

𝕷𝖔𝖓𝖉𝖔𝖓

CHATTO & WINDUS, PICCADILLY

1882

CONTENTS

OF

THE SECOND VOLUME.

CHAPTER XXV.

THE DRAMA.

PAGE

The theatres—Dorset Gardens—Its demolition—Performances—
Lincoln's Inn Fields—Theatre Royal, Drury Lane—Its com-
pany—Mrs. Tofts—The Queen's Theatre, Haymarket—Its
foundation stone—Its operas—Pinkethman's theatre at
Greenwich—The Queen and the stage—Her reforms—
Strolling players—Behaviour at the theatre—Orange wenches
—Stage properties—Actors—Betterton—Verbruggen—Cave
Underhill—Estcourt—Dogget—Colley Cibber—Wilks—Booth
—Pinkethman—Minor actors—Actresses—Mrs. Barry—Mrs.
Bracegirdle—Mrs. Oldfield—Mrs. Verbruggen—The ballet

CHAPTER XXVI.

OPERA—CONCERTS—MUSIC.

Introduction of Italian opera—Its rapid popularity—Mixture of
languages—Handel—His operas, and visit here—Singers—
—Abel—Hughs—Leveridge—Lawrence—Ramondon—Mrs.
Tofts—Her madness—Foreign singers—Margherita de l'Epine
—Nicolino Grimaldi—Isabella Girardeau—Composers—Dr.
Blow—Jeremiah Clarke—Dean Aldrich—Tom D'Urfey—
Henry Carey—Britton, the small coal man—His concerts—
His death—Concerts and concert rooms—Gasparini, the
violinist—Musical instruments—Musical scores   .   .   .   28

CHAPTER XXXV.

THE STREETS.

CHAPTER XXXVI.

CARRIAGES, ETC.

CHAPTER XXXVII.

THE MOHOCKS.

CHAPTER XXXVIII.

DUELLING.

CHAPTER XXXIX.

THE ARMY AND NAVY.

CHAPTER XL.

CRIME.

CHAPTER XLI.

PRISONS.

CHAPTER XLII.

WORKHOUSES, HOSPITALS, ETC.

APPENDIX.

ILLUSTRATIONS

TO

THE SECOND VOLUME.

SOCIAL LIFE

IN THE

REIGN OF QUEEN ANNE.

CHAPTER XXV.

THE DRAMA.

The theatres—Dorset Gardens—Its demolition—Performances—Lincoln's
Inn Fields—Theatre Royal, Drury Lane—Its company—Mrs. Tofts—
The Queen's Theatre, Haymarket—Its foundation stone—Its operas
—Pinkethman's theatre at Greenwich—The Queen and the Stage—
Her reforms—Strolling players—Behaviour at the theatre—Orange
wenches—Stage properties—Actors—Betterton—Verbruggen—Cave
Underhill—Estcourt—Dogget—Colley Cibber—Wilks—Booth—Pink-
ethman—Minor actors—Actresses—Mrs. Barry—Mrs. Bracegirdle—
Mrs. Oldfield—Mrs. Verbruggen—The ballet.

THE drama was fairly supported in Queen Anne's time
although there were never more than three theatres open at
once, and generally only two. It was not an age for either
striking actors or immortal plays; but, as to the former, they
were hard-working, and some of them have left a name behind them renowned in the history of the stage; and, for the
latter, they were, although somewhat coarse in humour, not
so licentious as the plays of the three preceding reigns. It is
impossible, within the limits of this book, to do more than
generalise on the drama of that day—its history has materials
in it for a book to itself.

There were four theatres: Dorset Gardens, Lincoln's

Inn Fields, Drury Lane, and the Queen's Theatre, Hay-market.

Dorset Gardens Theatre was in Salisbury Court, in Salisbury Square, Fleet Street, and was built, it is said, from designs by Sir Christopher Wren, and to have been decorated by Grinling Gibbons. It fronted the river one way, was consequently easy of access by 'the silent highway,' and its façade was very pretty, although not elaborately ornamented. It was opened on Nov. 9, 1671, by the Duke of York's Company, when they left the playhouse in Little Lincoln's Inn Fields. It gradually got disreputable, and in 1698 was used for the drawing of a penny lottery. Ward thus describes its condition in his time. 'By this time we were come to our propos'd landing Place, when a Stately Edifice (the Front supported by Lofty Columns) presented to our View. I enquired of my Friend what Magnanimous Don Cressus Resided in this Noble and Delightful Mansion? Who told me, No Body as he knew on, except Rats and Mice; and perhaps an old superannuated *Jack Pudding*, to look after it, and to take Care that no Decay'd Lover of the Drama should get in and steal away the *Poet's Pictures*, and sell 'em to some Upholsterers for *Roman Emperours*; I suppose there being little else to lose, except Scenes, Machines, or some such Jim Cracks. For this, says he, is one of the Theatres, but now wholly abandon'd by the Players; and 'tis thought, will in a little time be pull'd down.'[1] The neighbourhood around about he describes as something awful in its character, and he was not particular to a shade.

The following advertisement[2] will show the style of amusement it afforded its patrons :—

'Being the last time of Acting till after May Fair.
At the Theatre in *Dorset Gardens*, this day being *Friday* the 30th of *April* will be presented A *Farce* call'd, *The Cheats* of Scapin. And a Comedy of two Acts only, call'd, *The Comical Rivals*, or the School Boy. With several Italian Sonatas by Signior *Gasperini* and others. And the *Devonshire Girl*, being now upon her Return to the City of *Exeter*, will perform three several Dances, particularly her last new Entry in

---

[1] *London Spy.*   [2] *Daily Courant*, April 30, 1703.

imitation of *Mademoiselle Subligni*, and the *Whip of* Dunboyne by Mr. Claxton her *Master*, being the last time of their Performance till Winter. And at the desire of several Persons of Quality (hearing that Mr. *Pinkeman* hath hired the two famous French Girls lately arriv'd from the Emperor's Court) They will perform several Dances on the Rope upon the Stage, being improv'd to that Degree, far exceeding all others in that Art. And their *Father* presents you with the *Newest Humours of Harlequin* as perform'd by him before the Grand Signior at *Constantinople*. Also the Famous Mr. *Evans* lately arriv'd from *Vienna*, will shew you Wonders of another kind, Vaulting on the Manag'd Horse, being the greatest Master of that Kind in the World. To begin at Five so that all may be done by Nine a Clock.'

In the *Daily Courant* May 13, 1703, there was an attempt to revive it, but it was unsuccessful. 'The Queen's Theatre in *Dorset Garden* is now fitting up for a new *Opera* ; and the great Preparations that are made to forward it and bring it upon the Stage by the beginning of *June*, adds to every body's Expectation, who promise themselves mighty Satisfaction from so well order'd and regular an Undertaking as this is said to be, both in the Beauties of the Scenes, and Varieties of Entertainments in the Musick and Dances.'

It opened spasmodically, now and then : on July 9, 1706, with an opera called 'Arsinoe, Queen of Cyprus.' Mrs. Tofts as Arsinoe ; a prologue spoken by Cibber, and an epilogue by Estcourt ; and on Aug. 1 there was an opera called 'Camilla' played. And we hear the last of it in the autumn of this year.[1] 'By the *deserted Company* of Comedians of the Theatre Royal. At the Queen's Theatre in Dorset Gardens, on Thursday next being the 24th of October, will be Acted a Comedy, call'd The RECRUITING OFFICER.[2] In which they Pray there may be *Singing by Mrs. Tofts* in English and Italian. *And some dancing*.' On the 30th they played 'Master Fido, or the Faithful Shepherd,' 'acted all by women' —a not absolute novelty, but which showed how hard up they were for something new to draw. And there were five more performances that year.

[1] *Daily Courant*, Oct. 22, 1706.   [2] By George Farquhar.

B 2

But all attempts to galvanise it into life failed, and in the *Daily Courant* of June 1, 1709, we read, 'The Play House at Dorset Stairs is now pulling down, where there is to be sold old Timber fit for Building or Repairs, Old Boards, Bricks, Glass'd Pantiles and Plain Tiles, also Fire Wood, at very reasonable rates.'

Lincoln's Inn Fields was another theatre which had very varying fortunes during this reign. In 1705, when the company left for their new home in the Haymarket, it was to let. Betterton took it for a night for his benefit on March 3 of that year, and Cave Underhill for his on March 31. It was not re-opened till Sept. 12, 1706, and was played in only six nights that year. It was rebuilt by Rich, but was not again acted in during Queen Anne's reign.

One advertisement of its performances may be given as exemplifying their variety.[1] 'At the Desire of several Persons of Quality. For the Benefit of Mrs. *Prince*. At the Theatre in *Little Lincoln's Inn Fields*, the present *Tuesday* being the 8th of *June*, will be presented the last New Tragedy call'd, *The Fair Penitent*.[2] With four Entertainments of Singing (entirely New) by the Famous Signiora *Francisca Margarita de l'Epine*; to which will be added the Nightingale Song[3]; it being the last time of her Singing whilst she stays in *England*. The Instrumental Musick composed by Signior *Jacomo Greber*. With a Country Wedding Dance by Monsieur *Labbé*, Mrs. Elford, and others. Also a new Entertainment of Dancing between *Mazetin* a Clown, and two Chairmen. With the Dance of *Blouzabella* by Mr. *Prince*, and Mrs. Elford. By reason of the Entertainments the Play will be shortened. Boxes 6s. Pit 4s. Gallery 2s. 6d.' These seem to have been the benefit prices at this theatre, the normal ones being 5s., 3s., and 2s.

Dorset Gardens and Lincoln's Inn Fields theatres were the dramatic failures; the 'Theatre Royal in Drury Lane,' as it was called, was an exception, and stood its ground fairly during the Queen's reign. It was built by Killigrew, at a cost of £1,500, on the site of a plot of ground called the

---

[1] *Daily Courant*, June 8, 1703.   [2] By N. Rowe.
[3] Can this be an early work of Carey's? See Appendix.

' Riding Yard,' which was obtained on lease from the Duke of Bedford, and opened in 1663. The actors there were called Her Majesty's servants, and had the right to dress in scarlet, the royal livery.

In the summer time, when the quality was dispersed at the various Spas, the dramatic company followed them to their fashionable resorts, as also did Powell and Clinch. This, at all events, was the case in the early days of Anne's rule. ' Her Majesty's Servants of the Theatre Royal being return'd from the Bath, do intend, to morrow being *Wednesday* the Sixth of this instant *October* to act a Comedy call'd *Love makes a Man, or, the Fop's Fortune*.[1] With Singing and Dancing. And whereas the Audiences have been incommoded by the Plays usually beginning too late, the Company of the said Theatre do therefore give Notice that they will constantly begin at Five a Clock without fail, and continue the same Hour all the Winter.' [2]

Later in this reign they stopped in London, but did not play every day. ' Not Acted these 15 years. By Her Majesty's Company of Comedians. At the Theatre Royal in Drury Lane, on Tuesday next, being the 1st of July, will be Reviv'd the 2nd Part of the Destruction of Jerusalem,[3] by Titus Vespasian. The Parts of Titus by Mr. Booth, Phraartes Mr. Mills, Tiberius Mr. Keen. John, Mr. Powell. Berenice Mrs. Rogers, Clarona Mrs. Bradshaw. N.B. The Company will continue to Act on every Tuesday and Friday during the Summer Season. By Her Majesty's Command[4] no Persons are to be admitted behind the Scenes.' [5] At one time, as Cibber narrates, it was even closed altogether.

The theatre was used occasionally for other than dramatic performances. Here is one : ' At the Theatre Royal in *Drury Lane*, this present *Tuesday* being the 14th of *December* will be perform'd, *The Subscription Musick.* Wherein Mrs. *Tofts* Sings several Songs in Italian and English. With a new piece of Vocal and Instrumental Musick never perform'd before, composed by Mr. *Leveridge*. And several new Entries and Entertainments of Dancing by Monsieur *l'Abbe,* Mon-

---

[1] By Colley Cibber.   [2] *Daily Courant,* Oct. 5, 1703.
[3] By J. Crowne, 1677.   [4] See p. 10.   [5] *Daily Courant,* June 28, 1712.

sieur *Du Ruell*, Monsieur *Charrier*, Mrs. *Campion*, Mrs. *Elford*, the *Devonshire* Girl, and others.   No Person to be admitted into the Pit or Boxes but by the Subscribers Tickets, which are deliver'd at Mr. *White's* Chocolate house.   The Boxes on the Stage and the Galleries are for the Benefit of the Actors. The Stage Boxes 7s. 6d. the first Gallery 2s. 6d. the Upper Gallery 1s. 6d.   To begin about Five a Clock.   No Person to stand on the Stage.'[1]

That the ordinary prices, which they never advertised, were much lower than these, is shown by an advertisement in the following year.   'And by reason of the extraordinary Charge in the Decoration of it, the Prices will be rais'd. Boxes 5s. Pit 3s. First Gallery 2s. Upper Gallery 1s.'

Before quitting this short notice of Drury Lane Theatre reference must be made to an incident in which Mrs. Tofts the singer was interested.   'ANN *Barwick* having occasion'd a Disturbance at the Theatre Royal in *Drury Lane* on *Saturday* Night last the 5th of *February*, and being thereupon taken into Custody, Mrs. Tofts, in Vindication of her own Innocency, sent a Letter to Mr. *Rich*, Master of the said Theatre, which is as followeth.

SIR, I was very much surpriz'd when I was inform'd, that *Ann Barwick*, who was lately my Servant, had committed a Rudeness last night at the Play-house, by throwing of Oranges, and hissing when Mrs. *l'Epine* the Italian Gentlewoman Sung.   I hope no one can think that it was in the least with my Privity, as I assure you it was not.   I abhor such Practises, and I hope that you will cause her to be prosecuted, that she may be punish'd as she deserves.

I am, Sir, Your humble Servant,

KATHARINE TOFTS.

To Christopher Rich Esq. ; at the
Theatre Royal. Feb. 6. 1703.'[2]

Misson gives a description of its interior, which, from his invariable truthfulness, can be relied on.   'The Pit is an

---

[1] *Daily Courant*, Dec. 14, 1703.   [2] *Ibid.* Feb. 8 1704.

Amphitheater, fill'd with Benches without Back boards, and adorn'd and cover'd with green Cloth. Men of Quality, particularly the younger Sort, some Ladies of Reputation and Vertue, and abundance of Damsels that hunt for Prey, Sit all together in this place, Higgledy piggledy, chatter, toy, play, hear, hear not. Farther up, against the Wall, under the first Gallery, and just opposite to the Stage, rises another Amphitheater, which is taken up by Persons of the best Quality, among whom are generally very few Men. The Galleries, whereof there are only two rows, are filled with none but ordinary People, particularly the Upper One.'

Italian opera was coming mightily into vogue, but a new theatre was needed for its performance, so a company was formed, capital 3,000*l*. in 100*l*. shares, which covered a subscription for life ; and Sir John Vanbrugh was entrusted with its building. The members of the Kitcat Club were large subscribers ; and Cibber says, 'Of this Theatre I saw the first Stone laid, on which was inscrib'd *The little Whig*,[1] in Honour to a Lady of extraordinary Beauty, then the celebrated Toast and Pride of that Party.' But this seems an inaccuracy, for in a newspaper-cutting of March 19, 1825, it says, 'Removing that portion of the walls of the Italian Opera House, immediately adjoining the cellar of Mr. Wright, on Saturday last, the workmen discovered the first stone of the old building, laid in 1704. The stone was in a perfect state, and in the cavity formed for the purpose of receiving them were found several coins of the reign of Queen Anne ; a brass plate which covered the cavity bore the following inscription : " April 18, 1704. In the third year of the happy reign of our Sovereign Lady Queen Anne, this corner stone of the Queen's Theatre was laid, by his Grace Charles Duke of Somerset, Master of the Horse to her most sacred Majesty." '

The outside was imposing : an arcade, as now, ran along the front of the building, the length of which was relieved by a dome in the centre, and on the balustraded parapet were eight statues on pedestals. But, if Cibber is to be trusted, the inside was so badly constructed acoustically that 'scarce

[1] Lady Sunderland, second daughter of the Duke of Marlborough. *See* Vol. I. p. 28.

one Word in ten could be distinctly heard in it,' and the con-
sequence was that the roof had to be remodelled and made
flat.

Vanbrugh and Congreve opened this theatre on Easter
Monday, April 9, 1705, and Mrs. Bracegirdle spoke a prologue, written by Dr. Garth, in which are the lines, alluding
to the Haymarket :—

> Your own magnificence you here Survey,
> Majestick Columns stand where Dunghills lay,
> And Cars triumphal rise from Carts of Hay.

The play on this occasion was, according to Cibber, 'a
translated Opera, to *Italian* Musick, called the *Triumph of
Love.*' This, he says, only ran three days, and then Sir John
Vanbrugh produced his comedy called 'The Confederacy.'
Downes[1] says, 'It (i.e. the Italian Opera) lasted but 5 Days,
and they being lik'd but indifferently by the Gentry ; they in
a little time marcht back to their own Country. The first
play *Acted* there was *The Gamester.*'

It is singular that neither of these authorities are correct,
and luckily we have the advertisements left to guide us. It
is, however, somewhat strange that there should have been no
public announcement in the newspapers of its opening ; but
the first advertisement published is in the *Daily Courant*,
April 14, 1705 : 'At the Queens Theatre in the Haymarket,
this present Saturday being the 14th of April, will be reviv'd,
The Indian Emperor, or the Conquest of Mexico by the
Spaniards. The Part of Cortez to be perform'd by Mr.
Powel ; with Entertainments of Dancing, as also Singing by
the new Italian Boy. By Her Majesty's Sworn Servants.'

The next play was 'The Merry Wives of Windsor,' on
April 23 ; *on the 27th* ' *The Gamester* ' ; and Downes says ' The
Confederacy' was played long after.

This theatre was, undoubtedly, the most fashionable ;
and its prices, at times, were far above its rivals. Take, for
example[2]: 'At the Desire of several Persons of Quality. At
the Queen's Theatre in the Hay Market, on Saturday next,
being the 7th of February, will be presented an Opera call'd

---

[1] *Roscius Anglicanus*, 1712.   [2] *Daily Courant*, Feb. 4, 1708.

Camilla. The Part of Metius (to which are added several new Select Songs) to be perform'd by the famous Signior Gioseppe Cassani, lately arrived from Italy. With several new Entertainments of Dancing by Monsieur Cherrier, Monsieur Debargues, Mrs. Santlow, Mrs. Evans, and others. The Boxes to be open'd to the Pit, and no Person to be admitted but by Tickets, which will be deliver'd out on Friday and Saturday Morning at White's Chocolate House, at a Guinea each Ticket. The Number of Tickets not to exceed 450.' On the 6th same month the performance was lowered to half a guinea. Stage boxes, half a guinea ; first gallery, 5s. ; upper gallery, 2s.'; and on Feb. 10 admission was still further lowered.

Congreve soon gave up his share, and Sir John Vanbrugh was also glad to get rid of this 'bad egg'; so after Jan. 10, 1708, it was transferred to Owen Mac Swiney for operatic performances, one of which we have just mentioned.

Pinkethman, the indefatigable, had a theatre at Greenwich, which he worked during the summer months, though the exact time is unknown. In an advertisement of his moving picture (*Daily Courant*, May 9, 1709) he says it may be seen ' next Door to his New Play House, where variety of Plays are Acted every Day as in London.' He could not long have started, as in the *Tatler* (No. 4, April 18, 1709) it says, ' We hear Mr. *Penkethman* has removed his ingenious Company of Strollers to Greenwich. But other letters from Deptford say, the company is only making thither, and not yet settled ; but that several Heathen Gods and Goddesses, which are to descend in machines, landed at the King's Head Stairs last Saturday. *Venus* and *Cupid* went on foot from thence to Greenwich ; *Mars* got drunk in the town, and broke his Landlord's head, for which he sat in the Stocks the whole Evening ; but Mr. *Penkethman* giving Security that he should do nothing this ensuing Summer, he was set at liberty. The most melancholy part of all was, that *Diana* was taken, and committed by Justice Wrathful ; which has, it seems, put a stop to the Diversions of the Theatre at Blackheath. But there goes down another *Diana* and a *Patient Grissel* next tide from Billingsgate.'

Queen Anne was not a patron of the drama. She never went to the theatre, and, as far as I can learn, seldom had dramatic performances at court. 'On Sunday, being the Queen's Birth Day, her Majesty receiv'd the usual Compliments on that occasion, and yesterday there was an extraordinary appearance of the Nobility and Gentry of both Sexes at St. James's upon the same account. The Play call'd, All for Love,[1] was Acted in the presence of the Court.'[2] And this was such an extraordinary event that even another newspaper informed its readers of the astounding fact. Downes remarks on this : 'Note From *Candlemas* 1704 to the 22d of April 1706. There were 4 Plays commanded to be *Acted* at Court at St. *James'*, by the *Actors* of both Houses viz. First *All for Love.* The Second was *Sir* Solomon *or the Cautious Coxcomb.*[3] The next was *The Merry Wives of* Windsor, *Acted* the 23rd of *April*, the Queen's Coronation Day. The last was *The Anatomist or Sham Doctor* ;[4] it was perform'd on *Shrove Tuesday*, the Queen's Birthday.'

But though she would not go to the theatres, she heartily took their reformation in hand, as the following proclamation shows :—

'ANNE R.

'WHEREAS. We have already given Orders to the Master of Our Revels, and also to Both the Companies of Comedians, Acting in *Drury Lane*, and *Lincolns Inn Fields*, to take Special Care, that Nothing be Acted in either of the Theatres contrary to Religion or Good Manners, upon Pain of our High Displeasure, and of being Silenc'd from further Acting ; And being further desirous to Reform all other Indecencies, and Abuses of the Stage, which have Occasion'd great Disorders, and Justly give Offence ; Our Will and Pleasure therefore is, and We do hereby strictly Command, That no Person of what Quality soever, Presume to go Behind the Scenes, or come upon the Stage, either before, or during the Acting of any Play. That no Woman be Allow'd

---

[1] *All for Love, or the World Well Lost*, by Dryden.
[2] *Postman*, Feb. 5/8, 1704.
[3] A translation from the *École des Femmes* of Molière, and attributed to John Caryll.   [4] By Edward Ravenscroft, 169..

or Presume to wear a Vizard Mask in either of the Theatres.
And that no Person come into either House without Paying
the Prices Establish'd for their Respective Places.

'All which Orders We strictly Command all Managers,
Sharers, and Actors of the said Companies, to see exactly
Observ'd, and Obey'd. And We Require and Command all
Our Constables, and others appointed to Attend the Theatres,
to be Aiding and Assisting to them therein. And if any
Persons whatsoever shall disobey this Our Known Pleasure
and Command, We shall Proceed against them as Con-
temners of Our Royal Authority, and Disturbers of the
Publick Peace.

'Given at our Court at St. *James's* the 17th Day of
January.

'In the Second Year of our Reign.'

Luttrell, writing on January 20, 1704, says : ' This day,
the lords ordered thanks to the Queen for restraining the
play houses from immorality.'

This proclamation, however, did not have the desired
effect, for another appeared in March the same year :
'WHEREAS great Complaints have been made to He-
Majesty, of many indecent, prophane and immoral Ex-
pressions that are usually spoken by Players and Mountebanks contrary to Religion and Good Manners. And thereupon Her Majesty has lately given Order to *Charles Killigrew, Esqre.* ; Her Majesty's Master of the Revels, to take
especial care to correct all such Abuses. The said Master of
the Revels does therefore hereby require all Stage Players,
Mountebanks, and all other Persons, mounting Stages, or
otherwise, to bring their Several Plays, Drolls, Farces, Interludes, Dialogues, Prologues, and other Entertainments, fairly
written, to him at his Office in *Somerset House*, to be by
him perused, corrected and allow'd under his hand, pur-
suant to Her Majesty's Commands, upon pain of being
proceeded against for contempt of Her Majesty's said
Order,'[1] etc. Another proclamation appeared in the *Gazette,*

---

[1] *Daily Courant,* March 9, 1704.

Nov. 13/15, 1711, forbidding anybody to stand upon the stage or go behind the scenes.

That these proclamations were not strictly attended to is evidenced by the notices scattered over the newspaper advertisements, till 1712, that no persons were allowed on the stage, or behind the scenes, by her Majesty's command ; but, after this last proclamation, the practice seems to have been stopped.

Anne was determined that her orders should be carried out, and looked after the small fry as well as the big fish. 'Whereas the Master of the Revels has received Information, That several Companies of Strolling Actors pretend to have Licenses from Noblemen, and presume under that pretence to avoid the Master of the Revels, his Correcting their Plays, Drolls, Farces, and Interludes ; which being against Her Majesty's Intentions and Directions to the said Master : These are to signifie. That such Licenses are not of any Force or authority. There are likewise several Mountebanks Acting upon Stages, and Mountebanks on Horseback, Persons that keep Poppets, and others that make Shew of Monsters, and strange Sights of living Creatures, who presume to Travel without the said Master of the Revels' Licence,'[1] etc., and goes on to say that their exhibitions must be licensed by him, under penalty.

These strolling actors seem to have been poor enough, and might fairly come under the category of 'vagabonds by Act of Parliament' if the account Steele[2] gives of them be in any way correct : 'We have now at this Place a Company of Strolers, who are very far from offending in the impertinent Splendour of the Drama. They are so far from falling into these false Gallantries, that the Stage is here in its Original Situation of a Cart. *Alexander* the Great was acted by a Fellow in a Paper Cravat ; The next Day the Earl of *Essex* seemed to have no Distress but his Poverty : and my Lord *Foppington* the same Morning wanted any better means to shew himself a Fop Man by wearing Stockings of different Colours. In a Word tho' they have had a full Barn for many Days together, our Itinerants are still so wretchedly

[1] *London Gazette*, Feb. 1/5, 1705.   [2] *Spectator*, No. 48.

poor, that without you can prevail to send us the Furniture you forbid at the Play House, the Heroes appear only like sturdy Beggars, and the Heroines Gipsies.

'No person to be admitted to keep Places in the Pit' seems a singular order, were it not explicable by the fact that people used to send their footmen to keep places for them until their arrival, and that the manners of these gentry gave great offence to the habitués of the pit. The proper place for the footmen was the upper gallery, which was allowed to them free, supposing they were in attendance on their masters. We have seen Pinkethman's power over them, but their behaviour generally was rough and noisy. In the *Female Tatler*, Dec. 9, 1709, is this notice : 'Dropt near the Play house, in the Haymarket, a bundle of Horsewhips, designed to belabour the Footmen in the Upper Gallery, who almost every Night this Winter, have made such an intolerable Disturbance, that the Players could not be heard, and their Masters were obliged to hiss them into silence. Whoever has taken up the said Whips, is desired to leave 'em with my Lord Rake's Porter, several Noblemen resolving to exercise 'em on their Backs, the next Frosty Morning.'

The bad behaviour was not wholly confined to the lackeys, for Addison[1] alludes to that of some ladies whilst at the Theatre : 'A little before the rising of the Curtain, she broke out into a loud Soliloquy, *When will the Dear Witches enter?* and immediately upon their first Appearance, asked a Lady that sat three Boxes from her, on her Right Hand, if those Witches were not charming Creatures. A little after, as *Betterton* was in one of the finest Speeches of the Play, she shook her Fan at another Lady, who sat as far on the Left Hand, and told her with a Whisper that might be heard all over the Pit, We must not expect to see *Ballon* to-night. Not long after, calling out to a young Baronet by his Name, who sat three seats before me, she asked him whether Macbeth's wife was still alive ; and before he could give an Answer, fell a talking of the Ghost of Banquo.'

Steele,[2] too, tells of the bad conduct of a beau, which curiously illustrates the necessity of Anne's proclamations :

[1] *Spectator*, No. 45.   [2] *Ibid.* No. 240.

'This was a very lusty Fellow, but withal a sort of Beau, who getting into one of the Side boxes on the Stage before the Curtain drew, was disposed to shew the whole Audience his Activity by leaping over the Spikes ; he pass'd from thence to one of the Entering Doors, where he took Snuff with a tolerable good Grace, display'd his fine Cloaths, made two or three feint Passes at the Curtain with his Cane, then faced about and appear'd at t'other Door : Here he affected to survey the whole House, bow'd and smil'd at random, and then shew'd his Teeth, which were some of them indeed very white : After this he retired behind the Curtain, and obliged us with several Views of his Person from every Opening.'

And, again, take this short sketch : 'And our rakely young Fellows live as much by their Wits as ever ; and to avoid the clinking Dun of a Boxkeeper, at the End of one Act, they sneak to the opposite Side 'till the End of another ; then call the Boxkeeper saucy Rascal, ridicule the Poet, laugh at the Actors, march to the Opera, and spunge away the rest of the Evening. The Women of the Town take their Places in the Pit with their wonted Assurance. The middle Gallery is fill'd with the middle Part of the City : and your high exalted Galleries are grac'd with handsome Footmen, that wear their Master's Linen.'[1]

Such then was the appearance in front of the stage ; and, to thoroughly realise the scene, we must remember, *en passant*, that necessary individual the ' Candle Snuffer,' and those bold young women, whose class Nell Gwynne made famous, the ' Orange Wenches.'

Four or five hours in such theatres were almost insupportable without some slight refreshment, and this was supplied by these girls, who continually circulated throughout the audience. Their class is sufficiently alluded to in a passage in the *Spectator*, No. 141 : 'A Poet sacrifices the best Part of his Audience to the Worst ; and as one would think neglects the Boxes, to write to the Orange Wenches.' They seem to have fulfilled other duties besides supplying refreshment :—

> Now turn, and see where loaden with her Freight,
> A Damsel Stands, and Orange-wench is hight ;

[1] *Humours of the Army*, Chas. Shadwell, 1713.

See ! how her Charge hangs dangling by the Rim,
See ! how the Balls blush o'er the Basket-brim ;
But little those she minds, the cunning *Belle*
Has other Fish to Fry, and other Fruit to sell ;
See ! how she whispers yonder youthful Peer,
See ! how he smiles, and lends a greedy Ear.
At length 'tis done, the Note o'er Orange wrapt
Has reach'd the Box, and lays in Lady's Lap.[1]

Bad weather occasionally militated against the poor players. 'Her Majesty's Servants at the Theatre Royal (the weather being chang'd) intend to act on Wednesdays and Fridays till Bartholomew Fair.'[2] This and bad trade made them look out for novelties, such as acting a play the characters in which were sustained entirely by women, or having amateurs on the stage. 'At the Theatre Royal in Drury Lane, to morrow being Friday the 7th of July, will be reviv'd a Play call'd, The Orphan, or, the Unhappy Marriage.[3] All the Men's parts to be perform'd by young Gentlemen for their Diversion.'[4] Or they would try the effect of 'a New Prologue by a Child of 4 years of Age,' or 'a New Epilogue by Mrs. Pack in a Riding Habit, upon a Pad-Nagg representing a Town Miss Travelling to Tunbridge.'

The properties of a theatre have always been a fair whetstone for men to sharpen their humour on, and the writers of the time of Queen Anne were not behindhand in this respect. When Drury Lane was closed by order, in 1709, the *Tatler* (No. 42) made very merry over the miscellaneous effects :—

'Three Bottles and a half of lightning.

'One Shower of Snow in the whitest French Paper.

'Two Showers of a browner sort.

'A Sea, consisting of a dozen large waves ; the tenth bigger than ordinary, and a little damaged.

'A dozen and a half of Clouds, trimmed with black, and well conditioned.

'A Mustard bowl to make Thunder with.

'The Complexion of a Murderer in a Bandbox ; consist-

---

[1] *The Stage*, N. Rowe.   [2] *Daily Courant*, July 26, 1704.
[3] By Thos. Otway.   [4] *Daily Courant*, July 6, 1704.

ing of a large piece of burnt Cork, and a Coal black Peruke,'
etc.

At the death of Peer, the property man at this theatre,
the *Guardian* extracted much fun from a catalogue of articles
under his care.

Rowe goes into poetry on the same subject—thus :—

> Hung on the selfsame Peg, in Union rest
> Young *Tarquin's* Trowsers, and *Lucretia's* Vest,
> Whilst without pulling Quoives *Roxana* lays
> Close by *Statira's* Petticoat her Stays
>
> .   .   .   .   .
>
> Near these sets up a Dragon drawn Calash,
> There a Ghost's Doublet delicately slash'd,
> Bleeds from the mangled Breast, and gapes a frightful Gash.
> In Crimson wrought the sanguine Floods abound,
> And seem to gutter from the streaming Wound.
> · Here Iris bends her various painted Arch,
> There artificial Clouds in sullen Order march,
> Here stands a Crown upon a Rack, and there
> A *Witch's* Broomstick by great *Hector's* Spear ;
> Here stands a Throne, and there the *Cynick's* Tub,
> Here *Bullock's* Cudgel, there Alcida's Club :
> Beads, Plumes, and Spangles, in Confusion rise,
> Whilst Rocks of Cornish Diamonds reach the Skies.
> Crests, Corslets, all the Pomp of Battle join,
> In one Effulgence, one promiscuous shine.

The actors of this reign, with a few exceptions, were
not people of much genius. After these few, some were
respectable, the rest bad ; but, although the play was the
proper place of amusement to go to, and there were seldom
more than two theatres open at once, yet we find it comparatively languishing, the companies frequently playing only
twice a week, or the theatre closed altogether. Doubtless
the tragedy was stilted, and the comedy was akin to buf-
foonery. As witness to the latter let Addison[1] testify : ' It
would be an Endless Task to consider Comedy in the same
Light, and to mention the innumerable Shifts that small Wits
put in practice to raise a Laugh. *Bullock* in a short Coat, and
Norris in a long one, seldom fail of this Effect. In ordinary
Comedies, a broad and a narrow Brim'd Hat are different

[1] *Spectator*, No. 44.

characters. Sometimes the Wit of the Scene lies in a Shoulder belt, and sometimes in a Pair of whiskers.'

The ' Phœnix of the Stage,' as Anthony, or Tony, Aston calls Betterton, stands pre-eminent among the actors. Born in 1635, he was an old man when Queen Anne came to the throne ; and he died on April 28, 1710, from the effects of gout, which he aggravated by acting when the fit was on. His last performance was on April 13, 1710, and it is thus described in the *Daily Courant* of that date : ' At the Desire of several Persons of Quality. For the Benefit of Mr. Betterton. At the Queen's Theatre in the Hay market this present Thursday being the 13th April will be Reviv'd, The Maid's Tragedy.[1] The part of Melantius by Mr. Betterton, Amintor by Mr. Wilks, Calianax by Mr. Pinkethman, Evadne by Mrs. Barry, and all the other parts to the best Advantage. To which will be added Three Designs, Representing the Three Principal Actions of the Play, in Imitation of so many great Pieces of History Painting, where all the real Persons concern'd in those Actions will be Plac'd at proper distances, in different Postures peculiar to the Passion of each Character.'

Totally unfit, from illness, to act, he had resort to violent remedies to enable him to go through his part, which he did, with his gouty foot in a slipper, but the exertion killed him. A great favourite of Charles II., that king not only sent him to Paris, to see and report on the French theatres, but appointed him to teach the nobility for court theatricals, whilst his wife tutored the future queens Mary and Anne— in fact, the latter settled a pension of 100*l.* per annum upon her, after her husband's death. Pepys describes him as ' the best actor in the world,' and so he undoubtedly was—in his age. Aston[2] describes him thus : ' He had little Eyes, and a broad Face, a little Pock fretten, a Corpulent Body, and thick Legs, with large Feet. . . . His Voice was low and grumbling ; yet he could Tune it by an artful *Climax*, which enforc'd universal Attention, even from the *Fops* and *Orange Girls*. He was incapable of dancing even in a Country Dance.'

---

[1] By Beaumont and Fletcher.   [2] *Supplement to Cibber.*

Room must be found for one little anecdote which Aston tells of him. ' Mr. *Betterton* had a small Farm near *Reading*, in the County of *Berks* ; and a Countryman came, in the Time of *Bartholomew Fair*, to pay his Rent. Mr. *Betterton* took him to the Fair, and going to one *Crawley's* Puppet Shew, offer'd *Two Shillings* for himself and *Roger*, his Tenant.—No, no, Sir, said *Crawley ; we never take Money of one Another.* This affronted *Mr. Betterton*, who threw down the Money, and they entered.'

Among the actors of the time he was looked up to as a king. Downes[1] says : ' I must not Omit Praises due to Mr. Betterton. The first and now only remains of the old Stock, of the Company of Sir *William Davenant* in *Lincolns* Inn Fields ; he like an old Stately Spreading Oak now stands Fixt, Environ'd round with brave Young Growing Flourishing Plants. . . . Mr. *Dryden* a little before his Death in a Prologue, rendring him this Praise :—

> He like the Setting Sun, still shows a Glimmery Ray
> Like Antient ROME Majestick in decay.'

He was buried in Westminster Abbey on May 2, 1710, and Steele[2] wrote a long panegyric upon him, saying he ' ought to be recorded with the same respect as Roscius among the Romans.'

He died, not in want, but in comparatively poor circumstances, and he must have been a man of some culture, as the following advertisement, soon after his death, shows :[3] ' This Day will be Continued the Sale by Auction of the *Prints*, and *Books of Prints and Drawings*, of Mr. *Tho Betterton* deceased, &c.'

Verbruggen, although he died in 1708, played in Queen Anne's reign. But little is known of him, except that he was a tragedian, and was the original Oronooko. A contemporary character of him is ' A fellow with a crackt voice, he clangs his words, as if he spoke out of a broken drum.'[4] Downes says, ' his Person being tall, well built and clean, only he was a little In Kneed, which gave him a shambling Gate ;'

[1] *Roscius Anglicanus*, 1708.   [2] *Tatler*, 167.
[3] *Harl. MSS.* 5996, 100.   [4] *Comparison between the two Stages.*

and he adds, ' *Verbruggen* was Nature without Extravagance
—Freedom without Licentiousness—and vociferous without
bellowing.'

Cave Underhill was another veteran, of whom Steele
writes[1] when making an appeal to the public to support
him : 'he has been a comic for three generations ; my father
admired him extremely when he was a boy.' He took a
benefit at Drury Lane on June 3, 1709, when 'Hamlet' was
played, and he took his favourite part of the gravedigger.

Leigh was another old actor who died in this reign.

Estcourt deserves notice. He was born in 1668, and, at
the age of 15, ran away from his father's house, and joined a
company of strollers at Worcester. He was recovered, and
apprenticed to an apothecary in London ; again ran away, and
led a wandering life for some years, till we find him engaged
at Drury Lane. Downes describes him as '*Histrio Natus* ;
he has the Honour (Nature enduing him with an easy, free,
unaffected Mode of Elocution) in Comedy always to Lœtificate
his Audience, especially Quality.' He was a pet of the Duke
of Marlborough, and was *Providore* of the famous Beefsteak
Club, where he wore a small gold gridiron suspended from his
neck by a green ribbon. He retired from the stage some
time before his death, and took the 'Bumper' in St. James
Street, where he Lœtificated his customers in another manner.
Steele puffed him in the *Spectator*, and wept over his decease
in the same periodical.[2]

The name of Dogget is, perhaps, as well known to us as
any actor of the time. An Irishman by birth, he came to
England and joined a travelling troupe ; afterwards being
good enough to play at both Drury Lane, and Lincoln's Inn
Fields. In fact, he was joint manager of the former with
Wilks and Cibber, but gave it up in 1713, because Booth was
forced on him as a co-partner ; and he never returned to the
theatre, either as a regular actor or as manager. It must have
been a blow to him, for he was fond of money, and was then
reputed to have been worth £1,000 per annum. He was not
particular : he put his pride in his pocket, and had a booth
at Bartholomew Fair, the same as Pinkethman or Mills. He

[1] *Tatler*, 22.   [2] No. 468.

died at Eltham, in Kent, Sept. 22, 1721, and left in his will the
memorable Coat and Badge to be raced for, annually, on the
anniversary of the accession of George the First, to show his
attachment to the Whig party and the House of Brunswick.
Downes says of him, 'On the Stage, he's very Aspectabund,
wearing Farce in his Face ; his Thoughts deliberately framing
his Utterance Congruous to his Looks ; He is the only Comick
Original now extant.' Tony Aston says 'he was a little, lively
spract Man . . . a Man of very good Sense, but illiterate ;
for he wrote me Word thus—*Sir, I will give you a* hole, instead of (*whole*) *Share*. He dress'd neat, and something fine,
in a plain Cloth Coat, and a Brocaded Waistcoat.'

Colley Cibber was born in London Nov. 6, 1671, and is
known as much, or more, as a playwright, or poet, as an actor.
In his boyhood he tried for a scholarship at Winchester, but
failed ; afterwards he meditated going to the University, but
the Revolution of 1688 broke out, and he was for a short
time in the army as his father's substitute. He saw no service,
and soon became an actor, *i.e.* in 1690, and did not quit the
stage till 1730, in which year he was made Poet Laureate to
George II. He died Dec. 12, 1757. Downes tells us he was
'A Gentleman of his time who has Arriv'd to an exceeding
Perfection, in hitting justly the Humour of a starcht Beau or
Fop ; as the Lord *Fopington* ; Sir *Fopling* and Sir *Courtly*,
equalling in the last the late Eminent Mr. *Mountfort*, not
much Inferior in Tragedy, had Nature given him Lungs
Strenuous to his finisht Judgment.' Gildon,[1] however, falls
foul of him ; but then, the only good words he had were for
Betterton and Barry.

Ramble. But prithee look on this side ; there's Cibber, a poet and
fine Actor.

Critick. And one that's always repining at the success of others, and
upon the stage makes all his fellow actors uneasy.

Wilks, the best tragedian of the age, came of a good Wor-
cestershire family, and, from his association with actors, drifted
into the profession. He was remarkable for the carefulness
of his acting, and for the ease and good breeding he displayed

---

[1] *Comparison between the two Stages.*

upon the stage. He died in 1732 at the age of 76. What do his contemporaries say of him ? Downes says, ' Proper and Comely in Person, of Graceful Port, Mein and Air ; void of Affectation ; his Elevations and Cadences just, Congruent to Elocution.' The author of ' The Comparison between the two Stages ' can say nothing ill-natured of him, and Steele[1] speaks highly of him.

Ramble. Ay, but Powell——

Critick. Is an idle fellow, that neither minds his business, nor lives quietly in any community—

is a fair criticism on that actor, who, had he been but as steady or painstaking, might have rivalled Wilks; but he was a drunken, dissipated dog, a careless study, with a bad memory ; pursued by bailiffs, he sometimes walked with his sword drawn—once making an unfortunate ' officer ' retreat to the other side of the road, where he called out, ' We don't want you *now*, Mr. Powel.' Died Dec. 14, 1715.

Booth was the Aristo of the profession. He was not only nearly related to the Earl of Warrington, but in 1704 he married a daughter of Sir William Barkham, Bart., of Norfolk A scholar of the great and terrible Dr. Busby, he shone ir acting in the Latin plays at Westminster. He was intended for the Church, but he caught stage fever, ran away from school at the age of 17, and joined the theatre at Dublin When he came to London he became a pupil of Betterton's and profited by his master's instructions. He was joint patentee in Drury Lane, but he left the stage at the early age of 46. Died 1733.

Of the minor actors Pinkethman stands first. He was low comedy, and his great ambition was to please the gods We have heard a good deal about him in this book in his various characters as caterer for the amusement of the public Gildon, of course, can say nothing good of him.

Sullen. But Penkethman the flower of——

Critick. Bartholomew Fair, and the idol of the rabble ; a fellow that over does everything, and spoils many a part with his own stuff.

Be this as it may, he is very honourably mentioned through- out the *Spectator*, although Steele[2] gives him a good-humoured

---

[1] *Spectator*, 370.   [2] *Tatler*, 188.

rap over the knuckles. 'Mr. William Bullock and Mr. William Penkethman are of the same Age, Profession, and Sex. They both distinguish themselves in a very particular Manner under the discipline of the Crab-tree, with this only difference, that Mr. Bullock has the more agreeable Squall, and Mr. Penkethman the more graceful Shrug. Penkethman devours a cold Chick with great Applause ; Bullock's talent lies chiefly in Asparagus. Penkethman is very dexterous at conveying himself under a Table ; Bullock is no less active in jumping over a Stick. Penkethman has a great deal of money ; but Mr. Bullock is the taller man.'

The mention of Crab-tree seems to suggest that Pinkethman had been thrashed at some period of his career, as does a passage in another *Tatler* (No. 42), describing the theatrical properties at Drury Lane : 'Three oak Cudgels, with one of Crab-tree ; all bought for the Use of Mr. Pinkethman.'

That he must have been a fair actor is testified by the fact that he played in two out of the four performances at St. James's.

As far as I can find out, he seems first to have acted at the Theatre Royal in 1692, in the play of 'Volunteers, or the Stock Jobbers,'[1] when he played the part of Taylor (six lines only). He rose gradually, and was a painstaking actor, ever on the alert to court popular favour. He became rich. Downes says of him, ' He's the darling of *Fortunatus*, he has gain'd more in Theatres and Fairs in Twelve Years than those that have Tugg'd at the Oar of Acting these 50.' To realise this fortune he probably was saving in his habits, and not so lavish as some of his compeers—a fact which is exaggerated into a charge of meanness : see an Elegy on his Merry Andrew, John Edwards.[2]

> Dull'sneaking Pinkeman this loss bewail,
> And sing his Dirge o're half a pint of Ale,
> For if thou more didst spend at once, your Note
> You'd Change, and for your Charges cut your throat.

He seems to have retired from the stage after his benefit on May 23, 1724, and he died in 1740.

[1] By Thos. Shadwell.   [2] *Harl. MSS.* 5931, 251.

The other actors, Bullock,[1] Mills, Norris, *alias* Jubilee Dickey, Pack Johnson, etc., are unworthy any notice except to chronicle their names as actors of the time.

It is singular that the ladies of the stage of this period stand out so prominently for their talents. It must have been by natural genius, for they could have had little enough tradition to guide them, it being only forty or fifty years since the first woman ever trod the boards. Who she was seems to be somewhat obscure, but it probably was Mrs. Coleman, who played Ianthe in the first part of the ' Siege of Rhodes ' in 1656, but she did not speak. We know Kynaston, who kept Charles II. waiting whilst he was being shaved to play his part ; he of whom Pepys writes[2] thus : ' Kynaston, the boy, had the good turn to appear in three shapes ; first as a poor woman in ordinary clothes to please Morose ; then in fine clothes, as a gallant ; and in them was the prettiest woman in the whole house ; and lastly, as a man ; and then likewise did appear the handsomest man in the house.' Of him Betterton writes,[3] ' that it has been disputed among the Judicious, whether any *Woman* could have more sensibly touched the Passions.' He seems to have been the last of the male actors who took female parts, although in 1661 a woman actor was still a novelty. ' There saw the " Scornfull Lady, "[4] now done by a woman, which makes the play much better than ever it did to me.'[5] A Mrs. Sanderson is traditionally said to have been the first woman actress, and she played

[1] ' For the Benefit of Will. Bullock.
' At the Theatre Royal in Drury Lane, on Whitson Monday, being the 5th of June, will be reviv'd a Diverting Comedy call'd the Miser [Thomas Shadwell]. Written by the Author of the Squire of Alsatia ; the part of Timothy Squeez the Scriveners foolish Son to be acted by Will. Bullock. With Entertainments of Dancing by Monsieur du Ruell. And Mr. Clinch of Barnet will perform these several Performances, first an Organ with three Voices, then the Double Curtel, the Flute, the Bells, the Huntsman, the Horn, and Pack of Dogs, all with his Mouth ; and an old Woman of Fourscore Years of Age nursing her Grand Child ; all of which he does open on the Stage. Next a Gentleman will perform several Mimick Entertainments on the Ladder, first he stands on the top round with a Bottle in one hand and a Glass in the other, and drinks a Health ; then plays several Tunes on the Violin, with fifteen other surprizing Performances which no man but himself can do. And Will Pinkeman will dance the Miller's Dance and speak a comical joking Epilogue on an Ass. Beginning exactly at five a Clock by reason of the length of the Entertainments. At Common Prices.'—*Daily Courant*, June 2, 1704.
[2] *Diary*, Jan. 7, 1661.   [3] *The History of the English Stage.*
[4] By Beaumont and Fletcher.   [5] *Pepys*, Feb. 12, 1661.

Desdemona at the theatre in Clare Market on Dec. 8, 1660. Betterton says the mother of Norris, or Jubilee Dickey, 'was the first Woman who ever appeared on the Stage as an Actress.'

Anyhow, never was there a period that could show four such actresses as Mrs. Barry, Mrs. Bracegirdle, Mrs. Oldfield, and Mrs. Verbruggen.

Elizabeth Barry, the daughter of a barrister of good birth, was born 1658; so that she was not in her first youth at the accession of Anne. Her father so encumbered his estate that it became necessary for his children to seek their fortunes as best they might. She chose the stage, and Sir Wm. Davenant took her in hand, but gave her up as hopeless. The Earl of Rochester, however, having wagered that by proper instruction she should be the finest actress on the stage in less than six months, she took such pains that when, in 1677, she played the Hungarian Queen in the tragedy of 'Mustapha,'[1] before Charles the Second and the Duke and Duchess of York, she created an absolute furore : so much so that the Duchess took lessons from her, and not only gave her her wedding suit, but her coronation robes when she became queen. She died on November 7, 1713, and was buried at Acton, where her daughter, by the Earl of Rochester, was already interred. Aston, speaking of her personal appearance, says : 'And yet this fine creature was not handsome, her Mouth op'ning most on the Right Side, which she strove to draw t'other way, and, at Times, composing her Face, as if sitting to have her Picture drawn. Mrs. Barry was middle siz'd, and had darkish Hair, light Eyes, dark Eye-brows, and was indifferently plump : Her Face somewhat preceded her Action, as the latter did her Words ; her Face ever expressing the Passions ; not like the Actresses of late Times, who are afraid of putting their Faces out of the Form of Non-meaning, lest they should crack the Cerum, White Wash, or other Cosmetic, trowel'd on.'

Betterton says Mrs. Bracegirdle was the daughter of Justinian Bracegirdle of Northamptonshire, Esq., whilst Aston, who calls her 'the *Diana* of the Stage,' says 'The

---

[1] By the Earl of Orrery.

most received Opinion is, that she was the Daughter of a
Coach Man, Coach maker, or Letter out of Coaches in the
Town of *Northampton*, but I am inclinable to my Fathers
Opinion, (who had a great Value for her reported Virtue)
that she was a distant Relation, and came out of *Stafford-
shire* from about *Wallsal* or *Wolverhampton*.' She is believed
to have been born about the year 1674, and somehow came
to be placed, when an infant, under the care of Betterton and
his Wife, who naturally brought her up to the stage. So
young did she enter her future profession that she acted as
a page in 'The Orphan,'[1] at the Dorset Garden Theatre in
1680, when only six years old. She was not only remarkable for her magnificent acting, but for the exceeding purity
of her life, which no breath of scandal could sully ; although
it could not be said it was from want of temptation. Congreve writes of her :—

> Pious *Celinda* goes to Pray'rs,
>   Whene'er I ask the Favour ;
> Yet, the tender Fool's in Tears,
>   When she believes I'll leave her.
> Wou'd I were free from this Restraint,
>   Or else had Power to win her !
> Wou'd she cou'd make of me a Saint,
>   Or I of her a Sinner !

And D'Urfey, in his ' Don Quixote,' sings of her :—

> Since that our Fate intends
>   Our Amity shall be no dearer,
> Still let us kiss and be Friends,
>   And sigh we can never come nearer.

She was wonderfully charitable, and would go daily about
the slums of Clare Market relieving the necessitous ; and
woe be to anyone who should have dared to molest her—his
fate would have been speedy. She retired from the stage in
1707, but did not die till 1748. Her personal description is :
' She was of a lovely Height, with dark-brown Hair and Eye
brows, black sparkling Eyes, and a fresh blushy Complexion ;
and, whenever she exerted herself, had an involuntary Flush-
ing in her Breast, Neck and Face, having continually a

[1] By Thos. Otway.

chearful Aspect, and a fine Set of even White Teeth ; never making an *Exit*, but that she left the Audience in an Imitation of her pleasant Countenance.   Genteel Comedy was her chief Essay, and that too when in Men's Cloaths, in which she far surmounted all the Actresses of that Age ' (Aston).

Her great rival was Mrs. Anne Oldfield, who was born in Pall Mall in 1683.   Her father was in the Horse Guards, and on his death left his wife and daughter in very straitened circumstances.   Tradition says that she was living with her aunt, who kept the Mitre Tavern in St. James's Market, when Sir John Vanbrugh heard her read some plays : certain it is, he introduced her to Rich, in 1699, when she played Candiope, in ' Secret Love, or The Maiden Queen.'[1]   Mrs. Oldfield was far from being as immaculate in character as her rival.   Her last performance was on April 28, 1730 ; she died October 23, 1730, and was buried in Westminster Abbey.   Allusion has been made to her mode of burial at the commencement of this book (vol. i. p. 49).

Steele[2] gives her portrait thus : ' FLAVIA is ever well dressed, and always the genteelest woman you meet ; but the make of her mind very much contributes to the ornament of her body.   She has the greatest simplicity of manners of any of her sex.   This makes everything look native about her, and her clothes are so exactly fitted, that they appear, as it were, part of her person,' etc.

Ramble. There's Mrs. Rogers, Mrs. Oldfield, Mrs. Verbruggen——
Critick. The last is a miracle, but the others mere rubbish, that ought to be swept off the stage with the filth and dust.

Hers was a romantic history.   Her maiden name was Percival, and she married Mountford the actor, who was killed by Lord Mohun for protecting Mrs. Bracegirdle. Betterton says, ' Her Father Mr. *Percival* had the Misfortune to be drawn into the Assassination Plot against King *William* ; for this he lay under Sentence of Death, which he received on the same Night that Lord Mohun killed her Husband, Mr. *Mountfort.*   Under this, almost insuperable Affliction, she was introduced to the good Queen *Mary*, who

---

[1] By Dryden.   [2] *Tatler*, 212.

being, as she was pleased to say, *Struck to the Heart* upon receiving Mrs. *Mountfort's* Petition, immediately granted all that was in her Power, a Remission of her Father's Execution for that of Transportation. But Fate had so ordered it that poor Mrs. *Mountfort* was to lose both Father and Husband. For as Mr. *Percival* was going abroad, he was so weakened by his Imprisonment, that he was taken Sick on the Road, and died at *Portsmouth.*' She afterwards married Jack Verbruggen, and their married life is thus described by Aston : ' She was the best Conversation possible ; never Captious, or displeas'd at any Thing but what was gross or indecent ; for she was cautious lest fiery *Jack* shou'd so resent it as to breed a Quarrel ; for he wou'd often say *Dammee ! tho' I don't much value my Wife yet no Body shall affront her, by G—d* ; and his Sword was drawn on the least occasion, which was much the fashion in the latter End of King *William's* Reign.' She is described as being 'a fine fair Woman, plump, full featured, her Face of a fine smooth Oval.'

The theatre never solely depended upon the drama for its attractions, and there was generally a ballet of some description ; not, of course, such elaborate affairs as we have now, but performances by one or two artists, such as M. L'Abbé and Mrs. Elford. The dances were such as chacones, minuets, allmands, corantos, jigs, sarabands, etc., and we have already seen the pains taken with this art, and the elaborate instructions of its professors.

CHAPTER XXVI.

OPERA, CONCERTS, MUSIC.

Introduction of Italian opera—Its rapid popularity—Mixture of languages
—Handel—His operas, and visit here—Singers—Abel—Hughs—
Leveridge — Lawrence — Ramondon — Mrs. Tofts — Her madness—
Foreign singers—Margherita de l'Epine—Nicolino Grimaldi—Isabella
Girardeau—Composers—Dr. Blow—Jeremiah Clarke—Dean Aldrich
—Tom D'Urfey—Henry Carey—Britton, the small coal man—His
concerts—His death—Concerts and concert rooms—Gasparini, the
violinist—Musical instruments—Musical scores.

' 1673.4. 5 Jan.   I saw an Italian opera in Music, the first
that had been in England of this Kind,' writes Evelyn ; but
Pepys mentions it even earlier : ' 1667.8. Jan. 12.   With my
Lord Brouncker to his house, there to hear some Italian
musique, and here we met Tom Killigrew, Sir Robert
Murray, and the Italian, Signor Baptista,[1] who hath prepared a play in Italian for the Opera, which Sir T. Killigrew
do intend to have up ; and here he did sing one of the
Acts.'   There is, however, no record of either of these being
acted.   The first opera of which we have any record is a
translation of ' Arsinoë,' an Italian opera written by Stan-
zani of Bologna, for the theatre of that town, in 1677, and
here is the premier advertisement of opera in England.

'At the Theatre Royal in Drury Lane, this present
Tuesday being the 16th of January, will be presented a New
Opera never perform'd before, call'd Arsinóe Queen of
Cyprus, After the Italian manner, All Sung, being set to
Musick by Mr. Clayton.   With several Entertainments of
Dancing by Monsieur l'Abbee, Monsieur du Ruel, Monsieur
Cherrier, Mrs. Elford, Mrs. du Ruel, Mrs. Moss and others.
And the famous Signiora Francisca Margaretta de l'Epine

[1] Battista Draghi.

will, before the Beginning and after the Ending of the Opera, perform several Entertainments of singing in Italian and English. No person to be admitted into the Boxes or Pitt but by the Subscribers Tickets, to be delivered at Mrs. White's Chocolate House. The Boxes on the Stage and the Galleries are for the benefit of the Actors.'[1] The singers were all English ; and here we have the commencement of the subscription opera.

In the next two years there were but very few operas, although Addison wrote one called 'Rosamond.' During this period, too, the Queen's Theatre in the Haymarket was opened for opera, with what success we have seen.

The thin edge of the wedge, as regards Italian singing, was introduced in 1707, when Valentini Urbani, a Castrato, and a female singer called 'The Baroness,' came over here. They made their first appearance 'At the Theatre Royal in Drury Lane, this present Saturday, being the 6th of December, will be presented an Opera called "Camilla." All to be sung after the Italian manner. The Parts of Latinus by Mr. Turner, Prenesto by Signiora Margarita, part in Italian, Turnus by Signior Valentino, in Italian, Metius by Mr. Ramondon, Linco by Mr. Leveridge, Camilla by Mrs. Tofts, Lavinia by the Baroness, most in Italian, Tullia by Mrs. Lindsey.'[2]

What a curious mixture it must have been, some singing in Italian and some in English! but it was not the sole example, for when Italian opera was introduced into Germany the recitative was given in German and the airs sung in Italian.

Of course an innovation, and coming from a foreign source, roused the insular prejudices of John Bull. It was un-English. As Dennis, the critic, wrote[3] : 'And yet tho' the Reformation and Liberty and the Drama were establish'd among us together, and have flourish'd among us together, and have still been like to have fall'n together ; notwithstanding all this, at this present Juncture, when Liberty and the Reformation are in the utmost Danger, we are going

---

[1] *Daily Courant*, Jan. 16, 1705.   [2] *Ibid.* Dec. 6, 1707.
[3] *An Essay on the Operas after the Italian Manner*, 1706.

very bravely to oppress the Drama, in order to establish the luxurious Diversions of those very Nations, from whose Attempts and Designs, both Liberty and the Reformation are in the utmost Danger.'

With far greater sense and show of reason he says: ' If that is truly the most Gothick, which is the most oppos'd to Antick, nothing can be more Gothick than an Opera, since nothing can be more oppos'd to the ancient Tragedy, than the modern Tragedy in Musick, because the one is reasonable, the other ridiculous ; the one is artful, the other absurd ; the one beneficial, the other pernicious ; in short, the one natural, and the other monstrous. And the modern Tragedy in Musick, is as much oppos'd to the Chorus, which is the Musical part of the Ancient Tragedy, as it is in the *Episo-dique* ; because, in the Chorus, the Musick is always great and solemn, in the Opera 'tis often most trifling and most effeminate ; in the Chorus the Music is only for the sake of the Sense, in the Opera the Sense is most apparently for the sake of the Music.'

This mongrel style of performance, half Italian, half English, lasted till 1710. ' Pyrrhus and Demetrius' (a translation of ' Pirro e Demetrio' of Adriano Morselli) was the last opera thus played.   On Jan. 3, 1709, the prices of admission were considerably reduced : stage boxes from 15s. to 8s., first gallery from 5s. to 2s. 6d., and upper gallery from 2s. to 1s. 6d., and the pit was 5s.

Steele laughingly criticises [1] the performance of ' Pyrrhus and Demetrius.'   ' That the understanding has no part in the pleasure is evident, from what these letters very positively assert, to wit, that a great part of the performance was done in Italian ; and a great Critic fell into fits in the Gallery, at seeing not only Time and Place, but Languages and Nations confused in the most incorrigible manner.'

The opera of ' Almahide' (composer unknown, supposed to be Buononcini) was brought out at the Haymarket on Jan. 10, 1710, and was the first opera ever played entirely in Italian and by Italian singers.   These were Nicolini, Valentini, Cassani, Margarita, and Isabella Girardeau.   Still

[1] *Tatler*, No. 4.

John Bull must assert himself, and between the acts *inter-mezzi* were sung in English by Dogget, Mrs. Lindsey, and Mrs. Cross.

Another opera was that of 'Hydaspes' (by Francesco Mancini), which Addison [1] made terrible fun of, especially of a fight that took place between Nicolini and a lion. He had previously [2] unmercifully ridiculed 'Nicolini exposed to a Tempest in Robes of Ermine, and sailing in an Open Boat upon a Sea of Pasteboard,' 'the painted Dragons Spitting Wildfire, enchanted Chariots drawn by *Flanders* Mares, and real Cascades in artificial Landskips;' but then he might have been sore at the fate of his own opera, 'Rosamond,' which was not a success.

Towards the end of 1710 Handel, who was then twenty-seven years of age, came over to England, upon the invitation of several noblemen, whose acquaintance he had made at the Court of Hanover; and here he wrote, for Aaron Hill, who then managed the Haymarket Theatre, his opera of 'Rinaldo,' the first advertisement of which contains a silly blunder as to dates. 'By Subscription. At the Queen's Theatre in the Hay Market, this present Saturday being the 24th day of February, will be perform'd a new Opera, call'd Rinaldo. Tickets and Books will be delivered out at Mr. White's Chocolate House in St. James's Street, *to Morrow* and Saturday next.' [3] In 1712 appeared another of Handel's operas, 'Il Pastor Fido,' which was only performed four times.

On Jan. 21, 1713, was performed his opera of 'Theseus,' about which performance, however, there seems to have been some hitch, for we read [4]: 'Advertisement from the Queen's Theatre in the Hay Market.—This present Saturday the 24th of January, the Opera of Theseus composed by Mr. Hendel will be represented in its Perfection, that is to say with all the Scenes, Decorations, Flights and Machines. The Performers are much concerned that they did not give the Nobility and Gentry all the Satisfaction they could have wished, when they represented it on Wednesday last, having been hindred by some unforeseen Accidents, at that time

---

[1] *Spectator*, 13. [2] *Ibid.* 5.
[3] *Daily Courant*, Feb. 24, 1711. [4] *Ibid.* Jan 24, 1713.

insurmountable. The Boxes on the Stage Half a Guinea, the other Boxes 8s. The Pit 5s., the first Gallery 2s. 6d.' On Handel's first visit, in 1710, the Queen gave him a most flattering reception, and would fain have him remain here, offering him a pension; but he excused himself, as being already engaged to the Elector George of Hanover.

A few short notes about the singers will be interesting. Very early in Anne's reign mention is made of a singer of whom the only record I can find, is in the following advertisement, and some few others: 'To all the Nobility and Gentry. Whereas Mr. *Abel*, having been Honoured with the Commands of the Nobility and Gentry, to sing in Drury Lane 4 times; this is to give notice that the said Mr. Abel has not engaged to sing in any other Consort, till that Noble Performance be ended.' [1]

Hughes was a favourite concert singer, with a good counter-tenor voice; and, when opera first came in, he always played the best parts, until Valentini came over, after which he either died, or left the stage, for no more is heard of him.

Richard Leveridge had a fine and powerful bass voice, and stuck to the stage till he was more than eighty years old, singing in the pantomime at Covent Garden. He was not only an actor and singer, but a composer, having taken part in the composition of an English opera, called the 'Island Princess,' in 1699, and he also wrote and composed many Bacchanalian songs. Died 1758, aged 88.

Of Lawrence little is known, except that when the opera of 'Hydaspes' was brought out, on May 23, 1710, he was able to take a part in it, although an inferior one, and *sing it in Italian*. He had a tenor voice, and continued in Italian opera till 1717, when trace is lost of him.

Ramondon seems to have come upon the stage in 1705, and to have had a bass voice, as he took Leveridge's part in 'Arsinoë.' He seems to have left the stage with the opera of 'Pyrrhus and Demetrius,' but he published some songs in 1716, and set the song tunes in 'Camilla' for the harpsichord or spinet.

Mrs. Tofts was our English prima donna, and she too

[1] *Postman*, May 9'12, 1702.

possessed the then rare accomplishment of being able to sing in Italian. She was the daughter of a person in the family of Bishop Burnet, and, when she appeared on the stage, she won all hearts by her voice, figure, and performance. Her voice was more soprano than contralto.

We have seen her disclaimer when her servant insulted Madame de l'Epine ; and doubtless it was sincere, as she was an equal, if not a greater, favourite with the public. She retired from the stage, with a competence amassed by her exertions, in 1709. If we may believe the *Tatler* (No. 20), she had sad cause for leaving the stage, having lost her reason. 'The great revolutions of this nature bring to my mind the distresses of the unfortunate CAMILLA, who has had the ill luck to break before her voice, and to disappear at a time when her beauty was in the height of its bloom. This lady entered so thoroughly into the great characters she acted, that when she had finished her part she could not think of retrenching her equipage, but would appear in her own lodgings with the same magnificence that she did upon the stage. This greatness of soul had reduced that unhappy princess to an involuntary retirement, where she now passes her time among the Woods and Forests, thinking on the Crowns and sceptres she has lost, and often humming over in her solitude,

> I was born of royal race,
> Yet must wander in disgrace,[1]

etc. But for fear of being over heard, and her quality known, she usually sings it in Italian,

> Nacqui al regno, nacqui al trono
> E per sono
> I ventura pastorella.'[2]

A sad, very sad picture, if a true one.

At all events she must have got better, for she married a rich gentleman named Joseph Smith, a virtuoso, and patron of art ; and when he went to Venice, as English consul, she accompanied him.

---

[1] From the opera of 'Camilla.'
[2] Sic in orig., but it should read—
    'E pur sono
    Sventurata pastorella.'

In *Spectator* 443 is a letter, supposed to be written by her, from Venice.

Her mental malady, however, again seized her, and she lived in retirement, in a remote part of her own house, occasionally roaming about her garden, singing. She is supposed to have died about 1760.

She and her rival are thus celebrated in a song by Hughes (author of the 'Siege of Damascus'), called 'Tofts and Margaretta.'

> Music has learn'd the discords of the State,
> And concerts jar with Whig and Tory Hate.
> Here Somerset and Devonshire attend
> The British Tofts, and every note commend ;
> To native merit just, and pleas'd to see
> We've Roman arts, from Roman bondage free :
> There fam'd l'Epine does equal skill employ,
> Whilst listening peers crow'd to th' ecstatic joy :
> Bedford, to hear her song, his dice forsakes,
> And Nottingham is raptur'd when she shakes :
> Lull'd statesmen melt away their drowsy cares
> Of England's safety, in Italian Airs.
> Who would not send each year blank passes o'er,
> Rather than keep such strangers from our shore ?

Francesca Margherita de l'Epine came over here with a German musician named Greber, and was sometimes irreverently called 'Greber's Peg.' There is no doubt but that she sang very beautifully, and was without a rival on the stage, or in the concert room, after the retirement of Mrs. Tofts. She herself retired in 1718, and married Dr. Pepusch, the celebrated musician, who gave her another nickname, that of 'Hecate,' because of her swarthy complexion and unprepossessing countenance. However, she came well dowered, for she brought him a fortune of £10,000, a very large sum in those days. Swift, who evidently had a John Bull's dislike for everything foreign, writes from Windsor to Stella,[1] ' We have a music meeting in our town to-night. I went to a rehearsal of it, and there was Margarita, and her sister, with another drab, and a parcel of fiddlers ; I was weary, and would not go to the meeting, which I am sorry for, because I

---

[1] *Journal*, Aug. 6, 1711.

heard it was a great assembly.' She died about the year 1740.

The Cavaliere Nicolino Grimaldi,[1] commonly called Nicolini, was a Neapolitan, and came over to England in 1708, entirely on his own responsibility, hearing we were passionately fond of foreign operas. He had achieved a high reputation in Italy, and sustained it here, although foreigners were only tolerated, not liked. He first played in 'Pyrrhus and Demetrius,' and he left England June 14, 1712. His departure is thus chronicled by Addison[2] : 'I am very sorry to find, by the Opera Bills for this Day, that we are likely to lose the greatest Performer in Dramatick Musick that is now living, or that perhaps ever appeared upon a Stage. I need not acquaint my Reader, that I am speaking of *Signior Nicolini.*'

Of Isabella Girardeau we know little, save that her maiden name was Calliari, that she married a Frenchman, and sang from 1700 to 1720.

Of the musical composers living in Anne's reign, perhaps the oldest was Dr. Blow, who died in 1708. Then there was Tudway, who composed an anthem[3] on the occasion of Queen Anne visiting the University of Cambridge, in 1705, which gained him his doctor's degree, and he was afterwards made public Professor of Music to that university, where he was longer remembered for his punning proclivities than for his musical talents.

Jeremiah Clarke, who was coadjutor with Dr. Blow as organist at the King's Chapel, composed the beautiful anthem 'Praise the Lord, O Jerusalem.' He shot himself in 1707 when about forty years of age. There is a curious story told about his suicidal mania. Some weeks before he finally committed the rash act, he was riding to town, accompanied by a servant, returning from a visit to a friend in the country, when the fit seized him, and, dismounting by a field in which was a pond surrounded by trees, he tossed up whether he should hang or drown. The coin fell *on its edge* in the clay, and saved his life for that time.

Dean Aldrich was then alive (he did not die till 1710),

---

[1] *Cavaliere di San Marco.*   [2] *Spectator*, 405.
[3] 'Thou, O God, hast heard my vows.'

and he will be long remembered, not only for his 'Artis Logicæ Rudimenta,' but for his skill as a musical composer[1]; whilst no one at all conversant with Church music will forget the names of Drs. Crofts and Greene.

Among the secular composers was Tom D'Urfey, whose 'Pills to purge Melancholy' is a storehouse of song; but, with the exception of Henry Carey, whose 'Sally in our Alley' and 'Black Eyed Susan' are immortal, the opera and ballad composers of Anne's reign were of no great mark.

A most curious outcome of musical brotherhood was Thomas Britton, the small coal man, already casually mentioned. He must not be passed over under any circumstances, as it is perhaps the only instance of fraternity, absolute and equal, recorded in this reign, between the upper and lower ranks of society. It was of him that Prior wrote:—

> Though doom'd to small coal, yet to arts allied;
> Rich without wealth, and famous without pride,
> Music's best patron, judge of books and men;
> Belov'd and honour'd by Apollo's train.
> In Greece or Rome sure never did appear,
> So bright a genius, in so dark a sphere!
> More of the man had probably been sav'd
> Had Kneller painted, and had Virtue grav'd.

This singular man had a small coal shop in Aylesbury Street, Clerkenwell; and his room, which was over his coal stores, could only be reached by a breakneck ladder, as Ward remarks—

> Upon Thursdays repair
> To my palace, and there
> Hobble up stair by stair;
> But I pray ye take Care
> That you break not your shins by a Stumble.

Somehow, he had a soul above his vocation. He was a fair chemist, and a collector (with some knowledge) of old books and manuscripts. But the most curious part of all his surroundings was the fact that he was able to gather round him in his dirty little den, not only all the musical talent

---

[1] See *Christ Church Bells*, Appendix.

available, but titled *dilletanti*, and even elegant ladies came
to his *réunions*. It was quite the proper place to go to. Hear
what old Thoresby says,[1] 'In our way home called at Mr.
Britton's, the noted small coal man, where we heard a noble
concert of music, vocal and instrumental, the best in town,
which for many years past he has had weekly for his own
entertainment, and of the gentry &c. gratis, to which most
foreigners and many persons of distinction, for the fancy of it,
occasionally resort.' And no wonder, when the learned musical
Dr. Pepusch might be present, or Handel played the harpsichord, whilst Banister would take first violin. Still, it was a
peculiar place to meet in, and only shows what inconveniences
people will suffer for fashion's sake.

His death was almost as remarkable as his life. One of
his performers was injudicious enough to introduce to him a
friend of his who was a ventriloquist, who, without seeming
to speak, bade him, as from a far-off, sepulchral voice, fall
down on his knees at once and say the Lord's Prayer, for
that he should die within a few hours. Poor Britton did as
he was bid—then went home, took to his bed, and died in a
few days of sheer fright, a victim to practical joking.

There was a vast amount of musical taste at that time,
but of course it was not so highly developed as now. We
have seen that a dramatic performance was generally accompanied by a musical one, and the concerts, or *consorts*, as
they were then called, were numerous.

Owing probably to the mourning consequent on the
decease of William III., the first announcement of a concert
in Anne's reign that I can find is one postponed from April 30,
1702, to May 7, and this was to take place at Stationers'
Hall, a very usual place for such entertainments. In the
same newspaper is a notice that 'The Queen's Coronation
Song, compos'd and Sung by Mr. Abell is to be perform'd at
Stationers Hall near Ludgate, to Morrow, being the First of
May 1702 at 8 of the Clock at Night precisely, with other
Songs in Several Languages, and accompanied by the greatest
Masters of Instrumental Musick ; Each Ticket 5s.'

York Buildings was another favourite concert room, as

---

[1] June 5, 1712.

was also Hickford's Dancing Room.   This latter place, being at the extreme West End of London, bid for aristocratic patrons, and the prices were high ; indeed, the tickets for the following concert were the highest priced of any I have ever met with : '1707 To Morrow being Wednesday the 2nd of April, Signior Fr. Conti will cause to be perform'd at Mr. Hickford's Dancing Room in James Street, in the Hay Market over against the Tennis Court, the Consort of Musick compos'd by him for her Majesty, and which he had the Honour to have perform'd at Court the Day after the Act for the Union [1] pass'd. Signiora Margarita, the Baroness, and Signior Valentino will sing in it accompanied with several Instruments, and the Signior Conti will play upon his great Theorbo, and on the Mandoline, an instrument not known yet.   The Consort will begin at 7 a Clock at Night. Tickets to be had only at White's Chocolate House, and at the Smyrna Coffee House at a Guinea a ticket.' A high price—but consider the attractions.   All the available talent, together with a *Monstre* Instrument, and an entirely novel one !

Nowadays we should hardly expect concerts to be given at Chelsea Hospital, but it was different then, and ' Ladies of Quality' probably had as much influence then as they have now, and could get pretty well what they liked : '1702 In Honour of the Queens Coronation ; The Ladies Consort of Musick ; by Subscription of several Ladies of Quality (by permission) at the Royal College of Chelsea, on Monday the 25th of the present May, is to be performed once, a new Consort of Musick, by Mr. Abel and other voices ; with Instrumental Musick of all sorts ; To be placed in two several Quires on each side of the Hall ; a manner never yet performed in England.   The Hall to be well illuminated ; the said Consort to begin exactly at five a Clock, and to hold 3 full hours.   Each Ticket 5s. Notice that the Moon will shine, the Tide serve, and a Guard placed from the College to St. James's Park, for the safe return of the Ladies.'

The moon and tide were important factors then, as we find in a notice of 'a Consort of Musick' at Richmond Wells,

[1] The Royal Assent to this Act was given March 6, 1707.

Aug. 12, 1703: 'This Consort to be perform'd but once, because of the Queen's going to the Bath. *Note.* The Tide serves at 11 o'clock in the Morning and Light Nights.' So that the visitors were evidently expected to spend the whole day there.

Another suburban Spa (Hampstead) was famous for its concerts, and continued in favour during the whole of the reign.

'1705 On Saturday August the 4th In the great Room at the *Ship Tavern Greenwich* will be an extraordinary Consort of Vocal and Instrumental Musick, viz., Several Songs set by the best Masters ; Particularly a Song of two parts by Mr. Henry Purcel, never perform'd but once before in Publick,' etc.

Towards the latter end of the reign the character of some of these concerts seem to be altering. Take one at Stationers' Hall, Feb. 22, 1715, for instance : 'Among other choice Compositions, a celebrated Song of Mr. Hendel's by a Gentlewoman from Abroad, who hath never before exposed her Voice publickly in this kingdom. To which will be added an uncommon piece of Musick by Bassoons only. Country Dances when the Consort is over ; and such a Decorum kept that the most innocent may be present without the danger of an Affront.'

Concerts, as we see, were both vocal and instrumental. Of the vocal performers much has already been said ; of the instrumental, none are worth notice, except Gasparini, an Italian, who was an excellent violinist. The last and perhaps the least of them was : 'A Boy of about Eight Years of Age will perform an Italian Sonata on the Trumpet, who never yet perform'd in publick.' This musical treat took place at York Buildings, Feb. 24, 1703.

The instruments in domestic use were the chamber or house organ, many of which were frequently advertised for sale, the spinet, and harpsichord, or harpsicalls, which we know so well, thanks to the South Kensington Museum. Here, however, is a rare one: 'To be disposed of, a most excellent Harpsicord made by the Famous Sign. Gieronimo Senti, at Pesaro in Italy, having 2 Extraordinary fine Keys of Ivory, several Stops and Alterations besides the 2 Principals,

and one Octave, or the Spinet, which may be plaid seperately
or together, imitating most exactly the Theorba, and most
curiously the Arch Lute.' The flute was played, as were also
the lute, and the theorbo, a lute-like instrument. The other
stringed instruments were the bass viol and the violin,
Cremonas being then, as now, highly prized.

It was essentially an age for chamber music, with nice
little social gatherings, at which were played duets on the
flute, etc., or catches, rounds, and three-part songs were sung.
What we should call *good* music was thoroughly appreciated,
and Corelli, perhaps, was then the favourite composer. The
following advertisement will show the class of music then
in vogue (1706): 'To all Lovers of Musick. This day are
published, and to be sold at Isaac Vaillant's Book and Map-
seller in the Strand near Catherine Street, Per.[1] Opera 2 da,
Sonata di Camera for 2 Flutes and Bass, Marini Opera 6 ta,
12 Sonatas for 2 Violins, a Viol and double Basses, 6 Sonatas
and Solos transposed for the Flute, pr 5s. Mr Novel's 12
Sonatas for 2 Violins and double Basses, pr 6s., Six new
Sonatas for 2 Flutes and a Bass by Mr. Keller. Albicestilo,
Opera Nona, 12 Solos for the Violin, a new Book for the
Harpsichord by Mr. Anglebert, with several Overtures,
Minuets, Jigs &c. of Mr. Lully transposed for that instrument.
These books are printed by Steph Roger, most of them on
Royal Paper. At the abovesaid Vaillant's may be had the
new Edition of Corelli printed on Imperial Paper pr 32s. 6d.'

But all music was not as dear as this—for instance : 'The
Monthly Mask of Vocal Musick: the newest Songs, made for the
Theatres and other occasions Compos'd by Mr. John Welden
and Mr. Dan Purcel. Publish'd for November, which collections will be continued monthly for the year 1703 pr. 6d.
Also a Set of Lessons for the Harpsicord or Spinnet. Composed by Mr. John Eccles, Master of Her Majesties Musick
pr 6d.'

Music was printed either from engraved copper plates, as
in the case of 'The Nightingale,' which was engraved by
Thomas Cross, who worked in the very early part of the
century, or by movable types, as is the case with all music

---

[1] ? Perti, who lived to the age of nearly 100, and was alive in 1744.

taken from 'The Dancing Master.' But the Dutch hit upon
a cheaper plan, and made use of pewter plates, which they
stamped, and so were able to undersell the engraved music.
It is said they got 1,500*l.* by printing the opera of 'Rinaldo.'
One Richard Mears also engraved music, but he, finding his
trade interfered with by the Dutchmen, took to stamping. At
his death in 1743 almost the whole of the music printing in
the country was done by the son of the following advertiser :[1]
'Twenty four *New Country* Dances for the year 1710, with
proper *Tunes*, and *New* Figures, or direction to each *Dance*,
composed by Mr. Kynaston, all fairly *Engraven*, price 6*d*
NOTE The New *Country* Dancing *Master* is published, containing the Country dances for the three last years. Printed
for John Walsh. Servant in Ordinary to her Majesty.'

[1] *Tatler*, 88.

CHAPTER XXVII.

PAINTERS AND ARCHITECTS.

Woolaston—Murray—Hugh Howard—Lewis Crosse—Luke Cradock—
Charles Jervas—Richardson—Sir James Thornhill—Sir Godfrey
Kneller—Closterman—Pelegrini—Sebastian Ricci—Vander Vaart—
Laguerre—Dahl—Boit—Class of pictures in vogue—Water colours—
Drawings—Engravings—Sculpture—Grinling Gibbons—Architects—
Sir C. Wren—Vanbrugh.

THE sister art of painting was not well represented in this
reign—by native talent, at all events, except by Thornhill.
There was Wollaston, a portrait painter, who could only
command five guineas for a three-quarters canvas : he was
one of Britton's amateurs, and played both violin and flute.
He died at an old age in the Charter House. Thomas
Murray was another portrait painter.

There was Hugh Howard, to whom Prior indited an ode
commencing,

> Dear Howard, from the soft assaults of love,
>   Poets and painters never are secure ;
> Can I untouch'd the fair one's passions move,
>   Or thou draw beauty, and not feel its power ?

He was lucky, for through his acquaintances of high rank
he obtained the situation of Keeper of the State Papers, and
Paymaster of His Majesty's Palaces, when he still followed
the pursuit of art, by collecting prints and medals.

Lewis Crosse was a painter in water colours, and executed
miniatures. He also collected them, and his very valuable
collection was sold in 1722, two years before his death.
Luke Cradock, who was but a house painter, rose by his
own exertions to be an excellent painter of birds, and, like
H. S. Marks, Esq., R.A., his works were highly prized for

house decorations. According to Vertue, his pictures, soon after his death, fetched three or four times the prices paid for them.

Charles Jervas, who lived in this reign, and had been a pupil of Kneller, was a very good painter. He taught Pope to draw and paint, and Pope wrote an ' Epistle to Mr. Jervas,' in which he belauded him, as did also Steele [1] when he called him ' the last great painter Italy has sent us, Mr. Jervas '— alluding to his return from studying in Italy. He married a widow worth 20,000*l.*, and the praise he received with the affluence of his circumstances rendered him inordinately vain, as the two following anecdotes will show. He made a good copy of a Titian, and he thought he had actually out-done that master ; for, looking from one to the other, he complacently observed, ' Poor little Tit ! how he would stare !' The Duchess of Bridgewater sat to him for her portrait, that picture of which Pope says—

> With Zeuxis' Helen thy Bridgewater vie

—and he remarked that she had not a handsome ear. Her ladyship asked him his opinion of what *was* a handsome ear, to which his answer was – showing her one of his own.

Jonathan Richardson was, perhaps, the best English por-trait painter of his time ; and, after the deaths of Kneller and Dahl, stood prominent in that branch of his profession. Aikman and Alexander were also contemporary artists.

But perhaps the English artist of that time best known to us is Sir James Thornhill ; not only by his painting in the dome of St. Paul's, but by his masterpiece in the Hall of Greenwich Hospital. Indeed he was a worthy rival both of Verrio and Laguerre. Forty shillings per square yard was all he got for painting St. Paul's, and probably no more for Greenwich. For his decorations at Blenheim he only re-ceived twenty-five shillings per square yard ; and the Direc-tors of the South Sea Company would pay him no more for the work he did on their staircase and hall. There are a few other English painters, but they were of no note.

Of foreign artists in England, doubtless the greatest was

---

[1] *Tatler,* No. 4.

Kneller, who was born at Lubeck in 1648. He came over here in 1674, without the least intention of stopping ; but, having painted Charles II. and established a reputation, he made this country his home. Knighted by William, petted by Anne, baroneted by George I., he could scarcely expect greater honours. His principal works in Anne's reign were a bad portrait of the King of Spain, who paid a visit to the Queen, and was kept some time longer than he expected, by stress of weather ; seven portraits of admirals at Hampton Court, and the portraits of the Kit Cat Club, which have already been noticed. He was as vain as Jervas, if not more so. Pope tried to see to what extent his vanity would go. ' Sir Godfrey, I believe if God Almighty had had your assistance, the world would have been formed more perfect.' ' 'Fore Gad, Sir, I believe so too,' was the self-satisfied reply. He, however, was not devoid of wit, as his little encounter with Dr. Ratcliffe proves. They lived next to each other, and there was a door between the two gardens. Through this door Ratcliffe's servants used to come and pick Kneller's flowers ; so the painter sent word that he would have the door shut. A message came from the doctor that ' he might do anything with it but paint it,' to which the artist replied that ' he would take anything from him but his physic.' Kneller was painting the portrait of James II., which was to be a present to Pepys, when the King received the news of the landing of the Prince of Orange. He ordered the painter to proceed with his work, so that ' his good friend Pepys should not be disappointed.'

When Sir Godfrey moved from his house in Covent Garden, he had a sale of pictures, probably of little artistic value, or only copies.[1] ' At the late Dwelling House of Sir . Godfrey Kneller, in the Piazza's, Covent Garden, will be sold a Collection of Original Paintings, fit for Stair Cases, Chimneys, Doors or Closets. Some of the Masters they were done by are as follows : viz. Holben, Ruben, Van Dyke, Sr. Peter Lely, Antonio de Cortona, Solveta, Rosa, Snider, Vander Velde, Rostraten, Bombodes, Verelst and several other great Masters.' This auction was a failure : ' This is to give notice, That the Collection, &c., will be Sold out of hand at very reasonable Rates at the above mentioned place, beginning this present *Monday* being the 27th of March, the badness and uncertainty of the Weather having put a stop to the Auction.' [1]

John Closterman was the artist who painted the whole-length portrait of Queen Anne, now in the Guildhall. We get several notices of him from the newspapers : ' Mr. Closterman being obliged at Christmas next to go to Hannover, and afterwards to several Courts of Germany ; so that it is uncertain whether he will ever return to England. Such Persons of Quality and others, as have lately sate to him, are desired to take notice, that their Pictures will be finished out of hand, and deliver'd as they shall best please to order them.' [2]

In April of the next year he advertised that ' being oblig'd to leave England very suddenly, will sell all his pictures by Auction.' He had another sale of pictures on Feb. 28, 1711, which was probably after his death, the date of which is somewhat uncertain. He had married a worthless girl, who robbed him of all he possessed, and then ran away : this sent him mad, and he soon afterwards died.

Antonio Pelegrini made several designs for painting the dome of St. Paul's, and was paid for them. He painted staircases, etc., for the Dukes of Manchester and Portland, and for other noblemen. He died abroad.

His master, Sebastian Ricci, came over here, and painted the altarpiece in the chapel of Chelsea College ; but he, too, did not stop. Not so James Bogdani, a native of Hungary, who lived here between forty and fifty years. He painted fruit, flowers, and birds, and our royal palaces still possess examples of this master, which were purchased by Queen Anne.

John Vander Vaart,[3] of Haarlem, lived for over fifty years in Covent Garden, and died there. His *forte* was game. He

[1] *Daily Courant*, March 27, 1704. [2] *Ibid.* Aug. 6, 1705.
[3] In the *Postman*, Feb. 3 6, 1711, is an Advertisement of his, saying he intended retiring from business, and will sell his collection of pictures.

painted a piece of still life—a violin— on a door at Devonshire House, Piccadilly, that deceived everybody. This is
now at Chatsworth.

· Pope's line, 'Where sprawl the Saints of Verrio and
Laguerre,' naturally makes us think of these two masters, and
many were the ceilings which the latter painted in England.
He enjoyed royal patronage under both William and Anne,
designing for the latter some tapestry, illustrative of the
union between England and Scotland, in which were portraits
of the Queen and her ministers. He did the drawings, but
the tapestry was not made. His end was sudden : he died
of apoplexy in Drury Lane Theatre, whither he had gone to
attend the benefit of his son, who sang there in ' The Island
Princess.' [1]

Michael Dahl was a Swede, and a mighty portrait painter.
He was Kneller's rival, and yet they must have been friends,
for Sir Godfrey painted his portrait. He was a great pet of
Prince George of Denmark, and was also patronised by the
Queen.

Any account of the artists of this reign would be sadly
incomplete without mention of Boit, the enameller, who was
certainly the best, up to that time, after Petitot or Zincke.
He got large sums for his miniatures. Several now exist,
and one, especially good, of Queen Anne sitting, and Prince
George standing beside her, is at Kensington Palace. The
most important work on which he was engaged during his
stay in England was a large plate, about 24 in. by 18, for
which Laguerre painted the design in oil. It represented the
Queen, Prince George, and the principal members of the Court,
with Victory introducing the Duke of Marlborough and Prince
Eugene ; France and Bavaria were prostrate, and there were
the usual military accompaniment of standards and trophies
of arms. He got an advance of £1,000, and spent £700 or
£800 of it in erecting furnaces able to fire so large a plate ;
and, when he began to lay on colour, he got another advance of
£700. Then came the memorable disgrace of Marlborough,
and he was ordered to change Marlborough into Ormonde,
and Victory into Peace. Prince Eugene would not sit, and

---

[1] By P. A. Motteux.

no further progress was ever made with the picture. Boit ran away, on the Queen's death, much in debt, and got to France, where they were only too glad to receive him. There he died in 1726.

Those were not, as now, golden days for artists, who never dreamed of living in luxuriously furnished mansions of their own building. There were no exhibitions of art, nor did the middle class indulge much in oil paintings, which were principally confined to originals, or copies, of the Italian or Dutch and Flemish schools. Of course every gentleman who made the 'grand tour' brought some home with him, if only to show his taste in such matters ; and, through the fluctuations of fortune, there was generally a good supply of them in the market. The following extract from Swift's Journal to Stella will give some idea of the price of a copy, for it is scarcely likely to have been an original. '6 Mar. 1713. I was to day at an auction of pictures with Pratt, and laid out two pounds five Shillings for a picture of Titian, and if it were a Titian it would be worth twice as many pounds. If I am cheated, I'll part with it to Lord Masham ; if it be a bargain, I'll keep it to myself. That's my conscience.'

To give an idea of the range of art which these pictures occupied, let us take the names of the masters, with their spellings, as they appear in the advertisements. *Italian.* Giorgione da Castle Franco, Titian, Palma, Tintoret, Bassan, Cavalieri Gioseppi d'Arpino, Paulo Faranati, Camillo Procacino, Spaniolette, Bartolemeo, Pordenone, Andrea del Sarto, Leonardo da Vinci, Paulo Veronese, Gaspar Poussin, Julio Romano, Pollydore, Parmigiano, Baptista Franca, Corregio, Primaticcio, Schiavone, Claud Lorain, Fran, Bolognese, Mola, the Borgognon, Luca Jordano, Bourdon, Perosini, Scacciati, Daudini, Tempesto, and Guido Guavini.

Among the Dutch and Flemish Masters were : Van Dyke, Quentin Messias, Ostervelt, Vander Werff, Van de Velde, Cornelius Johnson, Vander Meer, Brayuinx, Griffiere Backhuysen, De Wit, Brawer, Wyck, Ostade, Hondecoeter, Saftleven, Boc, Percellus, Ryzeberg, Blœmœrt, Youngfranc, Bramer, Verelst, Palamedus, Levintz, Ruysdail, Hemskirk, Breughel, Holben, Rubens, Berchem, and Teniers.

And we have one advertisement where 'Among them are Portraicts a half length of the Queen of *England*[1] by *Ryly*; Sir *Tho More*; Lord *Cicil* in Queen *Elizabeth's* time, and the Lord *Francis Bacon.*'

People who could not afford oil paintings might buy water colours, and the following gives us the names of two famous artists: 'A choice collection of Limnings, by Mr. *Cooper* and old Mr. *Hoskins* now in the possession of his Son *John Hoskins* of *Chelsea*, will be sold by Auction. Likewise several Boxes of Limning Colours,' etc. These were, in all probability, miniatures.

Drawings, both in crayon and black lead, line engravings, and etchings were within the compass of most people's purses, and here is an advertisement which would create some interest even now at Christie's. 'At the Eagle and Child in Bedford Street, Covent Garden, &c. will be continued the Sale by Auction of a collection of Paintings, Drawings, and Prints, by the most famous Italian, and other great Masters. The Drawings are of the most celebrated Masters of the several Schools of Italy. A great number of them in Frames and Glasses. The Prints are in great perfection, a great many Etcht by the Masters themselves, others graved by the most eminent Gravers. There are a great many extraordinary rare Wood Cuts, they have been collecting these 30 Years with great industry and expense, most out of the chiefest Auctions in England, and others bought in Holland and France, by Mr. William Gibson,[2] Limner.'

We know the engravings of that time were very good: they were also very cheap, and of good subjects. 'You may have the Right Originals after the greatest Masters, as Raphael, Michael Angelo, Ruben, Julij Romana, all well graven, and 30 sorts of Altarpieces and Prints ready framed;' or one might buy ' A compleat Sett of the Prints of the Royal Palaces and Noblemen's Seats in England, neatly bound up together, or sold Singly for 1*s.* apiece ; and likewise a curious Collection of Italian and French prints, particularly the Original Battles

---

[1] Either Mary of Modena, Consort of James II., or Queen Mary.
[2] A miniature painter, pupil of Sir Peter Lely, and nephew of Gibson, the dwarf painter.

of Alexander ; the Galleries of Luxemburgh ; Poussin's Land-skips, and many others.' Good English Engravers were then very scarce : nearly all the illustratioris to books were engraved by foreigners, and very frequently in Holland.

Take the following for example—engraved in England, but by a foreigner : ' The Seven Cartons of Raphael d'Urbin drawn and engrav'd from the Originals in the Gallery at Hampton Court by S. Gribelin, are sold by C. Mather near Temple Bar in Fleet Street &c.—price 15*s*.' There was another set of these engraved in 1711 and 1712, by Michael Dorigny, who offered eight plates 19 in. by 25 to 30 for four guineas. Steele gives this venture a kindly puff in *Spectator* 226.

Sculpture was not at a premium, there being but one sculptor at all worthy of the name (of course except Gibbons), and he was Francis Bud, to whom, among other works, we owe the statue of Queen Anne in St. Paul's Churchyard, and the Conversion of St. Paul in the pediment of the cathedral.

The virtuosi got their statuary from Italy, and of course these classical gentlemen would be satisfied with nothing less than ' right Antiques.' ' Four Marble Figures lately come from Italy, with 2 half bodies. The Figures are Jupiter and Venus, Bacchus and his Mistress.'

There was a demand for plaster and leaden casts for garden ornamentation, and this was met by one Van Nost, who lived in ' Hide Park Road, near the Queen's Mead House,' who had a fine collection, which was sold after his death, in 1712. His widow also sold, at a great reduction in price, ' the fine Marble Figures and Bustos, curious inlaid Marble Tables, Brass and Leaden Figures and very rich Vauses.'

Grinling Gibbons, of course, bears the palm in the matter of carving in this age, and we must not forget that he carved in stone and marble as well as in wood. The statue of Charles II. in the old Royal Exchange, the base of Charles the First's statue at Charing Cross, and the marble pedestal of the equestrian statue of Charles II. at Windsor, together with the magnificent tomb of Baptist Noel, Viscount Camder, in the church of Exton, Rutlandshire, all testify to his ability when dealing with the more obdurate materials. As to his wood carvings, they are most numerous and widely spread.

In the choir of St. Paul's, at Chatsworth, at Burleigh, at Petworth, etc., are triumphs of his skill.

From sculpture to architecture is but a step ; and a reign that can boast of two such architects as Wren and Vanbrugh must of necessity rank high as favouring this art. If Wren had built nothing else but St. Paul's, his fame would have been immortal, and the other buildings with which he beautified London, thanks to the great fire, cannot add lustre to his name. In the architecture of his churches he was very uneven ; but it must not be forgotten that he had at that time so much work on hand, that thorough originality could not be expected in every case, and also, in very many instances he was hampered as to the expense. Not that he was an extravagant architect. The man who could build (even taking money at its different value then and now) St. Mary Aldermary for a little over 5,000*l.*, or St. Mary-le-Bow for 8,000*l.*— exclusive of the steeple, which cost nearly 1,400*l.* more—could not be accused of extravagance. We owe to him the Monument, Greenwich and Chelsea Hospitals, the Theatre and Ashmolean Museum at Oxford, and the library of Trinity College, Cambridge, besides a large number of churches, all still existing, and the Royal Exchange and Temple Bar, destroyed. In this reign he was thoroughly appreciated and honoured ; was knighted by Anne, was President of the Royal Society, and sat twice in Parliament ; and it was reserved to the Whigs in George the First's reign to deprive him of his places, and leave him uncared for in his old age.

The versatile Vanbrugh, who could be playwright or architect, poet, theatrical manager, or king-at-arms, adds much to the lustre of Anne's reign.

We have seen how Swift lampooned him on the building of his own house at Whitehall (vol. i. p. 61), and we all know Dr. Evans' epitaph upon him :—

> Lie heavy on him, earth, for he
> Laid many a heavy load on thee.

That he was as great an architect as Wren, cannot be for a moment entertained ; but that he was not without good taste and scientific knowledge, his two best works, Blenheim and Castle Howard, testify.

CHAPTER XXVIII.

SCIENCE, ETC.

Its infancy—Virtuosi—Gresham College—Visit to the Royal Society's Museum—Their curiosities—Their new house—Geology—Experimental philosophy—Courses of chemistry—Mathematics—List of patents—Hydraulic machinery—Savery's steam engine—Description.

EXACT science, as we understand the term, hardly existed. Sir Isaac Newton was just lighting the spark which has been fanned by succeeding generations into such a mighty flame. The Royal Society was an absolute laughing-stock, and men called virtuosi pottered about, looking (and doubtless thinking they were) mighty wise.

Any man who investigated nature after his lights, and with the imperfect materials which were at his command, was looked upon as a fool.

' The Will of a VIRTUOSO.'[1]

' I *Nicholas Gimcrack* being in sound health of mind, but in great weakness of body, do by this my last Will and Testament bestow my worldly Goods and Chattels in manner following.

' *Imprimis.* To my dear wife, One box of butterflies, One drawer of Shells, A female Skeleton, A dried Cockatrice.

' *Item.* To my Daughter *Elizabeth.* My Receipt for preserving dead Caterpillars. Also my preparations of winter May dew, and Embryo-Pickle.

' *Item.* To my little daughter *Fanny*, Three Crocodile's Eggs. And upon the birth of her first Child, if she marries with her mother's consent, the Nest of a Humming Bird.

' *Item.* To my eldest Brother, as an acknowledgment for the Lands he has vested in my Son *Charles*, I bequeath my last Year's Collection of Grasshoppers.

[1] *Tatler*, No. 216.

' *Item.* To his Daughter *Susanna*, being his only Child, I bequeath my English Weeds pasted on Royal paper, with my large Folio of Indian Cabbage.

' Having fully provided for my nephew *Isaac* by making over to him, some years since, a Horned Scarabœus, the Skin of a Rattle snake, and the Mummy of an Egyptian King, I make no further Provision for him in this my *Will*.

' My eldest Son *John* having spoke disrespectfully of his little Sister, whom I keep by me in Spirits of Wine, and in many other instances behaved himself undutifully towards me, I do disinherit, and wholly Cut off from any part of this my personal estate, by giving him a single Cockle shell.

' To my second son *Charles*, I give and bequeath all my Flowers, Plants, Minerals, Mosses, Shells, Pebbles, Fossils, Beetles, Butterflies, Caterpillars, Grasshoppers, and Vermin, not above specified ; as also my Monsters, both wet and dry ; making the said *Charles* whole and sole *Executor* of this my last *Will* and *Testament* ; He paying or causing to be paid, the aforesaid Legacies within the space of six Months after my Decease.   And I do hereby revoke all other *Wills* whatsoever by me formerly made.'

Clarinda. A Sot, that has spent £2000 in Microscopes, to find out the Nature of Eals in Vinegar, Mites in a Cheese, and the blue of Plums which he has subtilly found out to be living Creatures.

Miranda. One who has broken his brains about the nature of Magots, who has studied these twenty years to find out the several sorts of Spiders, and never cares for understanding Mankind.[1]

It is needless to say that Gresham College, then the home of the Royal Society, affords a wealth of merriment to Ward. It is ' Wise Acres Hall,' or ' Maggot Mongers' Hall ' ; but his description,[2] although whimsical, is truthful, and shows the puerility (as we might term it) of science in those days. ' My Friend conducted me up a pair of Stairs, to the Elaboratory-Keeper's Apartment and desir'd him to oblige us with a Sight of his Rarities ; who very curteously granted us the Liberty ; opening his Warehouse of *Egyptian Mummies*, old musty Skeletons, and other antiquated Trumpery : The first thing he thought most worthy of our Notice, was

[1] *The Virtuoso*, by Shadwell.   [2] *London Spy.*

the *Magnet*, with which he show'd some notable Experiments, it made a Paper of Steel Filings Prick up themselves one upon the back of another, that they stood pointing like the Bristles of a *Hedge hog*; and gave such Life and Merriment to a parcel of Needles, they danced the Hay, by the motion of the Stone, as if the Devil were in 'em; the next things he presented to our view, were a parcel of Shell Flies almost as big as *Lobsters*, arm'd with Beaks as big as *Jack-Daws* : then he commended to our observation that Wonderful Curiosity, the *Unicorn's* Horn; made, I suppose, by an Ingenious Turner, of the Tusks of an *Elephant*; it is of an excellent Virtue; and, by report of those that know nothing of the matter, will expel Poison beyond the *Mountebank's Orvieton*; Then he carry'd us to another part of the Room, where there was an *Aviary* of Dead Birds, Collected from the extream parts of *Europe*, *Asia*, *Africa*, and *America*; amongst which were an *East India* Owl, a *West India* Bat, and a Bird of *Paradise*, the last being Beautified with variety of Colours, having no discernable Body, but all Feathers, Feeding, when alive, upon nothing but Air, and tho' 'tis as big as a Parrot, 'tis as light as a Cobweb. Then he usher'd us among sundry sorts of Serpents, as the *Noy*, *Pelongy*, *Rattle Snake*, *Aligator*, *Crocodile* &c. That looking round me, I thought myself hem'd in amongst a legion of Devils; When we had taken a survey of these pin-cushion Monsters, we turn'd towards the Skeletons of Men, Women, and Monkeys, Birds, Beasts and Fishes; Abortives put up in Pickle, and abundance of other Memorandums of Mortality; that they look'd as Ghostly as the Picture of *Michael* Angelo's Resurrection; as if they had Collected their Scatter'd Bones into their Original Order, and were about to March in search after the rest of the Appurtenances.'

That this account is not exaggerated is shown by an extract or two of Dr. Green's catalogue of these curiosities.

'Tortoises, when turned on their backs, will sometimes fetch deep sighs and shed abundance of tears.

'A bone, said to be taken out of a Mermaid's head.

'A stag-beetle, whose horns, worn in a ring, are good against Cramp, &c.'

The Royal Society, however, under Newton's presidency, woke up wonderfully in Anne's reign, although they still pottered after such things as dissecting dolphins,[1] etc. In 1705 the Mercers' Company gave them notice to quit Gresham College, and they petitioned the Queen for a grant of land near Westminster, but the petition was refused. Then they applied to the trustees of the Cotton Library for permission to meet at Cotton House, Westminster, but could not obtain it. And so they tried for six years to get their own premises, and at last succeeded in buying the house (really two houses) of Dr. Brown, in Crane Court, Fleet Street, which house, but little altered, is now standing, and is in the occupation of the Scottish Corporation. This cost them 1450l., 550l. of which they paid out of their own funds, and borrowed the remainder at six per cent.; but it also required 1800l. to fit these houses for the requirements of the Society: yet somehow they managed to hold their first meeting there on Nov. 8, 1710.

Addison, in the *Tatler*,[2] cannot resist the temptation of making fun of this Society: 'When I married this Gentleman he had a very handsome estate, but upon buying a set of Microscopes he was chosen *a Fellow of the Royal Society, from which time I do not remember ever to have heard him speak as other people did*, or talk in a manner that any of his family could understand.' Steele,[3] too, must needs give a little stab: 'When I meet with a young fellow that is an humble admirer of these Sciences, but more dull than the rest of the Company, I conclude him to be a Fellow of the Royal Society.'

The science of geology was very little known, although Dr. Woodward, in his 'Natural History of the Earth,' notes its division into strata, but in that, as in all other sciences, they were but in a very elementary stage. They had only got as far as this : 'An Account of the Origin and Formation of Fossil-Shells, &c., wherein is proposed a Way to reconcile the two different Opinions, of those who affirm them to be the Exuviæ of real Animals, and those who fancy them to be Lusus Naturæ.'

---

[1] Thoresby.   [2] No. 221.   [3] *Tatler*, 236.

But science was making such steps that men were willing
to be taught, and consequently teachers were found. The
stage physical science had reached in 1706 is shown by the
following advertisement : 'For the Advancement of Experimental Philosophy, and for the Benefit of all such Gentlemen
as are willing to lay the best and surest Foundation for
all useful Knowledge : There are provided Engines for
rarifying and condensing Air, with all the Appurtenances
thereunto belonging ; also Barometers, Thermometers, and
such other Instruments as are Necessary for a Course of
Experiments, in order to prove the Weight and Spring of the
Air, its usefulness in the propagation of Sounds and Conversation of Life, &c., with several new and surprising Experiments concerning the production of Light in Vacuo :
Likewise Utensils proper for making the Hydrostatical
Experiments to determine the Laws of Fluids Gravitating
upon each other. By J. Hodgson and F. Hawksbee, Fellows
of the Royal Society. This Course will begin &c. . . . at
which times Lectures will be Read for the better understanding the Experiments, and for the drawing of such Conclusions
and Uses as flow from them. Those Gentlemen that are
desirous to be present must pay 2 Guineas, one at the time
of Subscription, and the other on the 3rd Night after the
Course begins.' Hawksbee continued these lectures till his
death, about 1710 or 1711.

Courses of chemistry had existed ever since the com-
mencement of the reign : *vide* ' A Course of Chimistry, com-
mencing the 27th of April, 1702, containing above 100
Operations, will be performed by George Willson at his
Elaboratory in Well Yard, by St. Bartholomew's Hospital in
Smithfield.' His fee was two and a half guineas.

What was meant by this course we cannot tell, but
there is another advertisement in 1712 which may throw
some light upon it : 'A Compleat Course of Chymistry
containing about 100 Operations, illustrated with the proper
Scholia, has been perform'd at the Laboratory of Mr.
Edward Bright, Chymist, in White Friars near Fleet
Street, to the entire Satisfaction of the Gentlemen that
attended it, &c. . . . In these Courses Endeavours are used

to demonstrate the Constituent Parts of each Medicine, their Virtues and Doses ; to which will be added many useful Observations applicable to the Practice of Physick.'

The higher branches of mathematics were also publicly taught in 1705 : 'On Tuesday next being the 2nd Day of October, at the Marine Coffee house in Birchin Lane, Mr. Harris will go on with the Public Mathematic Lecture ; beginning them with Geometry anew ; and he will explain largely the Uses of all the Propositions, as he goes along : with a particular regard to the principles of true Mechanick Philosophy.' This latter was highly necessary, for mechanics were in an exceedingly elementary state : even such a common thing as a wind dial was new, and wonderful, in 1706. 'The WIND DIAL, lately set up at Grigsby's Coffee and Chocolate House, behind the Royal Exchange, being the first and only one in any publick House in England, and having given great Satisfaction to all that have seen it, and being of Constant use to those that are in any wise Concerned in Navigation : We think it may not be improper to describe it to the Publick, viz. The Dial Board is fixed to the Ceiling of the Publick Ground room, upon which are all the points of the Compass in Gold Letters, and a Hand Points to each of them, continually as the Wind varies. The Hand is directed by an Iron work, which is turned by a Fan placed 90 foot high, to prevent the effects of Eddy Winds.'

Condensing sea water, in order to make it potable, is, if an old invention, quite a modern practice ; yet we see it in use in 1705. 'Mr. Walcot's Engines for making Sea Water Fresh and Wholesome, are sold by him at his Warehouse in Woolpack Alley in Houndsditch at reasonable rates being of great use and advantage for all Ships, especially such as go long voyages.'

Perhaps the best method of gauging the mechanical genius of the age is to examine the patents granted, and, as they are very few in this reign, a short list of them will fulfil this condition, and yet not be wearisome.

Jan. 1, 1703. A grant to George Sorocold, gent., of a new invention by him contrived and found out, for cutting and sawing all kinds of boards, timber, and stone, and twisting all kinds of ropes, cords, and cables, by the strength of horses or water.

. April 8, 1704. A grant to Benjamin Jackson, gent., of the sole use and exercise of a new invention for ordinary coaches, calashes, shazes, waggons, and other carriages and machines of that nature, that though the wheels or carriages may be overset, yet the bodies of them shall remain upright.

May 1, 1704. A grant to Nicholas Fain, gent., Peter Defaubre, and Jacob Defaubre, watchmakers, for making use of precious or more common stones, crystal or glass, as an internal and useful part of watches and other engines.

July 29, 1704. A grant unto Richard Cole, gent., of his invention of forming glasses into conical figures, and lamps for the better dispersing and casting of light.

April 12, 1706. A grant unto Henry Mill, gent., of his new invention of a mathematical instrument, consisting of several new sorts of springs for the ease of persons riding in coaches, chariots, calashes, and chaises.

June 6, 1706. A grant unto Robert Aldersey of his new invention in contriving a floating dam to carry lighters and other vessels over the greatest flats and shallows in any navigable river.

1706. A grant unto Thomas Savery, Esq., of his new invention for making double hand-bellows, which by the power of springs and screws will produce a continual blast.

July 26, 1709. A grant unto Jeremiah Wieschamer of his new invention of a mill or engine for the more easy grinding or pressing of sugar-canes with a less number of oxen, horses, or cattle than by those mills formerly used.

April 3, 1712. A grant unto Israel Pownoll of his new invented engine or machine for taking up ballast, sullage, sand, etc., of very great use in cleansing rivers, harbours, etc.

June 17, 1712. A grant unto Nicholas Lewis Mandell, Esq., and John Grey, carpenters, of their two new invented engines ; the one of a small size for the weighing and raising up any weight far beyond what can be performed by any crane or capstone ; and the other for raising water in a new and surprising manner, of great use in extinguishing fire.

April 2, 1714. A grant unto John Wilks of his new

invented engine or mill for grinding all sorts of wood dry for the use of dying.

May 27, 1714. A grant unto John Coster, gent., and John Coster, jun., gent., of their new invented engine for drawing water out of deep mines.

These are all the mechanical patents worthy of notice during Anne's reign. Hydraulic machinery was particularly useful, and attention was specially paid to its perfection. Here is the record [1] of a draining feat happily completed: 'The Lands in Havering and Dagenham Levels in Essex, having lain these 6 Years under Water, were, after a great deal of Industry and Expence happily recovered on the 29th Day of October past, being the same Day 6 years that that Breach happened. The Gentlemen concerned in that Undertaking have given to the Artificers and Labourers an Ox and a Sheep to be Roasted whole, and a Hog to be barbicui'd, with large Puddings in their Bellies, on the 13th of this present Instant, on the said Works.'

But few people remember that the steam engine was a living and working fact, and a commercial commodity, in Queen Anne's time, and this owed its being to the

SAVERY'S STEAM ENGINE.

general utility of hydraulic machinery. Salamon de Caus and the Marquis of Worcester are rivals as to the invention of a working steam engine, and Papin came very near to being successful, even going so far as to propel a ship with revolving

[1] *Daily Courant*, Nov. 11, 1713.

oars or paddles, which could in speed beat the king's barge manned by sixteen rowers. But it was reserved to Savery to make it commercially valuable. In 1698 he took out a patent. 'A grant to Thomas Savery gentł, of the sole exercise of a new invencon by him invented, for raising oʲ water, and occasioning mɔɛon to all sorts of Mill Works, by the impellent force of fire, which will be of great use for draining mines, serving towns wth water, and for the working of all sorts of Mills where they have not the benefit of water nor Constant winds, to hold for 14 years ; with usual clauses Testibus apud Westm̃ 25° die Julij anno supradɛ̃o.'

He could not have wasted much time in perfecting his invention and putting it on a sound commercial basis, for we find an advertisement in the *Postman*, March 28/31, 1702 'Captain *Savery's* Engines which raise Water by the force of Fire in any reasonable quantities and to any height, being now brought to perfection, and ready for publick use ; These are to give notice to all Proprietors of Mines and Collieries which are encumbered with Water, that they may be furnished with Engines to drain the same, at his Work house in *Salisbury Court, London*, against the Old Play house, where it may be seen working on *Wednesdays* and *Saturdays* in every week from 3 to 6 in the afternoon ; where they may be satisfied of the performance thereof, with less expence than any other force of Horse or Hands, and less subject to repair.'

He must, even then, have had some at work, for he says in the preface to his little work,[1] dated Sept. 22, 1701 : 'That the *attending* and working the *Engine* is so far from being so,[2] that it is familiar and *easie* to be learned by those of the *meanest Capacity*, in a very little time ; insomuch, that I have Boys of 13 or 14 years of *Age*, who now *attend* and *work* it to perfection, and were *taught* to do it in a few days ; and I have known some *learn* to work the Engine in *half-an-hour.*'

He had visions of its future power, and knew somewhat of its vast capabilities : ' Whereas this *Engine* may be made

---

[1] *The Miner's Friend, or, an Engine to raise Water by Fire described*, &c., by Thomas Savery, Gent. London. 1702.

[2] *I.e.* intricate and difficult to work.

large enough to do the *work* required in employing *eight, ten, fifteen,* or *twenty horses* to be constantly maintained and kept for doing *such a work* ; it will be improper to stint or *confine* its Uses and Operation in respect of *Water Mills.*' He then suggests that it would pump water to the top of a house, for domestic supply, for fountains, and in case of fire—or supply towns with water, draining fens, mines, and coal pits, nay, he even suggests their use, through the furnace and shaft, as ventilators. More than all, he says, ' I believe it may be made very *useful* to Ships, but I dare not meddle with that matter ; and leave it to the Judgment of those who are the best Judges of Maritain Affairs.'

His engine was as ingenious as it was simple. Two boilers with furnaces supplied the steam. This was admitted alternately, by means of a handle worked by a man or boy, into one of two elliptical receivers, where it condensed, formed a vacuum, and the water rushed in and filled its place—the same principle which is the foundation of that invaluable feed-pump, Giffard's injector. When full, the application of steam ejected it from the receiver, and forced it up the pipe, and so *de novo.* His idea was to utilise the water thus raised to turn a water-wheel, and thus get effective power for working machinery in mills.

CHAPTER XXIX.

LITERATURE, THE PRESS, ETC.

Authors—Public libraries—Their condition—George Psalmanazar—
Hack writers—Poverty of authors—Their punishment—The press—
Daily Courant—List of newspapers—*London Gazette—Postboy—Postman*—Dawk's *News Letter*—Dyer's—Evening papers—Dearth of
domestic news—Amenities of the press—Roper and Redpath—Tutchin
—His trial—Press remuneration—Mrs. Manley—The Essay papers
—The halfpenny stamp—Its effect—Advertising—Almanacs—List of
them—Moore's—The *Ladies' Diary—Poor Robin's Almanack*—Merlinus Liberatus—The Essayists and Partridge—His false death—His
elegy and epitaph—An amateur magazine.

WELL might the time of Anne be called the Augustan age
of literature. The writers of that day have lived till ours, and
will live, and be quoted as models of purity of style, as long
as, and wherever, the English language is spoken. In what
other age can such a wealth of literary names be found as
Addison, Steele, Swift, Pope, Warburton, Gay, Prior, Parnell,
Defoe, Vanbrugh, Congreve, Rowe! It was the grand
awakening of letters ; and, having good food provided for
them, the people appreciated it, and it undoubtedly laid the
foundation of the present reading age. Before this time
there had been no books, *i.e.* adapted to the general public,
to read. Truly, there were scholars here and there, and the
Universities were ever fountains of learning ; but literature
had not entered into every-day life, and we have to thank
Steele and Addison, who charmed the public taste by their
social and moral essays, into becoming first a reading, and
then a thinking, people.

There were men who loved their books—veritable biblio-
philes—and what choice editions they must have possessed !
Look at the huge volumes of title-pages which Bagford col-

lected as materials for his history of printing—which never was written—look at the treasures that have come down to us in the Cotton, Harleian, Royal, and Lambeth libraries ! A sale like that of the Sunderland library [1] convulses the literary world, and buyers come from all parts of the globe. Then, however, an advertisement like this was not uncommon : 'A curious Collection of Books, which was Collected by a great Antiquarian, in Greek, Latin, Spanish, French, Italian, and English, in all Faculties and Sciences, many of them very scarce, of the best Authors and Editions, as Aldus, Stevens, Elzevir and others,' etc.

We learn from Misson the state of our public libraries. He says : 'At present I know but three publick ones in this City ; those of the Chapter at *Westminster*, and *Sion College* (which are very much neglected, and in a sorry Condition in all Respects) and that which Dr. *Tenison*, Archbishop of *Canterbury*, has lately founded. The two former are going to Decay, and the latter is not yet quite form'd. Neither the one nor the other are much frequented. The King's Library at St. *James's* is also in a miserable state ; I am told, that Dr. *Bentley*, who has the keeping of it, in the room of Mr. *Instel*, does all he can to restore it ; but his Endeavours will be to no purpose, unless the Master of it has Leisure and Will to have an Eye to it himself. There have been Books in Pawn in the Hands of the Binders I know not how many Years. King *Charles II.* did but laugh at it. It is, nevertheless, a Pity that so many good Books, and so well bound, should be given up to the Mould and Moisture of the Air, to Moths and to Dust. The Library of Sir *Robert Cotton* is particularly famous for Manuscripts. The Royal Society have begun to Collect a pretty good one : the late Duke of *Norfolk*, who was of it, left them his. There are a great many Noble men in England that love Books, and have good Collections of them.'

A literary curiosity of this reign deserves to be, and must be, noticed. It is George Psalmanazar, the impostor who, for a while, deceived the majority of the English *literati*. He seems to have been born in France in 1679, and to have

[1] The Duke of Marlborough's collection, sold 1882.

received a good education. He wandered about as a pilgrim, and that either not paying, or else being dissatisfied with the life, he hit upon the extraordinary idea of passing himself off as a Formosan, and to do this he actually had to invent a new language and grammar. Accompanied by a clergyman named Innes, he came over to England, where he translated the Church Catechism into pretended Formosan, and he published a History of Formosa, and of his own adventures ; but the suspicions of the learned were aroused, and he was unmasked. He tried to fight against it for some time, and issued advertisements in the papers, that he could be seen, spoken with, and catechised, but to no purpose. He afterwards lived by doing hack work for the booksellers, and at his death he thoroughly confessed his imposture.

The hack writers of the time are thus humorously described in the *Guardian* (No. 58): 'According as my necessities suggest it to me, I hereby provide for my being. The last summer I paid a large debt for brandy and tobacco, by a wonderful description of a fiery dragon, and lived for ten days together upon a whale and a mermaid. When winter draws near, I generally conjure up my spirits, and have my apparition ready against long dark evenings. From November last to January I lived solely upon murders ; and have, since that time, had a comfortable subsistence from a plague and a famine. I made the Pope pay for my Beef and Mutton last Lent, out of pure spite to the Romish Religion ; and at present my good friend the King of Sweden finds me in clean linen, and the Mufti gets me credit at the Tavern.'

Literary men had their money troubles then as now— probably not more so—as many a melancholy tale of modern Grub Street could tell. Swift's society did some good. Take his Journal to Stella, Feb. 12 and 13, 1713, as an example : 'I gave an account of Sixty guineas I had collected, and am to give them away to two Authors to-morrow, and lord Treasurer has promised me a hundred pounds to reward some others. . . . I found a letter on my table last night to tell me that poor little Harrison . . . was ill, and desired to see me at night. . . . I went in the morning, and found him mighty ill, and got thirty guineas for him from Lord Bolin-

broke, and an order for a hundred pounds from the treasury
to be paid him to-morrow. . . . I was to see a poor poet, one
Mr. Diaper, in a nasty garret, very sick. I gave him twenty
guineas from Lord Bolinbroke, and disposed the other sixty
to two other authors.' This was practical benevolence, but
its record only shows the sad necessity there was for its
exercise.

Other troubles they had, and perhaps not the least of
them was the fear of personal violence. They hit hard in
those days, and people did not always take their castigation
meekly. Sometimes they took the law into their own hands,
and then woe be to the unfortunate author. Samuel Johnson
(author of *Julian*) in Charles the Second's reign was not only
publicly whipped, but was nearly murdered in his own house.
Tutchin, too, who wrote a poem on the death of James II.,
was waylaid, and so frightfully beaten that he died from
its effects. Defoe also frequently mentions attempts to injure
him. So Swift wrote to Stella,[1] ' No, no, I'll walk late no
more ; I ought to venture it less than other people, and so I
was told.'

In what condition was the press of that day ? Let Pope's
bitter pen answer—

> Next plunged a feeble, but a desperate, pack,
> With each a sickly brother at his back ;
> Sons of a day ; just buoyant on the flood,
> Then numbered with the puppies in the mud.
> Ask ye their names? I could as soon disclose
> The names of these blind puppies as of those.
> And monumental brass this record bears,
> These are—ah—no—these were—the gazetteers.[2]

When Anne succeeded to the throne on March 8, 1702,
the following newspapers were in existence: *The London
Post, English Post, Postman, Postboy, Flying Post, London
Gazette, Post Angel, New State of Europe,* and Dawks's and
Dyer's *News Letter* (the former of which was printed in
script letters, to look as much as possible like writing). The
whole of these were issued three times a week ; but three
days after Anne's accession came out the first daily paper in

---

[1] *Journal,* June 30, 1711.   [2] *Dunciad.*

England. *The Daily Courant* was born March 11, 1702, and this little fledgling, the precursor of the mighty daily press, measures but 14 in. by 8 in. It is printed only on one side of the sheet : the reason given for which is, to say the least, peculiar, reminding one of the lines :—

> My wound is great, because it is so small.
> Then were it greater, were it none at all.

' This Courant (as the Title shews) will be Publish'd Daily ; being design'd to give all the Material News as soon as every

A PRINTING PRESS.

Post arrives ; and is confin'd to half the Compass, *to save the Publick at least half the Impertinences of Ordinary News Papers.'* Probably the correct reason was that, being a new venture, it could not obtain advertisements. These, however, speedily came when it passed into the hands of Samuel Buckley (printer of the *Spectator*), and, in May, it was in a most flourishing state, the other side being entirely taken up with them, and it continued to have its fair share during the whole of the reign. There is nothing very striking about its news, but, as it is such a wonderful infant, I have reproduced this first number in its entirety, in the Appendix,[1] where it will serve as a model to show the kind of news contained in these newspapers. There now exist but two newspapers which were in being in Queen Anne's reign, namely, the *London Gazette* (but that has been kept alive through its official nursing), and—but one due to private enterprise—*Berrow's Worcester Journal*, which was established in 1709.

The other papers born in this reign, including the *Satirical* and *Essay* papers, are *The Observator, Gazette de Londres, Monthly Register, Letter Writer, Whitehall, Rehearsal, Diverting Post, A Weekly Review of the Affairs of France*, by Daniel De Foe, *Whipping Post, News Letter, General Remarks on Trade, Mercurius Politicus, St. James's, Kensington, Evening Post, A Review of the State of the British Nation, The Weekly Comedy, Generous Advertiser, Humours of a Coffee House, The British Apollo, Tatler, Athenian News, Examiner, Medley, Moderator, Evening Courant, British Mercury. Protestant Postboy, Hermit, Useful Intelligencer, Night Post, Spectator, Plain Dealer, Guardian, The Reconciler, The Mercator, Englishman, Britain, The Lover, The Patriot, Controller, Weekly Packet, Monitor.*

It would be a waste of time to follow the fortunes of all these papers; suffice it to say, that the majority of them had but a brief existence, and let us note only a few of the prominent ones. First of all the *London Gazette*, of which Misson says 'it is the truest and most Cautious of all the Gazettes that I know. It inserts no news but what is Certain, and often waits for the Confirmation of it, before it publishes it.' It was first published on Feb. 1, 1666, and still continues to this day as the official newspaper. It was first printed by Thomas Newcomb, of the Savoy, then by Edward Jones, who died in 1705. From Feb. 18 of that year to Feb. 26, 1708, it was printed by his widow, M. Jones. At the latter date, it appears as printed by J. Tonson, at Gray's Inn Gate, who, although he moved into the Strand, continued to print it during the remainder of the reign. It was somewhat smaller than the other papers, and its normal price was 1*d.*, but, if of extra size, owing to addresses

[1] See Appendix.

to the Queen, etc., it was 2*d.* It was published twice weekly, and was the only one of the newspapers that kept up the old style of reckoning time. It did not begin the new year till after March 25; thus, for the year 1702, all the Gazettes would be 1701 till March 25, after which they would be 1702 till that same date in 1703.

When Samuel Buckley took the *Daily Courant* in hand, he at once filled it with advertisements. He then lived at the *Dolphin,* in Little Britain ; afterwards at Amen Corner. Either he sold the *Courant,* or gave up printing it, for on Sept. 25, 1714, it was 'Printed by S. Gray, sold by Ferd. Burleigh in Amen Corner.' Perhaps he could not attend to two papers at once, for, on the copy of the *London Gazette* for Sept. 25/28, 1714, in the British Museum, is written 'first Gazette by Mr. Buckley.' Dunton[1] says of him : 'He was Originally a Book-seller, but follows Printing. He is an excellent *Linguist,* understands the *Latin, French, Dutch* and *Italian* Tongues ; and is Master of a great Deal of Wit. He prints *The Dayly Courant* and *Monthly Register* (which, I hear, he Translates out of the Foreign Papers himself).' Its usual price was 1*d.,* but there was a special edition published. ' The News

' LONDON GAZETTES HERE ! '

of every *Post Day's Courant,* is Constantly Printed with the *News* of the *Day before,* on a Sheet of Writing *Paper* a *Blank* being left for the Conveniency of sending it by the Post. And may be had for 2*d.'*[2]

Dunton thought the *Postboy* was the best for English and Spanish news, but the *Postman* was the best for everything. A French Protestant, named Fonvive, wrote the latter, and in the early part of Anne's reign the *Postboy* was written by Thomas, afterwards by Boyer, also a foreigner, who had

[1] *The Life and Errors of John Dunton,* Lond. 1705.
[2] *Daily Courant,* Sept. 21, 1705.

been tutor to the young Duke of Gloucester. Swift writes of him : 'One *Boyer*, a French dog, has abused *me* in a pamphlet, and I have got him up in a Messenger's hands. The secretary promised me to *swinge* him.   I must make that rogue an example to others.'

In the early days of the reign both these papers had manuscript postscripts, or supplements, when any fresh news arrived that was not in their last edition, they being published thrice weekly. 'This is to give Notice, that the *Post Boy*, with a Written Postscript, containing all the Domestick Occurrences, with the Translations of the Foreign News that arrives after the Printing of the said *Post Boy*, is to be had only of Mr. John Shank, at Nandoe's Coffee house, between the two Temple Gates ; and at Mr. Abel Roper's at the *Black Boy*, over against St. Dunstan's Church in Fleet Street.' 'The Author of this Paper having several times declared in Print that he is no ways directly nor indirectly concerned in the Written Postscripts to the *Post Man*, nor any other News but what is printed therein ; he thinks he has reason to complain of several People, who write to him from the Country about faults and mistakes contained in those Written Postscripts, putting him thereby to unnecessary Charges. He desires those Persons to forbear the same for the future, but if they are not satisfied with their written News (seeing they are not Contented with what is Printed), they may be furnished with written Postscripts at *Tom's* Coffee House in St. Martin's Lane, by a Person, who the Author hopes, will give them entire satisfaction.'

Later on in the century they printed these postscripts, but they were not safe even then. 'There being a Sham Postscript published last night, with an Advertisement, intending to impose the same upon people as a Postscript to the *Postman*, We think fit to desire again our Readers to buy no Postscripts to the *Postman*, but from the Hawkers they know, as the only means to stop that Villanous practice ; and when there is any material New, we shall take care to publish a Postscript, provided it be a Post Day, and not too Late.'   The *Post Boy* had two rough woodcuts, one on each side of the title : one of a Post boy on horseback, blowing his horn ;

the other a Fame, blowing a trumpet, on the banner of which
is inscribed *Viresque acquirit eundo*; whilst the *Postman*
has two woodcuts occupying the same position : one of a
ship in full sail ; the other of a post boy on horseback, blowing his horn.   They are the same size as the *Daily Courant*.

‘ Dawks's *News Letter*, For Thirty Shillings a Year, paying
a Quarter before Hand to J. Dawks at the West End of
Thames Street by Wardrobe Stairs, near Puddle Dock,’ was,
as before said, printed in imitation of writing.   It generally
contained a little more domestic news than the other papers,
and may be said to be the first evening paper.   ‘ This News
Letter continues to be published every Tuesday, Thursday,
and Saturday, in the Evening, and contains what is most
Remarkable, in any (or all) of the other News Papers ; to
which is added the Occurrences of the Day, and the Heads of
the Foreign Mails, which come in many times after the publication of the Printed Papers ; and is so contrived, that a Blank
Space is left for any Gentleman, or others, to write their private
Business to their Friends in the Country, so that they may
have therewith the Chiefest News stirring.’   Ichabod Dawks
started his *News Letter* on Aug. 4, 1696.   Steele mentions it
more than once in the *Tatler*, notably No. 178, where he says :
‘ But Mr. Dawkes concluded his paper with a courteous sentence, which was very well taken, and applauded by the whole
company.   “ We wish,” says he, “all our Customers a merry
Whitsuntide, and many of them.”   Honest Ichabod is as extraordinary a man as any of our fraternity, and as particular.’

The proprietor of the other news-letter, Dyer, got into
trouble more than once.   In 1694 he was summoned before
the Parliament, and reprimanded by the Speaker ‘ for his
great presumption ’ in printing the proceedings of the House.
And once again, in 1702, he was ordered to attend the House
to answer for his presuming to misrepresent the proceedings.
He did not attend, and the attorney-general was instructed
‘ to find out and prosecute him.’

In No. 18 of the *Tatler*, the joint production of Steele and
Addison, is an excellent *résumé* of the foregoing newspapers.
‘ There is another sort of gentlemen whom I am much more
concerned for, and that is the ingenious fraternity of which I

have the honour to be an unworthy member ; I mean the News Writers of Great Britain, whether Post Men or Post Boys, or by what other name or title soever dignified, or distinguished. The case of these gentlemen is, I think more hard than that of the Soldiers, considering they have taken more towns, and fought more battles. They have been upon parties and skirmishes, when our armies have lain still ; and given the general assault to many a place, when the besiegers were quiet in their trenches. They have made us masters of several strong towns many weeks before our generals could do it ; and completed victories, when our greatest captains have been glad to come off with a drawn battle. Where Prince Eugene has slain his thousands, *Boyer* has slain his ten thousands. This gentleman can indeed be never enough commended for his courage and intrepidity during the whole war : he has laid about him with an inexpressible fury ; and, like the offended Marius of ancient Rome, made such havoc among his countrymen, as must be the work of two or three ages to repair. It must be confessed, the redoubted *Mr. Buckley* has shed as much blood as the former ; but I cannot forbear saying (and I hope it will not look like envy) that we regard our brother *Buckley* as a kind of *Drawcansir*,[1] who spares neither friend nor foe ; but generally kills as many of his own side as the enemies. It is impossible for this ingenious sort of men to subsist after a peace ; every one remembers the shifts they were driven to in the reign of King Charles the Second, when they could not furnish out a single paper of News, without lighting up a Comet in Germany, or a fire in Moscow. There scarce appeared a letter without a paragraph on an earthquake. Prodigies were grown so familiar, that they had lost their name, as a great Poet of that age has it. I remember Mr. *Dyer*, who is justly looked upon by all Fox hunters in the nation as the greatest statesman our country has produced, was particularly famous for dealing in whales ; insomuch, that in five months' time (for I had the Curiosity to examine his letters on that occasion) he brought three into the mouth of the River Thames, besides two porpoises, and a

---

[1] The name of a principal character in the Duke of Buckingham's comedy of *The Rehearsal.*

Sturgeon. The judicious and wary Mr. *Ichabod Dawks* hath all along been the rival of this great writer, and got himself a reputation from plagues and famines ; by which, in those days, he destroyed as great multitudes, as he has lately done by the sword. In every dearth of news, Grand Cairo was sure to be unpeopled.'

The *Evening Post* came out in Aug. 1706, and was 'Published by John Morphew near Stationers' Hall.' It seems to have been then a failure, but it was started again in 1709. The *Evening Courant*, which started July 1711, seems also to have had a very brief existence, as did also the *Night Post*, which was born the same year; but this latter seems to have had a longer life than its sister the *Courant*.

A NEWS MAN.

The domestic news in them was nearly *nil*—principally of the sailing of ships or bringing in of prizes. Foreign news was taken bodily from the foreign papers, as we see in the *Daily Courant*, in the Appendix ; and the home news was left to take care of itself. The *Gazette* generally had the Queen's Speech to Parliament, and sometimes the other newspapers would also have it, if on very special occasions, say on June 6, 1712, when the Queen communicated to Parliament the terms on which a peace might be made ; yet the only reference the *Flying Post* of June 5/7 has on the subject is, 'Yesterday Her Majesty went to the House of Peers, and made a long speech to both Houses.'

In fact, in all the twelve years of this reign, I only remember meeting with one long account of any piece of home news, and I cannot help thinking that was manufactured, as it is decidedly of the catchpenny and chapbook order. It was ' An

Account of the Apprehending and Taking of *Thomas Wallis,* alias *Whipping Tom,*' a wicked villain who got hold of unprotected females, when crossing the unfrequented fields near Hackney, and administered a fearful thrashing to them, 'with a great Rodd of Birch, that the Blood ran down their tender Bodies in a sad and dreadful manner.' His only excuse was his 'being resolved to be Revenged on all the Women he could come at after that manner, for the sake of one Perjur'd Female, who had been Barbarously False to him.' He 'believed that he had Whip'd from the 10th of *October* last to the 1st of *December*, about Three Score and Ten, including Widdows, Wives and Maids, and did intend, if he had not been taken, to have made them up to a Hundred betwixt this and *Christmas*, at which time he then intended to keep Hollyday till after Twelfday, and then began his Whipping Work.' And once, too, the *Postboy* (Jan. 27/29, 1713) broke out in a sarcastically humorous vein : 'On Monday last that Facetious and Merry Gentleman in the Pulpit, Mr. Daniel Burgess, departed this Life to the great Mortification of his Female Auditors.'

'Esq : Thomas Burnet (S–n of that vertuous, orthodox, pious, forgiving, impartial, sincere, never wav–ri–g (always standing to his T–x–t) modest, conscientious Di—ne, and by the Gr— of G–d in the fere of the L—d) was on Saturday last taken up, and carried to the Lord Viscount Bolinbroke's Office, for being the Author of that seditious and scandalous Pamphlet, call'd *A certain Information of a certain Discourse,* &c. (of which Libel Mr. Baker the Publisher lately swore he was the Author) and gave Sureties to appear the last Day of this Term ; his Bail were Guy Neville and Geo Trenchard Esqs : *What's bred in the B–ne will never be out of the Fl–sh.*'

Talk about the amenities of the press ! Here are one or two samples :—

Titus detected the *Tory Popish* Plot, *and* Abel's[1] inveterating a *Whiggish One.*
Titus was a foul Mouth Slanderer,—so is Abel.
Titus openly traduced the next Heir to this Crown—So has *Abel.*

[1] Abel Roper, who then conducted the *Post Boy.*

Titus deserv'd to be Hang'd—So does *Abel.*
Titus was low in Stature, but of Outrageous Principles—So is *Abel.*
Titus was protected in his Impudence—So is *Abel.*
But the Time's coming to change, *Titus* was call'd to Account for it
—so *will* Abel.
Titus was flogg'd and Pilloried—So will *Abel.*
Titus was despis'd by both Parties—So will *Abel.*
Titus died unpittied ;—So will *Abel.*
In fine,—*Titus was both Knave and Dunce* ;—So is Abel.[1]

One would imagine that after this flagellation Roper
would not be the first to assault a brother journalist, but
he fell foul of Ridpath, who conducted the *Flying Post,* and
this is how he did it : ' Yesterday, one George Ridpath, a
Cameronian, who formerly (as it is credibly reported) was
banished Scotland, for putting on Lawn Sleves, and administering —— to a Dog, in derision of the Church and Bishops,
was committed to Newgate for several scandalous Reflections
writ by him in a Paper formerly publish'd call'd the *Observator* ; and for being the Author of several notorious
Falshoods and scandalous Reflections on the Queen and
Government, in a paper call'd *The Flying Post.'* [2]

Ridpath,[3] of whom Dunton says ' His *Humility* and His
Honesty have establish'd his Reputation,' hit back by means
of an anonymous correspondent in the *Flying Post* :—

' Lynn Regis in Norfolk, Sep. 22.
' Sir,
' Having observ'd the false Account which that
Scandalous Wretch Abel Roper gave some time ago in his
Post Boy, about the Reception of Mr. Walpole here ; This is
to inform you 'tis a notorious Lye ; for that worthy Gentle-
man had a very honourable Reception, answerable to the just
Esteem which this Corporation has for him.'

A notice of one more sparring match must close this
subject—the same two papers. Says friend Abel[4] : ' In
the *Flying Post* of last Tuesday, we have a very unusual
Specimen of the Author's Modesty, in Owning and Recanting
the Lye he had so impudently fix'd on Dr. S——l in his

---

[1] *Protestant Post Boy*, Jan. 15/17, 1712.
[2] *Post Boy*, Sept. 6/9, 1712.
[3] Ridpath invented a manifold writer, which would take six or more copies at
once.   [4] *Post Boy*, Mar. 30/April 1, 1714.

former Paper. But 'tis very remarkable, That by endeavouring to excuse this Lye, he unluckily falls into his *Habitual
Sin* again, no less than *three* times in this single Paragraph.
. . . So little Credit is to be given to this Infamous Weekly
Libel, fill'd always with Lies of the Author's own Invention,
or such as are taken up at second-hand, and vouch'd by him
without the least Regard to Truth, Common Sense, or Common Honesty.'

After this, who can wonder if some editors had rather a
rough time of it, especially Roper. He gives us [1] one glimpse
of his condition : ' Last night *William Thompson* Esq., came
to the Proprietor of this Paper, and told him, That if he did
not insert the following Paragraph in his Paper of this Day,
*God Damn him, he would cut his Throat, and he had a Pen-
knife in his Pocket for that purpose* ; for which the Proprietor
of this Paper designs to prosecute him according to Law, but
thought fit to publish this, that the Nation may be Judges,
whether a Person of such a Character is proper to be employ'd
in his Station in the Law ? or, Whether our Constitution
ought to be entrusted in such Hands as will not scruple to
commit Murder when ever it may serve their Purpose.'

In 1704 the House of Commons took umbrage at some
remarks which John Tutchin, the conductor of the *Observator*,
had made on some mismanagement of public affairs (and
they were undoubted libels), and cited him, the printer, and
publisher before their Bar, to be brought in custody of the
Sergeant-at-Arms. Tutchin gave bail for his appearance ; and
his trial came on on Nov. 4, 1704.[2] He got off somehow, and
was never tried again. Earlier in life he had been tried at
the Bloody Assizes, where he had the brutal Jeffreys for his
judge, and he was sentenced ' to be imprisoned for Seven
Years ; that once every year he should be whipt through all
the Market Towns in Dorsetshire ; that he should pay a fine
of one hundred marks to the King, and find security for his
good behaviour during life. . . . Upon passing the Sentence,
the Clerk of the Arraigns stood up, and said, My lord, there
are a great many market towns in this County ; the sentence
reaches to a whipping about once a fortnight, and he is a

---

[1] *Postboy*, Sept. 12/15, 1713.   [2] Howell's *State Trials*, ed. 1812, v. 14.

very young man.   Aye, says Jeffreys, he is a young man but
an old rougue; and all the interest in England shall not
reverse the sentence I have past upon him.'   So poor
Tutchin's heart died within him, and he petitioned the King
that he ' will be mercifully pleased to grant him the favour of
being hanged with those of his fellow prisoners, that are
condemned to die.'   But to no avail.

His friends tried to buy him a pardon, but Jeffreys
frustrated all their efforts.   At length Tutchin fell ill of the
smallpox, and nearly died of it, being only tended by his
fellow-prisoners.   During his illness his mother bought his
pardon of Jeffreys [1]; then she fell sick of the smallpox, and
died.

Of Tutchin's trial in 1704 we have the following contemporary evidence from Luttrell: ' 18 May.   Mr. Tutchin,
author of the Observator, against whom a proclamation was
out at the desire of the House of Commons, has given 1000*l.*
bail to answer what shal be objected against him '; and on
May 29 he gave fresh bail.   His trial began, as we know, on
Nov. 4, and he was found guilty, but sentence was deferred.
On the 14th we hear ' Yesterday, Mr. Tutchin, found guilty of
publishing the Observator, appeared at the Queen's bench
Court, when his council inform'd the Court of an error in the
information, and the Attorney General desiring time to consider of it, Tutchin is to attend again on Saturday.'   The
point was the false dating of the writ ; and he attended on the
20th and 23rd, when it was argued ; and on Nov. 28 judgment was given in Tutchin's favour, ' the Attorney General
at liberty to try him again,' which he never did.

This trial is interesting, as it furnishes us with evidence as
to the pay of an editor, or rather author (for Tutchin wrote
the whole paper), of that time.   John How was the proprietor
of the paper, which appeared first on April 1, 1702.   In his
evidence is the following :—

---

[1] A scandalous practice then in vogue. 'Mr. Tutchin hereupon endeavoured
to get a pardon from the people who had grants of lives, many of them 500, some
1000, more or less as they had interest with the King.' Again : ' For it was
usual at that time for one Courtier to get a pardon of the King for half a Score,
and then by the assistance of Jeffreys to augment the sum to fourscore or a hundred.' In these ' Bloody Assizes ' 300 persons were condemned to death, and
nearly 1000 sold as slaves to the West Indian plantations.

How. About the latter end of March, 1702, I treated with Mr. Tutchin about writing an Observator, to be published weekly : the first of which was published in April 1702.   And all that have been printed since, I had from him to this year.

Att. Gen. You looked on these papers here : were those printed by the direction of Mr. Tutchin?

How. To the best of my knowledge, they were.   They were always brought from him to me.

Att. Gen. Was there any agreement made between you about the writing of it ?

How. Yes, it was agreed at first to write once a week ; and I was to give him half a guinea for it.[1] . . .

Sir T. Powis. Did you pay him for the Preface ?

How. Yes, and for the Index.[2] . . .

L. C. Justice. What did you give him for that Preface and Index?

How. I think it was ten shillings.

At the same time there were other libels afloat.   ' 30 May 1704.   Yesterday came out a proclamation by her Majestie for discovering and apprehending the author, printer, and publisher of a scandalous libel, intituled, Legions Humble Addresse to the Lords ; offering the reward of £100 for the author thereof, and fifty pounds for the printer thereof.'[3]

Was not Steele turned out of Parliament for libel ?   ' Resolved that Richard Steele, Esq[re], for his offence in writing and publishing the said scandalous and seditious libels, be expelled the House ;'[4] and the resolution was adopted by 245 votes against 152.

In 1709 Luttrell tells us : ' 15 Oct. The Authors of the Review and Female Tatler were presented by the grand jury as scandalous and a publick nuisance, and were ordered to be prosecuted.   1 Nov. This day the printer and publisher of the New Atlantis were examined touching the author Mrs. Manley ; they were discharged, but she remains in custody. 5 Nov. One Ball is taken up for writing scandalous papers on persons of quality ; but Mrs. Manley, the author of the New Atlantis, is admitted to Bayl.'

Few would be inclined to pity the profligate Mrs. Manley for any punishment she might have received for her scandalous libels in both the *Female Tatler* and the *New Atlantis;*

---

[1] Howell's *State Papers,* ed. 1812, pp. 1105–6.   [2] *Ibid.* p. 1108.
[3] *Luttrell.*   [4] *Journals of the House of Commons,* vol. xvii. p. 514.

but she was not punished. On the contrary, the ministry gave her employment for her pen.

The *Tatler* commenced the series of Essay papers. Steele is almost apologetic, in its first number, for having to make any charge. He elaborately calls attention to the expenses incurred in getting up such a paper, and adds 'these considerations will I hope make all persons willing to comply with my humble request (when my *gratis* stock is exhausted) of a penny a piece.' And an advertisement at the end of No. 4 says, 'Upon the humble petition of Running Stationers &c., this Paper may be had of them, for the future, at the price of one penny.' But there was a more expensive edition, whole-sheet *Tatlers*, having a double quantity of paper, with one half-sheet blank 'to write business on, and for the convenience of the post,' and they, of course, were more expensive. The *Tatler, Spectator,* and *Guardian* were all of Steele's creation ; they were born, and died, at his discretion ; and the *Spectator*, at least, was always laid on the Royal breakfast table. Their imitators were numerous, but short-lived ; in fact, the imposition of a halfpenny stamp massacred the innocents of the press in a wholesale manner.

This tax was evidently in contemplation some time before it became law. Swift writes to Stella, Jan. 31, 1711 : 'They are here intending to tax all little printed penny papers a halfpenny every half sheet, which will utterly ruin Grub Street, and I am endeavouring to prevent it.' It slept for a little, but it was smuggled at last into the 10th Anne,[1] cap. 19,

[1] The part of this Act specially bearing upon newspapers was a stamp duty for thirty-two years from August 1, 1712 : 'And be it Enacted by the Authority aforesaid, that there shall be Raised, Levied, Collected and Paid, to and for the Use of her Majesty, her Heirs and Successors, for and upon all Books or Papers Commonly called Pamphlets, and for and upon all News Papers, or Papers containing Publick News, Intelligence or Occurrences, which shall, at any time or times within or during the Term last mentioned, be Printed in Great Britain to be Dispersed and made Publick, and for and upon such Advertisements as are herein after mentioned the respective Duties following ; That is to say,

'For every such Pamphlet or Paper contained in Half a Sheet or any lesser Piece of Paper, so Printed, the sum of One half penny.

'For every such Pamphlet or Paper (being larger than Half a Sheet, not exceeding one Whole Sheet) so Printed, a Duty after the Rate of One Peny Sterling for every Printed Copy thereof.

'And for every such Pamphlet or Paper, being larger than One Whole Sheet, and not exceeding Six Sheets in Octavo, or in a Lesser Page, or not exceeding Twelve Sheets in Quarto, or Twenty Sheets in Folio, so Printed, a Duty after

and fairly hidden among duties on soap, paper, silk, linens,
hackney chairs, cards, marriage licences, etc.   It came into
operation on Aug. 1, 1712, and Swift makes merry over
the effect it will have on the struggling periodical literature.
' 19 July 1712. Grub Street has but ten days to live; then
an act of parliament takes place that ruins it, by taxing every
half sheet at a halfpenny.' '17 Aug. 1712. Do you know
that Grub Street is dead and gone last week?   No more
ghosts or murders now for love or money.   I plied it pretty
close the last fortnight, and published at least seven penny
papers of my own, besides some of other people's : but now
every single half sheet pays a halfpenny to the Queen.   The
Observator is fallen ; the Medleys are jumbled together with
the Flying Post ; the Examiner is deadly sick ; the Spectator
keeps up, and doubles its price ; I know not how long it

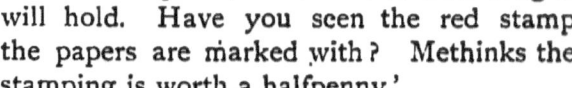

will hold.   Have you seen the red stamp
the papers are marked with ?   Methinks the
stamping is worth a halfpenny.'

The *Spectator* does not chuckle over the
fall of its humbler brethren.   Addison says[1]:
' This is the Day on which many eminent
Authors will probably Publish their Last
Words.   I am afraid that few of our Weekly

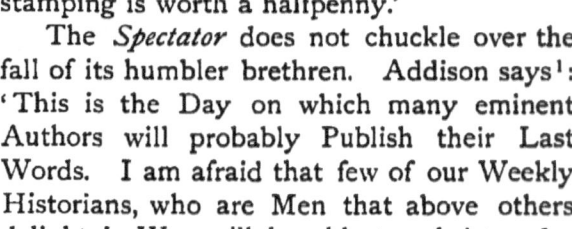

NEWSPAPER STAMP. Historians, who are Men that above others
delight in War, will be able to subsist under
the Weight of a Stamp, and an approaching Peace.   A
Sheet of Blank Paper that must have this new Imprimatur
clapt upon it, before it is qualified to Communicate any thing
to the Publick, will make its Way in the World but very
heavily.   In short, the Necessity of carrying a Stamp, and
the Improbability of Notifying a Bloody Battel, will, I am
afraid, both concur to the sinking of those thin Folios, which
have every other Day retailed to us the History of *Europe*
for several Years last past.   A Facetious Friend of mine who

the Rate of Two Shillings Sterling for every Sheet of any kind of Paper which
shall be Contained in One Printed Copy thereof.
' And for every Advertisement to be Contained in the *London Gazette* or any
other printed Paper, such Paper being Dispersed or made publick Weekly, or
oftner, the Sum of Twelve Pen e Sterling.' Acts of Parliament were exempt.
[1] No. 445, July 31, 1712.

loves a Punn, calls this present Mortality among Authors, *The Fall of the Leaf.'*

All the papers, except the *Spectator*, rose their price just the value of the stamps ; but that 'Society Journal' charged 1*d.* extra—a fact which caused no little grumbling—and which made Addison put forth all his powers of special pleading to vindicate (see No. 488).

The imposition of 1*s.* duty on advertisements had no deterrent effect upon them ; this 'backbone of the paper' continued as before. There is nothing that I have found to guide us as to the prices of advertisements, except in one case—and I hardly think that can be called a representative one. It is that of a short-lived paper called 'THE GENE-ROUS ADVERTISER OR Weekly Information of TRADE and BUSINESS. To be published every *Tuesday*, and *Friday*, and 4000 of them always carefully Distributed and Given away *Gratis* each Day, in and about the City's of *London* and *Westminster*.' It enjoyed its brief existence in 1707. The terms were not excessive under the circumstances: 'Advertisements . . . will be taken by the Men who carry this PAPER about ; Who will take them in very Carefully and Cheap *viz.* after the Rate of 3*d.* for every Fifty letters.'

Advertisements, with the exception of those of quack doctors and their medicines, were very much as now. Book-sellers, public amusements, things lost, things for sale, etc., give those old sheets a strange similarity to those we are so familiar with.

Even the poor almanacs were taxed. The *Protestant Post Boy*, Nov. 15/17, 1711, says, 'Whereas, by an Act made last Sessions of Parliament, a Duty was laid on all Almanacks, and a Penalty of Ten Pounds is for any one that shall Sell any Almanacks without being first Stampt as the Law directs; and whereas the said Tax &c. has made a great Attraction in the Price, this is to give Notice to all Retale Buyers, or others that the Prices are as follows.

'An Almanack Bound in Red Leather, with Paper to Write on, of any Sort. Ninepence.

'An Almanack of any Sort Sticht. Six Pence.

'Any Sheet Almanack Four Pence.'

It is hardly worth while to give an exhaustive list of the almanacs then in vogue. One advertisement [1] will be ample for the purpose: 'On Thursday next (15 Nov.) will be published the following Almanacks for the Year 1706. viz. Andrews, Chapman, Coley, Dove, Gadbury, Ladies Diary, Moor, Partridge, Pond, Poor Robin, Salmon, Saunders, Tanner, Wing, Colepepper, Dade, Fly, Fowl, Perkins, Rose, Swallow, Trigge, Turner, White, Woodhouse.'

Out of which, that by Francis Moore, physician, the 'Vox Stellarum,' is still published. Doubts have been thrown on the reality of this gentleman, but it is certain that he did live, and Lysons speaks of him as having lived in Calcotts Alley, High Street (then called Back Lane), Lambeth, where he practised the combined professions of astrologer, physician, and schoolmaster. He also lived in Southwark and in Westminster. There is an engraving of him extant, evidently done in Queen Anne's reign, by Drapentier, who also engraved the portrait of Dr. Burgess. Moore is represented as a fat-faced man in a full-bottomed wig. The legend is 'Francis Moore, born in Bridgenorth, in the County of Salop, the 29th of January 1656/7.' His almanac was first published in 1698.

The *Ladies' Diary*, which commenced in 1704, was only suspended in 1841, when it was incorporated in the *Gentleman's Diary*.

'Poor Robin, an ALMANACK of the Old and New Fashion; or an EPHEMERIS of the best and newest Edition; wherein the Reader may find (that is to say if he reads over the Almanack) many most excellent remarkable things worthy his and others choicest Observation. Containing a Two-fold Calendar. *viz*, The Old, Honest, Julian, or English Account, and the Round head's, Whimzey heads, Maggot heads, Paperscull'd, Slender-witted, Muggletonian, or Fanatick Account, with their several Saints Days, and Observations upon every Month. Being the BISSEXTILE or Leap Year. *Written by* POOR ROBIN *Knight of the Burnt Island, a Well-wisher to the Mathematicks.*'

[1] *Daily Courant*, Nov. 10, 1705.

THE TWO AND FORTIETH IMPRESSION.

Reader, this is the two and Fortieth Year,
Since first our Book did to the World appear :
And we do think 'tis stored with more knacks
Than may be found in other Almanacks.
Laugh if you will, but yet this always mind,
If you your Eyes laugh out, you will be blind.

London : Printed by *W. Bowyer* for the Company of Stationers. 1704.

Such is a title-page of this almanac, which, when first started, is thought to have been written by Herrick. It only ceased its publication in 1828. As this was a genuinely humorous book, in a time when pure fun was hardly understood, a very brief description may be permitted. It had a comic chronology, such as :—

	Years since
Geese without or Hose or Shoes went bare.	5603
Maids did Plackets in their Coats first wear.	4805
Plumbs were first put into Christmas Pies.	1472
The Hangman did the riding Knot devise.	3999
Coffee came first to be us'd in *London*.	0049
By Rebellion many a Man was undone.	0050
Women did at *Billingsgate* first scold.	0973
Summer was hot Weather, Winter cold.	5782 &c. &c.

And every month had its appropriate poem, thus :—

This is the merry Month of May,
When as the Fields are fresh and gay ;
And in each Place where 'ere you go
Are people walking to and fro.
On every Place you cast your Eye,
Hundreds of people you may Spy,
The Fields bestrewed all about,
Some pacing home, some passing out ;
Some woo their Lovers in the Shadows,
Some stragling to and fro the Meadows.
Some of this Chat, some of that Talk,
Some Coacht, some horst, some afoot Walk.
Some by *Thames* Bank their Pleasure taking,
Some Silabubs 'mong Milkmaids making ;
With Musick some on Waters rowing ;
Some to the adjoining Towns are going.
To *Hogsdon, Islington, Totenham Court*,
For Cakes and Cream is great Resort, &c.

Also each month has its appropriate prose.

'Observations on January. Now a good Fire, and a Glass of brisk Canary is as Comfortable as the thing called Matrimony.   Cold Weather makes hungry Stomachs, so that now a piece of powder'd Beef lin'd with Brews,[1] vociferating Veal, and a Neat's Tongue, that never told a Lye, is excellent good food ; but to feed on hope, is but a poor Dish of Meat to dine and sup with after a two Days Fast.   If thou art minded to go a Wooing this Cold Weather, do it with Discretion, for he that doth make a Goddess of a Puppet, merits no Recompense but mere Contempt.'

PARTRIDGE AND BICKERSTAFF.

Besides these, there was plenty of proverbial philosophy, interspersed with divers merry tales, and eccentric receipts, the whole going to form a compilation perfectly unique for its time.

Perhaps the chief among the serious astrological, and predicting, almanacs was '*Merlinus Liberatus*, by JOHN PARTRIDGE, Student in Physick and Astrology, at the *Blue Ball* in *Salisbury Street*, in the *Strand, London.*' Not, perhaps, that he would have lived in story, much more than his fellows, had it not have been for the fun that Swift, Steele,

[1] Broth.

and Addison made of him. Swift set the ball rolling, in his
sham 'Predictions for the year 1708, by Isaac Bickerstaff'
(his pseudonym), in which he says: ' My first prediction is
but a trifle, yet I will mention it to show how ignorant those
sottish pretenders to astronomy are in their own concerns.
It relates to Partridge the Almanack maker. I have con-
sulted the star of his nativity by my own rules, and find he
will infallibly die on the 29th of March next, about eleven at
night, of a raging fever ; therefore, I advise him to consider
of it, and settle his affairs in time.' This was a happy
thought, born of the fact that Partridge had prophesied the
downfall and death of Louis XIV. Early in April 1703
Swift published ' The accomplishment of the first part of Mr.
Bickerstaff's predictions, being an account of the death of
Mr. Partridge, the Almanac maker, on the 29th of March,
1708, in a letter to a person of honour.'

From that moment Partridge was dead. It was no use
his publicly stating that he was alive. The wits had decreed
his fate, and dead he was. His elegy and epitaph were
printed, in the grisly manner common to those productions.
They are too long for reproduction, but are too good not to
quote from.

> WELL, 'tis as *Bickerstaff* has guest,
> Tho' we all took it for a Jest ;
> *Patrige* is Dead, nay more, he dy'd
> E'er he could prove the good Squire ly'd.
> Strange, an Astrologer should Die,
> Without one Wonder in the Sky ;
> Not one of all his *Crony* Stars,
> To pay their Duty at his Hearse !
> No Meteor, no Eclipse appear'd !
> No Comet with a flaming Beard !
> The Sun has rose, and gone to Bed,
> Just as if *Patrige* were not Dead ;
> Not hid himself behind the Moon,
> To make a dreadful Night at Noon :
> He at fit Periods walks through *Aries*,
> Howe'er our Earthly Motion varies,
> And twice a Year he'll cut th' *Æquator*,
> As if there had been no such Matter.
> ⠀ Some Wits have wondered what Analogy
> There is 'twixt *Cobling* and *Astrology* ;

How *Patrige* made his *Opticks* rise,
From a *Shoe Sole* to reach the Skies ;

.   .   .   .

Besides, that slow pac'd Sign *Bootes*
As 'tis miscall'd, we know not who 'tis ;
But *Patrige* ended all Disputes,
He knew his Trade, and call'd it *Boots.*
The *Horned Moon* which heretofore
Upon their Shoes the *Romans* wore,
Whose Wideness kept their Toes from Corns,
And whence we claim our *Shoeing horns,*
Shews how the Art of *Cobling* bears
A near Resemblance to the Spheres, &c.

THE EPITAPH.

HERE Five Foot deep lyes on his Back
A *Cobler, Starmonger,* and *Quack,*
Who to the Stars in pure Good will,
Does to his best look upward still.
Weep all you Customers that use
His *Pills,* his *Almanacks,* or *Shoes.*
And you that did your Fortunes seek,
Step to this Grave but once a Week,
This Earth which bears his Body's Print,
You'll find has so much Virtue in't,
That I durst Pawn my Ears, 'twill tell
What 'eer concerns you full as well,
In *Physick, Stolen Goods,* or *Love,*
As he himself could, when above.[1]

Congreve, or Rowe, took up cudgels for the poor man, and wrote and published ' Squire Bickerstaff detected, or the astrological impostor convicted, by JOHN PARTRIDGE, student in Physick, and Astrology.' What was the use ? Not only were the above squibs being sold about the streets for a halfpenny, but Swift had to annihilate his opponents by his ' Vindication of Isaac Bickerstaff Esq. against what is objected to him by Mr. *Partridge,* in his Almanack for the present year, 1709.'

Steele, even in the very first *Tatler,* could not forbear poking fun at Partridge. 'I have, in another place, and in a paper by itself, sufficiently convinced this man that he is

[1] *Harl. MSS.* 5931-85.

dead, .and, .if he has any shame, I do not doubt but that by this time he owns it to all his acquaintance; for though the legs and arms and whole body of that man may still appear, and perform their animal functions; yet since, as I have elsewhere observed, his art is gone, the man is gone.' And so the banter was kept up, at intervals, all through the *Tatler.*

As an almanac writer he, in fact, did die in 1709, for that was the last he really published—although an almanac is still sold bearing the same title. He really, and corporeally, died in 1715, and was buried in Mortlake Churchyard, where, on a flat black marble stone, was the following inscription :—

'Johannes Partridge Astrologus,
et Medicinæ Doctor.
Natus est apud East Sheen,
in Comitatu Surrey,
18 Januarii, 1641,
et mortuus est Londini 24 Junii, 1715.
Medicinam fecit duobus regibus, unæque Reginæ;
Carolo scilicet secundo, Willielmo Tertio,
Reginæque Mariæ.
Creatus est Medicinæ Doctor
Luguduni Batavorum.'

The almanac stamps seem to have prompted crime and forgery, owing to their price; for the *London Gazette*, Feb. 7/10, 1713 has, 'Whereas divers Almanacks, or Papers serving the purpose of an Almanack, with false Stamps, have been lately Printed and Sold in several Parts of England, contrary to a late Act of Parliament, and prejudicial to Her Majesty's Revenue; and others, tho' with the true Stamps, have been Printed and Sold Contrary to the Right of the Company of Stationers, for which divers Persons are now under Prosecution, and all others will be Prosecuted when discover'd : This notice is given to prevent all Persons incurring the like Trouble and Penalties.'

It seems strange, and somewhat in advance of the time, to hear of an amateur magazine being started—but, at all

events, such a thing was proposed. ' Any Gentleman or
Lady that is desirous of having any short Poem, Epigram,
Satyr &c. (published ?) if they please to communicate the
Subjects to the Authors of the Diverting Muse, or the
Universal Medley, now in the Press and will be continued
Monthly ; or, if they have any Song or other Poem of their
own that is New and Entertaining, if they please to direct
them for Mr. George Daggastaff, to be left at Mr. Hogarth's
Coffee House in St. John's Gateway near Clerkenwell, the
former shall be done Gratis, and inserted in the Miscellany
abovemention'd, as also the latter, both paying the Postage
or Messenger.'[1]   This liberal offer does not seem to have met
with the anticipated response, for I have looked in vain, in
the Catalogues of the British Museum and elsewhere, and
can find no mention of the ' Diverting Muse.'

[1] *Daily Courant*, June 23, 1707.

CHAPTER XXX.

MEDICAL.

List of diseases—Quackery—Bleeding, etc.—Physicians—Surgeons—
Apothecaries—Dissension between the physicians and apothecaries—
The dispensary—Pharmacopœias—Some nostrums—Prescriptions—
Cupping—Treatment of lunatics—Physicians' carriages—Dr. Radcliffe
—Sir Samuel Garth—Sir Hans Sloane—Dr. Mead—His duel with
Woodward—Study of Anatomy—Surgical instruments—Oculists—Sir
William Read—Roger Grant—The Queen touching for the evil—
Description of the ceremony—Quacks' remedies—Quack harangues.

PEOPLE got ill then as now, and, judging by the following
list, there were just about as many diseases, only scientific
names had not taken the place of the old homely nomencla-
ture. This is taken from a list of deaths from all causes :
' Age. Ague and Fever, Appoplex and Suddenly, Bleach,
Blasted, Bloody Flux, Scouring and Flux. Burns and Scalds.
Bleeding, Calenture, Cancer, Gangrene and Fistula, Wolf,
Canker, Soremouth and Thrush, Colick and Wind, Cough
and Cold, Consumption and Cough, Convulsion, Cramp,
Dropsie and Tympany, Excessive drinking, Falling Sickness,
Flox and Small Pox, French pox, Gout, Grief, Head Ach,
Jaundice, Jaw-faln, Impostume, Itch, King's Evil, Lethargy,
Leprosie, Liver-grown, Spleen and Rickets, Lunatick, Meagrom,
Measles, Mother, Palsie, Plague, Plague in the Guts, Pleurisie,
Purples and Spotted Fever, Quinsie and Sore Throat, Rising
of the Lights, Rupture, Scal'd head, Scurvy, Sores and Ulcers,
Spleen, Shingles, Stitch, Stone and Strangury, Sciatica,
Stopping of the Stomach, Surfet. Swine Pox. Teeth and
Worms, Tissick, Vomiting, Wen.'

Of these, the most deaths resulted from consumption
and cough, next ague and fever, then flox and smallpox.
The infant mortality was terrible—the great cause of death

being put down as teeth and worms.   Consumption even now
baffles the skill of our physicians.   Quinine was then used
for ague and fever, not as the crystal alkaloid, but in the
rough bark, which was sold as 'Jesuits Bark,' at prices
ranging from 4s. to 10s. per lb.   Smallpox, inoculation or
vaccination being unknown, was a fearful scourge, and spared
no one—helped, as it was, by the all but utter ignorance of
sanitary science, to the value of which we, in this generation, are only awaking.

Quackery was rampant, probably because people did not
have much belief in the healing powers of the regular practitioners.   Herbs and simples were much in use ; and not
only were there fearful remedies concocted by fair hands in
the still-room, but naturally every old woman had faith in
the traditional medicaments handed down to her by her forefathers.   Also the empiricism of the alchemists still lingered
—see the following advertisement : 'Whereas the Viper hath
been a Medicine approv'd by the Physicians of all Nations ;
there is now prepar'd the Volatile Spirit compound of it, a
Preparation altogether new, not only exceeding all Volatiles
and Cordials whatsoever, but all the Preparations of the
Viper itself, being the Receipt of a late Eminent Physician,
and prepar'd only by a Relation.   It is the most Sovereign
Remedy against all Faintings, Sweatings, Lowness of Spirits,
Vapours &c.—As also in all Habits of Body or Disorders
proceeding from Intemperance, eating of Fruit, drinking of
bad Wine, or any other poysonous or crude Liquors, and is
good to take off the ill Effects or Remains of the Bark or
Jesuits Powder.'

Bleeding and *purging*—these were the main remedies
relied on in those old days ; something to make the patient
remember his illness by, as he did his doctor's bill, by the
quantity of medicine he had swallowed.   Brown, satirist as
he was, was truthful, even to coarseness, and neither he nor
Ward told lies in order to round a sentence, or point an
epigram.   This is how Brown[1] makes a fashionable physician
describe his practice : 'He pays well, and takes Physick
freely : besides I particularly know his Constitution ; after

[1] *The Dispensary*, by Thos. Brown.

Bleeding, he must take a Purge or two, then some Cordial
Powders, Dulcifiers of the Blood, and two or three odd things
more. . . . I tell you 'tis an easie thing for a Man of Parts to
be a Surgeon ; do but buy a Lancet, Forceps, Saw ; talk a
little of Contusions, Fractures, Compress and Bandage ; you'll
presently by most People, be thought an excellent Surgeon.
. . . I myself have turn'd out several Doctors out of Families
because they would not prescribe Physick *plentifully*, and in
large Quantities. I have perswaded my Patients, that they
did not well understand their Distemper ; so have brought in
another who has *swingingly dos'd 'um.* I could tell you of a
Sir *Harry* that paid an £100 for Physick in six Weeks, and I
accepted it, being a Friend, without requiring one Penny for
my own Fees.'

The profession then, as now, was divided among Physicians,
Surgeons, and Apothecaries ; and the relative position of two
of them is mentioned by Addison[1] : ' An Operator of this
Nature might act under me with the same regard as a Surgeon
to a Physician ; the one might be employ'd in healing those
Blotches and Tumours which break out in the Body, while
the other is sweetning the Blood and rectifying the Constitution.' The Apothecaries, of course, kept shops for the supply
of drugs.

In the great fire of 1666 the College of Physicians, which
was at Amen Corner, was burnt down, and a new one built,
which was used till 1825, in Warwick Lane :—

> Not far from that most celebrated Place,
> Where angry Justice shews her awful Face ;
> Where little Villains must submit to Fate,
> That great ones may enjoy the World in State ;
> There stands a Dome, majestick to the sight,
> And sumptuous Arches bear its oval height ;
> A golden Globe plac'd high with artful skill,
> Seems, to the distant sight, a gilded Pill.
> —*The Dispensary*, by Dr. Garth, Canto 1, ed. 1699.

This was the building that the profession thought was mainly
built by the munificence of Sir John Cutler ; but after his

[1] *Spectator*, No. 16.

death his executors demanded 7,000*l.* for money *lent*, and
were eventually repaid 2,000*l.*   Pope wrote of Cutler :—

> His Grace's fate sage Cutler could foresee
> And well (he thought,) advis'd him, ' Live like Me.'
> As well his Grace replied, ' Like you Sir John ?
> That I can do, when all I have is gone.'

Ward[1] sums up the physician's privileges : ' What Priviledges, said I, extraordinary are Granted to them in their
Charter, above what are held by other Physicians who are not
of their Society ?   Many, replied my friend, and these in particular, viz. No Person, tho' a Graduate in Physick of *Oxford*
or *Cambridge*, and a Man of more Learning, Judgment and
Experience than one half of their Members, shall have the
Liberty of practising in, or within Seven Miles of *London*,
without License under the Colledge Seal ; Or in any other
part of *England*, if they have not taken some Degree at one
of the Universities ; They have also power to administer an
Oath, which they know by Experience is as practicable to be
broke the next Day, as 'tis to be taken ; They can likewise
Fine and Imprison Offenders, in the Science of Physick, and
all such who presume to Cure a Patient, when they have
given 'em over, by more excellent Measures than ever were
known by their Ignorance ; They have also the Priviledge of
making By Laws, for the Interest of themselves, and Injury
of the Publick, and can purchase Lands in Right of the Corporation, if they could but find Money to pay for 'em ; they
have authority to examine the Medicines in all Apothecaries
Shops, to Judge of the wholesomeness and Goodness of many
Drugs and Compositions they never yet understood ; They
are likewise exempt from troublesome Offices, as *Jury men*,
Constables, &c.'

A visiting physician's fee was a guinea, but a consulting
one's less. ' The Worshipful Graduate in the noble Art of
Man slaughter, receiv'd us with a Civility that was peculiar
to him at the sight of four Half Crowns.'   A suit of black
(velvet if possible), a full-bottomed wig, a muff, and a gold-
or silver-headed cane formed the outward adornment of the
physician.

[1] *London Spy.*

. The surgeons, not being incorporated till 1800, had no special meeting-place ; but the apothecaries had their Hall in Water Lane, Blackfriars, which had been built in 1670, and is thus described by Garth :—

> Nigh where *Fleet Ditch* descends in sable Streams,
> To wash his sooty Naiads in the *Thames* ;
> There stands a Structure on a Rising Hill,
> Where *Tyro's* take their Freedom out to kill.
> —*The Dispensary*, Canto 3, ed. 1699.

Professional etiquette was, as a rule, strictly adhered to, and these divisions did not interfere with each other, although Brown[1] intimates that it was done occasionally: ' *Gallypot. . . .* " For tho' I am an Old Apothecary, I am but a Young Doctor. For I visit in either Capacity, either as an Old Apothecary, which is as good as a Young Doctor, or as a Young Doctor, and that's as good as t'other again." *Trueman.* " But I thought you had left off Shop, and stuck only to your Doctorship ?" *Gallypot.* " So I do *openly*, but *privately I keep a Shop*, and side in all things with the Apothecaries against the Doctors." '

This allusion refers to a curious dissension which had arisen in the profession. The physicians at the latter end of the seventeenth century were undoubtedly an ignorant and unscientific race ; and the apothecaries, finding that if they did not know as much, they could soon do so, began to prescribe on their own responsibility, as Pope[2] says :—

> So modern 'pothecaries taught the art
> By Doctor's bills, to play the Doctor's part ;
> Bold in the practice of mistaken rules,
> Prescribe, apply, and call their Masters fools.

The physicians naturally resented this, and, making a pretext that the apothecary's charges were so enormous as to render their prescriptions useless to the poor, they eventually set up a Dispensary of their own at the College, where they sold medicines to the poor at cost price. And this accusation was warranted, if we can believe Brown. ' Pray how do ye at your end of the Town prize a Dose of common Purging

[1] *The Dispensary.*   [2] *Essay on Criticism.*

Pills?'   'Why, Brother, about Eighteenpence, sometimes
Two Shillings, with an *Haustus* after them of Three and Sixpence.'   'And can you live so?   I believe all the things cost
you at least a Shilling out of Pocket.'   'No, God forbid!
How could I live then?   Indeed they cost me about Sixpence, and I take but Five Shillings and Sixpence, sometimes
less, and I think that's honest Gains.'

This Dispensary was the cause of great disturbance, and
split the profession into Dispensarians and anti-Dispensarians,
and a naturally acrimonious feeling sprang up, which was
only allayed by the obnoxious Dispensary being given up,
when things fell back into their old groove.

The Pharmacopœias then in use were 'Lasher's,' 'Bate's
Dispensary,' 'Hartman's Family Physitian,' and 'Salmon's
Collectanea Medica'[1]; and very curious indeed were some of
the medicines prescribed, as 'Live Hog Lice,' 'Burnt Cork
quenched in Aqua Vitæ,' 'Red Coral,' 'New Gathered Earth
Worms,' 'Live Toads,' 'Black tips of Crabs Claws,' 'Man's
Skull,' 'Elk's hoofs,' 'Leaves of Gold,' 'Man's bones calcined,'
'Inward skin of a Capon's Gizzard,' 'Goose dung, gather'd in
the Spring time, dry'd in the Sun,' 'Stone of a Carp's head,'
'Unicorn's horn,' 'Boar's tooth,' 'Jaw of a Pike,' 'Wind pipes
of Sheep cleansed and dryed in an Oven, Wind pipes of
Capons in like manner prepared,' 'Sea Horse tooth rasped,'
'Frog's livers,' 'White dung of a Peacock dryed,' 'Toads and
Vipers flesh,' 'Cuttle fish bone,' and many others even more
repulsive than these.

How would one like to take this medicine for smallpox?
'*Pulvis Æthiopicus*, the Black powder. R. Live Toads, No.
30 or 40, burn them in a new Pot, to black Cinders or Ashes,
and make a fine pouder. Dose ʒss. or more in the Small
Pox &c. and is a certain help for such as are ready to die:
some also commend it as a wonderful thing for the cure of the
Dropsie.'

'*Pulvis Ictericus*, A Pouder against the Yellow Jaundice.
R. Goose dung gather'd in the Spring time, dry'd in the Sun,

---

[1] A very long list of medical works of the time can be seen at the end of
Dr. Garth's poem of *The Dispensary*, ed. 1699, B. M. $\frac{840 \text{ h. } 6}{2.}$

and finely pouder'd ℥ij., the best Saffron ℈i., white Sugar
candy ℥ij., mix and make a pouder.   Dose ℈ij. twice a day in
Rhenish wine, for six days together.   Or thus—℞. Roots of
Turmerick, white Tartar, Mars prepared. A ℥ss. Earthworms,
Choice Rhubarb ℈ij., mix and make a powder.   Dose ℈j. in a
little Glass of White Wine.   An Acquaintance of mine, a
Learned Physician, usually makes both the Compositions into
One, and assures me that he never found it once to fail.'

'*Ranarum Hepata*, Livers of Frogs. ℞. They are prepared
by drying them upon Colewort Leaves in a Closed Vessel,
and then poudring them. S.A. Dose ℈ss. against the Epilepsie,
Quartan Ague &c.   If they be dryed and preserved with the
galls adjoyning, the medicine will be stronger and better ; and
may then be given Morning and Evening à ℈j. ad ℈ij. in any
fit Vehicle.'

'*Corrus Epilepticus*.   The Antepileptick Crow or Raven.
℞. The greater Crow, deplumate, and eviscerate it, casting
away its Feet and Bill ; put into its Belly the Heart, Liver,
Lungs, Bladder of the Gall, with Galangal and Aniseeds,
A ℥iv. bake it in a new Earthen Vessel well shut or closed in
an Oven with Household Bread ; after it is cooled, separate
the Flesh from the Sides or Bones, and repeat this Operation
of baking the second or third time, but taking great care that
it may not be burnt, then reduce it into a fine pouder.   S.A.
Dose ℈j. every day, to such as are afflicted with the Falling
Sickness ; it is a famous remedy.   That there may be a more
excellent Composition than this, we doubt not, and are confident it may be improv'd to a greater advantage ; the Composition in our *Seplasium. lib.* 6. *cap.* 21. *sect.* 11. seems to
excel it, which is this.   ℞. Of Ravens Flesh in pouder (as
the former Prescript advises) ℈iij. Viper pouder, ℈j native
Cinnamon ℈j (ad ℈ss.) mix and make a subtile Pouder for two
Doses, to be given at Night going to Bed.'

The above are all from one book, published 1706, and
could be multiplied to almost any extent, from this and the
other Pharmacopœias, were it necessary ; but enough has been
quoted to show the ignorance and empiricism of the medical
practitioners of that day.

All remedies, however, were not of the foregoing descrip-

tion, and many receipts seem admirably fitted to effect their
desired purpose, the great fault with them being that they
were overloaded with extraneous compounds, which could not
possibly do the patient any good, and must necessarily add
greatly to the cost, if only the extra time taken in their preparation be counted.   Bleeding and purging, as before said,.
were the remedies really relied on, and bleeding took place on
the slightest occasion.   Not only the lancet, but cupping, was
employed ; indeed, cuppers attended nearly every Bagnio or
bath, as Ward says: 'I'll carry you to see the *Hummuns*,
where I have an honest old Acquaintance that is a Cupper.'
He describes the operation thus :[' By the Perswasions of my
Friend, and my Friend's Friend, I at last consented ; upon
which the Operator fetch'd in his Instruments, and fixes three
Glasses at my Back, which by drawing out the Air, stuck to
me as close as a *Cantharides* Plaister to the Head of a
Lunatick, and Sucked as hard as so many Leeches, till I
thought they would have crept into me, and have come out
on t'other side.   When by Virtue of this *Hocus Pocus* Strata-
gem, he had conjur'd all the ill blood out of my Body, under
his glass Juggling Cups, he plucks out an ill favour'd Instrument, at which I was as much frighted, as an absconding
Debtor is at the sight of a Bill of Middlesex, takes off his
Glasses, which had made my Shoulders as weary as a Porter's
Back under a heavy Burthen, and begins to Scarifie my
Skin, as a Cook does a Loin of Pork to be Roasted ; but
with such Ease and Dexterity, that I could have suffer'd him
to have Pink'd me all over as full of Eyelet holes, as the
Taylor did the Shoemakers Cloak, had any Malady requir'd
it, without Flinching ; when he had drawn away as much
Blood as he thought Necessary, for the removal of my pain,
he cover'd the Places he had Carbonaded, with a new Skin,
provided for that purpose, and heal'd the Scarifications he had
made, in an Instant.'

    'A *Cantharides* Plaister to the Head of a Lunatick' shows
us somewhat how those poor unfortunates who were bereft
of their senses were treated.   Of Bethlehem Hospital I will
speak in another place, regarding it more as a prison for the
safe keeping of mad people than as an hospital, where, by any

means, those cloudy intellects could be brightened up and cleared.

If the relatives or friends could afford it, they were put under the charge of some one, as now, who would pretend to try and cure them; but then, unlike the present time, there was not even the form of a visitation to hear complaints, or to report on ill-treatment. 'At the Pestle and Mortar on Snow Hill, is a Person who has had great Experience and success in curing Lunaticks, he has also conveniences for Persons of both Sexes, good and diligent Attendance for the best ranks of People, and having for several years past, perform'd it to the satisfaction of many Families: He therefore makes this Publick, to inform, where on very reasonable rates the same Cure shall be industriously endeavour'd, and (with God's Blessing) effected.' Does it not look like a model for a modern advertisement? How Dr. So and So, assisted by a large staff of well-trained domestics, etc.

Here is an advertisement of a private Mad House. It being industriously given out by some malicious Persons, That the House of the Late Claudius Gillat at Hoxton, for the Accommodation of Lunaticks, is shut up; These are to Certify, that the said House is still kept by William Prowting, Apothecary, who has all Conveniences fitting for such persons; as a large House, pleasant Gardens, &c., and gives Liberty to any Physician, Surgeon or Apothecary, of administering Physick to those that are recommended by them.'

Another Advertisement, however, lets a little light into the treatment of the mentally afflicted: 'A Dumb young Man broke his Chain last Wednesday Night, and left his Friends from their House in Compton Street, next door to the Golden Ball Alehouse, Soho, and those that will take Care to bring him Home, shall be Rewarded. He has been Mad these 23 Years.'

Garth thus describes a prosperous physician :—

> Triumphant Plenty, with a chearful grace
> Basks in their Eyes, and sparkles in their Face.
> How sleik their looks, how goodly is their Mien,
> When big they strut behind a double Chin.
> Each Faculty in blandishments they lull,
> Aspiring to be venerably dull.

Like his descendant of modern times, who cannot possibly be clever in his profession unless he drives two horses to his brougham, the physician of Queen Anne's reign had to have his coach ; but then it must have at least four horses—of course he must be vastly cleverer if he could drive six—but still, his equipage must be well appointed, and in the fashion. Of course he need not go to the extent Radcliffe did ; but Radcliffe made himself the laughing-stock of the town, both by the gaiety of his turn-out and by a rumour getting abroad that he had started it with the idea of favourably impressing a young and wealthy lady, to whom this old Adonis of sixty would needs pay his addresses—in which scheme, alas for the doctor ! he was not successful.   Steele could not resist having a bit of fun over it.   ' This day, passing through Covent garden, I was stopped in the piazza by PACOLET, to observe what he called the Triumph of LOVE and YOUTH. I turned to the object he pointed at, and there I saw a gay gilt Chariot, drawn by fresh prancing horses ; the Coachman with a new Cockade, and the lacqueys with insolence and plenty in their countenances.   I asked immediately, "What young heir or lover owned that glittering equipage ?"   But my companion interrupted : " Do you not see there the mourning Æsculapius ? "   " The mourning ? " said I.   " Yes Isaac," said Pacolet, " he's in deep mourning, and is the languishing, hopeless lover of the divine HEBE,[1] the emblem of youth and beauty.'[2]

His rival Hannes set up a beautiful carriage, etc., and it excited universal attention.   Some friend told him that Hannes' horses were the finest he had seen.   ' Ah,' snarled old Radcliffe, ' then he'll be able to sell 'em for all the more.'

The principal physicians of Anne's reign were Dr. Radcliffe, Sir Samuel Garth, Sir Hans Sloane, and Dr. Mead.

The first was born in 1650, took his M.D. degree in 1682, came to London in 1684, and, somehow, at once got into good practice.   He was called in to the poor little Duke of Gloucester, when too late to be of any service, and consoled

---

[1] Miss Tempest, one of Queen Anne's Maids of Honour.
[2] *The Tatler*, No. 44.

himself by soundly rating the two physicians, Sir E. Hannes and Sir Rd. Blackmore, for their previous conduct of the case. But he was not the court physician, for which he had himself to thank. The Queen, when the Princess Anne, got somewhat hypochondriac, after the death of her sister Queen Mary, and sent for Radcliffe to come at once to see her. He was at a tavern in St. James's, enjoying his bottle. He knew there was nothing the matter, and physicians were not so smooth-tongued as they are now ; so he very rudely refused to go, and sent back a message that it was all fancy, and that her Royal Highness was as well as anyone else. Next morning he presented himself at the palace, only to be informed that he had been dismissed, and that Dr. Gibbons had already received his appointment. The Queen would never forgive him ; but, on her death-bed, he was sent for to attend her, when he returned as answer that 'he had taken physic and could not come.' The Queen died, and great was the popular wrath against the doctor for his refusal. He might have saved her life, said the people ; and after the manner of their kind, they sent him threatening letters ; nay, a friend of his moved that he might be summoned to attend in his place in Parliament (he was member for the town of Buckingham) in order to be censured for not attending her Majesty. He did not long survive her, dying on Nov. 1, 1714.

One anecdote told of him is too good not to be repeated. He would never even pay a tradesman without squabbling over the account. A paviour had been repairing the pavement in front of his house, and when he applied for his money was told he had spoiled it, and then covered it with earth to hide his bad work. 'Doctor,' replied the man, 'mine is not the only bad work the earth hides.'

Sir Samuel Garth took his degree of M.D. in 1691, was elected a Fellow of the College in 1692, and took a prominent part in the famous dispute as to the Dispensary—writing in 1699 his poem of that name, which had at once a large sale. Garth wrote many poems, translated Ovid, and it was to him that Dryden owed his public funeral, for, as Ward says, 'they had like to let him pass in private to

his Grave, without those Funeral Obsequies suitable to his
Greatness, had it not been for that true *British* Worthy, who,
Meeting with the Venerable Remains of the neglected Bard
passing silently in a Coach, unregarded to his last Home,
ordered the Corps, by the consent of his few Friends that
Attended him, to be Respited from so obscure an Interment ;
and most Generously undertook at his own Expence, to
revive his Worth in the Minds of a forgetful People, by
bestowing on his peaceful Dust a Solemn Funeral Answerable
to his Merit.'   He had the body removed to the College of
Physicians, where it lay in state previous to its removal, with
great pomp, to Westminster Abbey.

He was a member of the Kit Cat Club, and the story is
told of him that one day at a meeting of that club he sat so
long over his wine that Steele reminded him of his duty to his
patients.   Garth replied that ' it was no matter whether he
saw them that night or next morning, for nine had such bad
constitutions that no physician could save them, and the
other six had such good ones that all the physicians in the
world could not kill them.'   He died Jan. 18, 1719.

The name of Sir Hans Sloane is undoubtedly the most
familiar to the ears of this generation of all the doctors of
that time ; especially to Londoners, Sloane Street and Square,
and Hans Place, being all reminiscences of him, through the
marriage of his daughter Elizabeth with the second Baron
Cadogan.

He was of Scotch extraction, but born in Ireland, in 1660.
Already a Fellow of the College of Physicians and Royal
Society, he accompanied as physician the Duke of Albemarle
(who had been appointed Governor of the West Indies) to
Jamaica.   The Duke soon died out there, and Sloane returned
to England with a large collection of the flora and fauna of
the countries he had visited.   To this voyage may be attributed the foundation of the British Museum, for it gave him
the taste for collecting rarities of every description, and, to
prevent his museum from being dispersed after his death, he
bequeathed it to the nation, on condition of the payment of
20,000*l.* to his family.   Montague House was purchased to
contain the curiosities ; and from this small beginning has

arisen that marvellous national collection, the finest in the world. Honours flowed in upon him, and, after a very busy life, he died at a good old age in 1752.

Dr. Rd. Mead was born in 1673. Clever in his profession, and the author of many medical treatises, undoubtedly he owed much of his position to Radcliffe, whose patronage he secured by the most unblushing adulation. He took advantage of every opportunity, such as moving into the larger house of a physician recently dead ; and should have amassed a large fortune, as for many years he was earning between 5,000*l.* and 6,000*l.* per annum. Although his consulting fee was one guinea and his visiting fee two, he would attend either Batson's, or Tom's, Coffee Houses (the former being a noted place of resort for medical men), and thither would come the apothecaries, for whom he would write prescriptions, without seeing the patient, at half a guinea each. He is remarkable as the doctor who fought a duel. It was with Woodward, who had not only attacked him in his ' State of Physick and Diseases,' but insulted him in public. Matters came to a climax one day when they were leaving Gresham College, and, under the arch leading from the outer to the Green court, Mead's patience gave way. He drew, and called upon Woodward to defend himself or beg his pardon. Whether they ever actually fought or not is not known, although there is a *bon-mot* about Mead disarming Woodward and telling him to beg for his life. ' Never till I am your patient,' was his reply. Certain it is that Woodward gave in, and Mead lived in peace.

Mead was called in consultation when the Queen was in her last illness, and he plainly gave his opinion that she would not survive, but he did not attend her. He died Feb. 16, 1754, and was buried in the Temple Church.

There must have been some hot blood in the profession in those days, for Luttrell says : ' 6 July, 1704. Mr. Coatsworth, an apothecary in St. Martin's Lane, convicted in Easter term, upon an information in the Queen's bench, for assaulting Dr. Ratcliffe, at Tom's Coffee House, by spitting in his face, upon some words that arose betwen them, was upon Monday fined 100 marks, which he paid into Court.'

The practice of surgery was attended with some difficulties, for there were no public schools of anatomy as now : nay, it was as late as 1667 that Evelyn presented to the Royal Society, as a wonderful curiosity, the Table of Veins, Arteries, and Nerves which he had caused to be made in Italy.

We see that anatomy had to be taught privately, but still that there were professors who were capable of teaching. ' On Monday the 13th Instant, Mr. *Rolfe* Surgeon in *Chancery Lane* intends to begin at his House a compleat Course of Anatomy on Human Bodies, *viz.* Osteology, Myology, and Enterology, to be continued every Monday, Wednesday, and Friday.' The knife was freely used, and the instruments were far from clumsy ; but conservative surgery was also practised, and many orthopædic mechanical appliances were in use. 'Charles Roberts, who makes Steel Stays, Strait Stockings, Steel Boots, Collars, Cheiques and Swings, and by many years practice, having brought the same to great perfection, is perswaded to give this publick notice for the benefit of such who suffer by Deformity.'

The barbers also bled and drew teeth, as many now do.

The oculists of that day were particularly pushing, and puffed and lied themselves into notoriety with vigour. Chief of them was Sir William Read, oculist to her most gracious majesty ; and if anybody wishes to see how much that tender organ the eye can be abused by an oculist, let him read his ' Short but Exact Account of all the Diseases Incident to the Eyes.' Originally a tailor in a small way of business, he managed, somehow, to rise so as to become the Queen's sworn oculist, and to be knighted ; nor only so, but was able to keep up a good establishment and a magnificent equipage. One thing is certain—he thoroughly knew the value of advertising ; and the accompanying illustration is taken from one of his handbills, probably about 1696. In it he gives a list of wonderful cures he has wrought, how he has cured wry necks, harelips, cut out cancers, trepanned skulls, operated on wens and polypuses, cured dropsy, cut off a man's leg, and given sight to numerous people who were born blind.

His knighthood is thus recorded in the *Gazette* of July 30/Aug. 1, 1705 : ' Windsor 27 July. Her Majesty was

this day Graciously pleased to confer the Honour of Knight-
hood upon William Read Esq. Her Majesty's Oculist :n
Ordinary, as a Mark of her Royal Favour for his great
Services done in Curing great Numbers of Seamen and
Soldiers of Blindness *gratis.*' This he advertised to do all

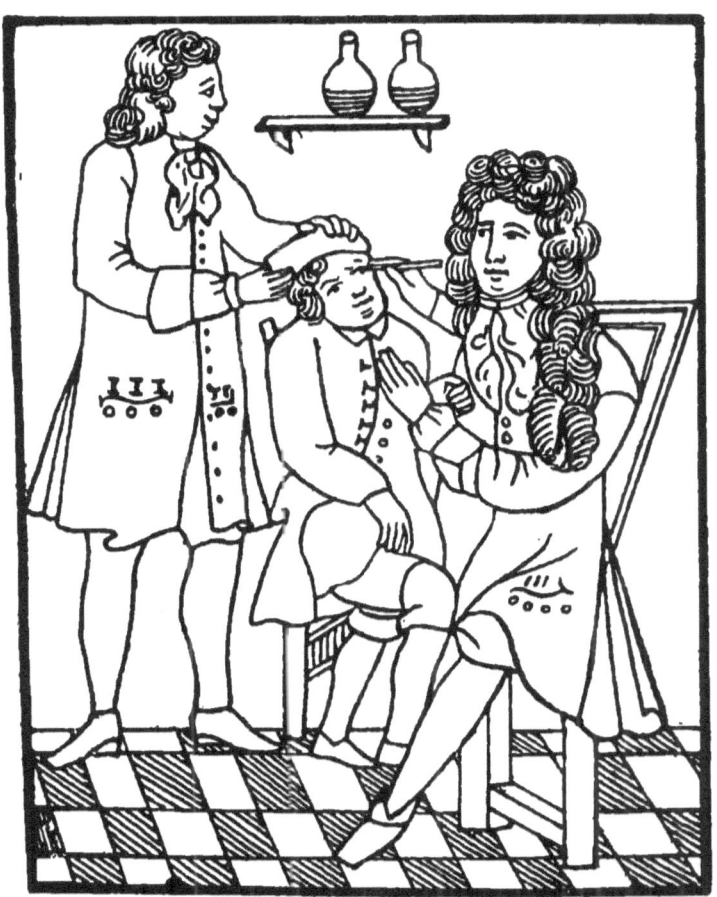

SIR WILLIAM READ OPERATING.

through the war ; and when the Palatines came over here he
publicly offered to attend any of them for diseases of the eye
gratis. And now, forsooth, he advertised that ' Lady Read '
would attend to patients as well ; and some Grub Street poet
wrote a poem, called ' The Oculist,' ' Address'd to Sir *William*

Read, Knt.,' with a long and fulsome dedication.   One part
of the poem runs :—

> Whilst *Britain's* Sovereign Scales such WORTH has weig'd,
> And ANNE her self her smiling Favours paid :
> That Sacred Hand does Your fair Chaplet twist,
> Great READ her own Entitled OCULIST.
>
> . . .   .
>
> When the Great ANNE'S warm Smiles this Favourite raise,
> 'Tis not a Royal Grace she gives, but pays.

Swift[1] writes to Stella of Read's sumptuous way of living:
' Henley would fain engage me to go with Steele and Rowe
&c. to an invitation at Sir William Read's.   Surely you have
heard of him.   He has been a Mountebank, and is the
Queen's Oculist ; he makes admirable punch, and treats you
in gold vessels.   But I am engaged, and won't go.'

His rival, who was also the Queen's sworn oculist, was
Roger Grant, who, report said, was originally a tinker, and
afterwards an anabaptist preacher in Southwark.

> Her Majesty sure was in a Surprise,
> Or else was very short sighted ;
> When a *Tinker* was sworn to look after her Eyes,
> And the Mountebank *Read* was *Knighted*.

He also advertised largely, and published lists of his cures, with
certificates from the mayor and aldermen of Durham, Northampton, Coventry, Hull, etc., touching the authenticity of his
cures.   How these were procured is fully explained in a little
tract called ' A Full and True ACCOUNT of a *Miraculous*
CURE of a Young MAN in *Newington*, That was Born BLIND,
and was in Five Minutes brought to Perfect Sight, by Mr.
ROGER GRANT, Oculist,' 1709.   The case in question was
advertised by Grant in the *Daily Courant* of July 30, 1709,
and the little book ruthlessly exposes the fraudulent manner
in which the certificate was obtained.

As has been said before, quackery was universal ; nay, it
had the sanction of being practised by royalty, for was not
the Queen an arch quack when she touched for the ' evil '?
She was the last of a long line of sovereigns, from Edward

---

[1] *Journal*, April 11, 1711.

the Confessor, who exercised the supposed royal gift of healing ; but this salutary efficacy was not confined to the royal
touch alone, if we can believe a little story of Thoresby's[1]:
' Her Mother Mary Bailey of Deptford, after she had been
twelve years blind by the Kings evil was miraculously cured by
a handkerchief dipped in the blood of King Charles the First.'

Misson was present the last time James the Second touched,
and has left us a graphic account of the ceremony : ' The King
was seated in a Chair of State,[2] rais'd two or three Steps. The
Reverend Father *Peter*, with his little Band and his sweeping
Cloak was standing at the King's Right Hand. After some
Prayers, the diseased Person, or those that pretended to be so,[3]
were made to pass between a narrow double Rail, which fac'd
the King. Each Patient, Rich and Poor, Male and Female, fell
upon their knees, one after another, at the King's Feet. The
King putting forth his two Hands, touch'd their two Cheeks ;
the Jesuit, who held a Number of Gold Medals, each fasten'd
to a narrow white Ribband, put the Ribband round the
Patient's Neck at the same Time that the King touch'd him,
and said something tantamount to what they say in *France*,
The King touches thee ; God cure thee. This was done in a
Trice ; and for fear the same Patient should crowd into the
File again, to get another Medal,[4] he was taken by the Arm,
and carry'd into a safe place. When the King was weary of
repeating the same action, and touching the Cheek or Chin,
Father *Peter* the Almoner, presented him with the End of
the String which was round the Patient's Neck. The Virtue
pass'd from the Hand to the String, from the String to the
Cloaths, from the Cloaths to the Skin, and from the Skin to
the Root of the Evil : After this Royal Touch, those that
were really ill were put into the Hands of Physicians ; and
those that came only for the Medal, had no need of other
Remedies.' This last sentence explains a great deal.

William III. did not touch, but gave away the money
hitherto spent on the touch pieces, etc., in charity. But
Anne, as a thoroughly legitimate English monarch, and a

---

[1] *Diary*, July 14, 1714.   [2] In the Banqueting Hall, Whitehall.
[3] On this occasion there were 300.
[4] These ' touch pieces ' had on one side St. George overcoming the dragon,
and were called 'angels.'

Stuart to boot, kept up the fiction of her curative powers. She tried it on Dr. Johnson, but it had no effect ; and his recollections of the ceremony were very vague.   ' He had,' he said, ' a confused but somehow a sort of solemn recollection of a lady in diamonds, and a long black hood.'   But then the staunch old Jacobite used to declare that ' his mother had not carried him far enough ; she should have taken him to ROME ' (to the Pretender).

Anne touched the very first year of her reign, for Luttrell [1] says, ' The Service and Attendance belonging to the Ceremony of touching for the King's Evil went for Bath last Week, her Majesty desiring to touch there.'   Illness sometimes prevented her : ' Her Majesty did not touch yesterday for the evil as design'd, having the gout in her hands.' [2]

It evidently required some little interest to get touched, for Swift writes [3] to Stella : ' I visited the Duchess of Ormond this morning . . . I spoke to her to get a lad touched for the Evil. . . . But the Queen has not been able to touch, and it now grows so warm, I fear she will not at all.'

Notices were duly posted in the *Gazette* as to when she touched or not, and in that of May 24/28, 1705, we find one which would lead us to imagine that some unfair practice had arisen : ' It is also Her Majesty's Command, That all Persons who shall then apply to be touched, shall bring a Certificate to Her Majesty's Serjeant Surgeon, signed by the Minister and Churchwardens of the Parish where such Person shall then reside, that they never had before received the Royal Touch, as been heretofore accustomed.'

It is impossible to take up a newspaper of that time without encountering some quack advertisements, and the quantity of handbills [4] still preserved, show how they must have flooded the place.   There was the ' Volatile *Spirit* of BOHEA TEA,' ' Pilula Salutiferens,' ' Spirit of Scurvy Grass,' ' Balsamick Pills,' ' Elixir Minerale,' ' Green Cathartick Elixir,'

---

[1] Oct. 8, 1702.   [2] *Luttrell*, March 20, 1703.   [3] *Journal*, May 8, 1711.

[4] ' If the pale Walker pants with weak'ning Ills,
His sickly Hand is stor'd with Friendly Bills :
From hence, he learns the seventh born Doctor's Fame,
From hence he learns the cheapest Tailor's name.'

—*Trivia*, book 2.

'The Hysterick Tincture,' 'The White Cardialgic Powder,' 'The Volatile Cordial Pill,' 'Tinctura Benedicta,' 'Electuarium Mirabile,' 'Electuary of the Balm of Gilead.' What a list might be made of them! See what Addison says of them in the *Tatler* (224). The heading to one is given as a sample of the style of art in the handbill.

This 'Paris Pill and Electuary' is described as follows 'The Price of a Box of the Pills is 2s. 6d. and a Pot of the Electuary 1s. 6d. of wch Pills and Electuary two Boxes & one Pot will be sufficient for any one not very far gone in the Distemper, and Double the Number will heal the Patient if in great Extremity. Sold by J. Sherwood Book Seller at Popings aley Gate fleet street, With a paper of Directions.'

A QUACK.

In another advertisement of 'Dr. Anderson's, or the Famous Scots Pills,' you are requested to 'Beware of Counterfeits, especially an Ignorant pretender, one Muffen, who keeps a China Shop, and is so unneighbourly as to pretend to sel the same Pills within 3 Doors of me.'

But the quacks were not all stationary; as at present, some were peripatetic, who, after the fashion of these wanderers, had an eloquence of their own, which only Ward can do justice to. Here is a short extract [1] of the 'patter' of those days. 'Gentlemen, you that have a Mind to be Mindful of preserving a Sound Mind in a Sound Body, that is, as the Learned Physician Doctor *Honorificicabilitudinitatibusque* has

[1] *London Spy.*

it, *Manus Sanaque in Cobile Sanaquorum*, may here, at the
expence of twopence, furnish himself with a parcel, which
tho' it is but small, yet containeth mighty things of great Use
and Wonderful Operation in the Bodies of Mankind, against
all Distempers, whether *Homogeneal* or *Complicated* ; whether
deriv'd from your *Parents*, got by *Infection*, or proceeding
from an ill Habit of your own Body.

'In the first place, Gentlemen, I here present you with a
little inconsiderable Pill to look at, you see not much bigger
than a Corn of Pepper, yet in this Diminutive *Pampharmica*,
so powerful in effect, and of such excellent Vertues, that if
you have Twenty Distempers lurking in the Mass of Blood,
it shall give you just Twenty Stools, and every time it
operates, it carries off a Distemper ; but if your Blood's
Wholesome, and your Body Sound, it will work you no more
than the same quantity of Ginger bread.   I therefore call it,
from its admirable Qualities, *Pilula Ton dobula*, which signifies
in the Greek, *The Touch Stone of Nature* ; For by taking of
this Pill you will truly discover what state of Health or
Infirmity your Constitution is then under.

'In the next place, Gentlemen, I present you with an
excellent outward application, call'd a Plaister ; good against
Green Wounds, old Fistulas and Ulcers, Pains and Aches,
Contusions, Tumours or King's Evil, Spasms, Fractures, or
Dislocations, or any Hurts whatsoever, received either by
Sword, Cane, or Gun Shot, Knife, Saw, or Hatchet, Hammer,
Nail or Tenter hook, Fire, Blast or Gunpowder, &c.   And
will continue its Vertue beyond Credit ; and as useful seven
years hence as at this present Moment, that you may lend it
to your Neighbours in the time of Distress and Affliction ;
and, when it has perform'd Forty Cures 'twill be ne'er the
Worse, but still retain its Integrity.   *Probatum Est*,' etc.

Dr. Zachary Pearce, Bishop of Rochester, who wrote
No. 572 of the *Spectator* (altered by Addison), gives an
amusing account of one of these quacks.   'I remember one
of those Public-spirited Artists at *Hammersmith*, who told his
Audience "that he had been born and bred there, and that,
having a special Regard for the place of his Nativity, he was
determined to make a Present of five Shillings to as many as

would accept of it." The whole Crowd stood agape, and
ready to take the Doctor at his Word ; when putting his
Hand into a long Bag, as every one was expecting his Crown
Piece, he drew out a handful of little Packets, each of which
he informed the Spectators was constantly sold at five Shillings and six pence, but that he would bate the odd five Shillings to every Inhabitant of that Place ; the whole Assemb y
immediately closed with this generous Offer, and took off all
his Physick, after the Doctor had made them vouch for one
another, that there were no Foreigners among them, but that
they were all *Hammersmith* Men.' The whole article is an
amusing *exposé* of the quackery then at its height. 'I
unluckily called to mind a Story of an Ingenious Gentleman
of the last Age, who, lying violently afflicted with the Gout,
a Person came and offered his Service to Cure him by a
Method, which he assured him was Infallible ; the Servant
who received the Message, carried it up to his Master, who,
enquiring whether the Person came on Foot, or in a Chariot ;
and being informed he was on Foot: *Go*, says he, *send the
Knave about his Business : Was his Method as infallible as
he pretends, he would long before now have been in his Coach
and Six.'*

CHAPTER XXXI.

SPAS AND BATHING.

Bath—Manners of the company there—Description of Bath—Its gaieties —Sale of the water—Tunbridge—Epsom—Hampstead—Other spas— Turkish baths—Controversy on hot and cold bathing—The Hum- mums—Description of a Turkish bath—Other bagnios—Cold bathing and baths.

IT was a great time for our English spas, and 'Spaw Water' was a favourite drink with the temperate. Chief of all, for its curative qualities, and for its society, was Bath, or 'The Bath,' as it was called ; and, as it occupies such a prominent position in the social life of this time, more than a passing notice of it is required. Misson's description of it is short but businesslike. 'This Town takes its Name from the Baths for which it is famous. Several in *Switzerland* and *Germany* are called *Baden* for the same reason. In Winter *Bath* makes a very melancholy Appearance ; but during the Months of *May, June, July*, and *August*, there is a concourse of genteel Company, that peoples, enriches, and adorns it ; at that Time, Provisions and Lodgings grow dear. Thousands go thither to pass away a few Weeks, without heeding either the Baths or the Waters, but only to divert themselves with good Company. They have Musick, Gaming, Public Walks, Balls, and a little Fair every Day.'

The manners of this 'concourse of genteel company' are thus described by Steele.[1] 'In the Autumn of the same Year I made my Appearance at *Bath*. I was now got into the Way of Talk proper for Ladies, and was run into a vast Acquaintance among them, which I always improved to the *best Advantage*. In all this Course of Time, and some Years

---

[1] *Spectator*, No. 154.

following, I found a Sober, Modest Man was always looked
upon by both Sexes as a precise unfashioned Fellow of no
Life or Spirit. It was ordinary for a Man who had been
drunk in good Company, or passed a Night with a Wench, to
speak of it next Day before Women for whom he had the
greatest Respect. He was reproved, perhaps, with a Blow of
the Fan, or an Oh Fie, but the angry Lady still preserved an
apparent Approbation in her Countenance : He was called a
strange wicked Fellow, a sad Wretch ; he shrugs his shoulders,
swears, receives another Blow, swears again he did not know
he swore, and all was well. You might often see Men game
in the Presence of Women, and throw at once for more than
they were worth, to recommend themselves as Men of Spirit.'

Perhaps the most graphic description of daily life at Bath
is given in a sixpenny pamphlet entitled ' A Step to the Bath
with a Character of the place' (London, 1700). It is published
anonymously, but I have no doubt in my own mind that it
was written by Ward, as it is exactly his style, and is published by his publisher. Of course, in his writings, we must
not look for polished language ; but his descriptions are accu-
rate, and as such well worth having. He thus describes the
place :—

' The first we went to, is call'd the *King's* ; and to it joyns
the Queen's, both running in one ; and the most famous for
Cures. In this *Bath* was at least fifty of both Sexes, with a
Score or two of Guides, who by their Scorbutic Carcasses,
and Lackered Hides, you would think they had lain Pickling
a Century of Years in the Stygian Lake ; Some had those
Infernal Emissaries to support their Impotent Limbs : Others
to Scrub their Putrify'd Carcasses, like a Race Horse. . . . At
the Pump was several a Drenching their Gullets, and Gor-
mandizing the Reaking Liquor by wholesale.

' From thence we went to the Cross Bath, where most of
the Quality resorts, more fam'd for *Pleasure* than *Cures.*
Here is perform'd all the Wanton Dalliances imaginable ;
Celebrated Beauties, Panting Breasts, and Curious Shapes,
almost Expos'd to Publick View : Languishing eyes, Darting
Killing Glances, Tempting Amorous Postures, attended by
soft Musick, enough to provoke a *Vestal* to forbidden Plea-

sure, Captivate a *Saint*, and charm a *Jove*: Here was also different Sexes, from *Quality* to the Honourable *Knights*, Country *Put*, and City *Madam's*. . . . The Ladies with their floating *Jappan* Bowles, freighted with Confectionary, Kick-Knacks, Essences and Perfumes, Wade about, like *Neptun's* Courtiers, suppling their Industrious Joynts. The Vigorous Sparks, presenting them with several Antick Postures, as Sailing on their Backs, then Embracing the Element, sink in Rapture. . . . The usual time being come to forsake that fickle Element, *Half Tub Chairs*, Lin'd with Blankets, Ply'd as thick as *Coaches* at the *Play House*, or *Carts* at the *Custom House*.

Bathing being over for that Day, we went to walk in the Grove, a very pleasant place for Diversion ; there is the *Royal Oak* and several Raffling Shops : In one of the Walks, is several Sets of Nine Pins and Attendants to wait on you : Tipping all Nine for a Guinea, is as common there, as two Farthings for a *Porrenger* of *Barley Broth*, at the *Hospital Gate* in Smithfield. On several of the Trees was hung a Lampoon on the Marriage of one Mr. S—— a Drugmonger and the famous Madam S—— of London.

'Having almost tir'd ourselves with walking, we took a Bench to ease our weary Pedestals. Now, said my Friend, I'll give you an impartial Account of the Perfections, Qualities and Functions, of a few particular Persons that are among this Amphibious Crowd. . . . To give you a particular Description of each of 'em, will require a Week's time at least. Come, therefore, let's go to some Tipling Mansion, and Carrouse, till we have Exhilerated our Drouthy Souls : To which I readily agreed. About five in the Evening, we went to See a great Match at Bowling : There was *Quality*, and Reverend *Doctors* of both Professions, Topping *Merchants*, Broken *Bankers*, Noted *Mercers*, Inns of Court *Rakes*, City *Beaus*, Stray'd *Prentices*, and *Dancing-Masters* in abundance. *Fly, fly, fly, fly*, said one ; *Rub, Rub*, rub, rub, cry'd another ; *Ten Guineas to five I Uncover the Jack*, says a third. *Damn these Nice Fingers of mine*, cry'd my Lord, *I Slipt my Bowl and mistook the Bias.* Another Swearing he knew the Ground to an Inch, and would hold five Pound his Bowl came in.

'From hence, we went to the *Groom Porters*, where they were a Labouring like so many *Anchor Smiths*, at the *Oake, Back Gammon, Tick Tack, Irish, Basset*, and throwing o: *Mains*. There was Palming, Lodging, Loaded Dice, Levant, and Gammoning, with all the Speed imaginable ; but the *Cornish* Rook was too hard for them all. The *Bristol Fair* Sparks had but a very bad bargain of it ; and little occasior. for Returns. *Bank Bills*, and *Exchequer Notes* were as Plenty, as *Pops* at the *Chocolate Houses* or *Patternoster Row*. Having satisfied our Curiosity here ; we left them as busie a shaking their Elbows, as the *Apple women* in *Stocks Market*, Wallnuts in *October*.

'And meeting with three or four more Acquaintance, we stroul'd to a *Bristol-Milk Dary-House*, and Enjoy'd our selves like brave *Bacchanalians*.'

This, then, was how the day was spent at Bath, with the exception of when some person of quality gave an entertainment to a select number of visitors—and this they were expected to do. Our writer describes his experience of one ' The Ball is always kept at the Town Hall, a very spacious Room, and fitted up for that Purpose. During which, the Door is kept by a Couple of Brawny Beadles, to keep out the Mobility, looking as fierce as the Uncouth Figures at *Guild-Hall*; there was Extraordinary Fine Dancing (anc how could it otherwise chuse, for Spouse and I had a Hanc in it). A Consort of Delicate Musick, Vocal and Instrumental, perform'd by good Masters ; A Noble Collation o: dry Sweet Meats, Rich Wine and large Attendance. The Lady who was the *Donor*, wore an Extraordinary Rich Favour, to distinguish her from the rest, which is always the Custom ; and before they break up to chuse another for the next Day, which fell upon a Shentlewoman of *Wales* ; but no ways Derogated from hur Honour, or Disparag'd her Country in the least, but hur was as Noble, and as Generous as e'er an *English* Shentlewoman of them all : To hur Honour be it Spoke.'

And he winds up the pamphlet with ' A Character of the Bath.'

''Tis neither Town nor City, yet goes by the Name of

both : five Months in the Year 'tis as Populous as *London,*
the other seven as desolate as a Wilderness.   Its chiefest
Inhabitants are Turn-spit-Dogs ; and it looks like *Lombard
Street* on a Saints day.   During the Season, it hath as many
Families in a House as *Edenborough* ; and Bills are as thick
for Lodgings to be Let, as there was for Houses in the
Fryars on the Late Act of Parliament for the Dissolution of
Priviledges ; but when the *Baths* are useless, so are their
Houses, and as empty as the new Buildings by *St. Giles*
in the *Fields ;* The *Baths* I can compare to nothing but the
Boylers in *Fleet Lane* or *Old Bedlam*, for they have a reaking
steem all the Year.   In a Word, 'tis a Valley of Pleasure, yet
a sink of Iniquity ; Nor is there any Intrigues or Debauch
Acted in *London*, but is Mimick'd here.'

The Water was bottled and sold, and in order to
guarantee its purity an advertisement was issued in 1706 :
' Notice is hereby given, that George Allen is now chosen
Pumper of the King's Bath Waters in Bath, and that the
true Waters are to be had of none but him who seals all
Bottles and Vessels with a Seal, whereon is the City Arms,
viz a Borough Wall and Sword, and round it these Words,
The King's Bath Water, George Allen, Pumper.'   It was
supplied in London fresh three times a week, as we find by
another advertisement of 1709.

Tunbridge ranked next to Bath as a fashionable resort,
and it is thus described in a contemporary play (' Tunbridge
Walks,' ed. 1703).

Loveworth. But *Tunbridge* I suppose is the Seat of Pleasure ; Prithee,
what Company does the Place afford?

Reynard. Like most publick Assemblies, a Medley of all Sorts, Fops
majestick and diminutive, from the long Flaxen Wig with a splendid
Equipage, to the Merchants' Spruce Prentice, that's always mighty neat
about the Legs ; Squires come to Court some fine Town Lady, and Town
Sparks to pick up a Russet Gown ; for the Women here are Wild Country
Ladies, with ruddy Cheeks like a *Sevil* Orange, that gape, stare, scamper,
and are brought hither to be Disciplined ; Fat City Ladies with tawdry
Atlasses, in Defiance of the Act of Parliament ; and slender Court Ladies
with *French* Scarffs, *French* Aprons, *French* Night Cloaths and *French*
Complexions.

Loveworth. But what are the Chief Diversions here?

Reynard. Each to his own Inclinations—Beaus Raffle and Dance—

Citts play at Nine Pins, Bowls, and Backgammon—Rakes, scoure the Walks, Bully the Shop keepers, and beat the Fidlers—Men of Wit ral y over Claret, and Fools get to the *Royal Oak* Lottery, where you may lose Fifty Guineas in a Moment; have a Crown returned to you for Coach Hire, a Glass of Wine, and a hearty wellcome. In short, 'tis a Place wholly dedicated to Freedom, no Distinction, either of Quality or Estate, but ev'ry Man that appears well Converses with the Best.

People, however, went to Tunbridge to *drink* the waters, not to *bathe* in them. So was it with Epsom Wells, which was decidedly lower in tone. From its easy access to London, it was crowded with citizens—and some very questionable characters. If Bath allowed some licence to its frequenters, Epsom gave more. ' But if you were not so monstrous lewd, the freedom of *Epsom* allows almost nothing to be scandalous.'[1]

The Epsom season began on Easter Monday, and one advertisement will sufficiently indicate its character. 170̃. 'The New Wells at Epsom, with variety of Raffling Shops, will be open'd on Easter Monday next. There are Shops now to be Let, at the said Wells for a Bookseller, Pictures, Haberdasher of Hats, Shoomaker, Fishmonger, and Butcher; with conveniences for several other Trades. ☞ It's design'd that a very good Conscrt of Musick shall attend and play there Morning and Evening during the Season ; and nothing will be demanded for the Waters drunk there.' Pinkethman would take his performing dogs down there, and Mr. Clinch, with the wonderful voice, would spend the season there. Morris-dancing and other sports were got up, and at last they had races, which have since evolved that national saturnalia the Derby.

They had not yet analysed these purgative waters, and consequently ' Epsom salts' were unknown, so that people, did they wish for them, must either go to Epsom, or buy the water in London, where almost all the other ' Spaw' waters could be procured. It is astonishing how they could drink the quantity they are recorded to have done—*i.e.* if those accounts are trustworthy. Brown, in one of his ' Letters from the Dead to the Living,' talks of a lady ' that has drank two

---

[1] *Epsom Wells*, Shadwell.

Quarts of *Epsom* Waters for her Mornings draught'; and
Shadwell, in 'Epsom Wells,' says :—

> *Brisket.* I vow it is a pleasurable Morning : the Waters taste so finely
> after being fudled last Night.   Neighbour *Fribbler*, here's a Pint to you.
> *Fribbler.* I'll pledge you Mrs. *Brisket*; I have drunk eight already.
> *Mrs. Brisket.* How do the Waters agree with your Ladyship?
> *Mrs. Woodly.* Oh, Soveraignly : how many Cups have you arrived to?
> *Mrs. Brisket.* Truly Six, and they pass so kindly.

There was, and even yet is, a mildly chalybeate spring at
Hampstead, which made that beautiful northern suburb very
fashionable.   The well has been lately altered, and the old
Assembly Rooms, which had lasted from Anne's time, were
pulled down in the early part of 1882.   Old gardens have
been grubbed up, and fine new villas set a-top of them.   It is
only a question of time as to when the trees in Well Walk
will die and be no more, and but a few houses will remain to
attest the glory of Hampstead in Queen Anne's time, when
the Kit Cats made it their summer meeting-place.   Like all
places of amusement then, the spirit of gambling had invaded
it, and either Swift or Steele notices that : ' By letters from
Hampstead which give me an account, there is a late institution there, under the name of a RAFFLING SHOP ; which is,
it seems, secretly supported by a person who is a deep prac-
titioner in the law, and out of tenderness of conscience, has,
under the name of his maid Sisly, set up this easier way
of conveyancing and alienating estates from one family to
another.'[1] Concerts of music were frequent here in the season,
as they were also at Richmond Wells, which opened in the
middle of May.

The medicinal powers of divers springs near London had
been known for generations, and we find them duly advertised
and puffed—Acton Waters, Dullidge and Northall Waters,
Lambeth Wells, Sadler's New Tunbridge Wells near Islington, 'at the *Musick House* by the *New River.*'   The London
Spaw, 'at the sign of the Fountain in the parish of St.
James's Clarken Well ; in the way going up to Islington'
(' the Poor may have it Gratis ') ; whilst in 1702 we find an
advertisement : ' This is to give notice, That at the King's

[1] *The Tatler*, No. 59.

Arms Inn in Haughton Street in Clare Market, over against
New Inn back Gate, is lately discovered a Spring of Purging
Water, known by the name of Holy-well, or the London
Water, exceeding for their Cathartic Excellency, all other
Purging Waters ; working in small quantities without neglect
of Business. This Water has been tried and approved of by
some of the best Physicians. To be had at the Pump, at the
place aforesaid at 2d. the Quart, and to those that buy it to
Retail it, at the Usual Rates.'

One of those in the country was Buxton, of which we get
the following notice in 1705 : 'Whereas the Bath House at
Buxton, in Derbyshire, so famous in the North for divers
Cures, hath of late Years been mismanaged, by disobliging
Persons of Quality and others usually resorting to the said
Bath ; this is therefore to give Notice to all Persons of
Quality and Gentry of Both Sexes, That Care has now been
taken, by his Grace the Duke of Devonshire, to remedy the
like Treatment, for the future, by sending down from London
a fitting and obliging Person sufficiently qualified : So that
now all Persons resorting to the said Bath will meet with
Civil Usage, and have the best of every thing for Man and
Beast at reasonable rates.' Then there were springs at Scar-
borough, Bury, Astrop, Croft, Holt, and Blurton Spaw Water,
which was belauded by Floyer. Of course these are not a
tithe of those which were locally famous, but were not pushed
into public notoriety.

Foreign mineral waters were in use, but evidently only for
medicinal purposes. 'Purging Spaw Waters newly brought
over from Germany, to be sold at the Two Golden Images in
King Street, near St. James's.' And they were sold at prices
varying from 12s. per doz. or 1s. per flask, to 15s. per doz.

Not only were the hot springs of Bath frequented for the
purposes of bathing, but the Turkish bath was peculiarly an
institution of this reign, and the 'Hummums' or 'Bagnios'
were well frequented, until the latter got an evil reputation,
and the name of Bagnio came to be regarded as synonymous
with a disorderly house. Some of the medical men of the
time took up the subject of bathing with relation to health,
and, as is generally the case, took opposite views ; some

advocating cold bathing, like Sir John Floyer and Dr. Ed
Baynard in 'ΨΤΧΡΟΛΟΨΣΙ'Α : or, the HISTORY of COLD
BATHING, Both Ancient and Modern,' 1706, or Dr. Browne,
who wrote in 1707 'An Account of the Wonderful CURES
perform'd by the COLD BATHS. With Advice to the Water
Drinkers at *Tunbridge, Hampstead, Astrope, Nasborough,* and
all the other *Chalibeate Spaws*'; whilst others took up the
cause of hot bathing, and decried the use of cold water, even
in immersion in Baptism, like Guidot, who in 1705 published
'An *Apology* for the *Bath*,' having previously printed a Latin
tract, '*De Thermis Britannicis.*'

Ward describes a visit to the Hummums in Covent
Garden with a friend, who suggested to him [1] 'if you will be
your Club towards Eight Shillings, we'll go in and Sweat,
and you shall feel the effects of this Notable Invention.'
Let him tell his experiences in his own words. 'We now
began to unstrip, and put ourselves in a Condition of endur-
ing an Hour's Baking, and when we had reduc'd our selves
into the Original state of Mankind, having nothing before us
to cover our Nakedness, but a Clout no bigger than a Fig
leaf, our Guide led us to the end of our Journey, the next
Apartment, which I am sure, was as hot as a Pastry Cooks
Oven to Bake a White Pot ; that I began immediately to
melt, like a piece of Butter in a Basting Ladle, and was afraid
I should have run all to Oyl by the time I had been in six
Minutes ; The bottom of the Room was Pav'd with Free-
stone ; to defend our feet from the excessive heat of which,
we had got on a pair of new-fashion'd *Brogues*, with Wooden
Soles after the *French* Mode, Cut out of an Inch Deal Board ;
or else like the Fellow in the *Fair*, we might as well have
walk'd cross a hot Iron Bar, as ventur'd here to have Trod
bare Foot. As soon as the Fire had tapt us all over, and we
began to run like a Conduit Pipe, at every Pore, our Rubber
arms his Right Hand with a Gauntlet of coarse hair Camlet,
and began to curry us with as much Labour, as a *Yorkshire
Groom* does his Master's best Stone Horse ; till he made our
Skins as smooth as a Fair Ladies Cheeks, just wash'd with
Lemon Posset, and greas'd over with *Pomatum.* At last I

[1] *The London Spy.*

grew so very faint with the expence of much Spirits, that I
begg'd as hard for a Mouthful of fresh Air, as *Dives* did for a
drop of Water; which our attendance let in at a Sash-Window,
no broader than a *Deptford* Cheese Cake ; but, however, it let
in a Comfortable Breeze that was very Reviving : when I had
foul'd many *Callico* Napkins, our Rubber draws a *Cistern* full
of Hot Water, that we might go in, and Boil out those gross
Humours that could not be Emitted by Perspiration. Thus,
almost Bak'd to a *Crust*, we went into the hot Bath to moisten
our Clay, where we lay Soddening our selves like *Deer's*
Humbles design'd for Minc'd Pies, till we were almost Par-
boiled . . . then after he had wiped me o'er with a dry Clout,
telling us we had Sweat enough, he reliev'd us out of Purga-
tory, and carried us into our Dressing Room ; which gave us
such Refreshment, after we had been stewing in our own
Gravy, that we thought ourselves as happy as a Couple of
English Travellers, Transported in an Instant, by a Miracle
from the *Torrid Zone* into their own Country. Our expence
of Spirits had weakened Nature and made us drowsie ; where
having the Conveniency of a Bed, we lay down and were
rubb'd like a couple of Race Horses after a Course.'

An advertisement of these baths tells us fully of the
extent of the accommodation they afforded. ' At the Hum-
mum's in Covent Garden are the best accommodation for
Persons of Quality to Sweat or Bath every day in the week,
the Conveniences of all kinds far exceeding all other Bagnios
or Sweating Houses both for Rich and Poor. Persons of
good Reputation may be accommodated with handsom
Lodgings to lye all Night. There is also a Man and Woman
who Cups after the Newest and easiest method. In the
Garden of the same House is also a large Cold Bath of
Spring Water, which, for its Coldness and Delicacy, deserves
an equal Reputation with any in use.'

There were also ' John Evans's Hummums in Brownlow
Street near Drury Lane,' ' John Pindar's (The German Sweating House) in Westmoreland Court, in Bartholomew Close,
near Aldersgate Street,' and ' The Queen's Bagnio in Long
Acre,' kept by Henry Ayme, chirurgeon ; where not only
could you have a bath for 5*s*., or two or more 4*s*. each, but

there was 'a lesser *Bagnio*, of a lower Rate, for the Diseased and Meaner Sort.' 'There is no Entertainment for Women after *Twelve* of the Clock at Night, but all Gentlemen that desire Beds, may have them for *Two Shillings* per Night, for one single Person, but if two lie together *Three Shillings* both ; which Rooms and Beds are fit for the Entertainment of Persons of the highest Quality, and Gentlemen.'

Then there was the Royal Bagnio in Newgate Street, at the Corner of what now is Bath (formerly Bagnio) Street. There was also Pierault's Bagnio, which was in St. James's Street, and was established about 1699. 'The charge of going in is 5*s.*—if lie all Night 10*s.* each. Here also is a *Cold Bath*, for which they take 2*s.* 6*d.* each Person.'

The disciples of cold bathing might be suited at 'A Convenient large Cold Bath, that is Erected upon an Excellent Cold Spring, adjoyning to the Bowling Green in *Queen Street* in the *Park, Southwark* . . . Prices 1*s.* and 6*d.* —The Chair 2*s.*'; and at No. 3 Endell Street was a bath which, tradition says, was used by Queen Anne. It was about twelve or fourteen feet square, and was originally lined with old blue and white Dutch tiles. I can find nothing confirming this tradition, which may or may not have a foundation in fact.

CHAPTER XXXII.

RELIGIONS.

Inactivity of the Church—Dulness of Sunday—Contempt of the clergy—
Low estimation of a chaplain—Dress of the clergy—Church furniture
— Traffic in benefices — Forged orders — Dr. Sacheverell —'The
modern champions'—Queen Anne's Bounty—Its history—Fifty new
churches—Protestant tone of Church feeling—The effigies on Queen
Elizabeth's birthday—Oppression of Roman Catholics—Religious
sects—Eminent Nonconformists—Daniel Burgess—Dislike to Quakers
—Examples—William Penn.

RELIGIOUS life in Anne's time was not active—at least in the
Church of England. Even the dignitaries of the Church,
with very few exceptions, were men of no mark, nor were
there any among the inferior clergy who could be called to
the higher estate, and so help to leaven and wake up the
Episcopate. For the Church was asleep, and with the exception of the Sacheverell episode—when the name of the
Church was dragged in to serve party purposes— nothing was
heard of it. There were priests in the livings then as now,
and they duly baptized, married, preached to, and buried
their flock ; but there was little vitality in their ministrations,
little or no zeal or earnestness as to the spiritual state of
those committed to their charge, and very little of practical
teaching, in the way of setting before them a higher social
standard for them to imitate. The Church services had no
life in them ; with the exception of the cathedrals the services
were *read*, and the soul-depressing parson and clerk duet had
its usual effect of deadening the religious sensibilities of the
so-called worshippers. Why ! Addison seems to think that
dear old Sir Roger was acting in a most praiseworthy manner
in dragooning all his tenants to church, otherwise he confesses
they would not have come ; but what spiritual good this

compulsory attendance did them he does not hint at—probably never thought of: ' My Friend Sir Roger being a good Churchman, has beautified the Inside of his Church with several texts of his own chusing: he has likewise given a handsome Pulpit Cloth, and railed in the Communion Table at his own expence. He has often told me, that at his coming to his Estate he found (his Parishioners) very irregular ; and that in order to make them kneel and join in the Responses, he gave every one of them a Hassock and a Common Prayer Book : and at the same time employed an itinerant Singing Master, who goes about the Country for that Purpose, to instruct them rightly in the Tunes of the Psalms ; upon which they now very much value themselves, and indeed out-do most of the Country Churches that I have ever heard.

' As Sir Roger is Landlord to the whole Congregation, he keeps them in very good Order, and will suffer no Body to sleep in it besides himself ; for if by chance he has been surprized into a short Nap at Sermon, upon recovering out of it he stands up and looks about him, and if he sees any Body else nodding, either wakes them himself, or sends his Servant to them. . . . As soon as the Sermon is finished, no Body presumes to stir till Sir Roger is gone out of the Church. The Knight walks down from his Seat in the Chancel between a Double Row of his Tenants, that stand bowing to him, on each Side ; and every now and then enquires how such an one's Wife, or Mother, or Son, or Father do, whom he does not see at Church ; which is understood as a secret reprimand to the Person that is absent.'[1]

He then contrasts this parish with a neighbouring one where the squire and parson are at variance—where all the tenants are *Atheists* and *Tithe Stealers*. Of course Addison's account is somewhat biassed by his own proclivities ; but we may take the tone of Church feeling throughout the country to have been exemplified by the state of Sir Roger's parish before the rather fussy, and certainly eccentric, knight entered upon his high-handed course of compulsory attendance.

How Sunday was spent in London let Misson say : ' The *English* of all Sects, but particularly the Presbyterians, make

[1] *Spectator*, 112.

profession of being very strict Observers of the Sabbath Day.

'I believe their Doctrine upon this Head does not differ from ours, but most assuredly our Scruples are much less great than theirs. This appears upon a hundred Occasions; but I have observ'd it particularly in the printed Confessions of Persons that are hang'd; Sabbath breaking is the Crime the poor Wretches always begin with. If they kill'd Father and Mother, they would not mention that Article, till after having profess'd how often they had broke the Sabbath. One of the good *English* Customs on the Sabbath Day, is to feast as nobly as possible, and especially not to forget the Pudding. It is a common Practice, even among People of good Substance, to have a huge piece of Roast Beef on *Sundays*, of which they stuff till they can swallow no more, and eat the rest cold, without any other Victuals, the other Six Days of the Week.'

Another quotation from Addison shows at all events his feeling as to the state of the Church at that time: 'After some short Pause, the old Knight turning about his Head twice or thrice, to take a Survey of this great Metropolis, bid me observe how thick the City was set with Churches, and that there was scarce a single Steeple on this side *Temple Bar. A most Heathenish Sight!* says Sir Roger: *There is no Religion at this End of the Town. The Fifty new Churches will very much mend the Prospect; but Church-work is slow—Church-work is slow.'* [1]

There is no doubt but that the Clergy as a body were but little thought of. Of course there were good and pious men then as now, but there is no disguising the fact that the majority showed an indifference to the spiritual well-being of the people, which could not fail to react upon themselves, and foster a feeling bordering upon contempt. Although those were not the days of deep thought, or scientific speculation, there was a great deal of freethought in existence; and although Atheists were professed to be looked upon, as they are now, as moral lepers, yet still there they were.

Perhaps one of the most curious symptoms of the times

[1] *Spectator*, 383.

was the exceeding popularity of Dr. John Eachard's satire, ' The Grounds and Occasions of the Contempt of the Clergy and Religion enquired into,' which, in 1705, had reached its *eleventh* edition. But the butt of all the satirists was the domestic chaplain. He was a member of the household of every person of position, yet he had no social status. Here is a contemporary account,[1] meant as a considerate warning to a friend, putting before him a chaplain's social position :—

> Some think themselves exalted to the Sky,
> If they light in some Noble Family :
> Diet, an Horse, and thirty pounds a year,
> Besides th' advantage of his Lordship's ear,
> The Credit of the business and the State,
> Are things that in a Youngster's Sense sound great.
> Little the unexperienc'd Wretch does know,
> What slavery he oft must undergo :
> Who, though in Silken Scarf and Cassock drest,
> Wears but a gayer Livery at best.
> When Dinner calls, the Implement must wait
> With holy words to consecrate the Meat,
> But hold it for a Favour seldom known,
> If he be deigned the Honour to sit down.
> Soon as the Tarts appear ; Sir *Crape*, withdraw,
> Those Dainties are not for a spiritual Maw.
> Observe your distance ; and be sure to stand
> Hard by the Cistern with your Cap in hand :
> There for diversion you may pick your Teeth,
> Till the kind Voider comes for your Relief.
> For meer Board-wages such their Freedom sell,
> Slaves to an Hour, and Vassals to a Bell :
> And if th' enjoyment of one day be stole,
> They are but Pris'ners out upon Parole :
> Always the marks of Slavery remain,
> And they, tho loose, still drag about the Chain.
>   And where's the mighty Prospect after all,
> A Chaplainship serv'd up, and seven years Thrall ?
> The menial thing perhaps for a Reward,
> Is to some slender Benefice preferr'd,
> With this Pròviso bound, that he must wed
> My Lady's antiquated Waiting Maid,
> In Dressing only skill'd, and Marmalade.
> Let others who such meannesses can brook,
> Strike Countenance to every Great Man's Look :

[1] ' A SATYR Address'd to a *Friend* that is about to leave the University, and come abroad in the World,' by Mr. John Oldham, ed. 1703.

Let those that have a mind, turn slaves to eat,
And live contented by another's Plate :
I rate my Freedom higher, nor will I
For Food, and Raiment truck my Liberty.

And Gay, too, in his *Trivia* (book 2) says :—

Cheese, that the Table's closing Rites denies,
And bids me with th' unwilling Chaplain rise.

Addison, commenting on this custom, and the chaplain's
status generally, remarks,[1] ' In this case I know not which to
censure, the Patron or the Chaplain, the insolence of power
or the abjectness of dependence. For my own part, I have
often blushed to see a gentleman, whom I know to have
much more wit and learning than myself, and who was bred
up with me at the University upon the same foot of a Liberal
Education, treated in such an ignominious manner, and sunk
beneath those of his own rank, by reason of that Character,
which ought to bring him honour.'

Again, in the *Guardian* (No. 163) his position is described :
' I have, with much ado, maintained my post hitherto at the
dessert, and every day eat tart in the face of my patron ; but
how long I shall be invested with this privilege, I do not know.
For the servants, who do not see me supported as I was in
my old lord's time, begin to brush very familiarly by me, and
thrust aside my chair when they set the sweetmeats on the .
table.'

A curious confirmation of one of Oldham's statements is
found in a little brochure of the early part of Anne's reign,[2]
' I turn away my Footman for aspiring to my Woman, her I
marry to my Lord's high Chaplain, and give her six Changes
of my old cast off Cloaths for her Dowry.'

Royalty, even, was not exempt from this failing of snubbing
the chaplains. Swift writes,[3] ' I never dined with the chaplains
till to day ; but my friend Gastrel and the Dean of Rochester
had often invited me, and I happened to be disengaged ; it is
the worst provided table at Court. We ate on pewter.'

---

[1] *Tatler*, 255.   [2] *The English Lady's Catechism.*
[3] *Journal to Stella*, Oct. 6. 1711.

The clergy, when they appeared in public, wore always both cassock and gown ; with the wig, of course, which was sometimes carried to excess, when it brought down the ridicule of the satirist, as in the following [1] 'humble petition of *Elizabeth Slender*, Spinster, Sheweth

'That on the twentieth of this instant December, her friend, *Rebecca Hive*, walking in the Strand, saw a gentleman before us in a gown, whose periwig was so long, and so much powdered, that your petitioner took notice of it, and said "she wondered that lawyer would so spoil a new gown with powder." To which it was answered, "that he was no lawyer,

but a clergyman." Upon a wager of a pot of Coffee we over took him, and your petitioner was soon convinced she had lost.

'Your petitioner, therefore, desires your worship to cite the clergyman before you, and to settle and adjust the length of *canonical Periwigs*, and the quantity of powder to be made use of in them,' etc.

The vestments, when officiating, were simple, consisting of a cassock and full surplice—the black gown being used for preaching.

A CLERGYMAN'S WALKING COSTUME.

The accompanying illustrations of a bishop and a prebendary are taken from the prints of Queen Anne's coronation—the bishop wears chimere and rochet, whilst the prebendary has his hood, and, as it was a festival, he wears what seems to be meant for a cope.

The church furniture was not very extravagant, as is exemplified by the following advertisement : 'Lost the 20th of August at Night, out of St. Bennets, Grace Church viz, a purple Velvet Cushion, with purple and gold Tassels ; The Covering of 2 Cushions very old of the same. The Vallins for the Pulpit of purple Velvet with purple and gold Fringe ; A Cover for the Communion Table of purple Velvet very old. S.B.G. 1641 Embroider'd on it ; A large Damask Table

[1] *Tatler*, 37c.

Cloath, and 2 Damask Napkins mark'd S.B.G.L.E. 2 large pewter Plates, mark'd S.B.G. 2 Surplices. 1 old, the other New, mark'd S.B.G.L.E. A Clark's Gown of black Callimanca with Loops, and faced with black Velvet.' The reward offered for this lot was three guineas.

Benefices were then trafficked in. 'The next Advowson or Presentation to a Church of about 200*l. per annum*, four score and ten Miles from *London*, is to be dispos'd of, on very reasonable Terms, to any Clergy man of a good Character for Learning and Morals. The present Incumbent upwards of 60 Years of Age.' Simony was, however, punishable, for

A BISHOP.   A PREBEND.

we read in Luttrell, July 4, 1702, 'The late bishop of St. Davids, who some time since was deprived of that bishoprick on account of Simony, being arrested for £1,000 costs of suit, is removed from the bailiff's house to Newgate.'

There were a few black sheep among the clergy. The *London Gazette* for Nov. 3/6, 1707, has an advertisement commencing, 'Where as one William Sale was some Years since Convicted in the Ecclesiastical Court at Canterbury, of having forged Holy Orders for himself, and for his own Father,' etc., and it goes on to cite him to appear before the Archbishop of Canterbury, or the Bishop of Rochester, and produce his true orders, if he had any—or, if not, he would be prosecuted.

And in the *London Gazette* for March 18/22, 1703, the
clergy are warned against one ' Abraham Gill (aged upwards
of 30 years, middle statur'd, some gray Hairs, wearing sometimes a light Wig, sometimes a darker, sanguine Complexion,
bold and Confident in Conversation, strong Voice, a North
Country Pronunciation, writing a Clerk like Hand, as having
been some time employ'd under an Attorney.   Travelling
the Country with a Woman and 3 or 4 Children, sometime
since forged Letters of Orders, under the Hand and Episcopal
Seal of the Lord Bishop of Chester,' etc.

Swift, too, writes,[1] ' I walked here after nine, two miles,
and I found a parson drunk, fighting with a seaman, and
Patrick and I were so wise as to part them, but the seaman
followed him to Chelsea, cursing at him, and the parson
slipped into a house, and I know no more.   It mortified me
to see a man in my coat so overtaken.'

It would be impossible to write of the Church of England
in Anne's reign without mentioning Dr. Sacheverell, whose two
famous sermons brought about his impeachment and sentence
to three years' suspension.   In them he condemned Dissenters
and those Churchmen who sympathised with them, lashing,
with his oratory, the high ones of the land—and Godolphin
especially, as was believed, under the name of 'Volpone.'
Then rose the war-cry of ' High Church and Sacheverell !'
which even the Queen could not avoid : ' God bless the Queen.
We hope your Majesty is for High Church and Sacheverell ; '
and presumably she was, for the very month his suspension
expired she presented him with the valuable living of St.
Andrew's, Holborn.   High Churchism then meant intolerance,
and Sacheverell was the puppet pulled by wires held by
others.

There is a curious contemporary skit which is worth
reproducing, for two reasons—first, as showing the style of
literature then used in party warfare ; and second, because it
gives an approximate illustration of the Hockley in the Hole
combatants mounted on the stage.   In fact, the whole thing
is a travesty on the bombastic challenges of those doughty
heroes.

[1] *Journal to Stella*, May 5, 1711.

'THE MODERN CHAMPIONS [1]

or

A Tryal of Skill to be Fought at her Majesty's Bear Garden, on Monday next, between a Jeroboam Tory and a Jerusalem Whig, with their two Seconds.

> When Gospel Trumpeter surrounded
> By long Ear'd Rout, to Battle Sounded
> And Pulpit, Drum Ecclesiastick
> Was beat with Fist instead of a Stick
> Then did Sir Knight ——

Prophetically sung by the learned Hudibras.

' THE MODERN CHAMPIONS.'

'I, JEHU HOTSPUR, known by the name of the High Church Champion, Defender of the Cause, against all Schismatical and Rebellious Saints whatever; Do Invite you Balthaser Turncoat, (of the Race of the Seditious ; Betrayers of their Country, and Rebels to their Lawful Sovereign ; Prolocutor and Contester for the Shameful and detested Cause of Moderation ; a Lukewarm Christian, and a False Brother of the Ch——h ; Dissenting from, and Prevaricating with,

---

[1] *Banks' Coll.*, Brit. Mus., 1890 *e.* 'The Combatants are Bishop (then Dr.) Hoadly and Dr. Sacheverell—the Seconds, Drs. Burgess and Harris.'

the Original Ordinances thereof) to meet and Fight me at the seven several sorts of weapons following, viz. :

Sword & Cloak	
Schism & Hypocrisy	
Tolleration	
Rebellion	JEHU HOTSPUR
Moderation	
Regicide and	
Anarchy	

So putting Trust in the Justice of my Quarrel, expect to find you at the Time and Place appointed, as you will answer the Contrary at your Peril.

'I BALTHASAR TURNCOAT, Chief Orator and Champion for the upright and blessed Principles of Moderation ; a True Blue Church Man, and Jerusalem Whig ; Receiving open Defiance from the said Jehu Hotspur avow'd Champion and Maintainer of the High Church Jacobite Cause (Sprung from the Loins of Jeroboam the Son of Nebat, who caused Israel to Sin ; a Race so wickedly malicious that they would have us all cut off, Root and Branch ; unless we fall down and worship the Calves of Dan and Bethel, whereby the Seed of Amalek may come to be restor'd) Will not fail, God Willing, to meet the Bold and Daring Inviter at the Time and Place appointed, and Oppose him at the several Weapons following, viz. :

Sword & Warming pan	
Non Resistance	
Passive Obedience	
Superstition	BALTHASAR
Jacobitism	TURNCOAT
Tyranny and	
Persecution	

Desiring a Clear Stage, and from him no Favour.

'N.B. Whoever brings this Ticket, will be admitted on the Day of Tryal.

'London.   Printed in the Year 1710—price 1*d.*'

Should anyone care to see to what depth the Church of England had sunk, as far as care of the fabric of the churches went, let him read 'Miscellany Accounts of the Diocese of Carlisle, &c., 1703-4,' by Wm. Nicholson, late Bishop of Carlisle : London, Geo. Bell & Sons, 1877.

The two most notable events in the reign, in connection with the Church, were the foundation of Queen Anne's Bounty, and the building of fifty new churches. In the times of the Crusades, a tax of first-fruits and tenths had been imposed for the purposes of prosecuting the Holy Wars, and it had never been taken off. Henry VIII., of course, seized upon it as his own royal perquisite, and so it continued. Charles II. found it handy to provide for his seraglio ; and probably, had it not been for the very strenuous exertions of Bishop Burnet with both William and Mary, and afterwards with Anne, it might never have reverted to the Church.

As it was, Queen Anne surrendered it in a most graceful manner, making it her birthday present to the nation in 1704. Her birthday (Feb. 6) fell that year on a Sunday, but she kept it on the Monday, and on that day sent a message to her faithful Commons that it was her desire to make a grant of her whole revenue derived from the first-fruits, and tenths, for the benefit of the poorer clergy. The Commons lost no time in passing a Bill in acquiescence with the royal wish, even broadening its basis—enabling other persons to make grants for the same purpose. This latter addition encountered some opposition in the Lords, but eventually became law.

The clergy were naturally grateful, and on Feb. 15 the clergy of both Provinces waited on her Majesty, with addresses of thanks for her kindness ; and the lower house of Convocation for the Province of Canterbury returned their thanks to the Commons for their readiness in complying with the Queen's desire. On April 3 of the same year the Queen gave her royal assent to the Act. That it was needed is evidenced by the fact that the Commissioners found there were 5,597 livings under 50*l.* per annum, which were capable of augmentation. The increase of the income of the poorer clergy was its first intention : now the scheme has widened, and grants towards building parsonage-houses, etc., are made. Still, Queen Anne's name remains attached to it in grateful remembrance.

It was estimated that it would bring in an income of 6,000*l.* per annum. How the fund is now administered may be learned from the following extract from the *Globe* of Feb. 15, 1882. 'In Convocation of York yesterday a Committee was appointed to report upon the constitution and management of Queen Anne's Bounty. It was stated that the income of the Bounty is 15,000*l.*, and that the cost of management is between 7,000*l.* and 8,000*l.*'[1] Comment on this is superfluous.

London was growing bigger, but with the extension of house-building there was no commensurate increase of church accommodation ; so the Upper House of Convocation presented an address to the Queen upon the subject, and the Lower House petitioned the House of Commons. The outcome of this was, that the Queen sent a message to the latter, calling their attention to the state of spiritual destitution, and recommending them to further 'so good and pious a work.' The Commons dutifully replied that, although they had an expensive war on hand, and heavy burdens to bear besides, yet they would be happy to do their part, and consequently the session of 1711 saw the royal assent given to an Act for building fifty new churches within the Bills of Mortality, to meet the expense of which was assigned the duty on coals, which had defrayed the expenses of building St. Paul's. Convocation returned thanks, and the fifty churches were eventually built.

The tone of the Church at that time was essentially Protestant. And no wonder. William the Deliverer was warm in men's memory ; and men, fearing a repetition of Roman supremacy, as in the times of the second James, unreasonably went in the opposite direction, probably without

---

[1] This statement was afterwards modified in the *Globe* of June 21, 1882. 'The Report of the auditor, Mr. Charles Garlant, states that the cost of administration of the 1ounty fund is approximately 17*s.* 6*d.* per cent. on the receipts and payments generally, and £2. 10*s.* per cent. if items on capital account are altogether excluded.'

much absolutely religious feeling prompting them.   More possibly it was

> ' The Church God Bless,
> The Queen no less,
> And all that do Profess
> The same Religion with Queen Bess.

But I'll warrant now, if we had a Bonfire in the Street, and such a Whig as Tom Double shou'd pass by, he wou'd refuse this Health, and then I shou'd break his Head.' [1]

Queen Bess was the Madonna of the Protestants, and ' her glorious Memory' was a watchword of the party.   Nov. 17, the anniversary of her accession to the throne, was celebrated in the same manner as Nov. 5 used to be, until police control interfered with it.   One Nov. 17 in Queen Anne's reign, that of 1711, was rendered historically famous by the steps the Government took in the suppression of this carnival.   A contemporary account [2] is as follows : ' Nov. 20. Upon information, That the Effigies of the *Devil*, the *Pope* and his *Attendants* were to be carry'd in Procession, and, according to Custom, burnt on *Saturday* last, the 17th Inst. being the Anniversary of Queen ELIZABETH'S Accession to the Crown, of ever Pious and most Glorious Memory, the Government apprehending that the same might occasion Tumults in this Populous City, thought fit to prevent it.   Accordingly, on *Friday* last, about Twelve a Clock at Night, some of Her Majesty's Messengers, sustain'd by a Detachment of Grenadiers of the Foot Guards, with their Officer, were order'd to go to an Empty House in *Angel Court, Drury Lane,* which being broke Open, they found in it the Effigies of the *Devil,* that of the POPE on his Right hand, and that of a Young *Gentleman* in a Blue Cloth Coat, with Tinsel Lace, and a Hat with a White Feather, made of Cut Paper, seated under a large Canopy ; as also the Figures of Four Cardinals, Four Jesuits, and Four *Franciscan Fryars*, and a large Cross about Eighteen Foot High ; all which, being put on several Carts were, about Two a Clock in the Morning, carry'd to the *Cock Pit*, and there lodg'd in a Room between the

---

[1] *The Weekly Comedy*, Jan. 2, 1708.
[2] *The Protestant Post Boy*, Nov. 17, 20, 1711.

Council Chamber, and the Right Honourable the Earl of *Dartmouth's* Secretary's Office.   Moreover, on *Saturday*, *Sunday*, and *Monday* the Trained Bands of *London* and *Westminster* were under Arms; so that there was no Pope *Burnt*, tho' we hear of one that was *Drown'd*.   It may, perhaps, appear strange that a Popular Rejoycing so grateful to this PROTESTANT City, which was never attempted to be quash'd but in *K. James* the Second's Reign, should, at this Juncture, be interrupted : But, to be sure, those who did it had very good Reasons for their Management.'

Swift, of course, gives Stella all the gossip about it, and says the Whigs laid out about a thousand pounds upon the proposed show.   'They did it by Contribution.   Garth gave five guineas ; Dr. Garth I mean, if ever you heard of him.' Swift afterwards went to see the effigies, and his report very much modifies his previous account: 'The fifteen images that I saw were not worth forty pounds, so I stretched a little when I said a thousand.   The Devil is not like lord treasurer ; they were all your odd antick masks, bought in Common Shops.'

The last of them is told in a paragraph of the *Post Boy*, July 1/3, 1712 : 'Yesterday, were disrobed at the Cockpit the Effigies of the Devil, the Person who has pretended to disturb the Settlement of the Protestant Succession of the House of Hanover, the Pope, Cardinals &c.   Our Enemies being now disarm'd, we will venture to say, that there will soon be a General Cessation of Arms.'

Protestant throats yelled out—

O ! Queen Bess, Queen Bess, Queen Bess,
Who sav'd us all from Popish Thrall?
O ! Queen Bess, Queen Bess, Queen Bess —

and bigoted, and intolerant Protestant legislators did their little utmost to oppress their Roman Catholic fellow-subjects, even in Ireland : 'Her Majestie, in council, has approved of several Irish acts sent over hither, which are to be return'd, to passe into laws ; among them is that for preventing the further growth of popery in that Kingdom, by which all the estates of Roman catholicks there after their death, shall be equally divided among all their children, unless the eldest turns protestant within a year after the father's decease, and if so, to enjoy the whole ; likewise by this bill all the Romish clergy, who are now tolerated there, are to be registered, and when they die, to be succeeded by protestants.'[1]

'Edinburgh, 14 Mar. 1704. Sir *James Stuart*, Her Majesty's Advocate, having represented to the Council, that there were several Popish Vestments, Trinkets, and others seized ; And that they were given to his Lordship, and in his Custody. The Lords of her Majesty's Privy-Council do hereby appoint and ordain the Vestments, Crucifixes and Trinkets, to be burnt at the Cross of *Edinburgh* to-morrow, being the 15th Instant, betwixt the hours of ten and twelve in the Fore noon. And appoints and ordains the Magistrates of *Edinburgh* to see the same effectually done : And appoints and ordains the Chalice, Patine, and such other of the said Trinkets, as are in Silver or Gold, to be melted down and delivered to the present Kirk Treasurer of *Edinburgh*, for the use of the poor thereof.'[2]

This order was duly carried out ; 'An Inventor whereof follows, *Imprimis* An Chalice and Patine for the Ilastic (?). *Item* Four Crucifixes. *Item* Two Surplices. *Item* Three Colliers. *Item* Four pair of Beeds, or Chapelets, with some Relicks of Saints. *Item,* Several Pictures, with Indulgencies and Pardons ; and particularly one with this Indulgence following : *viz.* the Archbishop of Mechline has granted Indulgence of forty days to those who shall bow their Knee before this Image once a day, considering devoutly the infinite Charity of Jesus Christ, who has suffered for us the Bitter Death of the Cross : And if any will perform this Devotion oftner, he shall so oft have new Indulgence for five days more extracted.'

'Information being given of several priests lurking about this Citty, the messengers the close of last week seized near Red Lyon Square 3 of them, viz, Gifford, Martin, and Matthews ; the last is committed to Newgate, but the others were admitted to bail, each in £1000, and 2 sureties in £500 apiece.'[3]

[1] *Luttrell*, Jan. 25, 1705.   [2] *Flying Post*, Feb. 17/20, 1705.
[3] *Luttrell*, Sept. 26, 1704.

On April 4, 1706, the Privy Council sent a circular to the Archbishop of Canterbury, which he in his turn sent round to the bishops, and they to their clergy, stating that her Majesty being acquainted 'with several Instances of the very great Boldness and Presumption of the Romish Priests and Papists in this Kingdom,' directed them 'to Require the Clergy in their several Dioceses to take an Exact and Particular Account of the Number of the Papists and Reputed Papists in every Parish with their Qualities, Estates and Places of Abode, and to return the same to their respective Diocesans, who are to return the same to your Grace, in Order to be laid before Her Majesty.'

This inquisitorial circular was followed on April 11, 1706, by 'A PROCLAMATION For the Putting in Execution the Laws in Force against such Persons as have or shall Endeavour to Pervert her Majesties Subjects to the Popish Religion,' and it recites that the Acts to be put in force were one of the 23 Eliz., 'An Act to Retain the Queen's Majesties Subjects in their due Obedience,' and one of the 3 Jas. I. 'An Act for the Discovering and Repressing of Popish Recusants.'

This seems to have been ineffectual, or the nation must have had another attack of Protestant fever, for on March 2, 1710, in a proclamation offering 100*l*. for the apprehension of some Sacheverell rioters, there are clauses, 'And we do strictly charge and command all Papists, who shall be above the Age of Sixteen Years, that they do, according to the Statutes in that behalf made, repair to their respective Places of Abode, and do not thence remove or pass above the Distance of five Miles— And that all such Papists and Persons reputed so to be (except Merchants, Traders, settled House holders, and other Persons excepted in the Statutes made in this behalf) do, on or before the eighth day of this Instant *March*, depart out of our said Cities and Suburbs of London and Westminster, and from all Places distant ten Miles from the Same.'

On March 15, 1711, another proclamation was issued for all Papists to remove from the cities of London and West-

minster, and, even at the very close of Anne's reign, we read[1] :
'At the Assizes held at Chelmsford in the County of Essex,
a Bill of Indictment was found against Hanmer, former'y
mention'd in this Paper, for that he, being a Popish Priest,
did say Mass according to the Custom of the Romish Church
in that Country ; to which Indictment he pleaded not Guilty,
and gave Suretys to try the same at the next Assizes.'

Misson gives a formidable list of religious sects then n
existence, to which, of course, owing to the vastly superior

wisdom and knowledge of this nine-
teenth century, we have enormously
added and improved upon. He says
that there were, in his time, in England, 'Antinomians, Hederingtonians,
Theaurian Joanites, Seekers, Waiters,
Brownists, Reevists, Baronists, Wilkin-
sonians, Familists, Ranters, Muggle-
tonians, &c., &c. All these, and nothing
at all, are just one and the same thing:
Christianity is overwhelm'd with Sects
enough already, without our studying to
multiply them chimerically. . . . Besides
the Religion which serves God in the
Church of *England*, and which is the
reigning Religion in *England*, there
are several Sorts of Sectaries ; the
Presbyterians are the Chief and most
numerous. . . . The Independents

A NONCONFORMIST
MINISTER.

were a Branch of Presbytery, but they are now united again.
Arminianism (if the Propositions of *Arminius* ought to give
the odious name of a Sect) is spread every where. Here and
there also you meet with a Millennarian ; but I know there is
a particular Society, tho' it makes but little Noise, of People,
who tho' they go by the Name of Sabbatharians,[2] make
Profession of expecting the Reign of a Thousand Years without participating in the other Opinions, which are ascrib'd to
the ancient Millenarians. These Sabbatharians are so call'd,

---

[1] *The Flying Post*, July 17/20, 1714.
[2] 'The Common people call them Seventh Day Men.'

because they will not remove the Day of Rest from *Saturday* to *Sunday*. They leave off Work betimes on *Friday* Evening, and are very rigid Observers of their Sabbath. . . . England hath also Anabaptists of Several sorts. . . . Within these few Weeks there is sprung up a new Sect of People, that say they are Mystical Theologists, and that take the name of *Philadelphians,'* etc.

This is very far from being an exhaustive list of the sects then in existence, and it is not worth while wasting time in hunting up the names and history of any more.

John Wesley was born in Anne's reign, and Matthew Henry died in it, whilst Calamy lived during the whole of it ;

A QUAKERS' MEETING.

but the most prominent nonconformist in London was Daniel Burgess, whose Theatre, or meeting-house, in Carey Street was gutted by the Sacheverell mob, and had to be repaired at the expense of Government. Of this meeting-house Brown says : ' For as it is not properly call'd the House of God, but Mr. *Burgess's,* so Mr. *Burgess,* not God, is there worshipped. Prayer and Praise is the proper Worship of God, but here they meet to hear *Daniel* lay about him, with his merry Stories and Theatrical Actions, which is at least an *Amusement* they think worth their while.'

And this is one of Daniel's ' merry Stories.' Preaching one day on ' the Robe of Righteousness,' he said : ' If any of

you would have a good and cheap suit, you will go to Monmouth Street ; if you want a *suit* for life, you will go to the
Court of Chancery ; but, if you wish for a suit that will last to
eternity, you must go to the Lord Jesus Christ, and put on
his Robe of Righteousness.'

Swift speaks of him in *Tatler* 66. ' There is my friend
and merry Companion *Daniel*. He knows a great deal better
than he speaks, and can form a proper discourse as well as
any orthodox neighbour.' And this, probably, is a true esti-
mate of his character. Anyhow, he *drew*, and his meeting-
house was the most popular in London.

A QUAKERS' MEETING.

There was an insane dislike to Quakers in Queen Anne's
reign, and I have not met with one kindly or sympathetic
remark about them in all my varied reading of these times.
On the contrary, they were represented as thoroughpaced
hypocrites, cheats, liars, immoral livers. The generic term
applied to a Quaker was Aminadab (why ?), and Aminadab
was everything that was sly and repulsive. We, who know
the quiet, simple folk, whose sect is fast dying out, because
they have obtained all the points they strove for, can never
for an instant imagine that their forefathers were the sly
hypocrites they were painted. Nor were they only lampooned

verbally—a Quaker could not be drawn without being cari-
catured into an unctuous rogue; their very plainness of
apparel, the men's plain hats and absence of wigs, and the
women wearing the old country steeple-crowned hat and
simply made gowns, were made the vehicles of sarcasm; the
poverty of their meeting-houses was typified by their preaching and sitting on tubs.

Still, all writers have their dab of dirt to throw at them,
and to show how universal it was, a few examples may be
given. *Swift*:[1] 'My friend Penn came there, Will Penn the
Quaker, at the head of his brethren, to thank the Duke for
his kindness to their people in Ireland. To see a dozen
scoundrels with their hats on, and the Duke complimenting
with his off, was a good sight enough.' *Misson*: 'The Quakers
are great Fanaticks; there seems to be something laudable
in them; to outward Appearance they are mild, simple in all
respects, sober, modest, peaceable, nay, and they have the
Reputation of being honest; and they often are so. But you
must have a Care of being Bit by this Appearance, which
very often is only outward;' and afterwards, talking of
females preaching, 'the Moment Mrs. Doctor spies a Ribbon,
the Spirit moves her, and she falls into one of her Fits; up
she gets on the Bottom of some Tub, with her pinch'd up
Cap, and her screw'd up Countenance; she Sighs, she Groans,
she Snorts through the Nose, and then out she bursts into
such a Jargon as no mortal Man can make Head or Tale of.'
Mrs. *Centlivre*, in the 'Beau's Duel': 'I carried her to wait on
a Relation of ours that has a Parrot, and whilst I was dis-
coursing about some private Business, she converted the Bird,
and now it talks of nothing but the Light of the Spirit, and
the Inward Man.' *Brown*: 'They would be thought the
only People of God; tho' their Chief Motive to that impudent
Ambition, is, that they may claim the Right of *Pillaging* and
Cheating all the World besides, as *Ægyptians*. They won't
swear, because they may chance to pay for that; but they
will lie Confoundedly, because they may chance to get by
that.' *Ward* gives an account of a visit to a Quakers' tavern,
which was 'intended chiefly for Watering the Lambs of Grace,

[1] *Journal to Stella*, Jan. 15, 1712.

and not to succour the Evil off-spring of a Reprobate Generation ;' and he says that 'when they were desirous to Elevate
their Lethargick Spirits with the circulation of a Bumper, one
fills it, and offers the prevailing Temptation to his left Hand
Companion, in these Words, saying, Friend, does the Spirit
move thee to receive the good Creature thus plentifully ? The
other replies, Yea, Do thou take and enjoy the Fruits of thy
own Labour, and by the help of Grace I will drink another as
full. Thus did the liquorish Saints quaff it about merrily,
after their precise Canting manner.' Even the *Tatler* (262)
has an advertisement, 'Drop'd on Sunday last, a small Roll
of Paper, in which was inclos'd the Draught of a *Quaker* hold-
ing forth in a Tub, &c.' These examples are quite sufficient
to show the universal dislike of this harmless sect, which could
only have been induced by the thorough contrast of their
homely attire, and plain speech, with the ornate dress and
exaggerated verbiage then in vogue.

Penn, indeed, was welcome at Court, and lived at Kensington, and afterwards at Knightsbridge, till 1706. He lived
all through Anne's reign, not dying till 1716.

CHAPTER XXXIII.

LEGAL.

The different branches of the law—Briefless Barristers—Green bags—
Forensic wigs—Attorneys—Knights of the Post—Lord Somers—Lord
Cowper: his abolition of New Year's gifts.

SPEAKING of lawyers, Addison says:[1] 'The Body of the Law
is no less encumbered with superfluous Members, that are like
Virgil's Army which he tells us was so crouded, many of
them had not Room to use their Weapons. This prodigious
Society of Men may be divided into the Litigious and Peaceable. Under the first are comprehended all those who are
carried down in Coach fulls to *Westminster Hall* every morning in Term time. *Martial's* description of this Species of
Lawyers is full of Humour:

> *Iras et verba locant.*

Men that hire out their Words and Anger; that are more
or less passionate according as they are paid for it, and allow
their Client a quantity of wrath proportionable to the Fee
which they receive from him. I must, however, observe to
the Reader, that above three Parts of those whom I reckon
among the Litigious, are such as are only quarrelsome in
their Hearts, and have no Opportunity of showing their
Passion at the Bar. Nevertheless, as they do not know what
Strifes may arise, they appear at the Hall every Day, that
they may show themselves in a Readiness to enter the Lists,
whenever there shall be Occasion for them.

'The Peaceable Lawyers are, in the first place, many of
the Benchers of the several Inns of Court, who seem to be
the Dignitaries of the Law, and are endowed with those
Qualifications of Mind, that accomplish a Man rather for a

---

[1] *Spectator*, 21.

Ruler, than a Pleader; These Men live peaceably in their Habitations, Eating once a Day, and Dancing once a Year, for the Honour of their Respective Societies.

'Another numberless Branch of Peaceable Lawyers, are those young Men, who being placed at the Inns of Court in order to study the Laws of their Country, frequent the Play House more than *Westminster Hall*, and are seen in all publick Assemblies, except in a Court of Justice. I shall say nothing of those Silent and Busie Multitudes that are employed within Doors in the Drawing up of Writings and Conveyances ; nor of those greater Numbers that palliate their want of Business with a Pretence to such Chamber Practice.'

Thus we see that the legal world then very much resembled the same now. Briefless barristers were as numerous then, and this seems to have been their life : 'Young Barristers troop down to *Westminster* at Nine ; Cheapen Cravats, and Handkerchiefs, Ogle the Semstresses, take a Whet at the *Dog*, or a Slice of Roast beef at *Heaven*, fetch half a dozen turns in the Hall, peep in at the Common Pleas, talk over the News, and so with their Green Bags, that have as little in them as their Noddles, go home again. Summon'd by pensive Sound of Horn to rotten roasted Mutton at Twelve ; Leave a Paper in their Doors to study Presidents and Cases for them all the Afternoon ; may be heard of at the Devil, or some neighbouring Tavern till One in the Morning.' [1]

We not only note, in this quotation, that the lawyers carried *green* bags, but we find, in contemporary literature frequent allusion to these bags, which certainly had been of the same colour ever since Charles the Second's time, and so continued until the reign of George III. Bands were worn, but they were not the little things they are now, and there was no distinctive wig—nay, some men were bold enough to wear their own hair. Lady Sarah Cowper has left a memorandum [2] respecting her father, Lord Cowper, which throws light on this subject : 'The Queen after this was persuaded to trust a Whigg ministry ; and in the year 1705 Ocb[r]. she made my father L[d] Keeper of the Great Seal in

[1] *A Comical View of London and Westminster.*
[2] *Lives of the Lord Chancellors,* etc., Lord Campbell.

the 41ˢᵗ year of his age—'tis said the youngest Lord Keeper
that had ever been.   He looked very young, and wearing his
own hair made him appear yet more so ; which the Queen
observing, obliged him to cut it off, telling him the world
would say she had given the Seals to a Boy.'   But it is said
that when he appeared at court in his wig, the Queen had to
look at him more than once before she recognised him.

So much for the barrister. Of the other branch, the attorney,
we hear very little.   Ward certainly portrays him in no very
bright colours.   ' He's an Amphibious Monster, that partakes
of two Natures, and those contrary ; He's a great Lover both
of Peace and Enmity ; and has no sooner set People together
by the Ears, but is Soliciting the Law to make an end of the
Difference.   His Learning is commonly as little as his
Honesty ; and his Conscience much larger than his Green
Bag.   Catch him in what Company soever, you will always
hear him stating of Cases, or telling what notice my Lord
Chancellor took of him, when he beg'd Leave·to supply the
deficiency of his Councel.   He always talks with as great
assurance as if he understood what he only pretends to know:
And always wears a Band, and in that lies his Gravity and
Wisdom.   He concerns himself with no Justice but the Justice
of a Cause: and for making an unconscionable Bill, he out
does a Taylor.'

The courts of law were conducted with as much decorum
and dignity as now ; but there is no doubt that false witnesses
could be hired—nay, they had a regular name—' Knights of
the Post' ; a name which certainly dates back as early as the
time of Charles I., when ' a roaring gul and Knight o' th' post '
were coupled together.   In Anne's time ' Knights of the Post
are to be had in the *Temple Walks* from Morning till Night, for
two Pots of Belch, and a Sixpenny slice of Boil'd beef' ; and
Ward's friend, the attorney, ' is so well read in Physiognomy,
that he knows a Knight of the Post by his Countenance ; and
if your Business requires such an Agent, he can pick you up
one at a small Warning.   He is very understanding in the
Business of the *Old Bailey* and knows as well how to Fee a
Jury Man as he does a Barrister.   He has a rare knack at
putting in Broomstick Bail ; and knows a great many more

ways to keep a Man out of his Money, than he does to get :t
him. Tricks and Quirks he calls the cunning part of the
Law ; and that Attorney that practises the most knavery, is
the Man for his Money.'

Queen Anne's reign was not prolific of great lawyers,
although Lords Somers, Cowper, and Harcourt were alive.
The two former had the felicity of being scarified by Mrs.
Manley in the ' New Atlantis.' The former, under the name
of Cicero, is accused of seducing a friend's wife, and then
imprisoning, and finally making away with, her husband ; and
the latter was charged with committing bigamy. His brother
Spencer Cowper, too, was unhappy in his connection with
the fair sex, he having been, with three others, arraigned for
being concerned in the murder of one Sarah Stout. He was
acquitted, and probably remembered the fact when afterwards
he was a judge, in which capacity he was very merciful. Lord
Cowper put an end to an old custom, by refusing to receive
New Year's gifts from the officers of his court and the
counsel of his Bar ; by which his wife says he lost 3,000*l.*
per annum ; but even then, although his salary was nominally
4,000*l.*, he managed, by fees to which he was entitled, to
make it up to 8,000*l.* If Evelyn is to be believed, he knew
how to take care of himself. ' Oct. 1705. Mr. Cowper made
Lord Keeper. Observing how uncertain greate officers are of
continuing long in their places, he would not accept it unless
£2000 a yeare were given him in reversion when he was put
out, in consideration of his loss of practice. His predecessors,
how little time soever they had the seal, usually got £100,000,
and made themselves barons.'

CHAPTER XXXIV.

THE RIVER.

Use as a highway—River slang—Rates of watermen—Description of wherries—Pleasure parties and barges—The Folly—Its frequenters—Gravesend tilt boat—Fares at the Horse Ferry—The Fleet Ditch.

THE River Thames was then a veritable 'silent highway,' in the sense of affording transport for passengers for short distances.   In fact, the wherries then took the places in a great measure of our present cabs ; and a cry of 'Next Oars' or 'Sculls,' when anyone made his appearance at the top of 'the Stairs,' was synonymous with 'Hansom' or 'Four Wheeler.'

Poor Taylor, the Water Poet, had, more than half a century before, sung the decadence of this highway, but it still fairly held its own, and was in great request.   When Sir Roger went with the Spectator to Spring Gardens, Foxhall (that naughty place where the 'wanton baggage' of a mask tapped the old knight on the shoulder, and asked him if he would drink a bottle of mead with her, and where Sir Roger told the mistress of the house 'He should be a better Customer to her Garden, if there were more Nightingales, and fewer Strumpets '), he never dreamed of going any other way than by boat.   He chose out the boatman with the wooden leg, and afterwards regaled him with the remains of their luncheon, to the waiter's astonishment.

Addison was writing a *superfine* paper 'for gentlemen, by gentlemen,' so he softens down the language for which the river was noted, and ignores the torrent of licentious ribaldry with which every boat greeted each other, and which was known as 'River Wit.'   He certainly hints at it, but simply touches it, and then changes the subject.   When Sir Roger,

in the kindliness of his heart and the forgetfulness of custom,
bids the passing boats Good Night, he merely says, 'But to
the Knight's great Surprize, as he gave the Good Night to
two or three young Fellows a little before our Landing, one
of them, instead of returning the Civility asked us what quee=
old Put we had in the Boat, and whether he was not ashamec
to go a Wenching at his Years? with a great deal of the like
Thames Ribaldry. Sir Roger seem'd a little shocked at first,
but at length assuming a Face of Magistracy, told us, *That if
he were a* Middlesex *Justice, he would make such Vagrants
know that Her Majesty's Subjects were no more to be abused by
Water than by Land.'*

But Brown gives us the unadulterated slang, which cannot
possibly be reprinted for general perusal—indeed, his whole
account of the river, although it is far too graphic to be
omitted, and it gives us certainly the best contemporaneous
description we have, must be somewhat expurgated to fit it for
modern tastes. 'Finding my Companion thus agreeable to
my Humour, I steer'd him down *Blackfryars* towards the
Thames side, till coming near the Stairs, where from their
Dirty Benches up started such a noisy multitude of old grizly
Tritons, in sweaty Shirts, and short-skirted Doublets, hollowing and hooting out *Next Oars* and *Skullers*, shaking their
Caps over their bald Noddles, seeming as overjoy'd to see us,
as if we had been Foreign Princes come out of stark Love
and Kindness to redeem them and their Families from Cruel
Popery and Slavery. I bawl'd out as loud as a Speaking
Trumpet, *Next Oars*, and away run Captain *Charon* from the
Front of his wrangling Fraternity, with a Badge upon his
Arm, that the World might behold whose Slave he was, and
hollow'd to his Man *Ben* to bring the Boat near, whilst the
rest withdrew to their Seats, calling one another *Louzy Rogue*
and *Sorry Rascal*, giving us a clear passage without further
Molestation.

'Upon my Word, says my friend, I am glad we are past
them, for this is one of the most ill looking Rabble, and from
whom I had more apprehensions of Danger, than from any I
have yet met with. 'Tis all, said I, but an *Amusement*, step
into the Boat, sit down Watermen, row us up to *Chelsea* : No

sooner had we put off into the middle of the Stream, but our *Charon* and his Assistant (being jolly Fellows) began to scatter their verbal Wildfire on every side of them, their first Attack being on a Couple of fine Ladies with a Footman in the Stern, as follows. . . . One of the Ladies taking Courage, pluck'd up a Female Spirit of Revenge, and facing us with the Gallantry of an *Amazon* made the following return ' . . Well ! that awful piece of river chaff, which is still popularly supposed to arouse the ire of ' bargees.' 'Who eat puppy pie under Marlow Bridge ?' was milk and water compared to the fearfully strong language this lady made use of, the mildest part of her speech being, ' talk not to a Woman, you surly Whelp, for you are fit for nothing, but like the Breed you come on, to crawl upon all four, and cry Bow wow at a Bear Garden.' And so on with every boat they met.

' After rowing for some time, we had arriv'd at that Port to which we had consign'd our selves, where we quitted our Boat, and offering old *Charon* Three Shillings, he swore he would have a Crown ; but having the printed Rates in my Pocket, I was forc'd to lug out my Oracle before the Freshwater Looby would be convinc'd of his Error ; and withal told him, Had it been in *London*, I would have carry'd him before my Lord Mayor, and have had him punish'd, for making, contrary to Law, so unreasonable a Demand. With that he takes the Money, and putting off his Boat, gave us a notable Farewel after the following manner—*viz.* You're a Couple of Niggardly Sons of —— ; I care not a —— for my Lord Mayor ; —— the Rogue that printed that Book ; —— take you for a Book-learn'd Blockhead ; and confound him that taught you to read ; and so we parted.'

Misson says, 'The little Boats upon the *Thames*, which are only for carrying of Persons, are light and pretty ; some are row'd but by one Man, others by two ; the former are call'd *Scullers*, and the latter *Oars*. They are reckon'd at several Thousands ; but tho' there are indeed a great many, I believe the Number is exaggerated. The City of *London* being very long, it is a great Conveniency to be able sometimes to make Use of this Way of Carriage. You sit at your Ease upon Cushions, and have a Board to lean against ; but generally they have no Covering, unless a Cloth, which the Watermen set up immediately, in case of Need, over a few Hoops ; and sometimes you are wet to the Skin for all this. It is easy to conceive that the *Oars* go faster than the *Sculls*, and accordingly their pay is doubled. You never have any Disputes with them ; for you can go to no Part either of *London*, or the Country above or below it, but the Rate is fix'd by Authority ; every Thing is regulated and printed.'

This, then, is a sample of the social amenities as then practised on the river, and the following are the

Rates of *Watermen* as they are set forth by the *Lord Mayor* and *Aldermen* of the City of *London*.[1]

	Oars.		Skull.	
	s.	*d.*	*s.*	*d.*
From London Bridge to Lime House, New Crane, Shadwell Dock, Bell Wharf, Ratcliff Cross	1	—		6
To Wapping Dock, Wapping new and old Stairs, the Hermitage, Rotherhith Church Stairs		6		3
From St. Olave's to Rotherhith Church Stairs, and Rotherhith Stairs		6		3
From Billingsgate and St. Olave's to St. Saviour's Mill		6		3
All the Stairs between London Bridge and Westminster		6		3
From either Side above London Bridge to Lambeth and Foxhall	1	—		6
From Temple, Dorset, and Black-fryers Stairs or Pauls Wharf to Lambeth		8		4
Over the Water directly between Foxhall and Limehouse		4		1

The Rates of OARS down the River.	Wh. F		Com.	
	s.	*d.*	*s.*	*d.*
From London to				
Gravesend	4	6		9
Grays or Greenhith	4	—		8
Purfleet or Erith	3	—		6
Woolwich	2	6		4
Blackwall	2	—		4
Greenwich, or Deptford	1	6		3
Up the RIVER.				
Chelsea, Battersey, Wandsworth	1	6		3
Putney, Fulham, Barnelms	2	—		4
Hammersmith, Chiswick, Mortlack	2	6		6
Brentford, Isleworth, Richmond	3	6		6
Twittenham	4	—		6
Kingston	5	—		9
Hampton Court	6	—	1	—
Hampton Town, Sunbury, Walton	7	—	1	—
Weybridge and Chertsey	10	—	1	—
Stanes	12	—	1	-
Windsor	14	—	2	—

[1] 'An Useful COMPANION : or a *Help at Hand*. Being a Convenient POCKET BOOK.' Lond. 1709.

The river, too, was naturally the place for picnics and
pleasure parties—although they were by no means so magnificent as the following :[1] 'I took five Barges, and the fairest
kept for my Company ; the other four I fill'd with Musick of
all sorts, and of all sorts the best ; in the first were Fiddles,
in the next Theorbo, Lutes, and Voices.   Flutes and such
Pastoral Instruments i' th' third.   Loud Musick from the
fourth did pierce the Air ; Each Consort vy'd by turns,
which with most Melody shou'd charm our Ears.   The fifth
the largest of 'em all was neatly hung, not with dull Tapistry,
but with green Boughs, Curiously Interlac'd to let in Air, and
every Branch with Jessemins, and Orange Poesies deckt.   In
this the Feast was kept.'

These pleasure barges were more or less ornate, and
varied from the ordinary boat, with a tilt of canvas or green
boughs to very elaborately carved and gilded ones.   The last
remaining, in our time, were the State barges of Her Majesty,
the Trinity Barge, and the Lord Mayor's and City Companies'
State barges.   The recollection of the water pageant, on a
sunshiny Lord Mayor's day, will never be effaced from the
memory of those among us who are old enough to have seen
it.   It was one of the prettiest sights I ever saw ; and a few of
these barges may still be seen, utilised at Oxford as College
Club boats.

Misson says of barges, ' They give this Name in England
to a Sort of Pleasure Boat, at one End of which is a little
Room handsomely painted and Cover'd, with a Table in the
Middle, and Benches round it ; and at the other End, Seats
for 8, 10, 12, 30 or 40 Rowers.   There are very few Persons
of Great Quality but what have their *Barges*, tho' they do
not frequently make use of them.   Their Watermen wear
a Jacket of the same Colour they give for their Livery,
with a pretty large Silver Badge upon their Arm, with the
Nobleman's Coat of Arms emboss'd in it.   These Watermen
have some Privileges, as belonging to Peers ; but they have
no Wages, and are not domestick Servants : They live in
their own Houses with their Families, and earn their Live-
lihood as they can.   The Lord Mayor of *London*, and the

[1] *The Lying Lover*, ed. 1704.

several Companies, have also their Barges, and are carry'd in them upon certain solemn occasions.'

Moored opposite Whitehall was a very large barge with a saloon, and promenade on the top, called the Folly, and this was a favourite place of entertainment. It was a fashionable resort in Pepys' time. He says, '13 Ap. 1668. Spent in the Folly 1s.'; and Queen Mary and some of her attendants pa.d it a visit. In Anne's reign it was used as a coffee-house, but it no longer was extremely fashionable, as the company was very mixed. As D'Urfey sung :—

> When Drapers' smugged apprentices,
> With Exchange girls mostly jolly,
> After shop was shut and all,
> Could sail up to the Folly.[1]

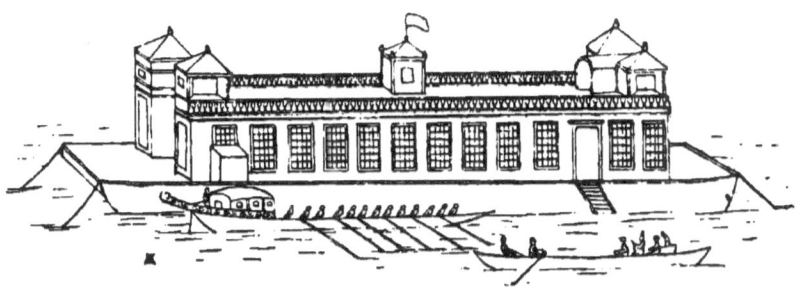

' THE FOLLY ON THE THAMES.'

' Pray, says my Companion (pointing to the Folly), what noble Structure is that floating upon the Water? I have often heard of Castles in the Air, and this seems to me to be a kind of an Essay towards such a windy Project. That Whimsical piece of Architect, said I, was design'd as a Musical Summer House for the entertainment of Quality; where they might meet. . . . But the Ladies of the Town, finding it as convenient a Rendezvous for their purpose . . . drove away their private Enemies, and entirely possess'd themselves of this moveable Mansion, which they have occupied ever since, very much to their advantage. . . . We no sooner enter'd but we had as many Ladies staring us in our Faces, as if we had been either handsom to admiration, or

[1] *A Touch of the Times.*

ugly to a Miracle . . . some dancing as they mov'd, to show
the Airyness of their Temper ; some ogling the Gallants, and
others crowded into Boxes like Passengers into a Western
Wherry, sat smoaking their Noses, and drinking Burnt Brandy,
to defend their Stomachs from the chill Air upon the Water.
. . . In short, it was such a confused Scene of Folly, Madness,
and Debauchery, that we step'd again into our Boat without
Drinking to avoid the Inconveniences that attend mixing
with such a Swarm of Caterpillars, who are always dangerous
to the Unwary, and destructive to the Innocent.'[1]

The ordinary freight barges were, both as to build and
rig, extremely similar to those of the present day, and there
was one passenger and freight sailing boat which went to the
then *Ultima Thule* of a Londoner's experience—the Gravesend Tilt boat—of which we have an interesting reminiscence
in the

'Rates for Carrying of Goods in the *Tilt Boat* between
Gravesend and London[2]—

	s.	d.
An Half Firkin	—	1
An Whole Firkin	—	2
An Hogshead	2	—
An Hundred Weight of Cheese, Iron, or any Heavy Goods	—	4
Sack of Salt, or Corn, Ordinary Chest, Trunck or Hamper	—	6
Every Single Person in the Ordinary Passage	—	6
The Hire of the Whole Tilt Boat	22	6

There was a horse ferry (from whence the name Horse-
ferry Road) between Westminster and Lambeth for passengers, horses, coaches, etc. The rates were—

	s.	d.
For a Man and Horse	—	2
„ Horse and Chaze	1	—
„ Coach and 2 Horses	1	6
„ „ „ 4 „	2	—
„ „ „ 6 „	2	6
„ a Cart Loaden	2	6
„ a Cart, or Waggon each	2	—

Whilst on the subject of the river Thames, mention of
one of its tributaries, the Fleet Ditch, should not be omitted.

[1] *A Walk Round London and Westminster.*   [2] *An Useful Companion.*

Taking its rise in Hampstead, it meandered along, until it fell into the river at Blackfriars, where it formed a wide and shallow mouth called a Fleet, which was once of such extent that ships of considerable burden could get up it some little distance. In Anne's time, however, it had become a black and fetid sewer. Nobody had a good word for it. Gay never mentions it without abuse.

> Or who that rugged Street would traverse o'er,
> That stretches, *O Fleet Ditch*, from thy black Shore.[1]

and—

> If where Fleet Ditch with Muddy Current flows.

Ward says, 'from thence we took a turn down by the Ditch side, I desiring my friend to inform me what great advantages this Costly Brook contributed to the Town, to Countervail the Expence of Seventy four Thousand Pounds, which I read in a very Credible Author was the Charge of its making: He told me he was wholly unacquainted with any, unless it was now and then to bring up a few Chaldron of Coles to 2 or 3 pedling *Fewel Merchants*, who sell them never the cheaper to the poor for such Conveniency: And as for those Cellers you see on each side, design'd for Warehouses, they are render'd by their dampness so unfit for that purpose, that they are wholly useless, except for Lightermen to lay themselves in, or to harbour Frogs, Toads and other Vermin. The greatest good that ever I heard it did, was to the undertaker, who is bound to acknowledge he has found better Fishing in a muddy Stream, than ever he did in clear Water.'

[1] *Trivia.*

CHAPTER XXXV.

THE STREETS.

Size of London—Pall Mall—London in wet weather—Early morning—
Street cries : a list of them—Roguery in the streets—Orderly regulations—State of the roads—Rule of the road—Street signs—Description of the streets—Milkmaids on May Day—Hyde Park : its
regulations—Lighting the streets—The streets at night.

LONDON, it is scarcely necessary to remark, was very circum-
scribed in its area compared to its overgrown present dimen-
sions. The northern bank of the river was well occupied from
Shadwell to Westminster, opposite Lambeth. On the west the
houses went down the northern side of Piccadilly, as far as
Apsley House ; but Bond Street was only partially built, and
there were no houses westward of it. The Edgware Road and
Tottenham (or, as it was then called, Hampstead) Road were
in existence, but few were the houses in either of them. At
the Back of Montague and Southampton Houses, and generally north of Theobald's Road and Clerkenwell, there was
nought but fields, dotted here and there with farmhouses—
with the hills of Hampstead and Highgate for a background.
Houses ceased, on the eastern side, after Shoreditch, and
shortly after passing Whitechapel Church ; so that a walk all
round inhabited London—skirting the north bank of the
river to begin with—might be done in about twelve miles.

Covent Garden was the centre of social life. Soho and
Leicester Squares, and thence westward, comprised the limits
of the court and fashionable society—that land of luxury for
which Gay sighed, but which yet was not perfect.

> O bear me to the Paths of fair *Pell Mell*,
> Safe are thy Pavements, grateful is thy Smell !
> At distance, rolls along the gilded Coach,
> Nor sturdy Carmen on thy Walks encroach ;

No Less would bar thy Ways, were Chairs deny'd,
The soft Supports of Laziness and Pride ;
Shops breathe Perfumes, thro' Sashes Ribbons glow,
The Mutual Arms of Ladies, and the Beau.—
Yet still ev'n Here, when Rains the Passage hide
Oft' the loose Stone spirts up a Muddy Tide,
Beneath thy careless Foot ; and from on high,
Where Masons mount the Ladder, Fragments fly ;
Mortar, and crumbled Lime in Show'rs descend,
And o'er thy Head destructive Tiles impend.

If, when it was wet weather, the ground was so bad in
'fair Pell Mell,' what was it elsewhere? Here is a litttle scene
out in the fields going to St. Pancras Church—a wedding
party.[1] 'The morning being rainy, methought the march to
this wedding was but too lively a picture of Wedlock itself.

A STREET SCENE.

They seemed both to have a month's mind to make the best
of their way single ; yet both tugged arm in arm : and when
they were in a dirty way, he was but deeper in the mire, by
endeavouring to pull out his companion, and yet without
helping her. The bridegroom's feathers in his hat all drooped ;
one of his shoes had lost an heel. In short, he was, in his
whole person and dress so extremely soused, that there did
not appear one inch or single thread about him *unmarried.*'[2]

Swift[3] gives an excellent metrical description of a shower
in those days.

Now in contiguous drops the flood comes down,
Threatening with deluge this devoted town.

[1] *Tatler*, No. 7. [2] A play upon the word unmarred (unspoilt). [3] *Tatler*, 238.

> To shops in crouds the draggled females fly,
> Pretend to cheapen goods, but nothing buy.
> The Templar spruce, while every spout's abroach,
> Stays till 'tis fair, yet seems to call a Coach.
> The tuck'd up sempstress walks with hasty Strides,
> While streams run down her oil'd umbrella's sides.
> Here various kinds, by various fortunes led,
> Commence acquaintance underneath a shed.
> Triumphant Tories and desponding Whigs
> Forget their feuds, and join to save their wigs.
> Box'd in a Chair the Beau impatient sits,
> While spouts run clattering o'er the roof by fits ;
> And ever and anon with frightful din
> The leather sounds ; he trembles from within.

Those gutter spouts, sending their streams not quite clear of the pavement, must have been a terrible nuisance to a generation of men innocent of umbrella or Mackintosh ; and Gay advises anyone, in wet weather, to maintain his privilege of taking the wall, but not to quarrel for it.

> When from high Spouts the dashing Torrents fall,
> Ever be watchful to maintain the Wall ;
> For should'st thou quit thy Ground, the rushing Throng
> Will with impetuous Fury drive along ;
> All press to gain those Honours thou hast lost,
> And rudely shove thee far without the Post.
> Then to retrieve the Shed you strive in vain,
> Draggled all o'er, and soak'd in Floods of Rain.
> Yet rather bear the Show'r, and Toils of Mud,
> Than in the doubtful Quarrel risque thy Blood.

Let us take the streets throughout the day ; and let, as usual, contemporary writers give their own account of them in their own language. Steele [1] begins with a description of London in the morning.

> Now hardly here and there an hackney Coach
> Appearing, show'd the ruddy morn's approach.
> The slipshod 'prentice, from his master's door,
> Had par'd the street, and sprinkled round the floor ;
> Now Moll had whirl'd her mop with dextrous airs,
> Prepar'd to scrub the entry and the Stairs.
> The youth with broomy stumps began to trace
> The kennel edge, where wheels had worn the place.

[1] *Tatler*, No. 9.

The small coal man was heard with cadence deep,
Till drown'd in shriller notes of Chimney sweep.
Duns at his Lordship's gates began to meet ;
And brick dust Mol. had scream'd thro' half a street :
The turnkey now his flock returning sees,
Duly let out a' nights to steal for fees.
The watchful bailiffs take their silent stands ;
And school boys lag with satchels in their hands.

It is only in the poorer neighbourhoods that street cries, nowadays, flourish, and it is only by a visit to them that we can at all realise the babel of sounds that the streets gave forth in the reign of Anne. Luckily, as they differ so much from anything we know of, and are so suggestive of the petty industries then practised, they have been preserved for us by Marcellus Lauron, in his somewhat scarce book,[1] from which many illustrations used in this book have been taken. Here is a list of them :—

Any Card Matches or Save Alls.
Pretty Maids, Pretty Pins, Pretty Women.
Ripe Strawberryes.
A Bed Matt or a Door Matt.
Buy a fine Table Basket.
Old Shoes for some Broomes.
Hot bak'd Wardens Hott.[2]
Small Coale.
Maids, any Cunny[3] Skins.
Buy a Rabbet, a Rabbet.
Buy a Fork or a Fire Shovel.
Chimney Sweep.
Crab, Crab, any Crab.
Oh Rare Shoe.[4]
Lilly White Vinegar 3 pence a quart.
Buy my Dutch biskets.

Ripe Speragas.
Maids, buy a Mopp.
Buy my fat Chickens.
Buy my flounders.
Old Cloaks Suits or Coats.
Fair Lemons and Oranges.
Old Chairs to mend.
Twelve pence a peck Oysters.
Troope, every One.
Old Satten, Old Taffety or Velvet.
Ha, Ha, Ha, Poor Jack.
Buy my Dish of great Eeles.
Buy a fine Singing bird.
Buy any Wax or Wafers.
Fine Writeing Inke.
A Merry new Song.
Buy a new Almanack.
Buy my fine singing Glasses.[5]

---

[1] *Habits and Cryes of the City of London.* 1709.   [2] Pies.
[3] Rabbit.   [4] Raree Show.   [5] Glass horns.

Any Kitchen Stuffe have you, Maids.

Knives, Combs or Ink hornes.

Four for six pence, Mackrell.

Any Work for John Cooper.

Four paire for a Shilling, Holland Socks.

Colly Molly Puffe.[1]

Six pence a pound fair Cherryes.

Knives or Cissors to grinde.

Long thread Laces, long and Strong.

Remember the Poor prisoners.

A Brass Pott, or an Iron Pott to mend.

Buy my four Ropes of Hard Onyons.

London Gazettes here.

Buy a White line, a Jack line, or a Cloathe line.

Any old Iron, take money for.

Delicate Cowcumbers to pickle.

Any Baking Pears.

New River Water.

This does not pretend to be an exhaustive list; in fact, they were so numerous and varied that, as Addison says (*Spectator*, 251), 'There is nothing which more astonishes a Foreigner, and frights a Country Squire, than the Cries of London. My good Friend Sir ROGER often declares, that he cannot get them out of his Head, or go to sleep for them, the first Week that he is in Town. On the contrary, WILL. HONEYCOMB calls them the *Ramage de la Ville*, and prefers them to the Sounds of Larks and Nightingales, with all the Musick of the Fields and Woods.' The whole of this *Spectator* is on street cries, and is very interesting reading.

Trim, in Steele's comedy of ' The Funeral,' tells a lot of ragged soldiers : ' There's a thousand things you might do to help out about this Town, as to cry—Puff—Puff Pyes. Have you any Knives or Scissors to grind—or, late in an Evening, whip from *Grub Street* strange and bloody News from *Flanders*—Votes from the House of Commons—Buns, rare Buns—Old Silver Lace, Cloaks, Sutes or Coats—Old Shoes, Boots or Hats.

> Successive Crys the Season's Change declare,
> And mark the Monthly Progress of the Year.

There was yet another noise in the streets, that of the

[1] An itinerant pastrycook, mentioned in *Spectator* 362, &c.

ballad-singer, or singers, for they generally went in couples. People were warned against them.

> Let not the Ballad-Singer's shrilling Strain
> Amid the Swarm thy list'ning Ear detain :
> Guard well thy Pocket ; for these *Syrens* stand,
> To aid the Labours of the diving hand ;
> Confed'rate in the Cheat, they draw the Throng,
> And *Cambrick* Handkerchiefs reward the Song.

The streets ought to have been kept in fair order, if the inhabitants had complied with the law ; but they evidently neglected it, and had to be reminded of their duties by a notice in the *Gazette*, April 12/14, 1711. According to 8 & 9 Will. III. cap 37, everyone had, on Wednesdays and Saturdays, to sweep and cleanse the road in front of their houses, buildings, or walls, and heap up the dirt for the scavenger to remove, under penalty of 10*s.*

That no one should throw any ashes, dirt, etc., into the open street before his house, under penalty of 5*s.*, or if it was thrown before any other building, 20*s.* ; but they must deliver the dust to the scavenger (2 Will. and Mary, cap. 8), who must come round daily to collect it, giving notice by ringing a bell or otherwise, or penalty 40*s.*

All householders, or, if empty, the owners of house, to keep the pavement before said house in repair, or pay 20*s.* per rod, and 20*s.* per week, till the same be sufficiently repaired.

While it was being done, the self-same sign was hung out as now—

> Does not each Walker know the Warning Sign,
> When Wisps of Straw depend upon the Twine
> 'Cross the Close Street ; that then the Pavior's Art
> Renews the Ways, deny'd to Coach and Cart.

The dust carts were not unmixed blessings—

> The *Dustman's* Cart offends thy Cloaths and Eyes
> When through the Street a Cloud of Ashes flies.

And there were other ways of 'offending Cloaths.'

> When Drays bound high, they never cross behind,
> Where bubbling Yest is blown by Gusts of Wind :

> And when up *Ludgate Hill* huge Carts move slow,
> Far from the straining Steeds, securely go,
> Whose dashing Hoofs, behind them, fling the Mire,
> And mark, with muddy Blots, the gazing Squire.

In walking the rule was the same as now : everyone should take the right-hand side of the path ; and the courtesies of giving way on special occasions are clearly pointed out in the following lines, showing there was a time to concede and a time to retain the right to the wall :—

> Let due Civilities be strictly paid.
> The Wall surrender to the hooded Maid ;
> Nor let thy sturdy Elbow's hasty Rage
> Jostle the feeble Steps of trembling Age :
> And when the Porter bends beneath his Load,
> And pants for Breath ; clear thou the crouded Road.
> But above all, the groaping Blind direct,
> And from the pressing Throng the Lame protect.
> You'll sometimes meet a Fop, of nicest Tread,
> Whose mantling Peruke veils his empty Head,
> At ev'ry Step he dreads the Wall to lose,
> And risques, to save a Coach, his red heel'd Shoes ;
> Him like the *Miller*, pass with Caution by,
> Lest from his Shoulder Clouds of Powder fly.
> But when the Bully, with assuming Pace
> Cocks his Broad Hat, edg'd round with tarnish'd Lace,
> Yield not the Way ; defie his strutting Pride,
> And thrust him to the Muddy Kennel's side ;
> He never turns again, nor dares oppose,
> But mutters Coward Curses as he goes.

The shops were low, and mostly with overhanging pent-houses, which were inconvenient.

> Where the low Penthouse bows the Walker's head,
> And the rough Pavement wounds the yielding Tread :
> Where not a Post protects the narrow Space,
> And strung in Twines, Combs dangle in thy Face.

The goods were very much exposed ; in fact, such conduct now in a shopkeeper would rouse the virtuous indignation of any metropolitan magistrate ; but there was generally an apprentice on the look-out. Our modern costermonger's barrows had a prototype. 'We mov'd on till we came to *Fleet Bridge*, where Nuts, Ginger bread, Oranges and Oysters, lay Pil'd up in Moveable Shops that run upon Wheeles, attended by Ill looking Fellows, some with but one Eye, and others without Noses.'[1]

The street signs, which were necessary, as houses were not numbered, were very numerous and large, and some were exceedingly costly. Misson was very much struck with them. 'At *London* they are commonly very large, and jutt out so far, that in some narrow Streets they touch one another ; nay, and run across almost quite to the other Side. They are generally adorn'd with Carving and Gilding ; and ·there are several that, with the Branches of Iron which support them, cost above a hundred Guineas. They seldom write upon the Sign the Name of the Thing represented in it ; so that here is no need of *Molière's* Inspector. Out of *London*, and particularly in Villages, the Signs of Inns are suspended in the middle of a great Wooden Portal, which may be look'd upon as a Kind of triumphal Arch to the Honour of Bacchus.'

Brown draws a vivid if somewhat unpleasant picture of the streets.[2] 'Some Carry, others are Carried : *Make way there*, says a gouty leg'd Chairman, that is carrying a Punk of Quality to a *Morning's Exercise* ; or a *Bartholomew* Baby Beau, newly launched out of a Chocolate House, with his Pockets as empty as his brains. *Make room there*, says another Fellow driving a Wheel-barrow of Nuts, that spoil the Lungs of the City Prentices. One draws, another drives. *Stand up there you blind Dog*, says a Carman, *Will you have the Cart squeeze your Guts out ?* One Tinker knocks, another bawls, *Have you a Brass Pot, Iron Pot, Kettle, Skillet, or a Frying Pan to mend ?* Whilst another yelps louder than *Homer's* Stentor, *Two a groat, and Four for Sixpence Mackerel.* One draws his Mouth up to his Ears, and howls out, *Buy my Flounders*, and is followed by an old burly Drab, that screams out the sale of her *Mades* and her *Souls* at the same Instant.

'Here a sooty Chimney Sweeper takes the Wall of a grave *Alderman*, and a *Broom man* justles the *Parson* of the

[1] *The London Spy.*
[2] *Amusements Serious and Comical, calculated for the Meridian of London.*

Parish.   There a fat greasie *Porter* runs a Trunk full butt
upon you, while another salutes you with a Flasket of *Eggs*
and *Butter*.   *Turn out there you Country Putt*, says a *Bully*
with a Sword two yards long jarring at his heels, and throws
him into the Kennel.   By and by comes a *Christning*, with the
Reader screwing up his Mouth to deliver the Service *a la
mode de Paris*, and afterwards talk immoderately nice and

dull with the Gossips, and the *Mid-
wife* strutting in the front, and young
Original Sin as fine as Fippence, follow'd with the Vocal Musick of Kitchen Stuff ha' you Maid, and a
damn'd Trumpeter calling in the
Rabble to see a Calf with Six Legs
and a Top Knot.   There goes a Funeral with the Men of Rosemary after
it, licking their Lips after three hits of
White, Sack and Claret at the House
of Mourning, and the *Sexton* walking
before, as big and bluff as a Beef
Eater at a Coronation.   A Poet
Scampers for 't as fast as his Legs will
carry him, and at his heels a brace
of *Bandog Bailiffs*, with open Mouths
ready to devour him and all the Nine
Muses.'

Let us turn to a prettier street
scene.   It is May Day, and, although
maypoles are banished to the country, where they still hold their own,

MILKMAID ON MAY DAY.   London celebrates it in another fashion.
The milkmaids hold their festival, and even Gay's 'Sallow
Milkmaid's' cheeks must have brightened at the prospect of
such a treat.   Confiding customers lent them silver plate, and
women's taste and a few ribbons make a gorgeous trophy.
Misson could not help being struck with it: 'On the First
of *May*, and the five or six Days following, all the pretty
young Country girls that serve the Town with Milk, dress
themselves up very neatly, and borrow abundance of Silver

Plate, whereof they make a Pyramid, which they adorn with Ribbands and Flowers, and carry upon their Heads, instead of their common Milk Pails. In this Equipage, accompany'd by some of their fellow Milk Maids, and a Bag pipe or a Fiddle, they go from Door to Door, dancing before the Houses of their Customers, in the Midst of Boys and Girls that follow them in Troops, and every Body gives them something.'

And Steele notices: [1] 'I was looking out of my parlour window this morning, and receiving the honours which MARGERY, the milk maid to our lane, was doing me, by *dancing* before my door *with the plate of her Customers on her head,*' etc.

In the daytime, after dinner, Hyde Park was the fashionable resort either for promenading, riding, or driving. 'Here the people take the Diversion of the Ring: In a pretty high place which lies very open they have surrounded a Circumference of two or three hundred Paces Diameter with a sorry Kind of Ballustrade, or rather with Poles plac'd upon Stakes, but three Foot from the Ground; and the Coaches drive round and round this. When they have turn'd for some Time round one Way, they face about and turn t'other: So rowls the World.' [1]

But it evidently was falling into evil habits, for on July 1, 1712, the Queen found it necessary to issue some rules and directions ' for the better keeping Hyde Park in good Order.' The gatekeepers were to be always on duty, and not to sell ale, brandy, or other liquors. No one should leap over the ditches, or fences, or break the latter down. ' No Person to ride over the grass on the South side of the Gravelled Coach Road . . . excepting Henry Wise, who is permitted to pass cross that Part of the Park leading from the Door in the Park Wall, next his Plantation.' No grooms or others were to ride over the banks, or slopes, of any pond. No stage coach, hackney coach, chaise with one horse, cart, waggon, or funeral should pass through the park; and no one should cut or lop any of the trees.

---

[1] *Tatler*, 166.   [2] Misson.

As evening drew on the lamps were lit, *i.e.* if there were not a full moon, or in the summer time ; but should the pavement be up, or a sewer open, a lantern was specially provided.

> Where a dim Gleam the paly Lanthorn throws
> O'er the mid' Pavement ; heapy Rubbish grows,
> Or arched Vaults their gaping Jaws extend,
> Or the dark Caves to Common Shores descend.
> Oft' by the Winds, extinct the Signal lies,
> Or smother'd in the glimm'ring Socket dies,
> E'er Night has half roll'd round her Ebon Throne ;
> In the wide Gulph the shatter'd Coach o'erthrown,
> Sinks with the Snorting Steeds ; the Reins are broke,
> And from the cracking Axle flies the Spoke.

Lighting was so far from universal that Thoresby [1] 'could not but observe that all the way, quite through Hyde Park to the Queen's palace at Kensington, has lanterns for illuminating the road in the dark nights, for the Coaches.'

'Instead of Lanterns, they set up [2] in the Streets of *London* Lamps,[3] which by Means of a very thick Convex Glass, throw out great Rays of Light, which illuminate the Path for people that go on Foot tolerably well. They begin to light up these Lamps at *Michaelmas*, and continue them till *Lady Day* ; they burn from Six in the Evening till Midnight, and from every third Day after the Full Moon to the sixth Day after the New Moon.'[4]

There was an improvement on the convex lamp, a new one, called the conic lamp, being introduced, and apparently answering very well. In the *Gazette*, Dec. 30 to Jan. 2, 1706–7, is this advertisement : 'Whereas Her most Gracious Majesty Queen Anne has been pleased to grant her Letters Patent for enlightening the Suburbs of London and City of Westminster, and all other Cities and Places in England, by new Invented Lights or Lamps called Conic Lamps, for 14 years ; and whereas the Letters Patent for the Convex Lamps are long since expired ; These are to certify whom it may

---

[1] *Diary*, June 15, 1712.   [2] At every tenth house.
[3] The invention of Edmund Heming.   [4] Misson.

concern, That by an Act of Parliament made in the 2d Year
of their late Majesties King William and Queen Mary of
ever Glorious Memory, all persons paying to any Lamps,
distanced by two of Her Majesty's Justices of the Peace,
are exempted from hanging out a Lanthorn and Candle
and indemnified from the Penalties contained in the said
Act.'

In 1709, however, is an advertisement of yet another
lamp. 'There is a new Sort of Light call'd a Globe Light,
at St. James's Coffee House, near St. James's Palace, which
is observ'd to enlighten the Street, and all Parts near it, with
a true steady Light, and no way offensive to the Eye. The
Person who contriv'd it and set it up, may be heard of
there, having obtain'd Her Majesty's Letters Patent for the
same.' [1]

Ward draws a picture of the streets at night, too repulsive
for reproduction—doubtless a true one—but one taken from
the very lowest haunts. Gay's gentle verse, on the contrary,
depicts more the inconveniences of the badly lit streets, and
their results :—

> That Walker, who regardless of his Pace,
> Turns oft' to pose upon the Damsel's Face.
> From Side to Side by thrusting Elbows tost,
> Shall strike his aking Breast against the Post ;
> Or Water, dash'd from fishy Stalls, shall stain
> His hapless Coat with Spirts of Scaly Rain.
> But if unwarily he chance to stray,
> Where twirling Turnstiles intercept the Way,
> The thwarting Passenger shall force them round,
> And beat the Wretch half breathless to the Ground.
>   Let constant Vigilance thy Footsteps guide,
> And wary Circumspection guard thy Side ;
> Then shalt thou walk unharm'd the dang'rous Night,
> Nor need th' officious Link-Boy's smoaky Light.
> Thou never wilt attempt to cross the Road,
> Where Alehouse Benches rest the Porter's load,
> Grievous to heedless Shins ; No Barrow's Wheel,
> That bruises oft the Truant School Boy's Heel,
> Behind thee rolling, with insidious Pace,
> Shall mark thy Stocking with a miry Trace.

[1] *Tatler*, Nov. 19/22.

Let not thy vent'rous Steps approach too nigh,
Where gaping wide, low steepy Cellars lie ;
Should thy Shoe wrench aside, down, down you fall
And overturn the scolding Huckster's Stall.
The scolding Huckster shall not o'er thee moan,
But Pence exact for Nuts and Pears o'er thrown.

.   .   .   .

Where the nail'd Hoop defends the painted Stall
Brush not thy sweeping Skirt too near the Wall ;
Thy heedless Sleeve will drink the colour'd Oil,
And Spot indelible thy Pocket soil.

CHAPTER XXXVI.

CARRIAGES, ETC.

Smithfield—Horse coursers—Waggons—Stage coaches : travelling in
them described—Bad roads — Posting—Hackney coaches : their
Fares—Hackney coachmen—State coaches—Other carriages—Suburban drives—A Mechanical coach—Mourning coaches—Harness—
Sedan chairs—Chairmen.

AMONG the many places swept away, and yet which many of
us well remember, is Smithfield, where both cattle and horses
were sold ; and Ward gives a very amusing account of the
horse sales there.   ' From thence we proceeded to the Rails,
where Country Carters stood Arm'd with their Long Whips,
to keep their Teams (upon Sale in a due *Decorum*,) who were
drawn up into the most sightly order with their fore feet
Mounted on a Dunghill, and their Heads dress'd up to as
much advantage as an Inns of Court Sempstress, or the
Mistress of a Boarding School : Some with their Manes
Frizzled up, to make 'em appear high Wither'd, that they
look'd as Fierce as one of *Hungess's* Wild Boars.   Others
with their Manes Plaited, as if they had been ridden by the
Nightmare : And the fellows that attended 'em made as
uncouth Figures as the Monsters in the Tempest ; amongst
these Cattel, here and there, was the Conductor of a Dung
Cart, in his Dirty Surplice, wrangling about the Price of a
Beast, as a wary Purchaser ; and that he ought not to be
deceived in the Goodness of the Creature, he must see him
stand three fair Pulls at a Post, to which the Poor Jade is
ty'd, that he may exert his Strength, and shew the Clown his
excellencies ; for which he strokes him on the Head, or claps
him on the Buttocks, to recompence his Labour.
    ' We went a little further, and there we saw a parcel of
Ragged Rapscallions, mounted upon Scrubbed Tits, scowring

about the Rounds, some Trotting, some Galloping, some Pacing, and others Stumbling.

' Pray friend, said I, what are those Eagle Look'd Fellows in their Narrow Brimm'd White Beavers, Jockeys Coats, a Spur in one Heel, and Bended Sticks in their Hands, that are so busily peeping into every Horses Mouth? . . . Those Blades, says my friend, are a Subtle Sort of *Smithfield Foxes*, called *Horse Coursers*, who Swear every Morning by the Bridle, that they will not, from any Man, suffer a Knavish trick, or ever do an Honest one.   They are a sort of *English Jews*, that never deal with any Man but they Cheat him ; and have a rare Faculty of Swearing a Man out of his Senses, Lying him out of his Reason, and Cozening him out of his Money ; If they have a Horse to sell that is Stone Blind, they'll call a Hundred Gods to Witness he can see as well as you can.   If he be downright Lame, they will use all the Asseverations that the Devil can assist 'em with, that it is nothing but a Spring Halt ; and if he be Twenty Years old, they'll Swear he comes but Seven next Grass, if they find the Buyer has not Judgment enough to discover the Contrary.'

This horse market was of importance to the metropolis, which was supplied from the country fairs, from which the horses came up in droves.   ' A Set of Geldings and Mares, just from a Journey to be sold Cheap.'   So many were wanted for riding, carriages, and draught purposes.   Horse-stealing was a crime so extremely prevalent, that it is difficult to take up a paper that does not contain an advertisement respecting a lost or stolen horse.

Some of the inland traffic was still done by means of pack-horses.   ' These are to give Notice to all Gentlemen or others that have occasion to send Goods, or travel from London to Exeter or Plymouth, or from Exeter and Plymouth, or any parts of Cornwall or Devonshire to London ; that they may be accommodated for Expedition by Pack Horse Carriage, who set out from the Cross Keys Inn in Wood Street London every Saturday, and from the Mermaid Inn in Exon every Monday.   Perform'd, if God permit, by Ebenezer Brookes.'   But there were also waggons, which, by the divine permission, started for every town of note in England.

Stage coaches ran to most of the towns ; and we may judge of the time they took over their journeys, Gloucester, 82 miles, in one day, and Hereford, 134 miles, in one day and a half. Their fares may be somewhat approximately guessed at : Bath, 16s. ; Bristol, 15s. to 18s. ; and Gosport, 9s. Steele gives an amusing description in the *Spectator* (No. 132) of stage-coach travelling: how the captain was subdued by the good plain sense of Ephraim the Quaker. 'We can not help it, Friend, I say ; if thou wilt, we must hear thee. . . . To speak indiscreetly what we are obliged to hear, by being hasped up with thee in this publick Vehicle is in some degree assaulting on the high road.' The captain took the rebuke in good part, and thorough good-fellowship prevailed. ' Faith, Friend, I thank thee : I should have been a little impertinent if thou hadst not reprimanded me.'

In ' A Step to the Bath' we get an insight into stage-coach travelling. 'Enquiring of the Tapster what Company I was like to have, he said more he believ'd than I desir'd ; for there was four Places taken just after I went, and three of the Passengers were in the House, and to Lye there that Night ; the other was for a Merchant of *Bristol.* Then ask-ing what those in the House were, he told me two Gentle-women and their Maid Servant, who were just going to Supper. Whereupon I bid him go and give my Service to 'em, and tell 'em I was to Travel with 'em to morrow, and should take it as a great favour, if they would please to Honour me so far, as to admit me of their Company, for I was alone. The Fellow brought word they desir'd me to walk in, and they should be very glad of mine. . . . Supper being ended, they call'd for a Bill, which was presently brought ; out I lugg'd and was going to Discharge, but they begg'd my Pardon, and would by no means suffer me ; tell-ing me that I must submit to the Rule that is generally observ'd in Travelling, for the Major of either Sex to Treat the Minor.'

They breakfasted at Colebrook, dined at Reading, and then drained the merchant's bottle of ' Right Nants '; after which one of the ladies told a story. They stopped at Theale to taste Old Mother Cleanly's bottled ale and plum cake ; then the merchant told a story ; and the day's journey terminated at Newbury. There they supped, and grumbled loudly at the bill. 'For a brace of Midling Trouts they charged us but a Leash of Crowns, Six Shillings for a Shoulder of Mutton and a Plate of Gerkins, Three and Sixpence for Six Rowles, and three Nipperkins of Belch ; and two Shillings more for *Whip* in drinking our Healths. Their Wine indeed was good, so was their price ; and in a Bill of two pound four Shillings, they made a mistake but of Nine ; I ask'd what Countrey-man my Landlord was? answer was made, Full *North* ; and Faith 'twas very Evident, for he had put the *Yorkshire* most damnably upon us.'

Next morning one of the ladies presented them with a pot of chocolate of her own preparing ; they refilled the merchant's bottle, and started, beguiling the way with stories. Came to Marlborough, where the road was so bad that the brandy bottle was broken ; and there they breakfasted. They seem to have dined at Calne or Chippenham, complaining bitterly of the roads, the last portion of which was got over at the rate of two miles in three hours. Here they stopped at a famous house, where 'there was more Coaches and Waggons drawn up before her Gate, than Hacks in *Palace Yard*, during the *Session of Parliament*, or *Term Time*. All her Entertainment is Loins of *Mutton* or *Rabbits* ; and she makes more Broth in a day than all the *Chop Houses* in *Castle Alley* in a Week.'

'Having Din'd, we proceeded on our Journey, but with a great deal of difficulty ; for the Road was so Rocky, Unlevel, and Narrow in some places, that I am persuaded the *Alps* are to be passed with less Danger,' and they finally reached Bath that evening.

The roads were bad almost everywhere, and no one travelled more than they could help. The coaches were heavy and strong, to stand the fearful wear and tear ; but, to the passengers, a journey was simply the time spent in torture. Even in London the stones jolted terribly. Says Ward 'When our *Stratford* Tub by the assistance of its

Carrionly Tits of different Colours, had outrun the Smoothness of the Road, and enter'd upon *London stones*, with as frightful a rumbling as an empty Hay Cart, our Leathern Conveniency being bound in the Braces to its good Behaviour, had no more Sway than a Funeral Herse, or a Country Waggon ; That we were jumbled about like so many Pease in a Child's Rattle, running at every Kennel Jolt a great hazard of a Dislocation : This we endured till we were brought within *White Chappel Bars*, where we lighted from our stubborn Caravan with our Elbows and Shoulders as Black and Blew as a Rural *Man* that has been under the pinches of an angry *Fairy.*'

Posthouses were at convenient stages all over the kingdom, and the postmaster was bound to provide horses for all comers, either to ride or drive. His duties and tariffs were as follows :—

'The Post Master is obliged to receive of every Person, Riding Post with Horses and Guide, thus 3*d.* per Mile for each Horse Hire and 4*d.* per Stage for a Guide.

'And no Person carrying a Bundle that doth not exceed 80 lbs. Averdupoise, shall be charged for it.

'If through the default of the Post Master, any Person Riding Post shall fail of being furnished, he shall forfeit 5*l.* Or if the Post Master cannot, or do not furnish any Person with Horses for Riding Post, then they are at Liberty to provide Horses for themselves ; but no Horses to be seized without the Owner's Consent.

'The other way that Gentlemen commonly Travel is in Stage Coaches, which is from about 2*d.* Farthing to 3*d.* per Mile. The Flying Coach is a Stage Coach, that is drawn by 6 Horses, and will sometimes run 90 or 100 *English* Miles on one day.

'It may also be noted that *Carriage* by Waggon or Pack Horses, is about 5 Shillings for carrying 112 Pound Weight 100 Miles ; and so in proportion ; though 'tis something cheaper in the Summer than Winter.'[1]

The hackney coach was a very useful institution, in spite of all said against it. We have read Ward's description of the bumping he had in one ; in another part of the *London*

[1] *British Curiosities in Nature and Art*, 1713.

Spy he says : 'Would you have me, said I, undergo the Punishment of a Coach again, when you Know I was so great a Sufferer by the last, that it made my Bones rattle in my Skin, and has brought as many Pains about me, as if troubled with the Rheumatism. That was a Country Coach, says he, and only fit for the Road ; but *London* Coaches are hung more loose, to prevent your being Jolted by the roughness of the pavement.'

The ordinary hackney coaches do not seem to have been provided with glasses. 'For want of Glasses to our Coach, having drawn up our Tin Sashes, pink'd like the bottom of a

HACKNEY COACH.

Cullender, that the Air might pass thro' the holes, and defend us from Stifling.'

By the 5 & 6 Will. and Mary, cap. 22, the number of hackney coaches was fixed at 700, and a tax was imposed of 4*l.* per annum each, 1*l.* to be paid every quarter day, besides a fine of 50*l.* for their first licence for 21 years ; and 8*l.* per annum on stage coaches.

To look after these hackney carriages there were five commissioners, at a salary each of 200*l.*, and their office was in Surrey Street, Strand. The fares were not very heavy, even taking the difference of the value of money into consideration, and the fact that they had two horses.

	s.	d.
For one day of 12 Hours	10	—
For One Hour	1	6
For every hour after the first	1	—
From any of the Inns of Court to any part of St. James's or City of Westminster, except beyond Tuttle Street	1	—

From the Inns of Court, or thereabouts, to the Royal
  Exchange   1 —
From any of the Inns of Court, to the Tower, Aldgate,
  Bishopsgate Street or thereabouts   1 6
And the same Rates back again, or to any Place of the like Distance.
And, if any Coachman shall refuse to go at, or exact more, for Hire,
  than the Rates hereby limited, he shall for every such Offence
  forfeit 40 Shillings.

In 1710 the number of coaches was increased to 800 by
the 9 Anne, cap. 23, which also provided that they were to
pay five shillings weekly, and were to go a mile and a half for
one shilling, two miles for one shilling and sixpence, above
two miles two shillings, and greater distances in the same
proportion.

The hackney coachmen petitioned against the tax, and
said they were willing to pay the old one. One petition was
entitled 'Some Reasons most humbly Offered to the Consideration of the Right Honourable the House of LORDS
and the Honourable the House of Commons ; by all the 700
Hackney Coachmen and their Widows to Enable them to pay
the Great Tax laid upon them ;' and another was 'The
Hackney Coachmen's case. Humbly presented to the Right
Honourable House of Commons with a proposal to raise for
her Majesty 200,000*l.* per annum.' This was proposed, very
coolly, to be done by laying a tax on all coaches and carriages
not licensed, on passengers going by stage coaches, and on
goods carried by waggons and packhorses.

The coaches were numbered, although I can only find one
notice of it : 'So that, rather than to stand a Vapulation,
one of them took Notice of his Number ;'[1] and the coachmen
were noted for their incivility. Of course they did not come
from a very high class, and the habits and language of the
lower class of that time were extremely coarse. 'We discharged our Grumbling Coachman, who Mutter'd heavily,
according to their old Custome, for t'other Sixpence ; till at
last moving us a little beyond our Patience, we gave an
Angry Positive Denial to his Unreasonable Importunities ;
for we found, like the rest of his Fraternity, he had taken
up the Miserly Immoral rule, viz. *Never to be Satisfied.'*

[1] *London Spy.*

Gay gently hints at their incivility :—

> If Wheels bar up the Road, where Streets are Crost,
> With gentle Words the Coachman's Ear accost :
> He ne'er the Threat, or harsh Command obeys,
> But with Contempt the spatter'd Shoe surveys.

And, according to him, they were not only surly but pug-
nacious.

> Now Oaths grow loud, with Coaches, Coaches jar,
> And the smart Blow provokes the sturdy War ;
> From the high Box they whirl the Thong around,
> And with the twining Lash their Shins resound :
> Their Rage ferments, more dang'rous Wounds they try,
> And the Blood gushes down their painful Eye.
> And now on Foot the frowning Warriors light,
> And with their pond'rous Fists renew the Fight ;
> Blow answers Blow, their Cheeks are 'smeared with Blood
> 'Till down they fall, and grappling, roll in Mud.

STATE COACH.

STATE COACH.

State coaches were very handsome, being elaborately
painted, carved, and gilt, a fine coach and many servants
being indispensable to a person of rank.

But even in that age of luxuriously appointed equipages
everyone was astonished at the magnificence of that of the

Venetian ambassador. Luttrell notes it on May 20, 1707 : 'Yesterday the Venetian ambassadors made their publick entry thro' this citty to Somerset House in great state and splendour, their Coach of State embroidered with gold, and the richest that ever was seen in England : they had two with 8 horses, and eight with 6 horses, trimm'd very fine with ribbons, 48 footmen in blew velvet cover'd with gold lace, 24 gentlemen and pages on horseback, with feathers in their hats.' And the novelty does not seem to have worn off, for, four years afterwards, Swift writes to Stella : ' This evening I saw the Venetian Ambassador coming from his first public audience. His coach is the most monstrous, huge, fine, rich, gilt thing that ever I saw.' He also writes her, Feb. 6, 1712 : 'Nothing has made so great a noise as one Kelson's Chariot, that cost nine hundred and thirty Pounds, the finest was ever seen. The rabble huzzaed him as much as they did Prince Eugene.'

Anybody with any pretension to wealth and fashion drove six horses, as says Mrs. Plotwell[1] : ' I must have Six Horses in my Coach, four are fit for those that have a Charge of Children, you and I shall never have any ;' and *Lucinda* tells Sir *Toby Doubtful*[2] : 'You'll at least keep Six Horses Sir . *Toby*, for I wou'd not make a Tour in High Park with less for the World ; for me thinks a pair looks like a Hackney.' The coachman, however, did not drive all six, one of the leaders being always ridden by a postilion. These carriage horses were heavy, long-tailed Flemish ones, and naturally went at a sedate and sober trot.

It was not everyone that could afford six, or even four, horses, so there were lighter vehicles, as the chariot, the calash, and the chaize or chaise. The latter was adapted for one or two horses, and sometimes was highly ornamented. ' A very fine CHAIZE, very well Carved, gilded and painted, and lined with blue Velvet, and a very good HORSE for it, are to be sold together, or apart &c.—The Horse is also a very good HORSE for the Saddle.'

' A very fine pair of young Stone Horses, and a very neat Chaize, well Carved, gilt and painted, and lined with Scarlet,

[1] *The Beau's Duel*, Mrs. Centlivre. [2] *Love's Contrivance*, Mrs. Centlivre.

and but little the worse for useing to be sold.' 'A Curious 4 Wheel Shaze, Crane Neck'd, little the worse for wearing, it is to be used with one or 2 Horses, and there is a fine Harness for one Horse, and a Reputable Sumpture Laopard Covering.'

The ordinary chaises, however, were much plainer, and they were built strongly, to stand the strain of bad pavements and roads ; but it is probable that very few were put to such a severe test as the following : 'At the Greyhound Inn in West Smithfield is to be sold a Two Wheel Chaise, with a Pair of Horses well match'd : It has run over a Bank and a Ditch 5 Foot High ; and likewise through a deep Pit within the Ring at Hide Park, in the presence of several Persons of Quality ; which are very satisfied it cannot be overturn'd with fair Driving. It is to be Lett for 7s. 6d. a Day, with some Abatement for a longer Time.'

There should be a history attaching to the following advertisement : 'Whereas, upon the 10th of Octob. last, a Gentleman brought a Calash and one Horse, to the Duke of Grafton's Head at Hide Park Corner, and on the 20th of the same Month fetched away the Horse, but left the Calash as a pawn for what was due for the same. If the Owner will come and pay what is due, he may have his Calash again, else it will be appraised and sold in 10 days time.' The innkeeper had waited six months before he advertised.

Here is another curious advertisement connected with coaches. 'Lost the 26th of February, about 9 a Clock at Night, between the Angel and Crown Tavern in Threadneedle Street, and the end of Bucklers Berry, the side Door of a Chariot, Painted Coffee Colour, with a Round Cypher in the Pannel, Lin'd with White Cloath embos'd with Red, having a Glass in one Frame, and White Canvas in another, with Red Strings to both Frames. Whosoever hath taken it up are desir'd to bring it to Mr. Jacob's a Coachmaker at the corner of St. Mary Ax near London Wall, where they shall receive 30s. Reward if all be brought with it ; or if offer'd to be Pawn'd or Sold, desire it may be stop'd and notice given, or if already Pawn'd or Sold, their money again.'

In very many advertisements of the sale of second-hand carriages, it is mentioned that the glasses are complete. One would imagine from this that glass was dear, but it was not particularly so. 'These are to give notice to all Persons that have occasions for Coach Glasses, or Glasses for Sash Windows, that they may be furnished with all sorts, at half the prises they were formerly sold for.' And it goes on to say that 12 inches square was 2s. 6d., and increased up to 22 inches, nearly at the rate of 6d. per inch, or 8s. 6d. ; 23 inches was 10s. 6d., and so on at about 2s. 6d. per inch to 28 inches, which was 20s., until it culminated at 36 inches square for £2 10s. If this, really, was half the previous cost, and if we reckon the difference in the value of money then and now perhaps some economical people would think twice before having a broken glass repaired.

There were also a 'Chasse marée Coach,' and a 'Curtin Coach for Six People.'

They used to take nice little drives, too, in these clumsy old carriages—but they took their time over the journey. Thoresby's 'kind friend Mr. Boulter, brought his chariot from Chelsea, purposely to carry him to see Hampton Court.' They started about eleven, and, 'having passed through the City, we passed the Gravel Pits,¹ and had a clear air (whither the Consumptive are sent by the physicians) and delicate pleasant Country to Acton and Brentford ; the Duke of Somerset's Seat at Sion House looked most charmingly, and was the first time I had observed the lime trees in the avenues cut in a pyramidal form, even to a great distance from the palace, which looked very Noble ; thence through Thistleworth and Twitnam, a very pleasant road.' After their visit to Hampton, they stopped for the night at Richmond Wells, returning next day *viâ* Kew, Mortlake, Putney, and Wandsworth.

His friend Boulter, on another occasion, 'took me in his Coach to Hampstead, where we dined with his mother ; and after viewing that pleasant town, and taking a view of the Country from the Hill beyond it, we took a tour to Highgate, Mussel Hill and other Country villages, and a pleasant Country, and returned by Islington and Newington home again.'

¹ At Kensington.

There was a mechanical curiosity which appeared in 1711, and of which the following is an advertisement. 'An Invention of a wonderful Chariot, in which Persons may travel several Miles an Hour, without the assistance of Horses, and Measure the Miles as they go ; it turns or goes back ; having the Praise of all Persons of Quality, and ingenious Men that have seen it. Note that it is convenient for any Gentleman that is incapable of walking thro' lameness, to ride about his Park or Garden, without damaging his Tarris-Walks or Grass-Plats. The Invention is so highly approv'd that there is one already bespoke by a Person of Quality, which is to go on four Wheels, and swing in the Nature of a large Coach ; which according to a modest Computation, will travel at the Rate of 7 or 8 Miles an Hour. If any Person of Quality is desirous to use them with Horses, they may either travel as far again in a Day as they can with another Coach, or can go as far with a Pair of Horses, as the Coaches hitherto in Use can with 6. Note that such as are bespoke for Parks or Gardens only, will come very reasonable, others at proportionable Prices.'

It was the fashion to use a mourning coach all the time mourning was worn, and this rendered it incumbent upon people to possess such a vehicle : consequently they were frequently advertised for sale—'At Mr. Harrison's, Coach Maker, in the Broadway, Westminster, is a Mourning Coach and Harness, never used, with a whole Fore Glass, and two Door Glasses, and all other Materials (the Person being deceased) ; also a Mourning Chariot, being little used, with all Materials likewise, and a Leather Body Coach, being very fashionable with a Coafoay Lining and 4 Glasses, and several sorts of Shazesses, at very reasonable Rates.'

The reins were not of leather, but of worsted, and sometimes of gay colours. Pepys, on that memorable May Day in 1669 when he started his pretty gilt coach, and had the horses' manes and tails tied with red ribbons, had 'green reins, that people did mightily look upon us.' French harness seems to have been most fashionable, although there is 'a pair of fine new Rumpee Town Harness' advertised ; and hammer-cloths were used on the coach-boxes. A singular industry sprang up—that of stealing these hammer-cloths. 'Lost off a Gentleman's Coach Box a Crimson Coffoy Hammer Cloth, with 2 yellow Laces about it.' 'Lost off a Gentleman's Coach Box, a Blue Hammer Cloth, trimm'd with a Gold colour'd Lace that is almost turn'd yellow.' 'Lost a Red Shag Hammock Cloth, with white Silk Lace round it, embroider'd with white and blue, and 3 Bulls Heads and a Squirrel for the Coat of Arms.'

The sedan chair was a conveyance that was getting into vogue in Anne's reign. Taking its name from the town of Sedan in France, it was first used in England in 1581, and in London in 1623.

In 1711 an Act (9 Anne, c. 23) was passed licensing 200

A SEDAN CHAIR.

public sedan chairs at ten shillings each yearly, and their fare was settled at 1*s.* per mile. Next year, another Act (10 Anne, c. 19) was passed, licensing 100 more, but keeping the fares unaltered.

Like coaches, their adornment was indicative of the wealth and position of their owners—although, perhaps, none ever came up to Anne's royal present.[1] 'The Queen has made a present of a chair value £8000 to the King of Prussia, which is ordered for Berlin.' Still they were highly orna-mental, as the following, which was the property of Sir Joseph Williamson, deceased, will show. 'A Cedan (or

---

[1] *Luttrell's Diary*, Dec. 10, 1709.

Chair) lin'd with Crimson Velvet, trim'd with Gold and Silver, and a new Mourning Chair &c.'

The prefix 'Sedan' was seldom used, and these conveyances were generally termed 'Chairs.' That they were considered somewhat of a novelty in Anne's reign is evidenced by that line of Gay's, 'Nor late invented Chairs perplex'd the way,' and also by the fact that then the public chairs were first licensed, and the number, a very small one, regulated.

They were not particularly comfortable, as the Marquis of Hazard describes [1] : 'Hey, let my three Footmen wait with my Chair there—the Rascals have come such a high trot—they've jolted me worse than a Hackney Coach—and I am in as much disorder as if I had not been drest to day.' And they were sometimes dangerous too.

> Or, box'd within the Chair, contemn the Street,
> And trust their Safety to another's Feet.
>
> .   .   .   .
>
> The drunken Chairman in the Kennel Spurns,
> The Glasses shatters, and his Charge o'erturns.

Gay evidently did not like either chairs or chairmen, for he warns his reader thus :—

> Let not the Chairman with assuming Stride,
> Press near the Wall, and rudely thrust thy Side :
> The Laws have set him Bounds ; his servile Feet
> Should ne'er encroach where Posts defend the Street.
> Yet who the Footman's Arrogance can quell,
> Whose Flambeau gilds the Sashes of Pell Mell?
> When in long Rank a Train of Torches flame,
> To light the Midnight Visits of the Dame?
> Others, perhaps, by happier Guidance led,
> May where the Chairman rests, with Safety tread ;
> When e'er I pass, their Poles, unseen below,
> Make my Knee tremble with the jarring Blow.

[1] *The Gamester.*

CHAPTER XXXVII.

THE MOHOCKS.

Scourers, etc.—Bully Dawson—Two outbreaks—That in 1712—Hawkubites—Exploits of the Mohocks—Sir Roger de Coverley—Swift's fear
of them—Emperor of the Mohocks—Gog and Magog—The Queen's
proclamation—Decline of the scare—Constables and watchmen.

IN every age and country young blood is hot blood, and
in this reign it was particularly so. The wild blood of the
Cavaliers still danced in the veins of the beaus in Anne's
time, and nightly frolics and broils were of frequent occurrence. They had their predecessors in this work—as Sir
Tope says in Shadwell's play of ' The Scowrers ' : ' Puh, this is
nothing, why I knew the *Hectors*, and before them the *Muns*
and the Titire Tus, they were brave fellows indeed ; in those
days a man could not go from the *Rose Tavern* to the *Piazza*
once, but he must venture his life twice.' And Whackum, in
the same play, describes the doings of the fraternity of
Scourers. ' Then how we Scour'd the Market People, over-
threw the Butter Women, defeated the Pippin Merchants,
wip'd out the Milk Scores, pull'd off the Door Knockers,
dawb'd the Gilt Signs.'

In Anne's reign these roysterers were called Mohocks—
why, I know not, except that it was then a sort of generic
term for North American Indians. In a later age this furore
was termed Tom and Jerryism ; but then it had an intelligible
origin, from Pierce Egan's ' Life in London, or the Day and
Night Scenes of Jerry Hawthorn Esq. and his elegant Friend
Corinthian Tom &c.' It still exists, although it has no
special name.

Brown, in his ' Letters from the Dead to the Living,' says

N 2

in that 'From Bully Dawson [1] to Bully W . . . . n': 'Therefore if ever you intend to be my Rival in Glory, you must
fight a Bailiff once a Day, stand Kick and Cuff once a Week,
Challenge some Coward or other once a Month, Bilk your
Lodgings once a quarter, and Cheat a Taylor once a year,
crow over every Coxcomb you meet with, and be sure you
kick every jilt you bully into submission and a compliance
of treating you ; never till then will the fame of W . . . . n
ring like *Dawson's* in every Coffee House, or be the merry
subject of every Tavern Tittle Tattle.'

There seem to have been two special outbreaks of
Mohocks—one in 1709, and the other in 1712. Of the first
Steele says [2] : 'When I was a middle-aged Man, there were
many societies of *Ambitious* young men in England, who,
in their pursuits after same, were every night employed in
roasting Porters, smoking Coblers, knocking down Watchmen, overturning Constables, breaking Windows, blackening
Sign Posts, and the like immortal enterprizes, that dispersed
their Reputation throughout the whole Kingdom.   One could
hardly find a knocker at a door in a whole street after a
midnight expedition of these *Beaux Esprits*.   I was lately
very much surprised by an account of my Maid, who entered
my bed chamber this morning in a very great fright, and told
me, she was afraid my parlour was haunted ; for that she had
found several panes of my Windows broken, and the floor
strewed with half-pence.   I have not yet a full light into this
new way, but am apt to think, that it is a generous piece of
wit, that some of my Contemporaries make use of, to break
windows, and leave money to pay for them.'

Gay notices the Mohocks, and their window-breaking,
thus :—

> Now is the Time that Rakes their Revells keep ;
> Kindlers of Riot, Enemies of Sleep.
> His scatter'd Pence the flying *Nicker* flings,
> And with the Copper Show'r the Casement rings.

---

[1] Bully Dawson is supposed to be the original of Captain Hackum in Shadwell's play of ' The Squire of Alsatia,' and is mentioned by Steele in No. 2 of
the *Spectator*, when he speaks of Sir Roger de Coverley having ' kick'd Bully
Dawson in a publick Coffee House for calling him Youngster.'

[2] *Tatler*, 77.

Who has not heard the *Scowrer's* Midnight Fame?
Who has not trembled at the *Mohock's* Name?
Was there a Watchman took his hourly Rounds,
Safe from their Blows, or new invented Wounds?
I pass their desp'rate Deeds, and Mischiefs done,
Where from *Snow Hill* black Steepy Torrents run;
How Matrons, hoop'd within the Hogshead's Womb,
Were tumbled furious thence, the rolling Tomb
O'er the Stones thunders, bounds from Side to Side
So *Regulus* to save his Country dy'd.

The greatest scare, however, was in March 1712, and that exercised the popular mind as much as the garotters of modern times. People, of course, were more frightened than hurt, and there is very little doubt but that this outbreak was much exaggerated. Still, we can only take the contemporary accounts, and this is one of them.

[1] 'THE TOWN RAKES, or the Frolicks of the *Mohocks* or *Hawkubites*. With an Account of their Frolicks last night, and at several other Times: shewing how they slit the Noses of several Men and Women, and wounded others; Several of which were taken up last Night by the Guards, and committed to several Prisons, the Guards being drawn out to disperse them.

'There are a certain set of Persons, amongst whom there are some of too great a Character, to be nam'd in these barbarous and ridiculous Encounters, did they not expose themselves by such mean and vulgar Exploits.

'These Barbarities have been carry'd on by a Gang of 'em for a considerable time, and many innocent Persons have receiv'd great Injury from them, who call themselves *Hawkubites*; and their mischievous Invention of the Word is that they take people betwixt *Hawk* and *Buzzard*, that is betwixt two of them, and making them turn from one to the other, abuse them with Blows and other Scoffings; and, if they pretend to speak for themselves, they then Slit their Noses, or cut them down the Back.

'The Watch in most of the Out-parts of the town stand in awe of them, because they always come in a body, and are

[1] Brit. Mus. $\frac{816 \text{ m. } 19}{74.}$

too strong for them, and when any Watchman presumes to demand where they are going, they generally misuse them.

'Last Night they had a general Rendezvouz, and were bent upon Mischief; their way is to meet People in the Streets and Stop them, and begin to Banter them, and if they make any Answer, they lay on them with Sticks, and toss them from one to another in a very rude manner.

'They attacked the Watch in *Devereux Court* and *Essex Street*, made them scower; they also slit two Persons' Noses, and cut a Woman in the Arm with a penknife that she is lam'd. They likewise rowled a Woman in a Tub down *Snow Hill*, that was going to Market, set other Women on their Heads, misusing them in a barbarous manner.

'They have short Clubs or Batts that have Lead at the End, which will overset a Coach, or turn over a Chair, and Tucks [1] in their Canes ready for Mischief.

'One of these Persons suppos'd to be of the Gang, did formerly slit a Drawer's Nose at *Greenwich*, and has committed many such Frolicks since. They were so outrageous last Night, that the Guards at *White Hall* was alarm'd, and a Detachment order'd to Patrole; and 'tis said, the Train Bands will be order'd to do Duty for the future, to prevent these Disorders; several of them were taken up last Night, and put into the Round Houses till order is taken what to do with them.'

The Spectator, whose living was by making the most of any popular subject of the hour, was specially exercised over the Mohocks. 'An outrageous Ambition of doing all possible hurt to their Fellow-Creatures, is the great Cement of their Assembly and the only Qualification required in the Members. In order to exert this Principle in its full Strength and Perfection, they take Care to drink themselves to a pitch that is beyond the Possibility of attending to any Motives of Reason and Humanity; then make a general Sally, and attack all that are so unfortunate as to walk the Streets through which they patrole. Some are knock'd down, others stabb'd, others cut and carbonado'd. To put the Watch to a total Rout, and mortify some of those inoffensive Militia, is reckon'd a Coup

---

[1] A tuck was a short sword.

d'éclat. The particular Talents by which these *Misanthropes* are distinguished from one another, consist in the various kinds of Barbarities which they execute upon their Prisoners. Some are celebrated for a happy Dexterity in tipping the Lion upon them ; which is perform'd by squeezing the Nose flat to the Face, and boring out the Eyes with their Fingers ; Others are called the Dancing Masters, and teach their Scholars to cut Capers by running Swords thro' their Legs ; a new Invention, whether originally *French* I cannot tell ; A third sort are the Tumblers, whose office it is to set Women on their Heads, and commit certain Indecencies or rather Barbarities on the Limbs which they expose.' [1]

Sir Roger de Coverley was even somewhat nervous about them when he went to the play—and 'asked me, in the next place, whether there would not be some danger in coming home late, in case the Mohocks should be Abroad ' ; and we learn how, finally, the party went to the theatre. 'The Captain, who did not fail to meet me there at the appointed Hour, bid Sir Roger fear nothing, for that he had put on the same Sword which he made use of at the Battle of *Steenkirk*. Sir Roger's Servants, and among the rest my old Friend, the Butler, had, I found, provided themselves with good Oaken Plants, to attend their Master upon this occasion.'

Swift was in mortal fear of them, and, in his ' History of the Four Last Years of Queen Anne,' declares it was part of a deliberate plan to raise riot, during which Harley might have been assassinated—and accuses Prince Eugene of setting it afloat. He writes Stella—in Letter 43—fragmentary jottings of his feelings during this period of terror. 'Did I tell you of a race of Rakes, called the Mohocks, that play the devil about this town every night, slit peoples noses, and bid them, &c. . . . Young Davenant was telling us at Court how he was set upon by the Mohocks, and how they ran his chair through with a Sword. It is not safe being in the streets at Night for them. The Bishop of Salisbury's son is said to be of the gang. They are all Whigs ; and a great lady sent to me, to speak to her father and to lord treasurer, to have a care of them, and to be careful likewise of myself ;

[1] *Spectator*, 324.

for she heard they had malicious intentions against the Ministers and their friends. . . . I walked in the Park this evening, and came home early to avoid the Mohocks. . . . Here is the devil and all to do with these Mohocks. Grub Street papers about them fly like lightning, and a list printed of near eighty put into several prisons, and all a lie ; and I almost begin to think there is no truth, or very little, in the whole Story. He that abused Davenant was a Drunken gentleman ; none of that gang. My man tells me, that one of the lodgers heard in a Coffee House, publicly, that one design of the Mohocks was upon me, if they Could Catch me ; and though I believe nothing of it, I forbear walking late, and they have put me to the Charge of some shillings already. . . . I came home in a Chair for fear of the Mohocks. . . . I came afoot but had my Man with me. Lord treasurer advised me not to go in a Chair, because the Mohocks insult Chairs more than they do those on foot. They think there is some mischievous design in those villains. Several of them, lord-treasurer told me, are actually taken up. I heard at dinner, that one of them was killed last night. . . . Lord Winchelsea told me to day at Court, that two of the Mohocks caught a maid of old Lady Winchelsea's at the door of their house in the Park, with a candle, and had just lighted out somebody. They Cut all her face, and beat her without any provocation. . . . I staid till past twelve, and could not get a Coach, and was alone, and was afraid enough of the Mohocks.'

This dreaded association was supposed to be under the orders of a chief or ' Emperor,' who wore a crescent on his forehead, and is so described both in the *Spectator* and in Gay's very amusing play of ' The Mohocks,' which is a delicious burlesque on the scare. Here is a sample of it. Some of the watch are talking about this dreaded band, and their doings. Says one : ' I met about five or six and thirty of these *Mohocks* —by the same token 'twas a very windy Morning—they all had Swords as broad as Butcher's Cleavers, and hack'd and hew'd down all before them—I saw—as I am a Man of credit, in the Neighbourhood—all the Ground covered with Noses— as thick as 'tis with Hail Stones after a Storm.' Says another :

'That is nothing to what I have seen—I saw them hook a
Man as cleverly as a Fisher Man would a great Fish—and
play him up and down from *Charing Cross* to *Temple Bar*—
they cut off his Ears, and eat them up, and then gave him a
swinging slash in the Arm—told him bleeding was good for
a fright, and so turned him loose.' A third relates his experience : ' Poh! that's nothing at all—I saw them cut off a
Fellow's Legs, and, if the poor Man had not run hard for it,
they had Cut off his Head into the bargain.' And the fourth
tells how ' Poor *John Mopstaff's* Wife was like to Come to
damage by them—for they took her up by the Heels, and
turn'd her quite inside out—the poor Woman, they say, will
ne'er be good for anything More.'

Gay also wrote another skit on these awful beings. ' An
ARGUMENT proving from History, Reason, and Scripture,
that the present *Mohocks* and *Hawkubites* are the GOG and
MAGOG mentioned in the Revelations, and therefore, That
this vain and Transitory World will shortly be brought to its
final Dissolution.' It is not particularly amusing, being a
parody on scriptural prophecy, and it winds up with the
following :—

> From Mohocks and from Hawkubites
>   Good Lord deliver me,
> Who wander through the Streets by Night
>   Committing Cruelty.
>
> They slash our Sons with Bloody knives,
>   And on our Daughters fall ;
> And if they ravish not our Wives,
>   We have good Luck withal.
>
> Coaches and Chairs they overturn,
>   Nay Carts most easily ;
> Therefore from GOG and eke MAGOG
>   Good Lord, deliver me.

Public feeling on the matter, however, was so strong, that
on March 17, 1712, the Queen issued a Royal Proclamation.
' Anne, R. The Queen's Most Excellent Majesty being
watchful for the Publick Good of Her Loving Subjects, and
taking notice of the great and unusual Riots and Barbarities
which have lately been committed in the Night time, in the

open Streets, in several parts of the Cities of *London* and *Westminster*, and Parts adjacent, by numbers of Evil dispos'd Persons, who have combined together to disturb the Publick Peace, and in an inhuman manner, without any Provocation, have Assaulted and Wounded many of her Majesty's good Subjects, and have had the Boldness to insult the Constables and Watchmen, in the Execution of their Office, to the great Terror of Her Majesty's said Subjects, and in Contempt and Defiance of the Laws of this Realm, to the Dishonour of Her Majesty's Government, and the Displeasure of Almighty God &c. &c. &c. . . . . Her Majesty doth hereby promise and declare, That whosoever shall before the First Day of *May* now next ensuing, discover to any of Her Majesty's Justices of Peace, any Person who, since the First Day of *February* last past, hath, without any Provocation, Wounded, Stabb'd or Maim'd, or who shall before the said First Day of *May*, without any Provocation, Wound, Stab, or Maim, any of Her Majesty's Subjects within the said Cities of *London* and *Westminster*, and Parts adjacent, so as such Offender be brought to Justice, shall have and receive the Reward of One Hundred Pounds, &c.'

Can the following advertisement have any possible relation to the midnight orgies of the Mohocks ? *Post Boy*, Dec. 18/20, 1712 : 'Lately found, several Pair of Stockings, some Night Caps, and several Pair of Shoocs, with two Brazill Rolling Pins, and some Brass Knockers of Doors.'

Brass knockers evidently were attractive, for in 1714 we find a genius advertising ' There is to be Sold at the Sign of the Plow on Fleet Ditch, New Fashion Brass Knockers of all Sizes that cannot be broke off so easily as any that have yet been made. However, this is to Satisfy all Gentlemen and others that do buy any of them, that if any should be broke off, upon their bringing me a Piece of that which I sold, I will give them gratis one as good and as large as they bought.'

The fright soon passed off, for we find Budgell[1] writing on April 8, 1712, that some began to doubt ' whether indeed there were ever any such Society of Men. The Terror which

---

[1] *Spectator*, 347.

spread itself over the whole Nation some Years since, on account of the *Irish*, is still fresh in most Peoples Memories, tho' it afterwards appeared there was not the least Ground for that general Consternation. The late Panick Fear was, in the Opinion of many deep and penetrating Persons, of the same Nature.' But there is no doubt there was a substratum of reality, mixed with a great deal of exaggeration.

The civil power was utterly unable to cope with riots of

THE WATCH.

this description. What were the watchmen like? From the time of Dogberry to the institution of the present police they have ever been a laughing-stock. Old, infirm men, badly paid, incumbered with a long staff and a lantern, perambulated the streets under the authority of a constable. Who cared for them? Certainly not a Mohock. Nay, their very honesty was called in question. 'Two of them like honest fellows, handed me home to my Chambers, without so much as stealing my Hat or picking my pockets which was a Wonder.'

Ward gives an amusing little sketch of their venality.

'Civil and Sober Persons, said he, how do I know that, Mr. *Prattle Box*? You may be Drunk for ought I know, and only feign yourselves Sober before my presence to escape the penalty of the Act.

'My Friend puts his Hand in his Pocket, plucks out a Shilling, Indeed, Mr. Constable, says he, we tell you nothing but

A CONSTABLE.

the Naked Truth. There is something for your Watch to Drink ; We know it is a late Hour, but hope you will detain us no longer.

'With that Mr. *Surly Cuff* directs himself to his right hand Janizary, Hem, hah, Aminidab, I believe they are Civil Gentlemen ; Ay, ay, said he, Master, you need not question it ; they don't look as if they had Fire balls about 'em. Well, Gentlemen, you may pass ; but Pray go civilly home. Here, Colly, light the Gentlemen down the Hill, they may chance to Stumble in the Dark, and break their Shins against the Monument.'

What sings Gay of watchmen ?

Yet there are Watchmen, who with friendly Light,
Will teach thy reeling Steps to tread aright ;
For *Sixpence* will support thy helpless Arm,
And Home conduct thee, safe from nightly Harm ;
But if they shake their Lanthorns, from afar,
To call their Breth'ren to confed'rate War,
When Rakes resist their Pow'r ; if hapless you
Should chance to wander with the Scow'ring Crew ;
Though Fortune yield thee Captive, ne'er despair,
But seek the Constable's consid'rate Ear ;
He will reverse the Watchman's harsh Decree,
Mov'd by the Rhetrick of a Silver Fee.
Thus, would you gain some fav'rite Courtier's Word ;
Fee not the petty Clarks, but bribe my Lord.

CHAPTER XXXVIII.

DUELLING.

Its prevalence—Bullying—Fielding's duels—Favourite localities—Its illegality—Col. Thornhill and Sir Cholmley Dering : their quarrel and duel—Duke of Hamilton and Lord Mohun—Story of their duel.

THE senseless custom of duelling was much in vogue in this reign, although perhaps it had not reached to the height it afterwards did. The custom of wearing swords rendered the arbitrament of every dispute liable to be settled by those weapons. A few hasty words and the sword was whipped out, and probably one or other of the combatants had reason to regret his loss of temper. Indeed, to such a pitch had it come, that the Code of Old John Selden, 'The duels or single combat,' printed in 1610, was reprinted in 1711 for the benefit of Queen Anne's subjects, as was also Sir William Hope's 'New Method of Fencing &c.' Fencing-masters naturally advertised. 'Peter Besson a Waldense, born in Piedmont, teaches the use of the Italian Spadroon ; and does invite all Gentlemen that are curious in the Sword to see him perform his Exercises at St. Amant's Coffee House by Charing Cross, Tuesdays, Thursdays, and Saturdays, from 10 of the Clock in the Morning till 1. He hath been in most Princes Courts of Europe, from whom he hath ample Certificates of his great Dexterity and Ability this Way, and in a very short time can make Gentlemen compleat Masters of this sort of Sword.' There were also the numerous fencing-masters who performed at Hockley in the Hole, who were always available as teachers.

Steele, who had himself fought his man and run him through the body, did all he could to discountenance the practice ; as he says in *Tatler* 25 : 'I shall talk very freely on a Custom which all men wish exploded, though no man has courage enough to resist it.' And not only does he write against it in that number, but also in Nos. 26, 28, 29, 38, and 39.

As a specimen of the hectoring and bullying then in vogue among a certain class, let us take the following extract from Ward [1]: 'As we came down *Ludgate Hill*, a couple of *Town Bullies* (as I suppose from their Behaviour) met each other, Damn ye, Sir, says one, why did you not meet me Yesterday Morning according to Appointment? Damn you, Sir, for a Cowardly Pimp, reply'd the other, I was there and waited till I was Wet to the Skin, and you never came at me.

A DUEL.

You lie like a Villain, says t'other, I was there, and stay'd the time of a Gentleman; and draw now, and give me Satisfaction like a Man of Honour, or I'll Cut your Ears off. You see, says the Valiant Adversary, I have not my Fighting Sword on, and hope you are a Man of more Honour than to take Advantage of a Gentleman. Then go home and fetch it, says *Don Furioso*, like a man of Justice, and meet me within an Hour in the *King's Bench Walks* in the *Temple*, or the next time I see you, by *Jove's Thunderbolts*, I will Pink as many Eylet holes in your Skin, as you have Button holes in your Coat; and therefore have a Care how you Trespass

[1] *London Spy.*

upon my Patience. Upon the Reputation of a Gentleman, I will Punctually meet you at your Time, and Place ; reply'd the other, and so they Parted.'

Very early in the reign we hear of duels. The *Flying Post*, Dec. 15/17, 1702, tells us of two. ' On Monday last Col. Fielding, commonly called Handsom Fielding, was dangerously wounded in a Quarrel with one Mr. Gudgeon, a Gentleman, at the Theatre Royal, Drury Lane. . . . On Tuesday night last, one Mr. Cusaick, an Irish Gentleman, and Capt Fullwood, quarrelled at the New Theatre in Lincoln's Inn Fields, and afterwards fought ; Captain Fullwood fell on the Spot, and Mr. Cusaick was dangerously wounded.'

In the same paper for Dec. 22/24, 1702, we read : ' Mr. Fullwood, who fought with Mr. Cusaick last Week in Lincoln's Inn Fields, was very decently buried on Sunday last in the Evening at St. Clement's Danes in the Strand. His Corps was brought from the Hay Market in a Hearse, attended by many Gentlemen of Note, and some of Quality ; they had all Favours and Gloves . . . . Two Gentlemen of the Guards fought a Duel in the Meuse ; one was kill'd upon the Spot, and the other dangerously wounded.'

We find ' handsom Fielding ' at it again in 1704. ' On Friday last my Lord de la Ware, and Mr. Fielding one of Her Majesty's Equerries, fought a Duel at Windsor : His Lordship was dangerously wounded.' [1]

There were pet places for these combats, as there were also in the later days of duelling with pistols, when Wimbledon Common, Wormwood Scrubs, and Chalk Farm were fashionable localities. In Anne's time the favourite spots were Lincoln's Inn Fields, or the fields at the back of Montague and Southampton Houses, St. James's Park, and Barn Elms between Putney and Mortlake. ' 29 May 1705. Saturday last, Mr. Kennet, a young Kentish gentleman of the Temple, was killed in a duel behind Montague House, supposed by one Mr. Medlicot, who made his escape.' [2] ' 23 June 1705. A duel was this week fought in St. James s

---

[1] *Daily Courant*, Sept. 18, 1704. [2] *Luttrell's Diary.*

Park between Foot Onslow Esq, and Dr Shadwell : the latter
wounded and disarmed.'

It was illegal to fight duels, but the law was seldom acted
on.   Still, it was put in force when appealed to.   '25 Feb
1703.   Upon Notice given, that Sir Stafford Fairborn and
admiral Churchill designed to fight a Duel, they were both
Confined, to prevent the same.'

Whilst on this subject, notice of two famous duels fought
in this reign must not be omitted—those between Col. Thornhill and Sir Cholmley Dering, and between the Duke of
Hamilton and Lord Mohun ; because they throw so much
light on the then procedure in these matters.

Swift[1] notices the former thus : 'Dr. Freind came this
morning to visit Atterbury's lady and children as physician,
and persuaded me to go with him to town in his Chariot.
He told me he had been an hour before with Sir Cholmley
Dering, Charles Dering's nephew, and head of that family in
Kent, for which he is Knight of the Shire.   He said he left
him dying of a pistol Shot quite through the body, by one
Mr. Thornhill.   They fought at sword and pistol this morning in Tuttle Fields ; their pistols so near, that the muzzles
touched.   Thornhill discharged first, and Dering having
received the shot, discharged his pistol as he was falling, so it
went into the Air.'

This duel created an immense sensation at the time, and
several accounts of the trial, etc., are preserved.   From one of
these[2] we will take our facts, premising that the trial took
place at the Old Bailey, May 18, 1711.   'The first Evidences
were such as related to the quarrel, begun at the *Toy* at
Hampton Court April 27th past, who depos'd that at an
Assembly of about Eighteen Gentlemen met there at that
Time, a Difference happen'd between the Deceas'd and the
Prisoner, upon their struggling and contending with each
other, the Wainscoat of the Room broke in, and *Mr. Thornhill*
falling down, had some Teeth struck out by Sir *Cholmley
Deering's* stamping upon him ; that upon this, the Company

[1] *Journal to Stella*, May 9, 1711.   [2] Brit. Mus. $\frac{E.\ 1992}{4.}$

immediately interpos'd to prevent further Mischief; and Sir *Cholmley* being made sensible of his fault, declar'd himself ready to ask Mr. *Thornhill's* Pardon which he did not think sufficient for the Injury done him in beating out his Teeth ; but upon his requiring further Satisfaction, Sir *Cholmley* reply'd, He did not know where to find him, which Mr. *Thornhill* said 'twas a Lie ; soon after this the company broke up, and 'twas observ'd that those Two Gentlemen went home in different Coaches.

'It appeared that after this the Deceas'd made overtures of Accommodation.'

At the trial the doctors deposed that Thornhill's injuries were very severe, that he had had fever, and might have died, had he not had an excellent constitution. As soon as he recovered a little, he sent his antagonist the following challenge.

'May the 8th, 1711.

' Sir, I shall be able to go Abroad to Morrow Morning, and desire you would give me a Meeting with your Sword and Pistols, which I insist on ; the Worthy Gentleman my Friend, who brings this, will concert with you for the Time and Place. I think *Tuttle Fields* will do well, *Hide Park* will not, this Time of the Year being full of Company.

' I am, Your Humble Servant,

' *Richard Thornhill.*'

His servant deposed that on the morning of the 9th of May ' Sir *Cholmley* came into his Master's dining Room with a Brace of Pistols in his Hands ; upon which he inform'd his Master, Sir *Cholmley* was there ; who thereupon came to him, and ask'd Sir *Cholmley* if he would drink a Dish of Tea, which he refus'd, but drank a Glass of Small beer. Mr. *Thornhill* having dress'd himself, they went together in a Hackney Coach to *Tuttle Fields*. Upon their being there, the Evidence depos'd, That they Came up like Two Lions with their Pistols advanc'd, and when within Four Yards of each other, discharg'd so equally together, that it could not well be discover'd who Shot first.'

Sir Cholmley fell, and the usual scene took place ; the

quondam friend rushed forward, and regretfully wished to be of service to the dying man. A surgeon was sent for, and before his death Sir Cholmley not only freely forgave his adversary, but admitted that 'this Misfortune was my own Fault, and of my own Seeking.'

For the defence 'Several Persons of Quality and Worth declared as to Mr. *Thornhill's* Character, That they never knew him to be of a Quarrelsome Disposition ; but that on the Contrary, Sir *Cholmley Deering* was given to be unwarrantably Contentious.'

The judge summed up very clearly, but against the prisoner, pointing out to the jury the difference between

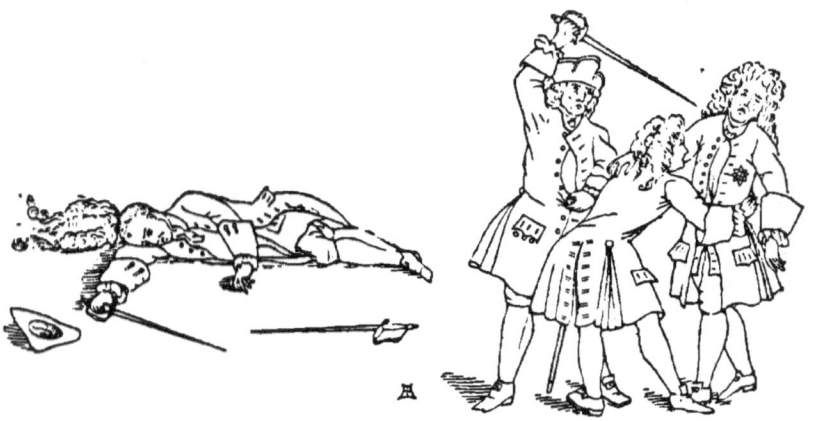

DUEL BETWEEN DUKE OF HAMILTON AND LORD MOHUN.

manslaughter and murder; but the jury brought in a verdict of manslaughter.

Thornhill did not survive his adversary long. Swift writes Stella, Aug. 21, 1711 : 'Thornhill, who killed Sir Cholmley Dering, was murdered by two men on Turnham Green last Monday Night. As they stabbed him, they bid him remember Sir Cholmley Dering. They had quarrelled at Hampton Court, and followed and stabbed him on horseback.'

His remorse at his killing Dering is commented on by Steele in *Spectator* 84, under the name of *Spinamont.*

The duel between the Duke of Hamilton and Lord Mohun has been frequently described ; and, had only the dissolute Mohun have been killed, few would have regretted its having taken place. As it was, the Duke being the leader of the Jacobite faction in Scotland, and Mohun being a violent Whig, the duel was invested with a political colouring; and the Tories, enraged at Hamilton's fall, did not scruple to call it a Whig murder, and denounce Lord Mohun's second, General Macartney, as having unfairly stabbed him; but from all the evidence [1] it is impossible to believe it.

The story of the duel is briefly this. The two noblemen were opposing parties in a lawsuit, and on Nov. 13, 1712, met in the chambers of a Master in Chancery, when the Duke remarked of a witness—'There is no truth or justice in him.' Lord Mohun replied, 'I know Mr. Whitworth; he is an honest Man, and has as much truth as your Grace.' This, fanned into flame by officious friends, was enough; and on Nov. 15, or two days afterwards, they fought, early in the morning, in Hyde Park; their seconds—Col. Hamilton and General Macartney—also fighting, or, as they expressed it, 'taking their share in the dance.' Lord Mohun fell, dead, and the Duke atop of him, mortally wounded. The seconds left off fighting, and went to the assistance of their principals; and it was then, it was averred, that Gen. Macartney treacherously stabbed the Duke.

Macartney fled; but Col. Hamilton remained, took his trial, and was only found guilty of manslaughter. He accused Macartney of the foul deed, and great was the hue and cry after him. The Duchess was naturally enraged, and offered a reward of 300*l.* for his apprehension, and the Government offered 500*l.* more, but he got off safely. When things were quieter, he returned, stood his trial at the Queen's Bench Colonel Hamilton's testimony was contradicted, and he was acquitted of the murder—but found guilty of manslaughter The punishment for this, by pleading benefit of clergy, which of course was always done, was reduced to a very minimum something amounting to the supposed burning of the hand with a barely warm or cold iron—and he was restored to his rank in the army and had a regiment given him.

[1] Brit. Mus. $\frac{515\ l.\ 2}{215.}$

CHAPTER XXXIX.

THE ARMY AND NAVY.

Sale of commissions—General practice—Its illegality—Arrears of pay—
Descriptions of officers—Army chaplains—The rank and file—Description of them—Irregularity of pay—Rations—Recruiting—
Bounty—Gaol birds—Vagrants—Desertions—Story of seditious
drummers—Train bands—The Navy: its deeds—Unpopularity of
the service—Pressing—Desertion—Rewards for capture—Pay—Description of Admiralty—Mercantile marine.

'COLONEL SOUTHWELL has sold his regiment for 5000*l.* to
Colonel Hansam of the guards;'[1] and doubtless the latter
made money by the transaction, for it seems to have been the
practice then for the colonel to sell the smaller commissions
in his regiment.   Hear what Brown says on the subject:[2]
'We observ'd there a *Colonel* and his *Agent*, upon whom a
pretty brisk Youth of about Seventeen attended at three or
four Yards distance in the Rear, and made his Honours upon
every occasion, we happen'd to place ourselves very near,
and immediately express'd himself as follows : "This young
Gentleman has a Particular Regard to your Honour, and a
desire to learn the Art of War under so experienc'd an Officer;
'tis true, he can't boast of any Antiquity of Blood or Service
in the Army, to recommend him to so considerable a Post, as
that of Ensign to your Honour.   But, Sir, he has deposited a
Hundred Guineas in the hands of Sir *Francis Child*, which,
I presume, will plead his Merit very weightily ; besides an
Acknowledgement to your humble Servant."   The Favour
was granted, and the young Beau dismiss'd to his satisfaction.'

This is not an exaggeration ; the thing was openly talked
about, and even advertised.   'This is to give Notice, That

---

[1] *Luttrell,* June 12, 1708.   [2] *A Walk round London and Westminster.*

Whosoever has a Mind to treat about the purchasing Commissions in the Army, either in old Regiments, or others, let them apply themselves to Mr. Pyne at his Coffee House under Scotland Yard Gate, near Whitehall, and they will be further inform'd about it.'

This advertisement seems to have aroused the authorities, for in the *Gazette* of Oct. 23/25, 1711, is the following official notice : ' Whereas a scandalous Advertisement has been twice published in the *Post Boy*, giving Notice, That whoever has a mind to treat about the Purchasing Commissions in the Army, either in the old Regiments or others, might apply to Mr. Pyne, at his Coffee house under Scotland Yard Gate near Whitehall, and they should be further inform'd about it ; which being directly contrary to Her Majesty's express Will and pleasure, sometime declar'd and signify'd, as well at home, as to all her Generals abroad, against the Sale of Commissions upon any account whatsoever ; it is thought fit to give this publick Notice, to prevent any abuses or Impositions that might happen therefrom ; and whoever shall discover to Her Majesty's Secretary at War, at his Office in Whitehall, the Authors of the said Advertisement, shall have due Protection and Encouragement.'

A colonel clothed his regiment too, and there must have been money made out of that : and a military conversation recorded by Brown throws much light on the manners of the army at that time. ' We had pass'd the *Horse Guards* and enter'd the oderiferous Park of *St. James's*, we found it a *High Change* on the *Parade*, Red Coats and Laced Hats spread everywhere. . . . Here is decided the Price of Commissions, which are openly bought and sold, as if a lawful Merchandize. . . . Here you may hear all this General's Miscarriages fully accounted for; that General's success magnify'd and describ'd ; that Colonel damn'd for being put over this Captain's Head ; that Agent curs'd for tricking the Regiment out of their Pay, or by raising such Contributions with the Colonel's Connivance, that Estates are now got at this end of the Town, as well as by Stock Jobbing in the City. Here honest *Pain*, and *Potter*, and divers others of that fraternity, take their mid-day's Perambulation, to Agree with

Spendthrift Officers, for advancing their Money at 30 per Cent.'

The pay of all ranks in the army was always in arrear and hard to be got at, so these agents had a fine time of it.

Lord Hardy. Were you at the Agent's?

Trim. Yes.

Lord Hardy. Well, and how?

Trim. Why, Sir, for your Arrears, you may have Eleven Shillings in the Pound; but he'll not touch your Growing Subsistence, under Three Shillings in the Pound Interest; besides which, You must let his Clerk *Jonathan Item*, Swear the Peace against you to keep you from Duelling, or insure your life, which you may do for Eight *per cent.* On these terms He'll Oblige you; which he would not do for any Body else in the Regiment, but he has a Friendship for you.

Lord Hardy. Oh, I'm his Humble Servant; But he must have his own terms, we can't Starve, nor must my Fellows want.[1]

Was an officer killed in action, his wife would be entitled to a pension—but it seems to have been somewhat problematical whether it would be available. 'One must Sneak to the Government, for a Pension of twenty Shillings a Week to Subsist half a Score Children, and hammer out the rest with Washing and Starching.'[2]

The 'Officer and Gentleman' hardly went together; the rough life of the camp told, and almost all contemporary writers agree in painting him as a swaggering, dicing bully. Farquhar's description[3] will serve for all :—

Silvia. I'm call'd Captain, Sir, by all the Coffee men, Drawers, and Groom porters in London; for I wear a Red Coat, a Sword, a Hat *bien troussé*, a Martial Twist in my Cravat, a fierce Knot in my Perriwig, a Cane upon my Button, Picquet in my Head, and Dice in my pocket.

Scale. Your Name : pray Sir.

Silvia. Capt. *Pinch* : I cock my Hat with a Pinch, I take Snuff with a Pinch, pay my women with a Pinch, In short I can do anything at a Pinch, but fight and fill my Belly.

In Bickerstaff's 'Lottery for the London Ladies,' another class of officer is spoken of. 'Young spruce *Beauish* non fighting *Officers*, often to be seen at *Man's Coffee House*, Loaded with more Gold Lace than ever was worn by a

---

[1] *The Funeral.*   [2] *Tunbridge Walks.*   [3] *The Recruiting Officer.*

thriving *Hostess* upon her *Red Petticoat*, all *Ladies* Sons of a
fine *Barbary* Shape, *Dance* admirably, *Sing* charmingly, speak
French fluently, and are the *Darlings* of their *Mothers*; have
large Pay for little Service, are kept at home by the Interest
of their Friends, to oblige the *Ladies*, and hate the thought of
going on Board Ships, because their nice Noses are unable to
endure the smell of *Tar*, or the stink of *Belg* Water; besides
they are as much afraid of dawbing their *Cloaths* as they are
of ventering their Carcases.'

Who can this be? 'The first Gentleman I happen'd to
cast my Eyes upon, was my old Friend and Fellow Collegian
Bartholomew Cringe. I wonder'd who in the Devil's Name
had equipt him with a Wig large enough to load a Camel
. . . His Sword in length resembled a Footman's, who
asserts the Reputation of his Mistriss, which, for divers good
Causes and Reasons, he is very nearly Concern'd in. His
Coat was as blue as the Sky; and his Hat boldly erected its
Sable Penthouse, to play with greater vivacity the ruddy
Complexion of its Owner. . . . Says he, Dear friend *Tom*,
you're surpriz'd to find your old Friend in this Place and
Habit. . I wear this Dress and Garniture as the Emblems of
my Militant Capacity. I have the Honour to perform the
Duties of my Office under the Protection of that worthy
Gentleman Lieutenant General —— in Quality of Chaplain
to his Regiment.'[1]

Even *their* commissions were the subject of traffic. 'If
any Gentleman that is Chaplain to a Regiment is willing to
dispose of his Commission, he is desired to acquaint therewith
the Master of the Tilt Yard Coffee House near Whitehall.'

What were the rank and file of this period? Hear a
contemporary opinion.[2] 'A Foot Soldier is commonly a Man,
who for the sake of wearing a Sword, and the Honour of
being term'd a Gentleman, is coax'd from a Handicraft Trade,
whereby he might Live comfortably, to bear Arms for his
King and Country, whereby he has the hopes of nothing but
to Live Starvingly. His Lodging is as near Heaven as his
Quarters can raise him; and his Soul generally is as near
Hell as a Profligate Life can sink him. To speak without

---

[1] *A Walk round London and Westminster.*   [2] *The London Spy.*

Swearing, he thinks a Scandal to his Post ; and makes many a Meal upon Tobacco, which keeps the inside of his Carcase as Nasty as his Shirt.   He's a Champion for the Church, because he Fights for Religion, tho' he never hears Prayers except they be Read upon a Drum Head.   He often leads a Sober Life against his Will ; but he never can pass by a Brandy shop with 2d. in his Pocket, for he as Naturally loves Strong Waters as a Turk loves Coffee. . . . He is a Man of Undaunted Courage ; and dreads no Enemies so much as he does the Wooden Horse, which makes him hate to be mounted ; and rather chuses to be a Foot Soldier.   He's a Man, that when upon guard, always keeps his word, and obeys his Officer as Indians do the Devil, not thro'·Love but Fear ; . . . When once he has been in a Battle it's a hard matter to get him out of it ; for where ever he comes he's always talking of the Action, in which he was posted in the greatest danger ; and seems to know more of the matter than the General.   Scars, tho' got in Drunken Quarrels, he makes Badges of his Bravery ; and tells you they were Wounds receiv'd in some Engagement, tho' perhaps given him for his Sawciness.   He's one that loves Fighting no more than other Men ; tho' perhaps a dozen of Drink and an affront, will make him draw his Sword ; yet a Pint, and a good Word, will make him put it up again.   Let him be in never so many Campaigns in *Flanders* he contracts but few Habits of a *Dutchman*, for you shall oftener see him with his Fingers in his Neck than his Hands in his Pockets.   He has the Pleasure once a Week, when he receives his Subsistence, of boasting he has Money in his Breeches ; and for all he is a Soldier owes no Man a Groat, which is likely enough to be true, because no Body will trust him.   Hunger and Lousiness are the two Distempers that Afflict him ; and Idleness and Scratching the two Medicines that Palliate his Miseries.   If he spends Twenty years in Wars, and lives to be Forty, perhaps he may get a Halbert ; and if he Survives Three Score, an Hospital.   The best end he can expect to make, is to Die in the Bed of Honour ; and the greatest Living Marks of his Bravery, to recommend him at once to the World's Praise and Pity, are Crippled Limbs, with which I shall leave him to beg a better Lively Hood.'

To a Coblers Aul, or Butcher's Knife,
  Or Porter's Knot, commend me ;
But from a Souldier's Lazy Life,
  Good Heaven pray defend me.

Here, then, we have an unvarnished description of the soldier of the period, his virtues, his vices, his destitution, his uncleanliness ; but the authorities could not afford to be too particular in those days, and, besides, the men did not get their

SOLDIERS.

pay regularly. True, they were *promised* that 'If any Able bodied Men are willing to serve Her Majesty in the Train of Artillery abroad, let them repair to Captain Silver, Master Gunner of England, at his House in St. James's Park, they shall enter into present Pay of Seven Shillings a Week, and be further encouraged and advanced as they shall deserve.'

Did they get this pay regularly ? I fear not always. Ward speaks of 'that unfortunate Wretch, who in time of War hazzards his Life for Six pence a day, and that perhaps ne'er paid him ;' and there is an ominous advertisement,[1] 'The Paymaster General of Her Majesty's Guards, Garrisons &c. in Great Britain, has given Notice, That Money is issued for the Subsistance of the Troops and Regiments under his Care, to the 24th instant, inclusive.' If it were the usual practice to have the money in hand, there would have been no necessity for advertising it in this case.

Discipline seems to have been rather lax just then, for in the *Gazette*, Oct. 11/14, 1712, there is a notice: 'Her Majesty is pleased to order, that all the Officers of the Regiments of Harvey, Peppar, Harrison, Wade, Bowles, Dormer, and Windress, do forthwith repair to the Castle of Dublin, and there receive such Orders as shall be given them by the Lords Justices of that Kingdom, upon pain of being checked of their Pay.'

The uniforms in the army were plain and serviceable ; the most picturesque being that of the Grenadiers, who, Evelyn says, were first introduced in 1678.

Some idea of the food given to the soldiers in garrison, may be gained by perusal of the following contract for rations.[2] 'The Most Honourable the Lord High Treasurer of Great Britain having receiv'd Her Majesty's Pleasure, That a Contract shall be made for Victualling Her Majesty's Garrisons at Minorca, to consist of about 4000 Men, and at Gibraltar, to consist of about 2000 Men, according to the Proportions underwritten for each Man for Seven Days, viz.

7 Pound of Bread, or (when desir'd by the Commanders in Chief) a pint of Wheat instead of a Pound of Bread.
' 2 Pound and half of Beef
' 1 Pound of Pork
' 4 Pints of Pease
' 3 Pints of Oatmeal
' 6 Ounces of Butter
' 8 Ounces of Cheese...'

Not a too liberal dietary for a soldier.

How did they recruit for the army ? for, during the long war which lasted nearly the whole of Anne's reign, men had to be furnished to fill the cruel gaps made by slaughter, wounds, and disease. First of all, a recruiting officer, with

---

[1] *Post Boy*, Oct. 7/9, 1712.   [2] *Gazette*, Sept. 23/27, 1712.

his. sergeant and drummer, would be quartered in some
country town, and 'beat up for recruits.' Of a recruiting
officer we get some notion in *Spectator* 132, and in Farquhars
play. Let Sergeant Kite himself tell us the qualifications
for a recruiting sergeant. 'So that if your Worship pleases
to cast up the whole Sum, viz. Canting, Lying, Impudence,
Pimping, Bullying, Swearing, Drinking, and a Halbard, you
will find the Sum Total amount to a Recruiting Sergeant.'
The Queen's shilling once being taken, or even sworn to have
been taken, and attestation made, there was no help for the
recruit, unless he was bought out.

In 1703 these means seem to have failed, for men could
not be got in sufficient quantities without the inducement of
a bounty. 'This is to give Notice, That his Grace the Duke
of Schombergh is raising a Regiment of Dragoons for Her
Majesty's Service; all such Persons who shall have a mind to
List themselves therein, may repair either to his Grace's in
Pall Mall, or to Mr. Brerewood in Norfolk Street, in the
Strand, near Temple Bar, Agent to the same, where such
Persons as have been formerly in the Army and are still
fit for Dragoons, shall receive 40s. in hand for Levy Money,
besides all fitting Accoutrements, and such as have not been
already in the Service shall have 30.s. and Accoutrements.'

In 1706 an Act was passed (4 & 5 Anne, cap. 21) 'For
the better recruiting Her Majesty's Army and Marines,' which
gave the power to justices, assisted by their subordinates, 'to
raise and levy such Able bodied Men as have not any lawful
Calling or Imployment or visible Means for their Maintenance
and Lively hood to serve as Soldiers.' A volunteer was to
have a bounty of 40s. given him, and 'shall not be liable to
be taken out of Her Majesty's Service by any Process other
than for some Criminal Matter.'

This shows to what straits they were reduced for men.
and the following exemplifies the class of recruits that were
then going into the army : 'Smith, who some time was
half hanged [1] and cut down, having accused about 35c
pickpockets, housebreakers, &c. who gott to be soldiers in
the guards, the better to hide their roguery, were last week

---

[1] See page 215.

upon mustering the regiments drawn out, and immediately shipt off for Catalonia ; and about 60 Women, who lay under condemnation for such Crimes, were likewise sent away to follow the Camp.'[1]

The Act of 1706 either fell partially in abeyance, or did not fulfil its requirements, for in the *Gazette* of Jan. 26/29, 1707–8, is a proclamation by the Queen calling attention to it, and promising, for the better carrying of it out, and 'for . the greater Incouragement of all Parish Officers to perform the Duty injoin'd them by that Act, That such Parish Officers, for every Person they should bring before the Magistrate, who should be Impressed should Receive the Sum of Twenty Shillings ; and that every Volunteer, for his better Incourage-ment to come into our Service, and List himself according to the Intention of the said Act, should Receive the sum of Four Pounds, and also that such Volunteer should be Discharg'd after Three Years Service, if he deserved it.'

This was the outcome of a fresh Act (7 Anne, cap. 2).

Of course these men deserted in shoals, but that they had always done, from the first year of the Queen's reign. The reward offered, by their officers, for their apprehension gener-ally ranged from one to two guineas, and occasionally they were entreated to return, of their own free will, when they would be forgiven. Once only can I find that a severe example was ever made of them, and that was in 1703. '6 Dec. This day a Soldier of Colonel Gorsuck's Company, was Shot in Hide Park for Desertion.' Probably they ran the gauntlet, as did that soldier in 1702 : 'Yesterday a Soldier ran the Gantlet (as he well deserved) in St. James's Park, for speaking some reflecting words on his late Majesty, and is to run twice more.'

In the last year of Anne's reign there were some wicked drummers, whose story is told very graphically in the *Post Boy*, Feb. 11/13, 1714. 'John Needham, Constable and Beadle of the Ward of Farringdon within, warding at Ludgate the Sixth Instant, (the Queen's Birth Day) by Order of the Lord Mayor and Court of Aldermen ; was sent for to the Crown Tavern on Ludgate Hill, to make a Gentleman Easy, who

[1] *Luttrell*, March 12, 1706.

was in Drink.   The Constable having made him and the rest
Friends, the Gentleman would have him to the Queen's Arms
Tavern, a little below, where they drank a Glass of Wine
together : But the Constable hearing some Drums beat, ran
into the Street, with his long Staff in his Hand, and the
Gentleman with him, who saw a very great Tumult of disorderly Persons arm'd with huge Clubs, and several with
Cleavers &c., and innumerable Lights, and Streamers.   Among
the rest came Three of H— M——'s Drummers beating their
Drums ; whereupon the Gentleman ran up to the Drum Head,
and ask'd, *Who they were for ?*   They said, *The House of
Hanover.*   He repli'd *G— D— you, what before the Queen is
dead?   Drummers, I'll give you Sixpence, beat a Point of War
for Queen* ANNE, *here by the Constable.*   But the Constable
said, *No, let them go into the Tavern, and beat out of the Crowd,
and they shall have Money and Wine too.*   So he made way
for them with his Staff, and they went into the Tavern, where
they beat and drank till the Tumult was gone by.   After
which, the Constable had them up to Ludgate, and from
thence to the Compter.   The next Evening, about Four a
Clock, he carry'd them before Sir William Withers, who
demanded their Names, and those of their Colonels, which
are as follows, Thomas Hawes under Colonel P——tt ; Charles
Bannister under Colonel E——ll ; and William Taylor under
Brigadier F——s belonging to the F—— R—— of G——'s.
And after Sir William Withers had examin'd them, and the
said Constable, and another Constable (whose Hat the Rioters
beat off, because he did not pull it off to them, tho' he was on
his Duty with his long Staff in his Hand) he was of Opinion
their Crime would amount to High Treason, and was so much
the blacker, because they were the Q——'s own S——ts, and
therefore Committed them to Newgate.'

In cases, however, of civil commotion, the train bands were
generally called out.   These citizen soldiers were ever the
laughing-stock of the wits of their day, and Steele cannot
help having his joke upon them.[1]   ' The Chief Citizens, like
the noble Italians, hire Mercenaries to carry arms in their
Stead ; and you shall have a fellow of desperate fortune, for

[1] *Tatler,* No. 28.

the gain of one half Crown, go through all the dangers of Tothill Fields, or the Artillery Ground, clap his right jaw within two inches of the touch-hole of a Musquet, fire it off, and huzza, with as little concern as he tears a pullet.'

He laughs, too, at the officers, and at their method of promotion. 'But the point of honour justly gives way to that of gain; and, by long and wise regulation, the richest is the bravest man. I have known a Captain rise to a Colonel in two days by the fall of stocks; and a Major, my good friend, near the Monument, ascended to that honour by the fall of the price of Spirits, and the rising of right Nantz.' And a great part of *Tatler* 41 is taken up by a laughing criticism on 'An Exercise of Arms,' which took place on June 29, 1709, and was supposed to represent the putting down of a revolt.

The sister service had no easy task under Anne, but were always hard at work, either at fighting, or convoying, or transport work, besides being always cruising about and snapping up prizes; and there were some good commanders in those days, whose names have descended to ours. What Englishman can forget the names of Benbow, Rooke, and Cloudesley Shovel? They were not always successful—as in the case of the first-named old sea-dog. On August 19, 1702, he sighted the enemy's squadron, under Du Casse; on the 20th he engaged—but not till the 24th did he come to close quarters. His ship, the *Breda*, was then able to close with the sternmost French ship, which he himself boarded three times, and was twice wounded. He afterwards had his right leg shattered by a chain shot, and was carried below, but would insist on being carried on deck, where he remained the rest of the action. He disabled his opponent, but her consorts came to her relief, when four cowardly captains of his basely deserted him, in spite of his signals; so he had to give up the pursuit, and proceeded with his squadron to Jamaica, where he died Nov. 4.

On Oct. 12, 1702, Sir George Rooke burnt the French and Spanish shipping in Vigo, and sacked the town. This, besides the damage done to the foreign navies, was notorious for the enormous quantity of booty taken, both in specie, snuff, and other goods. What the specie amounted to is not now known, but it was not so much as was expected, for by far the larger portion had been landed and sent into the interior of the country. Still it furnished a very handsome prize money for all concerned, although, as is usual in such cases, it was long before it was realised. A special coinage was made from this specie, and

AN ADMIRAL.

Ruding gives specimens of five-, two-, and one-guinea and half-guinea pieces— and silver crowns, half-crowns, shillings, and sixpences of this type. Some had the date 1702, others 1703, but in every case the word VIGO was under the Queen's bust. Luttrell gives a little anecdote about it. '20 Mar. 1703. This week £1000 of new mill'd money coyned out of the plate taken at Vigo was brought from the Tower to sir Christopher Musgrave's office in the exchequer, and lock't up for her majestie's use, haveing the word Vigo under the queen's effigie.'

It is not within the province of this book to go into details of the victories of the British navy in this reign, but we must not forget that Sir George Rooke won us, in 1704, the rock of Gibraltar.

The damage done to the French shipping during the long war must have been almost incalculable, not a daily paper or report from the sea-ports being without mention of some prizes.

Yet the service was not a popular one, at least with seamen, the way the navy was generally manned, by impress, being quite sufficient to make Jack fight shy of it. We hear of this impressing in the very first year of the reign. 'The Post Letters say there are 6 Press Ketches at Falmouth, which have pressed a considerable number of Men for her Majesty's Service.'[1] 'Irish Letters of the 26th past say, they continue to beat up for Soldiers at Dublin, where abundance list themselves, and that some Press-Ketches in that Harbour have pressed 400 Seamen within a few Days, and that a great many are voluntarily come in.'[2]

But though pressed, Jack was hard to hold, if he got a chance to get away. 'Hull, 1 March. Last week a Lieutenant came hither with a Press Gang, and had so good Success, that he soon Glean'd up a considerable number; but having no Vessel to put them on board, he turn'd them into an upper Room in the Town Gaol, and on Saturday they broke out through the top of the House and Escap'd.'[3]

All means were tried to get men, and a bribe was held out by the Act 1 Anne, cap. 19, which provided for the discharge of every male prisoner for debt under £20, and who had been in prison for six months, who should enlist either in the army or navy, and the same was afterwards tried by 4 & 5 Anne, cap. 6.

This serves to show the condition of the poor debtors, who were thus invited to *ameliorate* their position, by exchanging it for the 'Inferno' of a man-of-war of that period. Still we read early in 1704: 'There is great impressing of Seamen for Her Majesties Service, she being resolved to have the Navy early at sea.' The bounty system was tried, and on Dec. 14, 1704, the Queen issued a proclamation, offering two months' pay to every sailor voluntecring, and one month's to every landsman. This proclamation also vowed vengeance against deserters, ordered officers of press gangs to press no old men, boys, or infirm persons, and promised them 'Twenty Shillings for each Seaman, and Sixpence per Man for each Mile he shall be brought, if under

---

[1] *Flying Post*, April 2/4, 1702.   [2] *Ibid.* April 4/7, 1702.
[3] *Daily Courant*, March 4, 1703.

twenty Miles, and Ten Shillings for each Seaman that shall be brought above Twenty Miles, over and above the said Twenty Shillings.'

This arbitrary system of impressing was so cruel, that one feels heartily glad to find that it is possible there might be another side to the question, and that a man might be punished for it. 'Yesterday one Philpot was by the court of Queen's Bench fined 10 Nobles, and to stand in the pillory on Tower Hill, for wrongfully pressing one Gill, and taking 4 Guineas for his discharge.'[1] One man seems to have had the courage to speak against it, and I regret I have been unable to get his pamphlet. 'Just Published. The Old and True Way of Manning the Fleet, Or how to Retrieve the Glory of the English Arms by Sea, as it is done by Land; and to have Seamen always in readiness, without Pressing. In a Letter from an old Parliament Sea Commander, to a Member of the present House of Commons, desiring his Advice on that Subject. Printed in the Year 1707.'

The pay was not so bad, £4 a month;[2] but the service was unpopular—the officers were rough and foul-mouthed, whose creed was, 'I hate the *French*, love a handsome Woman and a Bowl of Punch'[3]—so the men deserted whenever they could. It was no use issuing proclamations offering a reward of twenty shillings for every such deserter delivered up on board ship; they kept their pay back, and tried to allure them from the joys of freedom and the shore by bidding them repair on board their ships to receive their pay due six months back, still keeping six months in hand. Jack was proof against such blandishments: so the authorities tried another plan—the magnanimous—and promised to forgive the deserters, if only they would come back; anything to get the dear fellows on board, all would be forgotten and forgiven, and joy and peace should reign henceforth. 'All such Seamen that are made run, for not repairing to their Duty, shall have their R's taken off, and be continued in Wages from the times they have been absent, provided they do forthwith repair on board.' As this is the only instance I can meet with of this bait being held out, one rather suspects

---

[1] *Luttrell*, July 14, 1709.   [2] *Ibid.* Oct. 31, 1702.   [3] *The Basset Table.*

Jack was not quite such a fool as they imagined him, and, once free, had no wish to get into the trap again.

Brown [1] gives a description of the Admiralty in his time : ' By this time we were come to the *Admiralty Office*, the outside invited us in, and here we found only a Company of Tarrs, walking to and fro with their Hands in their Pockets, as on the Quarter Deck aboard ; in one Room there was a company of Lieutenants, some had serv'd twenty Years without being rais'd, because they either knew not how to Bribe in the right Place, or were so tenacious of what they had so hardly purchas'd, that their only hopes were now *Half Pay* or *Superannuation*. In another place were Seamen's Wives with Petitions, and pressing Deputy B——, who was as surly to them, as a *true Whigg* in Office ; but tho' he demanded no Fee, he could be mollified by a little *Fellow feeling*, that like a Sop to *Cerberus*, let Petitions and Men pass too ; Then you fall in betwixt *Scylla* and *Charybdis*, the Clerks on one Side, and Sea Captains on the other ; where Cowards that have lost one Ship, easily get another ; and Men of Valour, without Interest, wait in vain for Preferment, from those who dispose of what they do not understand ; for here the *Land* determines of the *Main*, and he that never see the *North Foreland*, disposes of things, as if he knew all the Creeks and Bays, Shelves, Sands, and Nations of the Universe.'

From contemporary descriptions Jack's nature has not much altered since Anne's time. Ward thus sums him up : ' I could not but reflect on the unhappy Lives of these Salt Water kind of Vagabonds, who are never at Home but when they're at Sea, and always are wandering when they're at Home ; and never contented but when they're on Shore ; They're never at ease till they've receiv'd their Pay, and then never satisfied till they have spent it ; And when their Pockets are empty, they are just as much respected by their Landladies (who cheat them of one half, if they spend the other) as a Father is by his *Son-in-Law*, who has Beggar'd himself to give him a good Portion with his Daughter.'

In the mercantile marine, there was a large trade done

[1] *A Walk round London and Westminster.*

with India and China. Dampier fitted out his third semi-piratical expedition, Alexander Selkirk was discovered and brought home, and Captain Edward Cooke circumnavigated the globe. The map published in his book [1] is a very fair sample of hydrography. 'New Zealand, Dimens Land, and New Holland' are just indicated in their proper positions, but New Guinea is represented as being joined to the north of Australia, and California is shown as an island.

---

[1] *A Voyage to the South Sea and round the World perform'd in the Years* 1708, 1709, 1710, and 1711, etc.

CHAPTER XL.

CRIME.

Capital punishment—Its frequency—An execution described—Behaviour
on the scaffold and way to execution—Revival after hanging—*Peine
forte et dure*—Hanging in chains—Highwaymen—Claude du Val
lying in state—Ned Wicks and Lord Mohun : their swearing match
—A highwayman hanged—Highwaymen in society—Highway robberies—Footpads—Burglars—John Hall—Benefit of clergy—Coining
— Pickpockets — Robbery from children — Perjury — Sharpers—
Begging impostors — Gipsies — Constables — Private detectives —
Commercial frauds—' Society for the Reformation of Manners '—Sta-
tistics of their convictions—The pillory—Ducking-stool.

THE repression and punishment of crime is the duty of every
Government, and it was performed in Anne's reign as well as
an imperfect police would allow. Capital punishment was, of
course, more frequent than in our days, because there were
so many more offences punishable by it. In London alone,
from the commencement of Sir Thos. Abney's mayoralty in
1701, to the end of that of Sir Richard Hoare in 1713, 242
malefactors were hanged at Tyburn and other places.

It was of such frequent occurrence that men got callous
about it, nay, joked of it. ' Mr. Ordinary visits his melancholy Flock at *Newgate* by Eight. Doleful Procession up
Holborn Hill about Eleven. Men handsome and proper, that
were never thought so before, which is some Comfort however, Arrive at the fatal Place at Twelve. Burnt Brandy,
Women and Sabbath breaking repented of. Some few Penitential Drops fall under the Gallows. Sheriffs Men, Parson,
Pickpockets, Criminals, all very busie. The last concluding
peremptory Psalm struck up. Show over by One.'

Misson gives a far longer account, full of detail, of an
execution in those days. He says : ' Hanging is the most

common Punishment in *England*. Usually this Execution is done in a great Road¹ about a quarter of a League from the Suburbs of *London*. The Sessions for trying Criminals being held but eight Times a Year, there are sometimes twenty Malefactors to be hang'd at a Time.

'They put five² or six in a Cart (some gentlemen obtain leave to perform this journey in a coach) and carry them riding backwards with the Rope about their Necks, to the fatal Tree. The Executioner stops the Cart under one of the Cross Beams of the Gibbet, and fastens to that ill-favoured Beam one End of the Rope, while the other is round the Wretches Neck : This done, he gives the Horse a Lash with his Whip, away goes the Cart, and there swings my Gentleman Kicking in the Air.

'The Hangman does not give himself the Trouble to put them out of their Pain ; but some of their Friends or Relations do it for them. They pull the dying Person by the Legs, and beat his Breast to dispatch him as soon as possible. The *English* are People that laugh at the Delicacy of other Nations, who make it such a mighty Matter to be hang'd ; their extraordinary Courage looks upon it as a Trifle, and they also make a Jest of the pretended Dishonour, that in the Opinion of others, falls upon their Kindred.

'He that is to be hang'd, or otherwise executed, first takes Care to get himself shav'd, and handsomely drest, either in Mourning, or in the Dress of a Bridegroom. This done, he sets his Friends at Work to get him Leave to be bury'd, and to carry his Coffin with him, which is easily obtain'd. When his Suit of Cloaths, or Night Gown, his Gloves, Hat, Perriwig, Nosegay, Coffin, Flannel Dress for his Corps, and all those Things are bought and prepar'd, the main Point is taken Care of, his Mind is at Peace, and then he thinks of his Conscience. Generally he studies a Speech, which he pronounces under the Gallows, and gives in Writing to the Sheriff, or the Minister that attends him in his last Moments, desiring that it may be printed. Sometimes the Girls dress in White, with great Silk Scarves, and carry Baskets full of Flowers and Oranges, scattering these Favours all the Way they go. But

---

¹ Tyburn.   ² Usually three.

to represent Things as they really are, I must needs own that if a pretty many of these People dress thus gayly, and go to it with such an Air of Indifference, there are many others that go slovenly enough, and with very dismal Phizzes.

'I remember, one Day, I saw in the Park, a handsome Girl, very well drest, that was then in Mourning for her Father, who had been hang'd but a Month before at *Tyburn* for false Coinage. So many Countries, so many Fashions.'

There were sad and revolting scenes at the gallows. The notorious Captain Kidd, the pirate, went to his death drunk, which, as Paul Lorrain, the Ordinary of Newgate, observes, 'had so decomposed his Mind, that now it was in a very bad frame.' The rope broke, and he fell to the ground, which somewhat sobered him, and before he was finally strangled he listened to the chaplain's ministrations.

A previous chaplain, in 1691, was roughly treated by one Tom Cox, a highwayman,[1] 'for before he was turn'd off, Mr. *Smith*, the Ordinary, desiring him to join with the rest of his Fellow Sufferers in Prayer, he swore a great Oath to the contrary, and kickt him and the Hangman too off the Cart.'

When one Dick Hughes, a housebreaker, was in 1709 going to execution,[2] 'his wife met him at Saint *Giles's* Pound, where, the Cart stopping, she stept up to him, and whispering in his Ear, said, My dear, who must find the Rope that's to hang you, We or the Sheriff? Her Husband reply'd, The Sheriff, Honey; for who's obliged to find him Tools to do his Work? Ah! (reply'd his Wife) I wish I had known so much before, 'twould have sav'd me two Pence, for I have been and bought one already. Well, well, (said Dick again) perhaps it mayn't be lost, for it may serve a second Husband. Yes, (quoth his Wife) if I've any Luck in good Husbands, so it may.'

Another story is told, in the same book, of one Jack Witherington, a highwayman, who, when going up Holborn Hill to execution, 'he order'd the Cart to stop, then desiring to speak to the Sheriff's Deputy, who attends Criminals to the Place of Execution, he said to him, I owe, Sir, a small

---

[1] *History of the Lives of the most noted Highwaymen*, etc., by Capt. Alexander Smith, 1714.   [2] *Ibid.*

Matter at the Three Cups Inn, a little farther, for which I fear I shall be arrested as I go by the Door, therefore I shall be much obliged to you if you'll be pleas'd to carry me down *Shoe Lane*, and bring me up *Drury Lane* again to the Place for which I'm design'd. Hereupon the Deputy Sheriff telling him that if such a Mischance should happen, he would Bail him ; Jack, as not thinking he had such a good Friend to stand by him in time of Need, rid very contentedly to Tyburn.'

The system of strangulation then in vogue was favourable to the recovery of life, as is shown by the following extract from the *Flying Post*, Dec. 11/13, 1705 : 'Yesterday one John Smith,[1] Condemned last Sessions for House breaking, was carried from Newgate to Tyburn to be executed. Some minutes after he was turned off, a Reprieve came for him, and being immediately cut down, he soon reviv'd, to the admiration of all Spectators, and was brought back to Newgate.'

The Newgate Calendar reports that, ' being asked what were his sensations, after he was turned off; he answered, That at first he felt great pain, but that it gradually subsided, and that the last thing he could remember, was the appearance of a light in his eyes, after which he became quite insensible. But the greatest pain was, when he felt the blood returning to its proper channels.'

He received a free pardon a few weeks afterwards, and one would have imagined would have altered his ways, after so narrow an escape ; but he was apprehended for a similar offence, tried at the Old Bailey, and was acquitted on a point of law. Yet once more was he caught, and this time was acquitted by the death of the prosecutor. His ultimate fate is not known.

But this was nothing to the marvellous resuscitation of Anne Greene, who was hanged at Oxford Dec. 14, 1651, and was afterwards revived—and got quite well. She was condemned for the murder of her child, which was afterwards discovered to have been stillborn ; and that there was no deception in her execution her history[2] assures us, for she

[1] See page 203.   [2] Brit. Mus. $\frac{E.\ 625}{14.}$

was hanging by the neck for the space of almost half an hour,
some of her friends in the meantime thumping her on the
breast, others hanging with all their weight upon her legges ;
'sometimes lifting her up, and then pulling her down againe
with a suddaine jerke, thereby the sooner to despatch her out
of her paine ; insomuch that the Under-Sheriff, fearing lest
thereby they should breake the rope, forbad them to do so
any longer.'

And not only so, but when she was taken in her coffin to
Dr. Petty, the professor of anatomy, 'she was observed to
breathe, and obscurely to ruttle ; which being perceived by a
lusty fellow that stood by, he (thinking to do an act of Charity
in ridding her out of the small reliques of a painful life)
stamped several times on her breast and Stomack with all the
force he could.' This considerate treatment could not over-
come the girl's vitality, for by dint of bleeding and good
nursing she entirely recovered, and went to her own home,
taking with her her coffin, and a goodly sum of money, which
had been subscribed for her benefit, and which remained
after defraying all charges necessary to her recovery.

The scaffold still lingered on Tower Hill, but this was
reserved for political offenders.

A remnant of the barbarous use of torture still remained
(indeed, it was not abolished until the year 1772) in the
peine forte et dure. This punishment was inflicted when a
prisoner refused to plead 'guilty' or 'not guilty,' which was
then necessary before the trial could be gone on with. Now,
if a prisoner refuses to plead, he is regarded as pleading
'not guilty,' and the trial goes on. People have died under
this torture rather than plead, because by that means they
preserved their property to their friends, which would have
been confiscated had they pleaded and been found guilty of
felony.

Misson gives the following description of the ' *Peine forte
et dure or pressing to death.* When a Felon, punishable with
Death, takes a Resolution not to make any Answer to his
Judges, after the Second Calling upon, he is carry'd back to
his Dungeon, and is put to a Sort of Rack called *Peine forte
et dure.* If he speaks, his Indictment goes on, in the usual

Forms ; if he continues dumb, they leave him to die under that Punishment. He is stretch'd out naked upon his Back, and his Arms and Legs drawn out by cords, and fasten'd to the four Corners of the Dungeon : A Board or Plate of Iron is laid upon his Stomach, and this is heap'd up with Stones to a certain Weight.

'The next Day they give him, at three different times, three little Morsels of Barly Bread, and nothing to Drink :

' PEINE FORTE ET DURE.'

the next Day, three little Glasses of Water, and nothing to Eat : And, if he continues in his Obstinacy, they leave him in that Condition 'till he dies. This is practis'd only upon Felons, or Persons guilty of Petty Treason. Criminals of High Treason, in the like Case, would be condemn'd to the usual Punishment ; their Silence would Condemn them.'

Hanging in chains was a distinction to which highway-men and pirates were entitled, after having combinec murder with theft. It consisted of fastening the body into a sort of cage, made of iron hoops, and then hanging it upon the gibbet—which was bound to be on the very road where the crime was committed.

Highway robbery was, unfortunately, very common in this reign ; but the perpetrators were mostly pitiful wretches, whose career, while it lasted, was far from brilliant, and generally it was a very short one. All the romance of the highway died with Claude Du Val, who was executed on Jan. 21, 1670, in the 27th year of his age. His short career ended ingloriously, for he was taken, when drunk, at the ' Hole in the Wall,' in Chandos Street.

Whatever caused the furore over the poor rogue ? We are told :[1] ' There were a great Company of Ladies, and those not of the meanest Degree, that visited him in Prison, interceded for his Pardon, and accompany'd him to the Gallows, with swoll'n Eyes, and Cheeks blubber'd with Tears under their Vizards. After he had hang'd a Convenient Time, he was cut down, and by Persons well dress'd carry'd into a mourning Coach, and so Convey'd to the *Tangier* Tavern in *St. Giles's*, where he lay in State all that Night, the Room hung with black Cloth, the Herse cover'd with Scutcheons, eight Wax Tapers burning, as many tall Gentlemen with long Cloaks attending ; *Mum* was the Word, and great Silence expected from all that visited, for Fear of disturbing the sleeping Lion. And this Ceremony had lasted much longer, had not one of the Judges sent to disturb this Pageantry. . . . He was bury'd with many Flambeaus, and with a numerous Train of Mourners, most whereof were of the beautiful Sex ; he lyes in the Middle Isle of *Covent Garden* Church, under a White Marble Stone, whereon are curiously engrav'd the Du Val's Arms.'

The stories of their feats are very much alike, varied only in their degree of brutality. One however, if true, is somewhat out of the ordinary ruck, and it is told[2] of the same Lord Mohun ('Dog Mohun,' as Swift calls him) who fought the Duke of Hamilton.

'Another time *Ned Wicks* meeting with the late Lord

[1] Smith's *Lives of Highwaymen.*   [2] *Ibid.*

Mohun on the Road betwixt *Windsor* and *Colebrook*, attended only with a Groom and one Footman, he commanded his Lordship to stand and deliver, for he was in great Want of Money, and Money he would have before they parted. His Honour, pretending to have a great deal of Courage, swore he should fight for it then. *Wicks* very readily accepted the Proposal, and preparing his Pistols for an Engagement, his Lordship seeing his Resolution, he began to hang back, which his Antagonist perceiving, he began to be Cock on hoop, saying " All the World knows me to be a Man ; and tho' your Lordship was concern'd in the Cowardly murdering of *Mumford* the Player, and Captain *Cout*, yet I'm not to be frighten'd at that ; therefore down with your Gold, or else expect no Quarter." His Lordship now meeting with his Match, it put him into such a passionate Fit of swearing, that *Wicks* not willing to be outdone in any Wickedness, quoth he, " My Lord, I perceive you swear perfectly well *ex tempore* ; come, I'll give your Honour a fair Chance for your Moneys, and that is, he that swears best of us two, shall keep his own, and his that loseth." His Lordship agreed to this Bargain, and throwing down a Purse of 50 Guineas, which *Wicks* match'd with a like Sum ; after a quarter of an Hours Swearing most prodigiously on both Sides, it was left to his Lordship's Groom to decide the Matter ; who said, " Why, indeed your Honour Swears as well as ever I heard a Person of Quality in my Life ; but, indeed, to give the Strange Gentleman his Due, he has won the Wager if 'twas for a thousand Pounds. Whereupon *Wicks* taking up the Gold he gave the Groom a Guinea, and rid about his Business.'

A highwayman certainly carried his life in his hand—he was a *Wolf's head*, and, every man's hand being against him he was shot whenever he could be, and a reward of forty pounds was given for the capture of one of them. In 1712 one Joseph Reader, a miller of Shaftesbury, was attacked by a highwayman, who fired twice at him, and missed doing him any injury. The miller, judging that he had expended his ammunition, closed with him, knocked him off his horse with his cudgel, and beat him senseless. He then dragged him to a tree, and hanged him with his own belt. For this,

Reader was tried at Dorchester, and acquitted ; and a subscription was got up for him in court, which amounted to
over 30*l.*

Ward describes a typical highwayman : 'Another you needs
must take particular notice of, that pluck'd out a pair of *Pocket
Pistols*, and laid them in the Window, who had a great Scar
cross his Forehead, a twisted Wig, and lac'd Hat on ; the
Company call'd him *Captain* ; he's a man of Considerable
Reputation amongst *Birds of the same Feather*, who I have
heard say thus much in his Praise, that he is as Resolute a
Fellow as ever *Cock'd Pistol upon the Road* ; and indeed I do
believe he fears no Man in the World but the *Hang Man* ;
and dreads no death but *Choaking*.   He's as generous as a
Prince, treats any Body that will keep him Company ; loves
his friends as dearly as the *Ivy* does the *Oak*, will never leave
him till he has *Hug'd* him to his Ruin.   He has drawn in
twenty of his Associates to be Hang'd, but had always *Wit*
and *Money* enough to save his own Neck from the Halter.
He has good friends at Newgate, who give him now and
then a *Squeeze* when he is in full *Juice* ; and give him their
Words to stand by him, which he takes as a *Verbal Policy* of
Insurance from the *Gallows*, till he grows *Poor* thro' *Idleness*,
and then, (he has Cunning enough to know) he may be
Hang'd thro' *Poverty*.   He's well acquainted with the *Ostlers*
about *Bishopsgate Street*, and *Smithfield* ; and gains from
them Intelligence of what Booties goe out that are worth
attempting.   He accounts them very honest *Tikes*, and can
with all safety trust his Life in their Hands, for now and then
Gilding their *Palms* for the good Services they do him.   He
pretends to be a *Disbanded Officer*, and reflects very feelingly
upon the hard usage we poor Gentlemen meet with, who
have hazarded our Lives and Fortunes for the Honour of our
Prince, the Defence of our Country, and Safety of Religion ;
and after all to be *Broke* without our Pay, turn'd out without
any consideration for the dangers and difficulties we have
run thro' ; at this rate, *Wounds*, who the Devil wou'd be a
Soldier ? '

Their personal appearance—which, it is needless to say,
was not the gold-laced costume so beloved of the stage and

penny dreadfuls—is given in the following advertisement:
'Stolen from Sam. Brett Servant to Mr. Bayly of Romford
in Essex by two Highwaymen, one in a light colour'd Suit
trim'd with the same, a light coloured Wig and hood, the
other in a light colour'd Coat trim'd with Black Button holes
on each side, and dark brown Hair,' etc. And their style of
doing business may be learnt from the following: 'On
Wednesday night the Cambridge, Norwich, and Linn Stage
Coaches, were all 3 Robbed by one single Man in Epping
Forest.' 'Stafford 17 Feb. We have had great Robbing
lately in these parts by a Gang of Highway men: On the
30th past, they set upon the Shrewsbury Stage Coach and
plunder'd all the passengers; and afterwards met with 3
Country Attorneys, which they Robb'd also; one of them
having put 20 Guineas into his Shooes, the Rogues for haste,
cut the Straps of the Port Mantle, and threw the Shooes
away; after they were gone, the Attorney took up both
Shooes and Gold. On the 9th instant they set upon two
Drovers coming from New Castle Fair, took a great deal of
Money, kill'd one of them on the Spot, and dangerously
wounded the other. On the 11th May set upon the High
Sheriff of the County with his Lady and Servants, coming
from Lichfield Fair, took 60 Guineas from them, and cut off
one of the Servants Hands. Since which several of them are
taken, of which two are committed to Warwick Gaol, two to
Stafford, and two Men and three Women to Litchfield; one
of the Women was dress'd in Man's Apparel when they robb d
the Stage Coach.'

'The Mails due at London the 10th of Sept. from Ireland
and Chester, having been seiz'd by 3 Highwaymen between
Dunstable and St. Alban's, and several Letters opened. These
are to give Notice thereof, that care may be taken to prevent
the payment of such Bills as have by this means been in-
tercepted.'

Advertisements frequently occur of men being taken up
on suspicion of being highwaymen, but one would fancy
there could be but little doubt of the profession of this gentleman. 'There is now in Custody in her Majesty's Gaol of
Newgate in London, James Biswick, alias Bissick, a middle

size'd Man, Aged about 40, having a high Bridge Nose, a thin Visage, pale Complexion, stooping in the Shoulders, was Apprehended the 25th of August last, suppos'd to have committed divers Robberies on the Highway, he having in his Pockets a brace of Pistols loaded and prim'd, a Mask with Strings to it and other cords; also a black Jet Mare 13 Hands high, 7 years old, a Short Bob Tail, a Scar on the near knee, a Blood Spavin behind; is suppos'd to be Stolen, is to be seen at the Swan and Hoop near More gate.'

' The foot pads are very troublesome in the evenings on all the roads leading to this Citty, which renders them very unsafe,' writes Luttrell in 1702, and that he did not exaggerate, take these two instances occurring in that year. 'Last Wednesday Night, a Fencing Master coming to Town from Pancrass, was set upon by some Foot Pads, who, finding he had no Money about him, beat him so barbarously, that his Life is despaired of.' 'On Thursday night, between eight and nine, a Gentleman, who lives at Little Chelsea, was set upon by four Ruffians on this side Chelsea College, who knock'd him down, rifled him of all he had of Worth about him, and left him miserably bruis'd and beaten; but another Gentleman and his Man happening to come by, and seeing him, they together pursued the Rogues, recovered the Gentleman's Hat, Sword, Perriwig, and most of his Money, and took two of the Rogues, who are since committed; but the other two escaped with the Gentleman's Watch and Seal.' In 1703, ' 3 strowling Gipsies are ordered down to Huntington to be Tryed for Robbing two Women, and leaving them bound together on the Road Naked.' In 1704, 'A Gentleman going from St. James's to Kensington was met and attacked in Hide Park by two Foot Pads, who took from him his Sword, Watch, Perriwig, and Rings, in all to the value of 130*l.* and left him in a deplorable condition.' These are a few examples only, but they are sufficient to show us the insecurity of the public roads at that time.

The Newgate Calendar gives a long list of crime in this reign, but they are all of the ordinary type, murder, highway robberies, and burglaries with violence, which last was a capital offence; and so indeed it ought to be, were there many such burglaries as this: 'We hear that on Tuesday night last, five Housebreakers broke into Sir Charles Thorns House near Bedington in Surrey, and having Jagg'd¹ his Servants, got into his Bed Chamber. At their Entrance Sir Charles fir'd a Pistol at them, which unhappily miss'd doing Execution ; upon this they bound and Jagg'd him, and after-wards one of them attempted to insult his Lady ; at which Sir Charles being exasperated, with much struggling he got his Hands at Liberty, and flung a Perriwig block at the Villain's Head ; who in revenge stabbed Sir Charles, then cut his Throat from Ear to Ear, and left him Dead on the Spct. They afterwards Ransack'd the House, and it's said, carried off to the value of £900 in Money and Plate. The Lady Thorn is so ill by this barbarous Treatment, that her Life is despaired of.'

There was a most famous housebreaker in this reign— one John Hall, a chimney-sweep, who has a small literature entirely devoted to him—besides having dis-'honourable mention ' in the Newgate Calendar, and his biography written by no less a person than Paul Lorrain, the Ordinary of Newgate (who is mentioned both in *Tatler* 63 and *Spectator* 338). He had a long poetical elegy composed on him, after the fashion of the times—and an epitaph :—

Here lies Hall's Clay	At judgment day,	I'd better say
Thus swept away ;	He'd make essay	Here lies Jack Hall
If bolt or key	To get away :	And that is all.
Obliged his Stay	Be 't as it may,	

An Act passed in the fifth year of Anne's reign offered a Government reward of £40 and a pardon to any person con-cerned in breaking open houses, who shall discover two or more of his accomplices, upon their conviction ; whilst the 6 Anne, cap. 9, which deals with simple burglaries, housebreaking, or robbery in shops, etc., repeats the 10 Will. III., cap. 12, sec. 6, which provided that ' every Person and Persons, who should be convicted of or for any Theft or Larceny, and should have the Benefit of the Clergy allowed thereupon, or ought to be burnt in the Hand for such Offence : instead of being burnt

¹ Gagged.

in the Hand should be burnt in the most visible part of the left Cheek nearest the Nose;' and settles that henceforth they shall be burnt in the hand.

This 'Benefit of the Clergy' is thus described by Misson : 'About 600 Years ago in the reign of *William the Second*, the People of *England* were so strangely ignorant, that the very Priests could hardly read. The King, in order to bring the People out of such a State of Darkness made a Law, that in certain Cases (as Man Slaughter, Theft, (for the first Time) not exceeding the Sum of £5 Sterling, and committed without Burglary, or putting the Person robb'd into bodily Fear, Polygamy, &c.) the Convict might save his Life, and escape with no other Punishment but burning in the Hand, if he were so great a Scholar as to be able to read ; and tho' at present there is hardly the meanest Peasant in *England* but what can read, yet the Law is still in Force. They say to the Criminal, Thou N, who art convicted of having committed such and such a Crime, what hast thou to demand in Favour of thy self, to hinder Sentence of Death being pass'd upon thee ? The Criminal answers, I demand the Benefit of the Clergy. His demand is granted, and the Ordinary of *Newgate* gives him a Book, printed in the old *Gothic*[1] Letter, in which the Criminal reads a few Words. Then the Lord Mayor, or one of the Judges, asks the Ordinary *Legitne vel non ?* And the Ordinary answers *Legit ut Clericus.*

' However, when the Criminal has a Right to demand the *Benefit of the Clergy*, they seldom give themselves the trouble to examine whether they can read or no ; be he the greatest Scholar in the World, or the greatest Blockhead, tis all a Case, so he gives but a little Spite of Money to the Ordinary, who tells him in a low Voice (which the whole Court may hear) three or four words, which he pronounces, and there's an End of the matter. 'Tis always taken for granted that a Peer can read, and he is never burnt in the Hand when he claims *the Benefit of the Clergy.'*

By the 6 Anne, cap. 9, this ceremony of reading was abolished, although the privilege remained the same, and this

---

[1] Black letter, which was of later date than that text now termed Gothic.

singular custom was not altogether, and entirely, done away with until 1841, 4 & 5 Vict. 22.

Coining, as infringing the king's prerogative, and being a serious injury to the commonweal, was, of course, a capital offence. One can understand coiners of base metal being punished ; those who were cunning in 'the Art of making *Black Dogs*, which are Shillings, or other pieces of Money made only of Pewter, double Wash'd. What the Professors of this Hellish Art call *George Plateroon*, is all copper within, with only a thin Plate about it ; and what they call *Compositum*, is a mix'd Metal, which will both touch and cut, but not endure the fiery Test ' ; but by what reasoning should the following gentleman be found guilty of crime ? ' Sir Richard Blackham, formerly a Merchant, was at the sessions house in the Old Baily this week found guilty of Misprision of treason for melting down the coin of England, and making foreign coins of it.'[1]

The ordinary pickpocket was common enough. Let us hear what Gay says of him :—

> Here dives the skulking Thief, with practis'd Slight,
> And unfelt Fingers make thy Pocket light.
> Where's now thy Watch, with all its Trinkets, flown ?
> And thy late Snuff Box is no more thy own.
> But lo ! his bolder Thefts some Tradesman spies,
> Swift from his Prey the scudding Lurcher flies ;
> Dext'rous he scapes the Coach, with nimble Bounds,
> While ev'ry honest Tongue *Stop Thief* resounds.
> So speeds the wily Fox, alarm'd by Fear,
> Who lately filch'd the Turkey's callow Care ;
> Hounds following Hounds, grow louder as he flies,
> And injur'd Tenants joyn the Hunter's Cries.
> Breathless he stumbling falls : Ill fated Boy !
> Why did not honest Work thy Youth employ ?
> Seiz'd by rough Hands, he's dragg'd amid the Rout,
> And stretch'd beneath the Pump's incessant Spout :
> Or plung'd in miry Ponds, he gasping lies,
> Mud Choaks his Mouth, and plaisters o'er his Eyes.

In every age the question may be asked, ' Quis custodiet ipsos custodes ?' and it might have been *à propos* in 1703, when ' A Thieftaker was also brought upon his Tryal for

---

[1] *Luttrell*, Aug. 31, 1706.

Picking a Man's Pocket in Bartholomew Fair, and Acquitted ':
so, let us hope, he was innocent.

Of course, if people were so stupid as to bedizen their
children with gold chains, they could not well grumble, and
only had themselves to blame, if 'fat squat' wenches occasionally took advantage of their trustfulness and appropriated
the trinkets. 'A Child about 6 Years Old being led away
by a Fat Squat Wench, on Monday, being the 13th Instant,
at 5 of the Clock in the Evening, from Brook Street in
Ratcliffe to Golden Lane without Cripplegate, being robbed
of a Gold Chain marked A. H. and a Silver Thimble and
Purse. Whoever can discover the Wench, so as to be taken,
shall have a Guinea Reward, or if Pawn'd or Sold their Money
again at Thos. Townsend's at the Jamaica Coffee House in
Cornhill.'

As a rule, people were only too glad to get back their
property, and felonies were compounded in the most unblushing way—'No questions asked' being almost universally a
portion of an advertisement for missing or stolen property.

One parish was very zealous in its work of criminal purga-
tion. 'A Reward for Apprehending of Thieves in the Parish
of Stoak Newington, in the County of Middlesex, that shall
commit the Fact in the said Parish.

'Whosoever shall apprehend, or cause to be apprehended,
any Person or Persons for Felony or Burglary, or for any
petty Larceny, committed within the said Parish within one
year from the date hereof, shall receive for every person so
apprehended and convicted of petty Larcency, 40s. which
shall be paid by the Church Wardens of the said Parish, upon
demand, after Such Conviction, and the said Church Wardens
shall be at all Charges of the Prosecution, they being order'd
to do so at a Vestry held for the said Parish, on the 26th of
December 1704.'

'Knights of the Post' have been previously mentioned,
but, for a bit of hard swearing, the following anecdote will
hold its own. It is told of a vagabond who was hanged in
1704.[1] 'Another Time *Tom Sharpe* being very well dress'd,
he went to one Counçellor *Manning's* Chambers in *Gray's*

[1] Smith's *Lives of Highwaymen*, etc.

Inn, and demanded 100 Pounds which he had lent him on a Bond. The Barrister was surpris'd at his Demand, as not knowing him ; and looking on the Bond, his Hand was so exactly Counterfeited, that he could not in a manner deny it to be his own Writing ; but that he knew his own Circumstances were such, that he was never in any Necessity of borrowing so much Money in all his Life of any Man ; therefore, as he could not be indebted in any such Sum, upon the account of borrowing, he told *Tom*, he would not Pay 100 Pounds in his own Wrong. Hereupon *Tom*, taking his Leave, he told him, he must expect speedy Trouble ; and in the meantime, Mr. *Manning* expecting the same, sent for another Barrister, to whom opening the matter, they concluded it was a forg'd Bond ; whereupon Mr. Manning's Council got a general Release forg'd for the Payment of this 100 Pounds ; and when Issue was join'd, and the Cause came to be try'd before the late Lord Chief Justice *Holt*, the Witnesses to *Tom Sharpe's* Bond, swore so heartily to his lending of the Money to the Defendant that he was in a very fair way of being cast ; 'till Mr. *Manning's* Council moving the Court in behalf of his Client, acquainted his Lordship that they did not deny the having borrow'd 100 Pounds of the Plaintiff, but that it had been paid for above three Months. Three Months ! (quoth his Lordship) and why did not the Defendant then take up his Bond, or see it cancell'd ? To this, his Council reply'd, that when they paid the Money, the Bond could not be found, whereupon the Defendant took a general Release for Payment thereof ; which being produc'd in Court, and two *Knights of the Post* swearing to it, the Plaintiff was cast. Which putting Tom *Sharpe* into a great Passion, he cry'd to his Companions, as he was coming through Westminster Hall, Was ever such Rogues seen in this World before, to swear they paid that which they never borrow'd ?'

There were plenty of ' Chevaliers d'Industrie ' in those days, and many were the traps set for the gullible and unwary. ' Like a couple of Sweetners in search of a Country Gudgeon, who thro' Greediness of Gain, would Bite at his share in a drop'd Half Crown, a Gilded Ring, or Rug and Leather.'

Who can the various City Frauds recite,
With all the petty Rapines of the Night?
Who now the *Guinea Dropper's* Bait regards,
Trick'd by the Sharper's Dice, or Juggler's Cards?
Why shou'd I warn thee ne'er to join the Fray,
Where the Sham Quarrel interrupts the Way?
Lives there in these our Days so soft a Clown,
Brav'd by the Bully's Oaths, or threat'ning Frown?
I need not strict enjoyn the Pocket's Care,
When from the crouded *Play* thou lead'st the Fair;
Who has not here, or Watch, or Snuff Box lost,
Or Handkerchiefs that *India's* Shuttle Boast?

'To prevent People being imposed upon by Beggers, The President and Governors for the Poor of the City of London give Notice, that on the 18th of this instant April one Eliza Cozens was brought into the Workhouse for Begging, with a Paper on her Breast, viz. These are to certifie all Persons whom it may concern, that the Bearer hereof, Eliza Cosens, a Captive among the Turks for the Space of 11 years and more, and because she would not renounce the Christian Religion they cut out her Tongue. Being ransomed with some other poor Slaves 6 years ago, in the Reign of the late King William, coming to her Native Country of England, and having no Friend to help her, she being reduc'd to the utmost poverty. We whose Names are hereunto set, do grant her this Certificate for her more secure Travelling, that she might partake more easier of all good Christian's Charity wherever she comes.

Ralph Freeman   { Two of Her Majesty's Justices of the Peace for the County of Hartford, at our Meeting, being the Petty Sessions at Buttingford.
Thomas Burgrief

'This Woman hath a Tongue, and no Impediment at all in her Speech, and this Certificate seems to be as much a Counterfeit as herself. She is now at the Workhouse in Bishopsgate Street, to be seen by any that please.'

Another somewhat similar notice was issued by the same authorities, about one Mary Welch, and two children, who were sent to the workhouse 'for Begging on Horseback, Rapt up in Sheets and Blankets, pretending to be burnt in their Limbs by a Fire which consumed their House in Lincolnshire; the said Mary Welch usually begs in a Country Habit with a High Crown'd Hat, and this Trade she hath follow'd several Years. All which Fact is notoriously untrue, the said Mary and her two Children being sound of their Limbs, and no ways scorch'd by any Fire.'

And there are other advertisements of like import, of which the following is most worthy of notice, as the impostor got his deserts :—

'. . . There is now in their Workhouse in Bishopsgate Street, one Rob. Cunningham, a Man of about 40 years of Age, who went begging up and down this City, and other Places, with this Paper following :—

To the Pious Reader.

Remember that God gave out the Law,
To keep the People of the World in awe.
Hope without Faith availeth not indeed,
Faith without Works, you may be sure is dead ;
Without Charity there is no Salvation,
Poverty Causes a sorrowful Vexation.
Excuse the Writer, if bold he seems to be,
He is DEAF and DUMB, and desires Charity.
He came last from Londonderry,
Where he lost his Speech and Hearing.
The occasion may be told.
It was Sickness, Famine and Cold.
At last confin'd within the Town,
For a Dog's Head paid half a Crown.
He does now for a Pension wait,
The which he is promis'd to get.
But the old Proverb you may observe,
While the Grass grows the Horse may Starve.

Rob. Cunningham.

Surdus & Mutus Scotia Natus.

' This Man being Committed to the Workhouse for begging in the City in the Manner aforesaid, was there detected the 13th of this instant September before the Committee there present, he having no Infirmity in his Speech or Hearing, and he will shortly be sent a Soldier in her Majesty's Service. He is the 4th pretended Dumb Person who hath been here lately detected.'

Among the rogues and vagabonds may be classed the gipsies, who led their nomadic life then, as now, and their description one hundred and seventy years ago might be written to-day : ' As I was Yesterday riding out in the Fields with my Friend Sir Roger, we saw at a little Distance from us a Troop of Gypsies. Upon the first Discovery of them, my friend was in some doubt whether he should not exert the Justice of the Peace upon such a Band of Lawless Vagrants ; but not having his Clerk with him, who is a necessary Counsellor on these Occasions, and fearing that his Poultry might fare the worse for it, he let the Thought drop : But at the same time gave me a particular Account of the Mischiefs they do in the Country, in stealing People's Goods and spoiling their Servants. If a stray Piece of Linnen hangs upon an Hedge, says Sir Roger, they are sure to have it ; if the Hog loses his Way in the Fields, it is ten to one but he becomes their Prey ; our Geese cannot live in Peace for them : if a Man prosecutes them with Severity, his Hen roost is sure to pay for it ; They generally straggle into these Parts about this Time of the Year ; and set the Heads of our Servant Maids so agog for Husbands, that we do not expect to have any Business done as it should be whilst they are in the Country. I have an honest Dairy Maid, that crosses their Hands with a Piece of Silver every Summer, and never fails being promised the handsomest young Fellow in the Parish for her Pains. Your Friend the Butler has been Fool enough to be seduced by them ; and, though he is sure to lose a Knife, a Fork or a Spoon every time his fortune is told, generally shuts himself up in the Pantry with an old Gypsie for above half an Hour once in a Twelvemonth. Sweethearts are the things they live upon, which they bestow very plentifully upon all those that apply themselves to them. You see now and then some handsome young Jades among them : The Sluts have often white Teeth and black Eyes.' [1]

The laws were cruelly severe against them, as Misson notes. 'By Acts of Parliament and Statutes made in the Reign of *Henry* 8th and his two Daughters, all those People calling themselves *Bohemians* or *Egyptians*, are hangable as

[1] *Spectator*, 130.

Felons at the Age of 14 Years, a Month after their Arrival in *England*, or after their first disguising themselves. Before the Month is out, they escape with the Loss of their Goods, Money, &c., if they have any. This Law is not put in Execution: 'Tis true they have very few of those People in *England*.'

In 1704 the president and governors of the poor of London set a good example to the other municipalities of the kingdom by issuing a proclamation against ' Rogues, Vagabonds, and Sturdy Beggars,' and promised to anyone who should apprehend one of these objectionable persons, and, taking him before a justice of the peace, get him committed to the Workhouse, a reward of twelve pence ' towards the Charges of this so doing,' and it further recited the pains and penalties contained in the 29 Eliz. cap. 7, and 1 Jas. I. cap. 7, on those people who hindered their apprehension, and neglect of duty on the part of constables and others.

Perhaps it was as well to, now and then, remind the constables of their duties, for, if we may believe Ward, they were a very queer lot. ' He always walks Arm'd with a Staff of Authority, Seal'd with the Royal Arms, and all Wise People think the Fellow that Carries it a great Blot in the Scutcheon. . . . They are the only Encouragers of what they pretend to Suppress, Protecting those People, for Bribes, which they should punish ; Well Knowing each Bad house they break is a Weekly Stipend, out of their own Pockets.'

Here is a case in which they were made to eat the leek. ' On Tuesday last, at Guild Hall, came on the Tryal of the Constables for their insolent Behaviour the last Year, when the Honourable Plaintiffs, at the humble Request of the Defendants, out of pure Compassion for them and their indigent Families, were charitably pleas'd to forgive 'em, upon the following Submission : .

'WHEREAS we, *Francis Violet* and *John Bavis*, Constables of the Ward of *Broad Street*, did on the 8th day of Febr., 1707,[1] rudely Take the Right Hon. *Bazil*, Earl of *Denbigh*, and *William*, Lord *Craven*, Sir *Cholmley Dering*, Bar. *James*

---

[1] This of course should read 1708.

Buller, Esq. and *Thomas Leigh*, Esq. out of Mr. *Calwac's* House near the *Royal Exchange*, and commit 'em to the *Poultry Compter* ; We do hereby declare, That they were not Gaming, or any ways disorderly or offensive in their Behaviour : And that we were guilty of this great Imprudence, without any just Cause ; for which we are heartily sorry, and most humbly beg Pardon in open Court.   FRANCIS VIOLET.

JOHN BAVIS.'[1]

Pollaky and the private inquiry offices were foreshadowed by the subjoined. ' This is to give notice that those who have sustained any loss at Sturbridge Fair last, by Pick Pockets or Shop lifts : If they please to apply themselves to John Bonner in Shorts Gardens, they may receive information and assistance therein ; also Ladies and others who lose their Watches at Churches, and other Assemblies, may be served by him as aforesaid, to his utmost power, if desired by the right Owner, he being paid for his Labour and Expences.'

Nor do we enjoy the monopoly of gigantic commercial swindles and official peculations : human nature was pretty much the same. ' This day, one Mr. C——, a great exchange broker, who dealt mostly in Stocks, went off, as said, for above £100,000.'[2]

' 26 Oct., 2703. The Commons of Ireland divided, whether Sir Wm. Robertson, vice-treasurer there, not giving an account of about £130,000 of the publick money, should be uncapable of ever serving her majestie, and be committed to the Castle : noes, 96 ; yeas, 104.'

' 23 Dec., 1703. Yesterday the lords examined several Witnesses about abuses committed in Victualling the Fleet ; and it appearing that one Hoar, who made some discovery therein, had since been almost killed by persons in masks, the Commissioners of the victualling office were ordered to attend the 5th of January.'

' 7 Mar., 1704. The Commons considered the report of the Commissioners of accounts, wherein they charge the earl of Ranelagh with £72,000 of the publick money not accounted for, and Ordered an address to the queen, that the attorney-

---

[1] *The Post Boy,* March 5/8, 1709.   [2] *Luttrell,* Aug. 14, 1703.

generall may prosecute him in the exchequer by way of extent upon his estate.'

' 14 Mar., 1704. This day the Commons resolved, that the late Commissioners of the Victualling office, in neglecting to keep regular accounts, in making out perfect bills to clear imprests without vouchers, and in not keeping a regular course in payment of their bills, and not making regular assignments thereof, have been guilty of a breach of trust, and acted contrary to their instructions.

' That Philip Papillion, esq., late cashier of the Victualling (Office) has been guilty of a breach of his instructions, by paying several bills without being signed by three Commissioners.

' And that an addresse be presented to her Majestie to direct an immediate prosecution against him, to compell him to account according to the Course of the Exchequer.'

' 3 Oct., 1710. Yesterday Richard Dyot, esq., a justice of the peace for Middlesex, and one of the Commissioners of the stamp Office, was taken into Custody, being accused of counterfeiting stamps: implements for that purpose were taken in his house. Mr. Thomas Welham, deputy register of the prerogative office at Doctor's Commons, and others, were also seized and examined, being concern'd with him.'

These are not examples of a pleasant social state, and yet it seems that things might have been worse. ' I happen'd to be in a Company t'other day, among some persons who were very well acquainted with both *London* and *Paris*, where it was made a Question, Which of those two famous Cities was most debauch'd? 'Twas urg'd that the excessive Clemency of the *English* Laws gave *Room* for abundance of ill Actions that would not else be committed. Their Punishments have nothing terrible in them but Death. A Rack is not known among them ; and their Examination of Criminals is not at all severe. The Judges are extremely favourable to them ; false Witnesses lie under but a slight Penalty ; and there is a Relaxation which may be call'd an Inexecution of the Laws. Then as to Bankruptcies, and other Villanies of that Nature, the City of *London* is so full of privileg'd Places, where such Thieves may take Shelter, that upon the whole it must be

Confess'd there is much less Danger in being wicked at London than at *Paris*; and yet we came to a Resolution, That there is more Vice, and more Roguery at *Paris* than at *London*; more infamous Actions, more Cruelty, and more Enormity.'[1]

To remedy the very imperfect and lax enforcement of the laws, a society had been started in 1696, 'For the Reformation of Manners in the Cities of London and Westminster'; and in their eighth year (1703) they published a list of 858 'Leud and Scandalous Persons' convicted by their means in the previous year: in 1704, the convictions were 863; in 1707, only 706; whilst afterwards they increased enormously.

	1708.	1709.
Lewd and Disorderly Men and Women	1255	794
Keepers of disreputable and disorderly Houses	51	32
Keepers of Common Gaming Houses	30	10
Persons for—Exercising their Trades or ordinary Callings on the Lord's Day	1187	1523
Prophane Swearing and Cursing	626	575
Drunkenness	150	42

Looking at the above figures, the society must have done a sensible amount of good in morally purging the metropolis.

There were minor punishments: the stocks and the pillory, the former used for petty, the latter for somewhat graver, offences.

Defoe had to stand in the latter, and celebrated his defiance of his punishment in 'a HYMN to the PILLORY.' It was all very well for him to write—

> Hail *Hi'roglyphick* State *Machin*,
> Contriv'd to Punish Fancy in :
> Men that are Men, in thee can feel no Pain,
> And all thy *Insignificants* Disdain

—but even his proud boasting has to recognise unpleasantly

[1] Misson.

The undistinguish'd Fury of the Street,
Which Mob and Malice Mankind Greet,
No Byass can the Rabble draw,
But *Dirt* throws *Dirt* without respect to Merit or to Law.

Everyone is familiar with the general features of the pillory, but yet a contemporaneous account, by a keen-sighted witness, will materially help to bring it vividly before us. ' This Punishment is allotted for those who are convicted of any notorious Cheat, or infamous Imposture ; of having publish'd defamatory Libels against the King or Government ; of false Testimony, and of publick Blasphemy ; They are expos'd in a high Place, with their Heads put thro' two Pieces of notch'd Wood ; the uppermost whereof being made to slide down, shuts the Neck into the Notch. The Criminal's Hands are confin'd on each Side his Head in the same Manner ; and thus he stands in this ridiculous Posture for more or less time, or with more or fewer Repetitions, according to his Sentence. If the People think there is nothing very odious in the Action that rais'd him to this Honour, they stand quietly by, and only look at him ; but if he has been guilty of some Exploit dislik'd by the Tribe of 'Prentices, he must expect to be regaled with a hundred thousand handfuls of Mud, and as many rotten Eggs as can be got for Money. It is not lawful to throw Stones, but yet 'tis often done. Generally the honest Man wears a large Sheet of Paper like a Cravat, containing his Elogium in great Letters.' [1]

There was a lawful punishment for scolding women in the ducking stool, of which Gay sings :—

I'll speed me to the Pond, where the high Stool
On the long Plank hangs o'er the muddy Pool ;
That Stool, the Dread of every scolding Quean,
Yet, sure a Lover should not die so mean. [2]

The *cucking* stool is often used as being synonymous with *ducking* stool, but in reality it is not. The cucking stool is by far the more ancient, and is described in Domesday Book (speaking of Chester) as ' Cathedra Stercoris.' It was a solidly made chair with a hole in the seat, and a rail in front to keep the offender in ; and at first the punishment

---

[1] Misson.   [2] *The Shepherd's Week*—The Dumps.

was confined to exhibition of the scold in front of her house, where, for a certain length of time, she was exposed to the jeers of the neighbourhood.   Afterwards it was mounted on wheels, being then called a tumbrel, or trebucket, and moved about the town.   It then was improved by ducking the offending woman in some pond ; and at last permanent ones were set up in divers towns and villages, as described by Gay, and especially well by Misson, who says : ' The way of punishing Scolding Women is Pleasant enough ; They fasten an Arm Chair to the end of two Beams, twelve or fifteen Foot long, and parallel to each other : So that these two Pieces of Wood, with their two Ends, embrace the Chair, which hangs between them upon a Sort of Axel ; by which Means it plays freely, and always remains in the natural horizontal Position in which a Chair should be, that a Person may sit Conveniently in it, whether you raise it or let it down.   They set up a post upon the Bank of a Pond, or River, and over this Post they lay, almost in Equilibrio, the two Pieces of Wood, at one End of which the Chair hangs just over the Water ; they place the Woman in this Chair, and so plunge her into the Water, as often as the Sentence directs, in order to Cool her immoderate Heat.'

CHAPTER XLI.

PRISONS.

Dreadful condition of Prisons—Bridewell—Description of—Flogging—
Houses of Correction—Compters—Description of the Poultry compters
— 'Garnish' — Newgate — Description of — Marshalsea — Queen's
Bench—Fleet and Ludgate—Poor Debtors—Kidnappers—Country
prisons—Bankrupts.

PERHAPS one of the foulest social blots in this reign was the
loathsome pollution, moral and physical, of the prisons. It
was not that public attention was not called to it. Every
writer who touched at all upon the subject was loud in expos-
ing their terrible condition, and the villanies practised in them,
without effecting any amelioration in them ; and so they continued until the time of Howard. They are a portion of the
Social Life of the Reign of Queen Anne, and must be spoken
of ; but their description must be very modified, as the
plain, unvarnished statements made by contemporary writers
would not be held as exactly fitting for general perusal in
these days.

'A Prison is the Grave of the Living, where they are shut
up from the World, and the Worms that gnaw upon them,
their own Thoughts, the Jaylor, and their Creditors. A
House of Meagre Looks and ill Smells ; for Lice, Drink, and
Tobacco are the Compound. . . . Men huddle up their Life
here as a thing of no use, and wear it out like an old Shirt,
the faster, the better ; and he that deceives the time best,
best spends it. It is the Place where Strangers are best
Welcomed ; and their Joys are never greater than when they
hear of the increase of their miserable Companions, because
they are in hopes of a Garnish. This Place teaches Wisdom,

but commonly too late ; and a Man had better be a Fool
than come here to learn Wit.' [1]

The prisons in London, in their alphabetical order, were
as follows : Bridewell ; Clerkenwell House of Correction ;
Clerkenwell New Prison ; Counters, or Compters, in the
Poultry and Wood Street ; Fleet ; Gate House, Westmin-
ster ; Ludgate ; Marshalsea ; Newgate ; Queen's Bench ;
Westminster House of Correction ; and White Lyon Prison,
Southwark ; besides a sort of prison at Whitechapel, and one
exclusively for debtors in the precinct of St. Catharine's
Tower—a precinct which had the privilege of freedom of
arrest for debt, except by an order of the Board of Green Cloth.

Bridewell, which had originally been a royal residence,
was situated between Fleet Ditch and Bride Lane ; and ' It
is a prison and House of Correction for idle Vagrants, loose
and disorderly Servants, Night Walkers, Strumpets &c.
These are set to hard Labour, and have Correction according
to their deserts, but have their Cloaths and Diet during their
Imprisonment at the Charge of the House.' [2]

Ward, of course, is in his element in describing Bridewell[3] ;
but his account is not exaggerated. ' We then turn'd into the
Gate of a stately Edifice, my Friend told me was *Bridewell*,
which to me seem'd rather a Prince's Palace, than a House of
Correction ; till gazing round me, I saw in a large Room a
parcel of ill looking Mortals, pounding a Pernicious Weed,
which I thought from their unlucky aspects, seem'd to
threaten their Destruction. These, said I, to my Friend, I
suppose are the Offenders at Work ; pray what do you think
their Crimes may be ? Truly, said he, I cannot tell you ; but
if you have a mind to Know, ask any of them their Offence,
and they will soon satisfie you. Prithee Friend, said I, to a
Surly Bull neck'd fellow, who was thumping as lazily at his
Wooden Anvil, as a Ship Carpenter at a Log in the King's
Yard at *Deptford*, What are you Confin'd to this Labour for ?
My Hempen Operator, leering over his shoulder, cast at me
one of his hanging Looks, which so frightened me, I step'd
back, for fear he should have knocked me on the Head with

---

[1] *Hickelty Pickelty.*   [2] Hatton's *New View of London*, 1708.
[3] *London Spy.*

his Beetle, Why, Mr. *Tickletail*, says he, taking me, as I believe, being in Black, for some Country Pedagogue, I was committed hither by Justice Clodpate, for saying I had rather hear a Black bird Whistle *Walsingham*,[1] or a Peacock Scream against Foul Weather, than a Parson talk Nonsense in a Church, or a Fool talk Latin in a Coffee House: And I'll be judg'd by you who are a Man of Judgment, whether in all I said there be one Word of Treason to deserve a Whipping Post.

'The Impudence of this Canary Bird so dash'd me out of Countenance, together with his unexpected Answer, I had nothing to say, but heartily wish'd myself well out of their Company; and, just as we were turning back, to avoid their further Sawciness, another calls out to me, Hark you, Master in Black, of the same colour of the Devil, can you tell me how many thumps of this Hammer will soften the Hemp so as to make a Halter fit Easie, if a man should have occasion to wear one? A third crying out, I hope, Gentlemen, you will be so Generous to give us something to Drink, for you don't know but we may be hard at work for you? We were glad, with what Expedition we could, to escape their Impudence.

'Going from the Work room to the Common side, or place of Confinement (where they are Lock'd up at Night) through the frightful Grates of which uncomfortable Apartment, a Ghastly Skeleton stood peeping, that from his terrible Aspect, I thought some Power Immortal had imprison'd Death that the World might Live for ever. I could not speak to him without dread of danger, least when his Lips open'd to give me an Answer, he should poison the Air with his Contagious Breath, and Communicate to me the same Pestilence which had brought his infected Body to a dismal Anatomy: Yet mov'd with pity towards so sad an Object, I began to enquire into the Causes of his sad appearance, who, after a Penitential Look, that call'd for Mercy and Compassion, with much difficulty he rais'd his feeble Voice a degree above silence, and told me he had been Sick Six Weeks under that sad Confinement, and had nothing to comfort him but Bread and Water, now and then the refreshment of a little small beer. I asked him further what Offence he had Committed

---

[1] See Appendix.

that brought him under this unhappiness? To which he answer'd, He had been a great while discharg'd of all that was charg'd against him, and was detain'd only for his Fees, which for want of Friends, being a Stranger in the Town, he was totally unable to raise. I ask'd him what his Fees amounted to; who told me *Five Groats*—Bless me! thought I, what a Rigorous, Uncharitable thing is this.

'From thence we turn'd into another Court, the Buildings being like the former, Magnificently Noble; where straight before us was another Grate, which prov'd the Women's Apartments; we follow'd our Noses and Walk'd up to take a View of their Ladies, who we found were shut up as close

BEATING HEMP.

FLOGGING A WOMAN.

as Nuns; but like so many Slaves, were under the Care and Direction of an Over Seer, who walk'd about with a very flexible Weapon of Offence, to Correct such Hempen Journey Women who were unhappily troubled with the Spirit of Idleness. . . . They look'd with as much Modesty as so many *Newgate* Saints, canonized at the *Old Baily*; being all as Merry over their shameful Drudgery, notwithstanding their Miserable Circumstances, as so many Jolly Crispins in a Garret. . . .

'Being now both tired with, and amaz'd at the Confidence and Loose Behaviour of these Degenerate Wretches, who had neither Sense of Grace, Knowledge of Vertue, Fear of Shame, or Dread of Misery, my Friend reconducted me back

into the first Quadrangle, and led me up a pair of Stairs into
a spacious Chamber, where the Court was sat in great Grandeur
and Order. A Grave Gentleman, whose Awful Looks bespoke him some Honourable Citizen, being mounted in the
Judgment Seat, Arm'd with a Hammer, like a Change-
Broker at Lloyd's Coffee House—and a Woman under the
Lash in the next Room, where Folding Doors were open'd,
that the whole Court might view the Punishment; at last
down went the Hammer, and the Scourging ceas'd; that I
protest, until I was undeceiv'd, I thought they had sold their
Lashes by Auction. The Honourable Court, I observ'd was
chiefly Attended by Fellows in Blew Coats, and Women in
Blew Aprons. Another Accusation being then deliver'd by a
Flat Cap against a poor Wench, who having no Friend to
speak in her Behalf, Proclamation was made, viz. All you
who are willing E—th T——ll should have present Punishment, Pray hold up your Hands; Which was done accordingly; And then she was ordered the Civility of the House,
and was forced to shew her tender Back and Breasts to the
Sages of the Grave Assembly, who were mov'd by her Modest
Mein, together with the whiteness of her Skin, to give her
but a gentle Correction.'

The Houses of Correction at Clerkenwell, White Lyon
Prison at Southwark, and Westminster, were similar institutions. The new prison at Clerkenwell was simply a House of
Detention, where the prisoners awaited trial, and was intended
to ease Newgate.

Wood Street and Poultry Compters received not only
'debtors upon Actions in the Lord Mayor's and Sheriff's
Courts, but such as disturb the Peace of the City in the Night.'
Ward describes at considerable length a night spent in the
Poultry Counter. He says, 'The Turnkey was so civil to
offer us Beds, but upon such unconscionable terms, that we
thank'd him for his Love, but refus'd his *Courtesie.*' Afte--
wards he was put in the *Common side* of the prison, and this
is what it was like. 'When first we enter'd this Apartment,
under the Title of the *King's Ward*, the mixtures of Scenes
that arose from *Mundungus-Tobacco*, foul Sweaty *Toes*, Dirty
Shirts, stinking *Breaths*, and unclcanly Carcases, Poison d

our Nostrils far worse than a *Southwark* Ditch, a *Tanner's Yard*, or a *Tallow Chandlers* Melting Room.   The Ill looking Vermin, with long Rusty Beards swaddled up in Rags, and their heads, some cover'd with Thrum Caps, and others thrust into the tops of old Stockings ; some quitted their Play they were before engag'd in, and came hovering round us, like so many *Canibals*, with such devouring *Countenances*, as if a Man had been but a Morsel with 'em all crying out *Garnish, Garnish*, as a Rabble in an Insurrection, crying *Liberty, Liberty*.   We were forc'd to submit to their Doctrine of Non resistance, and comply with their demands, which extended to the Sum of Two Shillings each.   Having thus Paid our Initiation Fees, we were bid Welcome into the *King's Ward*, and to all the Privileges and Immunities thereof.'

We will not follow Ward through his night's experiences, which are far too graphically told—but in the morning, he says, ' Now I must confess, I was forc'd to hold my Nose to the Grate, and Snuff hard for a little fresh Air ; for I was e'en choak'd with the unwholesome Fumes that arose from their uncleanly Carcasses : Were the Burning of Old Shoes, Draymen's Stockings, the Dipping Card Matches, and a full Close Stool Pan, to be prepared in one Room, as a Nosegay to torment my Nostrils, it could not have prov'd a more effectual Punishment.'

More than once we have come across the word *Garnish*. The following scene will assist us in thoroughly grasping its meaning :—

Scene—Newgate.[1]

Storm. I defie the World to say I ever did an ill thing.   I love my Friend—but there is always some little Trifle given to Prisoners, they call Garnish ; we of the Road are above it, but o' t'other side of the House, Silly Rascals that come voluntarily hither.   Such as are in for Fools, sign'd their own *Mittimus*, in being bound for others, may perhaps want it : I'll be your faithful Almoner.

Bookwit. O, by all means, Sir.   (*Gives him Money.*)

Storm. Pray, Sir, is this your Footman ?

Bookwit. He is my Friend, Sir.

Storm. Look you, Sir, the only time to make use of a Friend is in

[1] *The Lying Lover.*

Extremity; do you think you cou'd not hang him, and save your self? Sir, my Service to you, your own Health. (*Gives it to next Prisoner.*)

1st Pris. Captain, your Health.

2nd Pris. Captain, your Health.

Storm. But perhaps the Captain likes Brandy better. So ho ! Brandy there—(*Drinks.*) But you don't perhaps like these strong Liquors. Sider ho ! Drink to him in it—Gentlemen all. But Captain, I see you don't love Sider neither. You and I will be for Claret then. Ay marry ! I knew this wou'd please (*Drinks*) you. (*Drinks again.*) Faith we'll make an end on't. I'm glad you like it.

Turnkey. I'm sorry, Captain *Storm,* to see you impose upon a Gentleman, and put him to Charge in his Misfortune. If a petty Larceny Fellow had done this—— But one of the Road !

Storm. I beg your Pardon, Sir, I don't question but the Captain understands there is a Fee to you for going to the Keeper's side (*Bookwit* and *Latin* give him Money) (Exeunt *Turnkey, Simon* following). Nay, Nay, you must stay here.

Simon. Why I am *Simon,* Madam *Penelope's* Man.

Storm. Then Madam Penelope's Man must strip for Garnish ; indeed, Master *Simon,* you must.

Simon. Thieves ! Thieves ! Thieves !

Storm. Thieves ! Thieves ! Why you senseless Dog, do you think there's Thieves in *Newgate?* Away with him to the Tap house. (*Pushes him off.*) We'll drink his Coat off. Come my little Chymist, thou shalt transmute this Jacket into Liquor, Liquor that will make us forget the evil Day. And while Day is ours, let us be Merry.

Perhaps the best contemporary account of Newgate is in a pamphlet, published in 1708, called 'MEMOIRS of the Right Villanous *John Hall*,' etc. ; and this is the scene attending the initiation of a prisoner into the *Common Side* :—

' Those Scholars that come here have nothing to depend on but the Charity of the Foundation, in which Side very exact Rules are observ'd ; for as soon as a Prisoner comes into the Turn Key's Hands Three Knocks are given at the Stair Foot, as a Signal a Collegian is coming up ; which Harmony makes those *Convicts* that stand for the *Garnish* as joyful as One Knock, the Signal of the *Baker's* coming every Morning, does those poor Prisoners, who, for want of Friends, have nothing else to Subsist on but Bread and Water : And no sooner are the Three Strokes given, but out jumps Four Trunchion Officers from their Hovel, and with a sort of ill mannerly Reverence receive him at the Grate ; then taking him into their Apartment, a couple of the good natured

Sparks hold him whilst the other Two pick his Pockets, claiming Six Pence apiece, as a Priviledge, belonging to their Office ; then they turn him out to the *Convicts*, who hover about him for *Garnish*, which is Six Shillings and Eight pence, which they, from an old Custom, claim by Prescription Time out of Mind for entring in the *Society*, otherwise they strip the poor Wretch, if he has not wherewithal to pay it.

' Then *Cook Ruffian* comes to him for Three pence for dressing the Charity Meat, which charitable disposed Persons send in every *Thursday*, whereon Earthen Dishes, Porringers, Pans, Wooden Spoons, and Cabbage Nets, are Stirring about against Dinner Time, whilst the Cook sweats in Porriging the Prisoners, who stand round him like so many poor Scholars begging at the Kitchin Door for College Broth.

' But yet the caged Person is not clear of his Dues, for next, Two other Officers, who have a Patent for being *Swabbers*, demand Three Half pence apiece more for clearing the Gaol of its Filth, which requires the Labour of *Sisiphus*, and is never to be ended. Then at the signal of the *Grey Pease* Woman, which is between Seven and Eight, he is conducted down Stairs, with an Illumination of Links, to his Lodging, and, provided he has a Shilling for Money, may lye in the *Middle Ward*, which (to give the Devils their due) is kept very neat and clean, where he pays One Shilling and Four Pence more to his Comrades, and then he is Free of the *College* and *Matriculated.'*

The *Lower Ward* was a shocking place, as was also a ' large Room call'd *Tangier*, which next to the *Lower Ward*, is the nastiest place in the Gaol. The Miserable Inhabitants hereof are Debtors.' There was a large room, called *High Hall*, for recreation, and a cellar where liquors were sold, in unlimited quantities, to moneyed prisoners. We can imagine the effects of drink among this depraved lot, and the fearful brawls and fights that took place ; but, were the riot very serious, then two pulls of the big bell, which hung over the *High Hall* stairs, would bring the turnkeys, who stood no nonsense among that unruly crew, and the ringleaders were ironed and thrown into dark dungeons.

The press-room, where non-pleading criminals were

pressed, and a room where the hangman seethed the quartered limbs of rebels and traitors in a mixture of pitch, tar, and oil, were among the apartments in Newgate. When the fettered prisoners were tried, if they did not give the gaolers half a crown to be put in the *Bail Dock*, they were put, men and women together, into the *Hold*, where a singular custom prevailed of a prisoner exacting a shilling apiece from the youngest for *Hold Money*; and were any one lucky enough to be acquitted, he had to spend a *Quit Shilling* for their delight.

Of the Marshalsea Prison Hatton says : ' It is now the County Gaol for Felons, the Admiralty Gaol for Piracy and other Offences committed at Sea, and is the Gaol to the Marshals court for Debt and Damage.' It was in Southwark ; and another contemporary [1] says it ' is situated on such a Cursed Piece of Land, that the Son is asham'd to be his Father's Heir in't. It is an infected Pest house all the Year long ; and *Lord have Mercy upon us* may well stand upon these Doors.'

The Gate House, Westminster, ' is the chief Prison for the City of *Westminster* Liberties, not only for Debt but Treason, Theft and other Criminal Matters ; the Keeper has that place by Lease from the Dean and Chapter of *Westminster.*'

The Queen's Bench Prison had ' its Rules of a considerable Extent and Allowance, somewhat better than in the Common Gaols, for which reason many Debtors elsewhere confin'd, do by *Habeas Corpus* remove into this Prison, which is the proper place of Confinement in all Cases tryable in the *Queen's Bench Court*, whether for Debt, Dammage, Treason, Murther, &c.'

The Fleet and Ludgate were purely for debtors, in contradistinction to the others, which accommodated not only debtors but criminals. Imprisonment for debt has not very long been done away with—indeed, it now exists, under the name of ' contempt of court ' ; and what renders it more illogical and oppressive, is that people can only be imprisoned for owing small sums, the debtors who operate on a larger scale having perfect immunity from restraint. However, in

[1] Smith's *Lives of Highwaymen.*

Anne's time large and small were taken indiscriminately; the smaller debtors, as being the weaker, naturally getting the worst of it; their chances of ever getting out being very remote. We have seen in Newgate that *Tangier* was the worst place but one in the gaol. 'The Miserable Inhabitants hereof are *Debtors*, who put what sorry Bedding they enjoy upon such an Ascent where Soldiers lye when on Guard at the *Tilt Yard*. But in this Apartment lye, besides *real Debtors*, such as are call'd your *Thieving Debtors*; who, having for *Theft* satisfy'd the *Queen*, by being Burnt in the Face, or Whipt, which is no Satisfaction to the wrong'd Subject, their Adversaries bring an Action of *Trover* against them, and keep them there till they make Restitution for Things stolen ... here is a lightsome Room call'd *Debtors' Hall*, so nam'd from such unfortunate Men lying there, where every Man shews like so many Wrecks upon the Sea; here the Ribs of £20, here the Ruins of a good Estate, Doublets, without Buttons, and a Gown without Sleeves; and a pair of Stairs higher lye Women that are *Fines* and *Debtors*, think-ing like their suffering Companions below them, every Year Seven till they get abroad.'[1]

The Warden of the Fleet must have made a good thing out of the necessities of his victims. If they had any money at all, he got it out of them. If their nature revolted at the moral and actual filth of the *Common Side*, they could rent a small room of him, the lowest price being about 8*s.* per week. This accommodation entailed paying besides 1*s.* 6*d.* a week to the chamberlain, and a double fee of 4*d.* to the chaplain. 'There are some who lie on the *Common Side*, or *Wards*, without Beds allowed to them, who pay but 1*s.* 2*d.* per week, and 34*s.* 4*d.* Commitment Fee, and 2*d.* per week to the *Parson*; but that place in the *Fleet* is Dark, Unwhole-some, and is a Curb upon the rest to pay those Great Rates the Gaoler Exacts; he unmercifully threatning all for *Non Payment*, with Dungeons and Irons, not distinguishing be-tween a Criminal and a Debtor.'

Ludgate was more comfortable, and rather more aris-tocratic; it was 'purely for Insolvent Citizens of *London*,

[1] *Hall's Memoirs.*

Beneficed Clergy, and Attorneys at Law. Fees at Coming in from the Counter—1*s.* 2*d.*; at going out—3*s.* 2*d.*; and to the Turnkey—1*s.* For their being here they pay on the Commons Side 1*s.* 2*d.* per Week, and on the Master's side— 1*s.* 9*d.* They have among the Prisoners a sort of Government, as a Steward chosen the 1st Tuesday in every Month ; also 7 Assistants.'[1]

But both here and at the Fleet, in spite of charitable bequests, there were some of the prisoners in a state of absolute destitution. To aid these, the prisoners took it in turns to perambulate the rules, and solicit help in money or kind, whilst another had to stand at the window-grating, rattling a box, and chanting the monotonous wail of ' Pray remember the poor Debtors ! '

' Passing under *Ludgate*, the other Day, I heard a Voice bawling for Charity, which I thought I had somewhere heard before. Coming near to the Grate, the Prisoner called me by my Name, and desired I would throw something into the Box. I was out of Countenance for him, and did as he bid me, by putting in half-a-Crown.'[2]

'REMEMBER THE POOR PRISONERS !'

Once in a debtors' prison, almost all hope had to be given up—even the release offered by Government on condition of joining the army or navy was limited to debtors of small amount, who must have been six months in prison ; and, besides, it was only going to other privations, and, in the army, almost certainly meant wounds or death. No wonder, then, if, when a man was in difficulties, he sometimes adopted the desperate resource of selling himself for a time in bondage to one of the Plantations. Poor wretch ! he knew it was bad to do so, by common report ; but he had to find out what the life of a 'Redemptioner' really was, by bitter experience.

[1] *New View of London.*   [2] *Spectator*, 82.

First, a little money advanced for his outfit ; then, on his
arrival at his destination, his body would be seized for his
passage money, which had been promised him free ; and then
he must be sold to Work for so many years, to some one who
paid his debt for him.   Put on the same footing, as to food
and government, with the convicts, his life was awful, whilst
his master always managed to keep him sufficiently in debt
for clothes and tobacco, &c., so that he never could free
himself.

Men were ever on the prowl, about London, to catch the
miserable. 'Those fine Fellows who look like Foot men
upon a Holy day, crept into cast Suits of their Masters, that
want Gentility in their Deportments answerable to their
Apparel, are Kidnappers, who walk the Change, and other
parts of the Town, in order to Seduce People, who want
Services, and young Fools crost in Love, and under an
uneasiness of Mind, to go beyond Seas, getting so much a
head of Masters of Ships, and Merchants who go over, for
every Wretch they trapan into this Misery.   Those Young
Rakes, and Tatterdemallions you see so lovingly herded, are
drawn by their fair Promises to sell themselves into Slavery,
and the Kidnappers are the Rogues that run away with the
Money.'[1]

Bad as the prisons where debtors were confined were in
London, they were infinitely worse in the country ; indeed,
one can scarcely credit the treatment they received.   There
is, however, a most interesting little book, called ' The Cry of
the Oppressed,' which goes minutely into the details in many
of the country prisons, and the engravings alone show the
cruel treatment debtors had to endure : catching mice for
subsistence ; being dragged on hurdles, dying of starvation
and malaria ; covered with boils and blains ; imprisoned in
underground dungeons ; assaulted by the gaolers ; having
to live with the hogs, with wooden clogs chained to their
legs ; having to herd with condemned criminals ; and being
tortured with thumbscrews, etc.

Nobody ever seems to have bothered their heads about it—
it was not their business.   Luttrell says, ' 3 Nov., 1702. This

[1] *London Spy.*

day ordered a Bill to be brought in for regulating the King's Bench and Fleet Prisons,' but nobody took sufficient interest in it, and it never became an Act.

Arrest for debt was so common in those days that we find that even the sacred person of an ambassador was not exempt. 'Saturday, 24 July, 1708. Thursday, the Muscovite envoy, who is leaving this kingdom, was arrested in his Coach in the Haymarket for a debt of £360, which he has since paid, but complained to her Majestie of the affront, who ordered the officers to be prosecuted, and promised him all possible satisfaction. 27 Jul. The Queen has ordered the persons who caused the Muscovite ambassador to be arrested to beg his pardon upon their knees.'[1]

In the *Daily Courant,* Oct. 11, 1705, is a most pathetic appeal from a bankrupt to his creditors. 'To the Creditors of James Folkingham, late of London, Merchant. The Mottos of Sic transit Gloria Mundi, and Hodie mihi, cras tibi, have been frequently made use of to express the uncertainty of Humane Affairs in all their Divisions, even from the greatest Monarch, to the Meanest Peasant, so I may occasionally lay Claim to them. This premised, I shall not entertain you Gentlemen, my Creditors, with the Number, Variety, and Severity of my Misfortunes, nor how far my folly, want of Judgment, Inadvertency, &c. may have contributed thereto ; but rather plead Guilty to the Indictment of having Injured you, unwillingly, of a great deal of Money, and my own near Relations of as much, and throw myself on your Mercy ; in order to entitule me to which, I promise upon Oath to resign all I have, and shall be required by the Persons deputed, directly or indirectly ; provided I may be forthwith set at Liberty, with a Security not to be molested hereafter. That my all is no more, is matter of Concern to me, as well as Disappointment to you. If God Almighty ever permit me to be able, my generous, honest Temper will oblige me to make you farther Satisfaction, for to Digg I will endeavour, tho' to Begg I am ashamed.

'Your Disconsolate Debtor and Humble Servant,

'JAMES FOLKINGHAM.'

[1] *Luttrell's Diary.*

In one case, that of Thomas Pitkin, a bankrupt linen draper, who absconded, an Act of Parliament (3 and 4 Anne, cap. 11) was passed for the relief of his creditors, and for his apprehension, and he was afterwards captured at Breda in Holland.

The Act of 4 and 5 Anne, cap. 4, 'to prevent Frauds frequently committed by Bankrupts,' gave liberty to a large number, the *Gazette* of June 6/10, 1706, having as many as forty-six bankruptcy petitions, whereas formerly seven or eight was an average.

CHAPTER XLII.

WORKHOUSES, HOSPITALS, ETC.

The London Workhouse—Life therein—Bedlam—Its building—Regulations—Descripticn of interior—Governors—Bartholomew Hospital—
St. Thomas's—Almshouses.

THE London Workhouse, in Bishopsgate Street, was, perhaps,
one of the first of these municipal institutions, and there the
rogues, vagrants, and sturdy beggars were really set to work,
and the women were employed in sewing or washing liner,
beating hemp, and picking oakum. The children, who were
either vagrants or parish children, were taught spinning wocl
and flax, sewing, knitting, winding silk, and making their
clothes and shoes ; but they also received some elementary
instruction in reading, writing, and arithmetic. Hatton thus
gives the daily life of these little ones : 'The Bell rings at 5
a Clock in the Morning to call up the Children, and half a1
Hour after, the Bell is rung for Prayers, and Breakfast ; at
7 the Children are set to work ; 20 under a Mistress to spin
Wool and Flax, to Knit Stockings, to wind Silk, to make
and Sew their Linen, Cloaths, Shooes, Mark &c. All the
Children are called down for an Hour every Day to Read,
and an Hour every day to Write (*viz.*) 20 at a time.

'At 12 a Clock they go to Dinner, and have a little time
to play till One, then they are set to work again till 6 a clock :
They are rung to Prayers, to their Supper, and allowed to
play till Bed time.

'Every Nurse combs her Children with a small tooth
comb 3 times a Week ; mends the Children's Cloaths ; makes
their beds, washes their Wards ; and sees that the children go
neat and clean, and that they wash and comb themselves
every day.

'Some Children earn a ½*d.*, some 1*d.* and some 4*d.* per day.

'The Children are taught their *Catechism*, and often Catechised by the Minister, especially every *Sunday.*

'When Children are grown up to 12, 13 or 14 years of Age they are put forth Apprentices to Masters of Ships, and other Sea faring Men, and to Handycraft Trades and others, and the Governors give with them a good ordinary Suit of Cloaths or 20*s.* in Money at the Election of the Master or Mistress.

'. . . The Seal or Badge of this Corporation is an Orphan, his Left Hand resting on the Head of a Sheep, with this Motto, *God's Providence is our Inheritance.*'

The hospitals, in the modern acceptation of the word, were Bethlehem, or Bedlam, St. Bartholomew's, and St. Thomas's—Guy's not having yet been founded.

Of Bethlehem Hatton says : 'It was formerly a mean House situate between the E. side of Moor-fields, and Bishops-gate Street. . . . This Hospital for poor distracted Persons, growing Old and Ruinous, and too small to accommodate so great numbers, for whom Applications were made ; the City of *London* granted to the Governours of the said Hospital, Ground on the S. Side of Moor-fields (a Situation much more Commodious as to Air &c.) for the benefit of Lunatick Persons, and in the year 1675, the present spacious Structure was begun to be erected, which was finished Anno 1676, being well built of Brick and Stone, the Wings at both ends and the Portico, being all adorned with each 4 pilasters,' etc. —'and on a Pediment over the Gate are the Figures of 2 Lunaticks curiously Carved.' These figures, which are now in the hall of Bethlehem Hospital, represent Raving and Melancholy Madness, and were the work of Caius Gabriel Cibber (father of the celebrated Colley Cibber). They are carved in Portland stone, and one of them was the portrait of Oliver Cromwell's porter, then in Bedlam.

In Anne's time it was not overcrowded. 'Distracted persons who went out cured in the Year ending at *Easter* 1707—59 ; buried in that time 24. Brought into the Hospital in 1706—82—and remaining at *Easter* aforesaid in this Hospital under Cure, 142.'

'The Method of receiving, continuing and curing Lunaticks in this Hospital is. When any Person is minded to get a Friend or Relation into the Hospital, it must be by Petition to the Committee who sit at *Bethlehem* 7 at a time weekly : this must be signed by the Church Wardens or other reputable Persons who know the Lunatick, and also recommended to the said Committee by one of the Governours ; and this being approved by the President and Governours, and enter'd in a Book, upon a vacancy (in their turn) an Order is granted for their being received into the House, where the said Lunatick is accommodated with a Room in a good Air, proper Physick, and Diet Gratis. The Diet is very good and wholesome, being commonly boyled Beef, Mutton or Veal and Broth with Bread for Dinners on Sundays, Tuesdays, and Thursdays, the other Days, Bread, Cheese and Butter, or on Saturdays Peas, Pottage, Rice Milk, Fermity or other Pottage ; and for Suppers they have usually Broth or Milk Pottage, always with Bread ; and there is this farther care taken, that some of the Committee go weekly to the said Hospital to see the Provisions weighed, and that the same be good and rightly expended.

'There is also care taken, That no distracted Person be abused by the Servants of the House &c. ; the Men Servants of the House attend the Lunatick Men, and the Women Servants the Women, and no loose Person or Apprentice is suffered to loyter away the time in this Hospital, nor any Person to be admitted to come or stay in (as a Spectator) after Sun Setting ; and the Servants are particularly enjoyned to keep good Hours.'

This looks admirable, *on paper*—but, practically, it was the reverse. It ranked, as we know, with the Lions and Westminster Abbey, as one of the principal sights of London. Ward describes a visit : 'Accordingly we were admitted in thro' an Iron gate, within which sat a Brawny *Cerberus* of an Indico Colour, leaning upon a Money box ; we turned in thro' another Iron Barricado, where we heard such a rattling of *Chains*, drumming of *Doors, Ranting, Hollowing, Singing* and *Running* that I could think of nothing but Don *Quevedo's* Vision, where the Damn'd broke loose, and put Hell in an Uproar.' He describes the lunatics as being filthy in their persons, their habits, and their conversation, and the visitors as no better than they ought to be: ''tis a new Whetstone's Park [1]—now the old one's Plough'd up, where a Sportsman at any Hour in the Day may meet with Game for his Purpose.' So he and his friend 'redeemed their Liberties from this Prison, at the Expence of Two Pence '—and went away.

There were the names of good men on the List of Governors—take that for 1711, for instance. All the aldermen were so, *ex officio*, and there were the Earls of Abingdon, Anglesea, Ailesford, Lords Craven, Gower, Harcourt, and St. John of Bletsoe ; the Earl of Scarsdale, Doctor *Jonathan Swift*, Dean of St. Patrick. The Earl of Thanet and Sir Philip York, the Attorney-General.

Of St. Bartholomew's Hospital Hatton says :—

This Hospital of St. Bartholomew's, the last Year 1706 cur'd and discharg'd of wounded, sick and maimed Souldiers, Seamen, and other diseased Persons from several Parts of the Queen's Dominions (and from Foreign Parts) who have been relieved with Money and other Necessaries, notwithstanding the greatest part of the Revenue of this Hospital was consumed by the lamentable Flames in 1666 to the Number of   } 2293

Buried in the year 1706, after much Charge on them   141

And at the beginning of the Year 1707, there remained Persons at the Charge of the Hospital under Cure   } 371

St. Thomas's Hospital escaped the fire of 1666, and also a very bad one that happened in Southwark May 26, 1676, when 500 houses were burnt. It performed its share of merciful work, for in 1706 it discharged (cured) 2,820 persons, buried 174, and had 362 in hospital.

Of almshouses there were plenty in existence, such as the Trinity, those of the different City companies, and of private benefactors ; but the stream of charity seems to have flowed, in this reign, in a different channel, that of founding charity schools, and I can find no new almshouses recorded.

---

[1] A narrow alley leading from Lincoln's Inn Fields to Holborn.

APPENDIX.

LILLI-BURLERO.

From 'The Dancing Master,' 15 Ed. 1713.
Brit. Mus. C. 31, b. 21.

H. PURCELL.

HUNT THE SQUIRIL.

LONGWAYS FOR AS MANY AS WILL.

'Dancing Master,' Ed. 1713.

⊙⊙⊙⊙ Men.
⟩⟩⟩⟩ Women.

NOTE.—Each Strain must be played twice over, to each Part of the Dance.

The first Man Heys[1] on the We. side, the 1st Wo Heys on the Men's side at the same time (*a*). The 1st Man Heys on the Men's side, the Wo, on the We. side, till they come into their own Places (*b*). The 1st cu. cross over and turn (*a*) then the 2 cu. do the same (*b*).

The 1st Man figures the Figure of 8 on the Man's side, his Partner follows after him the same time, then she slips into her own Place (*a*). Then the 1st Wo. cast off on the out side of the 3 Wo. and half figures with the 3 and 2 We. her Partner follows her at the same time, then the Man slips into his own Place (*b*) the 1st cu. being at the top, the 1 Man changes over with the 2 Wo. and the 1st Wo. changes over with the 2 Man, then Hands half round all four, the 1 cu. being at the top cast off (*a*). Then right and left quite round, and turn your partner (*b*).

MOLL PEATLEY.

LONGWAYS FOR AS MANY AS WILL.

⊙⊙⊙⊙ Men.
⟩⟩⟩⟩ Women.

'Dancing Master,' Ed. 1713.

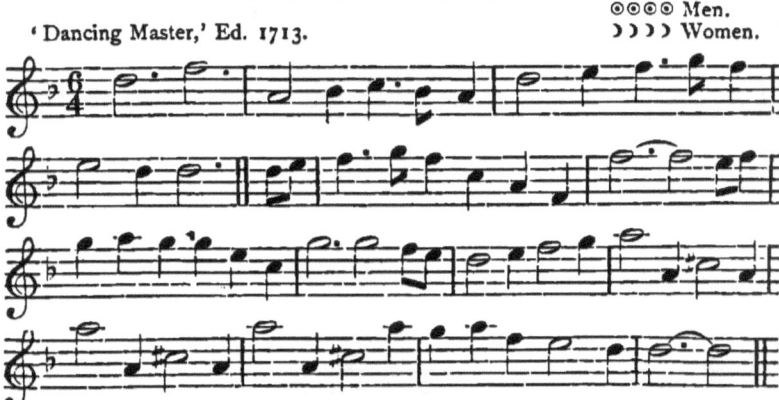

The 1 Man begins on the Women's side, the 1 cu. sides to the 2 cu. of one side, and then of the other side ; then hit your right elbows together, and then your left, and turn with your left hands behind, and your right hands before, and turn twice round ; and then your left Elbows together and turn as before, and so to the next.

[1] The figure half round is the Hey half round, the whole figure is the Hey all four round.
(*a*) For a strain of the tune played once over.
(*b*) For a strain played twice over.

A LIST

OF ALL THE PERSONS TO WHOM RINGS AND MOURNING WERE PRESENTED UPON THE OCCASION OF

MR. PEPYS'S DEATH AND BURIAL.

Persons	Rings of			Mourning
	20s.	15s.	10s.	
Relations viz				
Mr. Saml. & John Jackson his 2 Nephews	2			2 Suits & 10 Broad pieces to Samuel.
Capt. Sir Michel, his brother in Law	1			1 Suit.
Ditto, his daughter, Mrs. Mary Earl of Sandwich . . .		1		1 ,,
Dr. Montagu, Dean of Durham	1			
Mr. Pickering	1			
Mr. Roger Pepys of Impington		1		
Mr. & Mrs. Matthews . .	2			2 ,, & 10 Broad pieces to each.
Mr. Tim Turner, Minister of Tooting		1		
Mr. Bellamy		1		
Godchildren viz				
Mr. Saml. Gale, Mr. P.'s God-son		1		
Lt. Edwards do. . .			1	
Mrs. Frances Johnson, his Goddaughter . . .		1		
Domestics at his Death viz				
Mrs. Mary Skynner . .	1			1 Suit.
Ditto her Maid . . .				1 ,,
His own 7 men & women Servants . . .				7 ,,
Mr. Richard Gibson . .		1		
Mr. Paul Lorrain . .		1		
Ditto his Wife . . .			1	
John Wetton			1	
Saml. Holcroft . . .			1	
Mr. Pepy's former Servants and Dependents viz				
Mrs. Jane Penny . . .			1	1 Suit & 65 guineas.
Mrs. Jane Fane . . .		1		
Mrs. Mary Ballard . . .				1 ,,
Ditto her Husband . . .			1	
Mrs. Eliza Hughson . .				1 ,,
Ditto her Husband . . .			1	

Persons	Rings of 20s.	15s.	10s.	Mourning
'Retainers General viz — Physicians { Dr. Sloane .	1			1 Suit.
Dr. Shadwell .	1			1
Chirurgeon, Serjt. Bernard .	1			
Apothecary, Mr. Ethersey .		1		1 „
Lawyer, Judge Powis . .		1		
Scrivener, Mr. West . .		1		
Ditto, his Clerk, Mr. Martin .			1	
Goldsmith, Sir Rd. Hoare .	1			
Ditto, his Foreman Mr. Arnold		1		
Bookbinder, Mr. Beresford .			1	
Ditto his Sewer, Mr. Wetton .			1	
Self as Executor . . .	1			1 „
Edgley { Mr. & Mrs. Samuel .	2			2 „
Ditto their 3 Children		3		3 „
Mr. Arthur . .		1		
Blackburn, Mr. Wm. and Isaac		2		
Mr. Hewer's Relations — Crawley { Mrs. The Mother .		1		
Do. 2 Daughters Eliza & Margaret		2		
Mr. John } vide Navy		1		
Sergison Mr. . } Office		1		
Domestics . { Mr. Forbes, Chaplain . .		1		1 Suit.
Mr. Foster, Steward . .				
Ditto his Wife . . .			1	
Clapham . { Mr. Saville the Minister .		1		
Mr. Horne, late Lecturer .		1		
Mr. Pritchard, present Ditto .		1		
Mr. Urban Hall . . .		1		
Mr. Juxon		1		
Royal Society { Sir John Hoskins President .		1		
Mr. Abraham Hill . . .		1		
Mr. Hunt Operator . .			1	
Cambridge . { Dr. Quadring, Master of Mag. Coll.	1			
Dr. Bentley, Master of Trin. Coll.	1			
Oxford . . { Dr. Aldrich, Dean of Christ Church	1			
Dr. Wallis Professor . .	1			
Dr. Charlet, Master of University Coll.	1			
Dr. Gregory Professor . .	1			
Admiralty . { Mr. Burchett Secretary . .		1		
Sir Thos. Littleton Treasurer (a Supporter) . . .	1			
Sir Richd. Haddock, Controller		1		
Mr. Furzer Surveyor . .		1		
Mr. Sergison, Clerk of the Acts		1		
Mr. Atkins		1		

Persons	Rings of 20s.	Rings of 15s.	Rings of 10s.	Mourning
Commissioners { Mr. Tollett		I		
Mr. Hammond		I		
Mr. Lyddall		I		
Officers { Mr. Greenhill		I		
Mr. Tunewell		I		
Navy Clerks { Mr. Johnson		I		
Mr. John Crawley		I		
House keeper, Mrs. Griffin			I	
Auditors { Principal { Mr. Harley	I			
Mr. Bridges	I			
Deputys { Mr. Moody			I	
Mr. Bythell			I	
Clergy { Archbishop of Canterbury	I			
Bishop of London	I			
Dean of Worcester, who performed the Service	I			I Suit.
Dr. Smith	I			I ,,
Dr. Millington		I		
Dr. Gibson		I		
Archdeacon Baynard		I		
Mr. Coppyn - Munster of Crutched Fryars		I		
Ditto his Reader		I		
Earls of { Clarendon (a Supporter)	I			I ,,
Feversham (ditto)	I			I ,,
Honble. Mr. { Hatton (ditto)	I			I ,,
Vernon (ditto)	I			I ,,
Sir Anto° Deane (ditto)	I			I ,,
William Hodges	I			I ,,
Ditto His Son Mr. Hodges		I		
Ditto his Partner Mr. Haines		I		
Sir Henry Shere		I		
Sir Richard Dutton	I			
Sir William Gore		I		
Bowdler-Thomas		I		I ,,
Dégalénière Mons. et Mdlle.		2		
Dubois, Charles		I		
Evelyn, John, Grandfather & Grandson	2			I Suit Grand-father.
Gawden, Benjamin		I		
Houblon, Wynne & James	2			2 ,
Houghton, Apothecary		I		
Hunter, Saml.		I		I ,,
Isted		I		
Lowndes	I			
Martin, Joseph, Father & Son		2		
Monro			I	
Mussard		I		

S 2

Persons	Rings of			Mourning
	20s.	15s.	10s.	
Nelson		I		
Penn, William . . .	I			
Snow, Ralph		I		
Wind, Captain . . .	I			

LORD MAYOR'S DELIGHT.

LONGWAYS FOR AS MANY AS WILL.

'Dancing Master,' Ed. 1713.

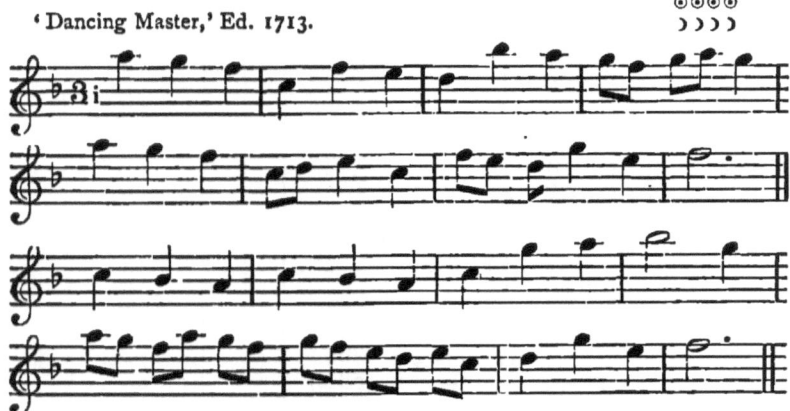

The 1 Man cast off below the 2 Man, then back to back with the
2 Wo. and stand in the 2 Man's place. The 1 Wo. cast off below the
2 Wo. and go back with the 2 Man being in the 1 Man's place, and stand
in the 2 Wo. place.

All four hands half round, then fall back and turn with one hand.
Cross over with your own Partner, then the 1 Couple Sett to their part-
ners and Cast off

WALSINGHAM.

Chappell's ' Popular Music of
the Olden Time.'

As I went to   Wal-sing-ham, To the shrine with speed;

Met I with a jol - ly pal - mer, In a pil - grim's weed.

Is in Queen Elizabeth's Virginal book, but is probably much older. Is mentioned very frequently; see 'Knight of the Burning Pestle.' Also Act 5 of Fletcher's 'The Honest Man's Fortune,' a servant says: 'I'll renounce my five mark a year, and all the hidden art I have in carving, to teach young birds to whistle *Walsingham.*'

THE CHILDREN IN THE WOOD.

Chappell's 'Popular Music of the Olden Time.'

Slowly.

Now pon-der well, You parents dear, These

words which I shall write; A dole-ful sto - ry

you shall hear, In time brought forth to light.

A LIST

OF SOME OF THE

COFFEE-HOUSES IN LONDON

DURING QUEEN ANNE'S REIGN, 1702–1714.

Adam's, Chancery Lane.
Adlamb's, Little Turnstile.
Admiralty, next the Admiralty Office.
Adulan's, Lincoln's Inn Fields
African, Leadenhall Street.
Alder's, Maiden Lane.
Alder's, Bull Inn Court, Ivey Bridge, Strand.
Aldersgate, without Aldersgate.
Alice's, at the Parliament House.
Allen's, Pope's Head Alley (formerly Bridge's).
Amsterdam (old), behind the Royal Exchange.
Anderton's, Fleet Street.
Andlaby's, Greek Street, Soho
Andrew's, Devereux Court, in Mid. Temple.
Andrew's, Bell Yard, Gracechurch Street.
Angel (the), Exeter Change.
Angel and Crown, Threadneedle Street.
Antegoe (the), Finch Lane.
Atkin's, Burr Street.
Auction (the), Burleigh Street.

Bagnio (the), Newgate Street
Baker's, Exchange Alley.
Baldrey's, next the Church, without Aldgate.
Bank (the), Grocer's Alley.
Barbadoes and Jamaica, Water Lane.
Barcelona, Birchin Lane.
Barndall's, Old Palace Yard.
Barnes's, Newgate Street.
Batson's, Cornhill.
Baulder's, Church Lane, Houndsditch.
Bay Tree (the), St. Swithin's Lane.
Bear Key (Quay).

Bedford (the), Tavistock Street.
Bedford Court, Covent Garden.
Bell (the), Bell Yard, Fleet Street.
Bell (the), Behind St. Clement's, Strand.
Bentley's, Opposite Bow Lane, Cheapside.
Best's, Cornhill.
Betts', Devonshire Street in Red Lion Square.
Betty's, Jermyn Street.
Bickerstaff's, Russell Street, Covent Garden.
Bigg's, Turnstile in Holborn.
Billingsgate.
Bird's, *Old* Palace Yard, Westminster.
Bird's, *New* Palace Yard, Westminster.
Bishop's, Aldersgate Street.
Blackborn's, Great Russell Street.
Black boy, Ave Maria Lane.
Black boy, Prescot Street, Goodman's Fields.
Blacknall's, Cross Street, Hatton Garden.
Bland's, Catherine Wheel Alley, Whitechapel.
Blenheim, by St. James's Church, Piccadilly.
Blue Coat, St. Swithin's Lane.
Blue Coat Boy, Thames Street.
Boam's, near Guildhall.
Boddy's, Peter Street, near Clare Market.
Bolland's, near the Bear in the Strand.
Bond's, near St. Dunstan's Church.
Booth's, Nicholas Lane.
Boulton's, Church Court, St. Martin's.
Bourne's, Cateaton Street.
Bourn's, Finch Lane.
Boyden's, Tower Street.

Bradshaw, near the Tennis Court Cockpit, Whitehall.

Bracqes, Silver Street.

Braxton, Henrietta Street, Covent Garden.

Bridges, Pope's Head Alley, Cornhill.

Bright's, Friday Street.

Brightman's, near Wapping Old Stairs.

Britannia, Bartholomew Lane.

Britannia, Charing Cross.

British, opposite Suffolk Street.

British, Great Wild Street, near Clare Market.

Brome's, King Street, Covent Garden.

Brown's, Bell Yard, near Temple Bar.

Brown's, Mitre Court, Temple.

Brown's, Fenchurch Street.

Brown's, King Street, Westminster.

Brown's, by the Nag's Head, Cheapside.

Brown's, Ormonde Street.

Buckeridge's, Aldersgate.

Bull's Head, Corner of Tower Street.

Burchill's (Capt. John), Crutched Friars.

Burton's, King Street, St. James's.

Button's, opposite Tom's, Covent Garden.

Camisards (the), St. Martin's Lane.

Carey's, Oxenden Street.

Carlisle, Laurence Lane.

Carolina, Birchin Lane.

Cecilia (Saint), St. Martin's Lane.

Chancery, Head of the Parliament Stairs.

Chapman's (Widow), Germain Street.

Child's, St. Paul's Churchyard.

Christian (the), West Smithfield Bars.

Clement's Inn, back side of St. Clement's.

Clifford's Inn, against the Temple.

Cole's, Birchin Lane.

Cole's (Wat), Bartholomew Lane.

Collin's, Old Fish Street.

Colton's, New Round Court, Strand.

Cooper's, Russell Court, Drury Lane.

Cope's, St. Martin's Court.

Couzen's, Maiden Lane, Covent Garden.

Covent Garden, Upper End of the Little Piazza.

Cowper's, Cornhill.

Cox's, near the Castle Tavern, Fleet Street.

Cross's, Carey Street, Lincoln's Inn Fields.

Crowforth's, near King Edward's Stairs.

Crown (the), behind the Royal Exchange.

Crown (the), Chancery Lane.

Crown (the), without Cripplegate.

Crown (the), Smithfield.

Daniel's, Gerrard Street.

Davis's, Bishopsgate Street.

Dennis', Finch Lane.

Dick's, from Will's, Bell Yard, Gracechurch Street.

Dick's, Fleet Street.

Digory's, by the Seven Dials.

Doctors' Commons, Carter Lane.

Dowglass's, or Duglace's, St. Martin's Lane.

Dowse's, near the Royal Exchange.

Draper's, opposite Leadenhall Gate.

Dunstan's (St.), Fleet Street.

Dutch (? Amsterdam), behind the Exchange.

East India, Leadenhall Street.

Edwardson's, Buckingham Street, York Buildings.

Elford's, George Yard, Lombard Street.

Eller's, Westminster Hall Gate.

Elliott's, Albemarle Street.

Essex (the), Mitre Court, Fleet Street.

Essex (the), Whitechapel.

Eteridge's, Birchin Lane.

Everitt's, Crutched Friars.

Exchange, Cornhill.

Exchequer, Mitre Court, Cornhill.

Faulck's, St. Martin's-le-Grand.

Fellowe's, opposite the Half Moon Tavern, Aldersgate Street.

Finch's, Minories.

Fitche's, Great Carter Lane.

Fountain, Cheapside.
Frampton's, Fenchurch Street.
Frank's, Little St. Andrew Street, Seven Dials.
Freeman's, Cheapside.
Friday Street, Friday Street, Cheapside.

Garraway's, Exchange Alley.
Garter (the), behind the Exchange.
Garter (the), at the Custom House.
Garter (the), Jermyn Street.
Gaunt, Pall Mall.
George's, top of the Haymarket.
George (the), Pall Mall.
George's, Piccadilly.
Gerald's, Queen Street, Westminster.
Gerrard's, Broad Street.
Gibson's, near Cripplegate.
Gilbert's, near St. James's Church.
Giles', Pall Mall.
Gillard's, Market Street, by Newport Market.
Gloucester, Cateaton Street.
Godlington's, Mitre Court, Fleet Street.
Grant's, Channel Row, Westminster.
Great Turnstile, High Holborn.
Grecian, Devereux Court, Temple.
Greyhound, King Street, Soho.
Greyhound, Monmouth Street.
Greyhound, Compton Street, Soho.
Grigsby's, Threadneedle Street (altered to Smith's in 1712).
Guildhall, King Street, Cheapside.
Gun (the), Mansfield Street, Goodman's Fields.
Gurney's, Garlick Hill, near Bow Lane.
Gyde's, Bow Lane.

Half Moon, Cheapside.
Hall's, Bell Savage Yard, Ludgate Hill.
Hall's, Great Wild Street, near Lincoln's Inn.
Ham's, near Lincoln's Inn, New Square.
Hamburg, Birchin Lane.
Hamlin's, Swithin's Alley, Cornhill.
Hammett's, at the Gate, London Bridge.

Hampton Court, Newport Street
Hanover, corner of Suffolk Street, Pall Mall.
Hanover, Finch Lane.
Hargrave's, without Bishopsgate Street.
Harris's, Love Lane.
Harris's, Ormonde Street.
Hart's, Lincoln's Inn.
Harwood's, Little Eastcheap.
Hatton's, Basinghall Street.
Hatwell, near St. Katherine's Stairs.
Haverse's, Whitechapel Bars.
Heming's, Holborn.
Hepworth's, Old Fish Street Hill.
Heyford's, Queen Street, Cheapside.
Hilliard's, Bread Street.
Hogarth's, St. John's Gate, Clerkenwell.
Holland's, Bridge Row.
Holland's, near St. Antholin's pump, Watling Street.
Holme's, Bartholomew Lane.
Hood's, Pudding Lane.
Howard's, behind the Exchange.
Howel's, Wild Street.
Hugh's, Charles Street, Westminster.
Hunt's, Friday Street.
Hurt's, against Katherine Street, Strand.

Italian (the), Katherine Street, Strand.
Ives's, Bartholomew Lane.

Jack's, Sweeting's Alley, by the Exchange.
Jack's, King Street, Cheapside.
Jack's (Thos.), Birchin Lane.
Jacob's, Threadneedle Street.
Jamaica, Cornhill, by the Ship and Turtle.
James's Street, St. James's Street (Elliot proprietor).
Jerusalem, near Garraway's.
Joe's, Hatton Garden.
Joe's, by Moorgate.
Joe's, Bucklersbury.
Joe's, St. James's Market.
John's, Fuller's Rents.
John's, Swithin's Alley (? same as Jack's).
John's, Birchin Lane.

John's, Great Old Bailey.
John's, Earl's Court, Bow Street.
John's, Shire Lane, Temple Bar.
John's, St. Martin's Lane.
John's, Gracechurch Street.
Johnson's, near St. James's Church, Piccadilly.
Jonathan's, Exchange Alley.
Jones's, Finch Lane.
Jones's, Mountford's Court, Milk Street.
Jones's, St. Martin's Lane.
Jordan's, near Rotherhithe Stairs.

Keeble's, Snow Hill.
Kentish, near the Custom House.
Kidd's, Catherine Street, Strand.
Kigg's, James Street, Golden Square.
Kimpton's, Fenchurch Street.
King's Arms, Customs House.
King's Head, in the paved Stones in West Smithfield.
Kirk's, Corner of Panton Square.
Knight's, Essex Street.
Knight's, Fish Street Hill.

Lamb's, opposite Devonshire Square, Bishopsgate.
Lane, King Street, Golden Square.
Laurence's, Freeman's Court, Cornhill.
Leadenhall, Leadenhall Street.
Leonard's, Finch Lane.
Lewenden's, Giltspur Street.
Lincoln's Inn, Chichester Rents.
Linnett's, George Alley, Snow Hill.
Lisbourne (Lisbon), Threadneedle Street.
Lloyd's, Lombard Street.
Lloyd's (Widow), at the Victualling Office Gate, Little Tower Hill.
London, Threadneedle Street.
London's, opposite Somerset House.
London Bridge,
London Stone, Cannon Street.
Lucas's,
Lyon's, near Doctor's Commons.
Lyth's, Freeman's Yard, Cornhill.

Macham's, West Smithfield.
Mackerell's, Bartlett's Buildings, Holborn.
Man's, Birchin Lane.

Man's, Chancery Lane.
Man's (old), Tilt Yard, Charing Cross.
Man's (young), Charing Cross.
Man's (young), Crooked Lane.
Man's (New), Charing Cross.
Manwaring's, Falcon Court, Fleet Street.
Margaret's, Cheapside.
Marine, Birchin Lane.
Marine, Piccadilly.
Marlborough (the), Wellclose Square.
Marlborough (the), Corner of Great Marlborough Street.
Martial's, White Horse Court.
Martin's, Guildhall Yard.
Martin's Street, Northumberland House.
Mason's, Bartholomew Lane.
Mawl's, within Newgate.
Mead's, Minories.
Meakin's, corner of East Cheap and Fish Street Hill.
Meare's, east end of St. Paul's.
Mears', by St. Austin's.
Mill's, Gerrard Street.
Mitchell's, at the Navy Office, Crutched Friars.
Mitre, Mitre Court, Fleet Street.
Moncrieth's, Threadneedle Street.
Montpellier's, behind the Exchange.
More's, Peter's Street, Bloomsbury.
Morris's, Essex Street, Strand.
Mynshill's, Three Crown Court, Southwark.

Nag's Head, Nag's Head Court, Gracechurch Street.
Nando's, Inner Temple Gate, Fleet Street.
Navy, against the Navy Office.
Ned's, in the Old Jewry.
Ned's, Birchin Lane.
Ned's, Ludgate Hill.
Ned's, Mitre Court, Temple.
Needham's, Castle Yard, Holborn Bars.
New England, Minories.
New Inn, Wych Street.
Nixon's, Mitre Court, Temple.
North's, King Street, Cheapside.
Norton's, near St. Margaret's Church, Westminster.
Norwich (the), Threadneedle Street.

Okely's, Old Bailey.
Oliver's, Westminster Hall Gate.
Owen's, Symond's Inn.
Oxford (the), without Temple Bar.
Ozinda's, St. James's Street.

Pall Mall, Pall Mall.
Palsgrave's Head, without Temple Bar.
Paris, Suffolk Street, Charing Cross.
Parliament, Old Palace Yard.
Paul's Street, St. Paul's Churchyard.
Pear's, Broad Street, Ratcliffe Cross.
Pen's, Queen Street.
Pensilvania, Birchin Lane.
Perry's, Great Russell Street.
Peter's, Threadneedle Street.
Pickering's, Cornhill.
Picket's, Clerkenwell Close.
Picking's, Clerkenwell Close.
Plantation (the), Water Lane.
Plough (the), Coleman Street.
Ponce's, or Pon's, Cecil Court, St. Martin's Lane.
Poole's, without Bishopsgate.
Portugal, Sweeting's Alley.
Potter's (Widow), St. James' Street.
Powell's, Cornhill.
Power's, near Queen's Arms, Pall Mall.
Pratt's, Cuteaton Street.
Prince's, Paul's Alley.
Prince of Orange, end of the Haymarket.
Purcell's, within the Nag's Head Tavern, Cheapside.

Queen's Arms, Custom House.
Queen's Square, near Petty France, Westminster.
Queen's Square, Devonshire Street, behind Red Lion Square.
Queen Street, Queen Street, Westminster.

Rainbow, Temple Bar.
Rainbow, Cornhill.
Rainbow, Corner of St. Martin's Lane.
Rainbow, by Fleet Bridge.
Rainbow, Ivy Lane.
Rainbow, Hoxton Square.

Rainbow, Newgate Street.
Randall's, Newport Street.
Rawle's, near the Maypole, Horsleydown.
Read's, Blackfriars, by Ludgate.
Rice's, Haymarket.
Richard's, near the Temple.
Rive's, by Clare Market.
Robin's, Exchange Alley.
Robin's, Basing Lane, near Cheapside.
Robinson's, Dean Street, Soho.
Robinson's, Berry Street, St. James's.
Rolls (the), Chancery Lane.
Rose (the), Covent Garden.
Royal (the), back gate of Lincoln's Inn.
Royal (the), St. James's Street.
Royal (the), Exchange Alley.
Royal Fishery (the), Thames Street.
Royal Union, by the Exchange.
Rowe's, Bridge Foot, Southwark.
Royce's, Clare Market.
Rudkin's, in the Rules of the Queen's Bench.

Salutation (the), Threadneedle Street.
Salutation (the), Tower Street.
Salutation (the), Bartholomew Lane.
Salter's (Don Saltero's), Chelsea.
Sam's, Ludgate Hill.
Sam's, near the Custom House.
Sandal's, opposite the Custom House.
St. Amand's, on the pav'd Stones over against Tom's.
Coffee House, in St. Martin's Lane.
Sarah's, Cornhill.
Sarah's, between Laurence Lane and King Street, Cheapside.
Sarah's, Fleet Street.
Say's, Ludgate Hill.
Scot's, near St. Dunstan's Church, Fleet Street.
Seager's, Haymarket.
Seago's, near Barnard's Inn.
Searl's, or Serle's, corner of Lincoln's Inn Square.
Serjeant's Inn, Chancery Lane.
Sews, Bow Lane, Cheapside.
Sheffield's, Temple Exchange.
Shipton's, Swithin's Alley.

Shiringham's, White Hart Court, Whitechapel.

Slaughter's, St. Martin's Lane.

Smart's Quay, near Billingsgate.

Smith's, Stock's Market.

Smith's, Gerrard Street, Soho.

Smith's, Silver Street, near Bloomsbury Market.

Smyrna (the), Pall Mall.

Smyrna (the), Peter's Alley, Cornhill.

Smyther's, Custom House.

South Sea, Broad Street.

Spentley's, near the Playhouse, Drury Lane.

Spurrett's, Bedford Court, Covent Garden.

Square's, Orange Street.

Squire's, Fulwood's Rents, Holborn.

Stal's, or Steel's, Bread Street.

Staple's Inn, Holborn.

Star (the), Mitre Court, Fleet Street.

Star (the), in the Mint.

Star (the), Crutched Friars.

Star (the), by the Royal Exchange.

Star (the), Exchange Alley.

Stephen's, Bloomsbury.

Steward's, 3 King's Court, by Water Lane, Fleet Street.

Storer's, King Street, by Old Street Square.

Stylyard, near the Stylyard, Thames Street.

Sun (the), behind the Exchange.

Sun (the), Queen Street, Cheapside.

Sun (the), Threadneedle Street.

Sun (the), Holbourne Conduit.

Sun (the), York Buildings.

Sun (the), Chancery Lane.

Sun (the Old), opposite the Navy Office.

Sunderland's, Warwick Lane.

Swan (the), Bloomsbury.

Swan's, Throgmorton Street.

Tarrant's, within Aldgate.

Tart's, Bartholomew Close.

Tawney's, Bell Savage Yard.

Tayler's, in the Mint.

Temple, Clifford's Inn Gate.

Templeman's, Charing Cross.

Thavies Inn, Bartlett's Buildings.

Tilt Yard, Whitehall.

Tom's, St. Martin's Lane.

Tom's, Half Moon Court, Ludgate Hill.

Tom's, in the pav'd Court, Fulwood's Rents.

Tom's, Devereux Court, Temple.

Tom's, Russell Street, Covent Garden.

Tom's (Old), Birchin Lane.

Towell's, West Smithfield.

Tower (the), Tower Street.

Turk's Head (the), Charles Street, Covent Garden.

Turk's Head (the), Essex Street.

Turk's Head (the), King's Gate Street.

Turk's Head (the), opposite the Fountain, Strand.

Turk's Head (the), Bell Savage Yard.

Turney's, Cornhill.

Twing's, Old Bailey Court.

Union (the), Exchange Alley.

Union (the), by King Edward's Stairs, Wapping.

Vernon's (Widow), Bartholomew Lane.

Viccar's, Court of Requests, Guildhall.

Victualling Office, Tower Hill.

Vigus's, Court of Requests, Westminster.

Vincent's, 3 Crown Court, Westminster.

Virginia (the), St. Michael's Alley.

Virginia (the), Birchin Lane.

Waghorn's, New Palace Yard, Westminster.

Waghorn's, Pope's Head Alley.

Wakeford's, Pudding Lane.

Walch's, Clare Market.

Wallsall's, Nag's Head Court, Bartholomew Lane.

Walton's, Warwick Lane.

Walton's, Denmark Street, Ratcliffe Highway.

Webb's, West Smithfield.

Wells (Mrs.), Scotland Yard Gate.

Whitehall, Buckingham Court, Charing Cross.

Wiat's, St. Olave's, Southwark.

Widow's (the), Half Moon Alley, Cheapside.
Widow's (the), Bedford Court.
Wijerts, Earl's Court, Drury Lane.
Will's, 1 Bow Street (Wm. Unwin, proprietor).
Will's, Threadneedle Street.
Will's, under Scotland Yard Gate.
Will's, Cornhill, by the Exchange.
Will's, Fuller's Rents.
Will's, St. Lawrence Lane.
Willet's, Threadneedle Street.
Willey's, or Willis's, near the Custom House.

William's, St. James's Street.
Wilson's, Cornhill.
Windsor's, opposite Northumberland House.
Wisdom's, King Street, Westminster.
Wither's, Jewin Street.
Wood's, in the Herb market, Leadenhall.
Wright's, Aldersgate Street.
Wright's, Artillery Lane.

Yate's, Leadenhall Street.
Yeates, West Smithfield.

CHOCOLATE HOUSES.

Chocolate House, on Blackheath.
The Cocoa Tree, Pall Mall.
Lindheart's, King Street, Bloomsbury.

The Spread Eagle, Bridge Street, Covent Garden.
White's, St. James's Street.

SIR ROGER DE COVERLEY.

In Chappell's ' Popular Music of the Olden Time,' the oldest account of this tune is given as follows : ' According to Ralph Thoresby's MS. account of the family of. Calverley, of Calverley in Yorkshire, the dance of *Roger de Coverley* was named after a knight who lived in the reign of Richard I. Thoresby was born in 1658. The following extract was communicated to Notes and Queries, vol. 1, p. 369, by Sir Walter Calverley Trevelyan, Bart. :—Roger, so named from the Archbishop (of York), was a person of renowned hospitality, since, at his day, *the obsolete known tune of Roger a Calverley* is referred to him, who, according to the custom of those times, kept his Minstrels, from that their Office, named Harpers, which became a family, and possessed lands till late Years, in and about Calverley, called to this Day Harper's roids and Harper's Spring.'

The earliest authentic notice I can find of it is in a very curious old tract, printed in the year 1648, or ten years before Thoresby was born, called 'A Vindication or justification of John Griffith, Esq., against the horrid, malitious, and unconscionable Verdict of Coroner's Jury in Cheshire : which was packt by means of that Pocky, Rotten, Lying Cowardly and most perfidious knave, Sir Hugh Caulverley Knight, onely to vent his inveterate Hatred and Malice against me.' And, on page 5, . Mr. Griffiths says : ' I purposely to vex Sir Hugh, and his Champion Dod, sent for a fidler, and during the time my fellow Coursers were drinking a Cup of Ale, we having run our Match, I and my Fidler, rid up to Sayton, and from one end of the town to the other, I made the Fidler play a tune called Roger of Caulverley : This I did to shew, that I did not fear to be disarmed by them, and they may thank themselves for it, for if they had not first endeavoured to mischief me, I should not trouble myself to have vext them.'

ROGER OF COVERLY.

'The Dancing Master,' 15 Ed. 1713.
    Brit. Mus. C. 31, b. 21.

CHRIST CHURCH BELLS IN OXON.

'Dancing Master,' Ed. 1713.   Dean ALDRICH.

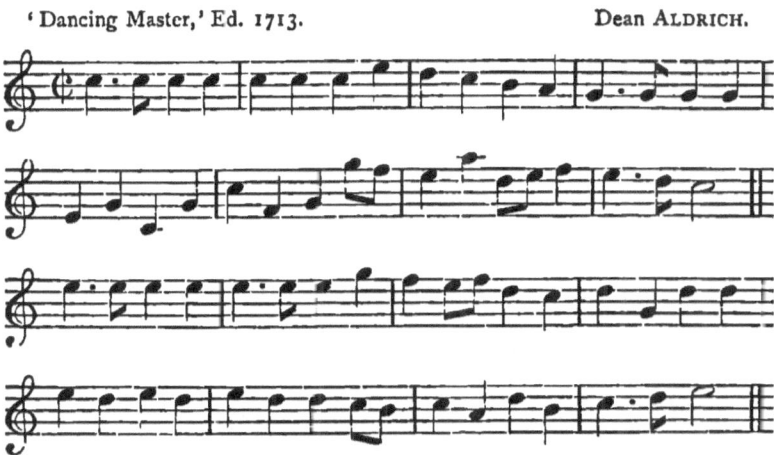

CHESHIRE ROUNDS.

LONGWAYS FOR AS MANY AS WILL.

'Dancing Master,' 1713.

The 1 Man casts off and his Partner follows him, the Man goes quite round ; the Woman slips up the middle ; the Woman casts off and goes quite round. The 1 Man slips up the middle, the 1 cu. cross over below the 2 cus. and cross up into their own places again, then right and left quite round into the 2 couples place.

THE NIGHTINGALE.

The Words by Mr. WELSTED.   Set by Mr. CAREY.

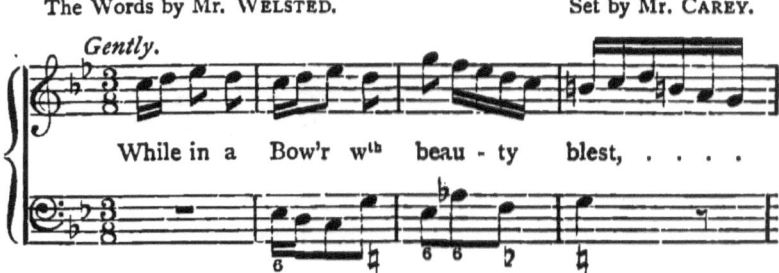

While in a   Bow'r wth beau - ty   blest, ...

sweet-ly re-new'd her plain - - tive Song, And

war - - - - bled through the Glade.

Melodious Songstress ! cry'd ye Swain,
To Shades, to Shades less happy go ;
Or, if thou wilt with us remain,
Forbear, forbear thy tuneful woe ;
While in LUCINDA'S arms I lie,
To Song, to Song I am not free ;
On her soft bosome, when I die,
I dis——cord find in thee.

BRIT. MUS. I. $\frac{530}{24}$.

THE END.

LONDON : PRINTED BY
SPOTTISWOODE AND CO., NEW-STREET SQUARE
AND PARLIAMENT STREET

www.ingramcontent.com/pod-product-compliance
Lightning Source LLC
Chambersburg PA
CBHW030627030726
47497CB00006B/1676